PENANCE FOR
JERRY KENNEDY

PENANCE FOR JERRY KENNEDY

George V. Higgins

ANDRE DEUTSCH

First published in Great Britain 1985
by André Deutsch Limited
105 Great Russell Street London WC1

First published in the United States of America
by Alfred A. Knopf, Inc.

ISBN 0 233 97795 3

Printed in Great Britain by
Ebenezer Baylis & Son Ltd
Worcester

PENANCE FOR
JERRY KENNEDY

1

THE DAY that Harry Mapes selected to win fame for his new dog was the same one designated by the Commonwealth for the trial of David Mackin. It was also a day on which Channel 8's remote broadcast crew decided to park the news van so that it blocked the crosswalk in front of the Norfolk Superior Courthouse in Dedham. David Mackin and I knew nothing about Harry Mapes and his new dog when we met there that morning, and that was just as well—I might not have showed up to defend David in court if I had known Harry Mapes would be there too, and David was all upset anyway. He stood there with the shoulders of his Burberry raincoat all hunched up around his ears and with his hands jammed down deep into the pockets, and he pressed his chin down against his neck so that his jowls bloomed out around his jaws—the position made him gargle slightly when he talked, and since he was shaking his head while he was doing that he sounded as though he had been partly underwater. "I don't like it," he said, "just the same. I don't like it at all. Can't you do something about this?" His horn-rimmed glasses skidded slightly on the bridge of his nose, from all the head fakes he was putting in the conversation, and he had to fish a gloved hand out to nudge them back in place.

"No," I said, as patiently as I could manage under the circumstances of standing foot to foot in a cold February drizzle in order to conduct a silly conversation with a client I disliked. "I can't do anything about it."

"They've got that thing blocking the crosswalk there," he said resentfully. "Is this what it's come to, that they can just park those damned things any damned where they please and nobody can do anything about it? Arrogant little bastards, aren't they?"

To hear David Mackin, Certified Life Underwriter, calling someone *arrogant* was like hearing Xaviera Hollander call someone *a loose woman.* I had trouble keeping a straight face. If I hadn't started off the day annoyed by the prospect of spending a good part of it with him, I would've laughed out loud. "David," I said, "that's not what I said. Somebody could do something about it. A Dedham cop, maybe, give them a citation for blocking a crosswalk. Or even one of the Staties, like the one, arrested you." David is the sort of guy that you jab every chance you get, just because he deserves so many more shots than he'll ever get in this world that God would punish you for wasting one. "But me, I don't have jurisdiction, see? To do that. So if it's me you're looking to for help, I've got to tell you that I'm going to disappoint you."

"Publicity," he said, shaking his head again. "I can't take publicity. Not over this, at least." I was glad he added that. David Mackin, C.L.U., top honcho in the Catholic Charities Annual Dinner Dance, fund raiser for the Norfolk County Crippled Children's Camp, with his lovely bride, Julia, prominent in the Boat Orphans Relief Fund, spent more time in a tuxedo with his mug pictured in the Quincy *Patriot Ledger* than he did in his office, scaring the bejesus out of underinsured, wealthy, and overweight middle-aged men.

"You shouldn't talk like that, David," I said, the cold drips running down my neck. He thought I was reproaching, not advising him. He looked at me sharply. "You look just like Richard Nixon when you talk like that," I said. "Sound just like him, too. Very dangerous to remind people of Richard Nixon when there are reporters around. Puts them in a frenzy." David did not find much humor in that. "Look," I said, going on to see if facts would improve his mood more than kidding did, "look at the van, all right? On top of it? The dishes are all down, right flat on the roof. The antennas? All collapsed for traveling, all right? That means they aren't broadcasting. Now look inside the truck, all right? Nobody inside the cab. That most likely means they went for coffee. Just like you and I should've, 'stead of standing here like a couple jerks in the freezing rain. They are not here for you this morning, David," I said. "They are here for somebody else. Or else they are here because this is a good place to sit around and see if something turns up. And besides, it's nice and close to One-twenty-eight, and if anything happens, north or south, they will get a call from the station and go cover it. So stop worrying, all right?"

"Like what?" David Mackin said. "Like what else could they be here for?"

I suppose a man who drives a vintage '57 Thunderbird with the vanity plate KIDS—his wife has a Volvo station wagon with LIFE, and if you ask her if she works for the magazine she will give you one uninterrupted hour of strenuous harangue on the equivalence of abortion and murder—finds it difficult to comprehend that there are actually large numbers of people right in Massachusetts who do not give a shit about him or what he happens to be doing at any given hour of the day or night. The possibility that nobody cares what he is doing, or whether he's enjoying it, is simply not one that occurs to him. "Like something big," I said. "A couple guys with a semi-trailer full of marijuana. Fifteen soldier boys from Devens that raped a rock-group honey in a schoolyard near the base. How the hell should I know, David? Anything. Anything but some damned insurance man that got shitfaced at a banquet and put his T-bird in the weeds on Groundhog Day. That, I can tell you definitely, isn't what they came here looking for."

"They're going to be inside, aren't they?" David said morosely. He jerked his head toward the old gray stone building where Sacco and Vanzetti got the death penalty with lots more dignity than he was showing on a drunk-driving charge. "In the courtroom there, I mean."

"They have a right to be," I said. "The television boys have got a right to go in there and take pictures of what everybody's doing in the courtrooms. And there's nothing I can do about that either."

"They shouldn't let them do that," David Mackin said. "This ought to be . . . this thing is hard enough, just going through it. You shouldn't have to be on television while it's happening."

I took him by the left arm and began to edge him toward the steps. "David," I said, "look, tomorrow morning in the U.S. District Court, I have a client coming up for sentencing. His name is Lou Schwartz. This guy is my accountant, has been for years. He is a nice man and it hurts me that I couldn't save him from this situation, but I couldn't and he knew it and the day is now upon us."

"Why are you telling me this?" David said, pulling back from my grasp. "Is it that you lose all your cases, Kennedy? Is that what you're telling me? All this stuff I heard, 'Hire Jerry Kennedy' and all that stuff, wasn't that correct?"

"David," I said, renewing my grasp, "I have given you my best prediction of what's going to happen to you. You will admit to sufficient facts so that a judge in a bad mood could put you in the can. You will do this on a deal with the prosecutor, who will so inform the judge. This will put the judge in a good mood, not a bad mood. It will also tie his hands so he can't put you in jail. He will tell you that you have to go to classes every night or something for the next three months or so. In those classes you will find out one point five ounces of alcohol constitutes one drink, and how many of those drinks you can have before some policeman stopping you acquires the right to arrest you. You will also watch some movies, it would be my educated guess. From those movies you will learn that people who drive cars while shitfaced often crack them up, sometimes hurting themselves but more often killing strangers who just happened to be passing by. You will also pay a fine and turn your license in, and you will not get that license back until the gentle winds of summer wash once more on old Cape Cod.

"I, on the other hand," I said, "will go from here back to my Boston office. There I will spend what this case leaves me of the day trying to dream up something that will reduce by a month or so the time Lou Schwartz is going to spend in Danbury, Connecticut. I am not optimistic about this. I am telling you about it because I thought it might help you to realize that your case isn't even close to being the end of the world as we know it, and because I know it is something that I have to get done sometime this morning, all right? So I can go and make a last-ditch effort to think of something that will save Lou Schwartz."

"Are you a man who likes his work, Mister Kennedy," David Mackin said sarcastically.

"There are days when I am not," I said. "There are also days I am. As I get along in years, there seem to be more of the first kind of days than there are of the second kind. On this kind of day what I hope chiefly is that my case is the first one out, and that therefore so am I. Then I get to go back to my office and sit down there with the door shut, and try to figure out where things started to go wrong."

2

THAT MORNING in Dedham, things had started to go wrong before David Mackin and I entered the damned courthouse. The docket clerk for Judge Dawes's session had put our case eighteenth on the list. There was a whole bunch of folks ahead of us whose cases had been opened back around Columbus Day, but some of them had just found out about the celebrations and were coming in to make apologies. Then there were all the people who had their lawyers come in early and attempt to see the prosecutors, only to be told to go to court and tell the judge they wanted conferences; then the judge would order their cases held for conferences, and instruct them to go find the selfsame prosecutors who had told them a couple hours earlier to go and find the judge. They would have their conferences and come back later in the day and belt the cases out on bargained guilty pleas, and the entire process would not take more than three or four hours longer than it might have if the prosecutors had conferred with the early lawyers in the first place. We sat there for all of those preliminary, useless exercises and we were still sitting there when the clerk called the seventeenth case, *Commonwealth* v. *Harry Mapes*. I had not noticed his name on the list. I slumped as far down in my chair as I could manage without sliding to the floor.

Harry Mapes is widely known in law enforcement circles. He is also famous among members of the bar. Harry's an engaging fellow, close to seventy—he gives his age as sixty-eight, but nothing he says is to be relied upon in any kind of detail. He has spent twenty-seven of those years confined of his liberty, as it is said, and he would have spent a great many more of them in that restricted setting had it not been for the diligent efforts of many, many lawyers.

None of those lawyers, so far as any of us have been able to determine, ever got a dime from Harry Mapes. Harry, that engaging rogue, believes prison is a hazard of his occupation, which is burglary, and that defense counsel is not only an entitlement of him who is about to be imprisoned, but an amusing diversion. He thinks a lawyer to defend him is something like a public toilet in a restaurant: when you are in the courthouse, and you need one, there is one there for your convenience, and you piss on it and then you go away. Back in the days when nobody paid anything for lawyers who represented indigents in felony cases—those charged with misdemeanors either got their own lawyers or went to the can without that wearisome formality—Harry gracefully accepted tendered services of volunteers, rewarding those who got him off with warm handclasps of appreciation and adversely criticizing those who attended his convictions. In the palmy early days of the Mass. Defenders, Harry deemed himself a sort of tutor for the rookie trial attorney, taking it upon himself to give the young lads and lassies pointers as they represented him. Now that the Defenders are swamped by the obligation to protect those charged with misdemeanors, and the unwary bastards like me are again in jeopardy of being court-appointed, Harry is again inspecting more mature counsel, and issuing evaluations. He thinks of himself as a discerning critic of the Massachusetts criminal defense bar.

That morning, before Luther Dawes, Harry answered to a charge arising from a break committed in the nighttime on a dwelling house in Cohasset. It belonged to a well-fixed executive who collected high-priced, detailed models of expensive racing cars. He also distrusted his fellow man, and had a silent burglar alarm rigged to alert the police when an uninvited person stepped on his oriental rugs. The cops found Harry perplexed before the glass case which housed a model of the Mercedes SSK.

"The fact the matter is, Your Honor," Harry said, accepting as he always does the invitation of any judge to contribute a great many well-chosen words to any session, any court, "and trying to look at this thing from a more or less objective point of view, you know what I mean, well, the fact the matter is, I haven't got a lawyer."

"No lawyer, Mister Mapes?" Dawes said, with exaggerated surprise. Luther Dawes is a patrician Yankee with a remote ancestral link to Samuel Dawes, the gentleman who actually did all the work that Paul Revere was credited with doing. That injustice appears still to weigh heavily upon members of the judge's family, and he seldom misses an opportunity to attract attention to himself. He is therefore a great favorite of the press and television people, especially the TV boys. His session, if he has anything to say about it, always offers, if possible, some comic relief, and he has a great deal to say about it. He preened when he talked with Harry, beaming with that blue-eyed Yankee twinkle I have always thought looked just a little watery, some evidence of an abiding fondness for a glass or four of gin after a long workday, and said: "Now that comes as something of a surprise, Mister Mapes, if I may say so. A man of your experience in this line, I'd think you'd almost have to have a lawyer on retainer."

That witty sally brought a lot of that suck-ass hearty chuckling that the hacks around the courthouse always force out of themselves when they draw a judge who thinks he is a regular charmer of a fellow. Mapes knew enough not to step on Dawes's line. He let it run its course while he stood and looked theatrically rueful. "I can't afford that, Your Honor, please," Mapes said, his timing and his bearing things he might have studied under Jack Benny. "I was never good enough at doing what I do, to pay for all the lawyers that I've needed when I get caught doing it."

That brought a huge burst of laughter from what had now become the audience. It's astonishing how fast rookie defendants and inexperienced lawyers catch on to the fact that the court officers and cops are ingratiating themselves with the judge by laughing at his simple-minded jokes, and at once join in the self-abasement with the older hands.

Judge Dawes's face showed much delight when he had finished laughing. "I take your point, Defendant," he said, very formally. "A life of crime's no bed of ease, is that it?"

Once again Mapes let the judge's laugh arise and fall. "I'm getting old, I guess," he said.

"So are we all, Mister Mapes," the judge said very gaily.

Mapes shook his head. "It isn't that, Your Honor," he said. "Not just normal growing old. It's . . . I don't notice things the way I used to. That thing that they had in the carpet? I heard of those things, sure. In banks. In jewelry stores. In places where they handle lots of money in the normal course of things. But I never thought I'd see the day when somebody had a silent bell inside his own place where he lived. I never looked for it. I just don't notice things like I used to, I guess. I'm not up on these new gadgets that they're using to catch people like me."

"Times change, Mister Mapes," Judge Dawes said, acting like he shared Mapes's chagrin. "Those who don't change with them get in trouble."

"I know," Mapes said. "I think it's drugs. There's all these kids out all the time, breaking into places that they never locked the doors in when I was growing up, and now everybody's jumpy and they got all these alarms." He shook his head. He sighed. "It isn't like it used to be."

Judge Dawes was at a loss for a new line. "Well," he said, clearing his throat, "that being the case, Mister Mapes, I have to ask you if you want a lawyer."

"I guess so, Judge," Mapes said forlornly. "I suppose I ought to have one."

"And from what you've said to me already," Dawes said, grimly jovial, "my guess is you either need a very good one, if you plan to try the case, or a very smart one, if you plan to plead it."

"Oh," Mapes said, "I plan to plead it. I've been in this situation enough times so I know when I haven't got a case."

The judge nodded sagely. "Very well, then," he said, and began to scan the gallery of lawyers sitting captive for his comedies inside the bar enclosure. "Mrs. Caldwell?" he inquired rhetorically, looking at the woman from the Mass. Defenders' Office, a tough lady in her late forties who was known to take no guff from anybody, even when it was guff that she richly deserved about rules of evidence and procedure that she'd never really mastered—all of the judges hated her, and with substantial reason. "Probably not," Dawes mused aloud, while she glared at him. "Press of work and all that sort of thing.

"Mister Collier," he said, shifting his gaze to Freddie, who sat cowering next to Mrs. Caldwell. Freddie is about sixty-five or so and appears to have spent all of his forty years before the bar in a state of near-hysteria. No one seems to know why this is. He is perfectly competent, careful never to accept cases which he does not understand, very well informed about the law—the son of a bitch actually keeps up to date reading the advance sheets of recent decisions, and serves willingly as a walking library for those of us who are a little lax along that line—and quite adequate examining witnesses, but nevertheless the poor bastard is scared to death every day he spends in court. "Give me the benefit of your thinking on this case of Mister Mapes's," Judge Dawes said to Freddie. "Is this one that you think you could handle?"

Freddie stood up, licking his lips and looking like a sixth-grader summoned to the headmaster for punishment. "If it please the Court," he said, "I've represented Mister Mapes before, and . . . I'd rather not do it again, if the Court would so grant."

Harry Mapes was gracious in the circumstances. "Your Honor," he said genially, "I remember Mister Collier, and I know what he means. I had to go to jail that time he had me, and he acted like it was my fault or something." He spoke like someone who had had a bad meal in a restaurant and wasn't going back there if he possibly could help it.

"Well, Mister Mapes," Dawes said, the thick white eyebrows shooting up for emphasis, "forgive my asking this, but whose fault was it that you had to go to jail for something that you did, if not your own?" That reaped another rippling chuckle from the multitude.

"I didn't mean that, Judge," Mapes said, "that it wasn't my fault, what I did. What I meant was Mister Collier. It was like he thought I should've said something that wasn't true, so that I would get off when I came to court." Among Harry's many excellent personal qualities is a broad streak of treachery. He not only does not recognize an obligation to be grateful at the very least to the lawyer who works for him for no money; he also treats the favor as a reason to damage the person's reputation afterwards, if the opportunity presents itself.

Judge Dawes to his credit didn't like that nasty small suggestion Mapes had made, hinting that Freddie Collier would have suborned perjury. Dawes prefers a cordial world where he's the main show-off, but nobody gets hurt unless he thinks it is necessary. He frowned at Mapes and cleared his throat. He looked at the next four lawyers seated in the bar enclosure, and quickly dismissed each of them for one reason or another, conflicting engagements in other courts, lack of experience in cases of repeat offenders, any flimsy argument which would get him down to me, whom he had most likely intended to appoint to represent Mapes from the instant that he saw me in the courtroom.

"*Mister* Kennedy," he said, his ruddy face displaying all the joy he felt in reaching me at last. Judge Dawes and I don't like each other, and we haven't since he was first named to the bench. Soon after he put his black dress on, I tried a piss-ant rape case before him and I did two things that he didn't like at all: I took the chance presented by a stupid prosecutor who had opened up the issue of the complainant's chastity, and asked all of the gaudy questions about what she liked to do, and how many times she'd done it, that I never could have put without that prosecutor's error. Judge Dawes thought that ungentlemanly, and he made that clear to me in a conference in his chambers. I told Judge Dawes that I didn't care what he thought and that what interested me was getting my defendant off. I said the jury deserved to know the lady was a tramp who'd changed her mind about my guy two days after he had screwed her. Judge Dawes told me he'd see to it my low-down tactics didn't work, and that he'd give my guy more time when that jury nailed him as the judge intended to make sure they did. That was when I did the second thing that annoyed him—I got my client off. And now that I think back on it, there may have been a third thing that got under his skin too—after he had furiously dismissed my man and adjourned court for that day, I stuck out my tongue at him. "I didn't realize you were here," he said expansively.

I stood up slowly and bowed toward him. "Your Honor," I said, "I have the Mackin matter, next case on the list. All that I think we'll need's a conference on it. I anticipate a plea, if the DA can see things my way." It was a perfectly innocuous speech. I had learned all I ever needed to know about Harry Mapes a good many years before; where Harry Mapes was concerned, I felt like the tomcat who had an affair with a lady skunk and said he liked as much of the experience as he could stand. I had Harry on a burglary in Brockton back when I was just starting out. He had gotten three fine cameras and a fair amount of jewelry out of a large house on the West Side and made a clean get-away. Then he had tried to sell it to an undercover cop. Harry was in his forties then, insouciant and somewhat inclined to brag. He told me his first arrest was as a juvenile—for burglary, of course—October 9th of 1928. "The same day," he told me proudly back then, "that Babe Ruth with a bum ankle hit three homers in the Series." I looked it up, his record and Babe Ruth's, and he was right on both accounts— the Yankees beat the Cards that day, 7–3 behind Waite Hoyt, and Harry had commenced his life of crime while Calvin Coolidge was still President.

"Well, then," Dawes said happily, "that means you'll have to hang around here for a while, after you have seen the DA and so forth, and you can talk to Mister Mapes. See what he has to say, and if it is a guilty plea as he seems to expect, dispose of his case too today without another trip."

I didn't want to do that. Harry went down to the House in Plymouth for two years of correction on that Brockton case I handled for him, and he took the leisure time there in the winter to sue me for ineffective assistance of counsel. I won the case of course, had it thrown out summarily, but it was an embarrassment and a damned inconvenience. The fact that I was one of about twenty lawyers Harry sued was no consolation to me whatsoever. "Your Honor," I said, "with all due respect to this honorable Court, I'd really rather not do that. I've had my differences with Mister Mapes before, and the experience of representing him is not one that I'm anxious to repeat." We're very formal in the courtroom setting. What I had said was that I hated the old bastard and would as soon see him hang as not. Both Judge Dawes and Harry Mapes knew that was what I meant.

"Well, Mister Kennedy," Judge Dawes said fruitily, "that often happens in the law, a difference of opinion that arises when the parties are excited by the combat of the case." He grinned at me hypocritically. "We all make it a practice to forget those things soon after they occur. Don't we? Otherwise, since you and I have had our little disagreements also, you would not be able to come here this morning with your private client."

One of the reasons I dislike Judge Dawes is that he's not above that sort of thing, threatening the lawyer with some harm to his client if the lawyer doesn't do what the judge wants. I have no desire to fight with judges—it makes my life harder and more complicated. But there are times when I have to do it, and I hate judges who take their revenge on me by coming down still harder on my clients. What Judge Dawes was saying on that February morning was that if I didn't take Mapes off his hands, he would vent his spleen on David Mackin, who would therefore be punished partly for driving after he had drunk too much and partly for hiring Jerry Kennedy to be his lawyer. "This was a little more than a sharp disagreement, Your Honor," I said hopelessly. "Mister Mapes sued me, and I'd be less than frank if I said that I didn't mind it."

Judge Dawes looked incredulously shocked. "Mister *Mapes,*" he said, "can this be so? You actually sued Mister Kennedy after he had represented you? Why, Mister Kennedy is one of the leading members of the trial bar. Would you mind if I asked him to deal with your case today? Bygones being bygones, and all that sort of thing?"

Harry Mapes would have accepted Dracula as his attorney, if Judge Dawes had recommended him. Harry Mapes plays showboating judges like Bobby Doerr played second base for the Boston Red Sox. He'll agree to anything the judge wants to make him happy, because Harry prefers happy judges as his audience for bullshit. "Your Honor," Harry said, now in the old weary-and-repentant-con routine that he's been practicing for years, "I was young when I had Mister Kennedy that time, lots younger than I am today, and I did some things then even when I was in jail that I am not too proud of. I know Mister Kennedy's a very famous lawyer, and if he will represent me, I'll be glad to have him."

The choice was to bite clean through my lower lip and accept the appointment, or make one final try to get out of it and then accept the appointment. I decided on the final try. I am, after all, a trial lawyer, and I'm supposed to be used to fighting hopeless causes. "Your Honor," I said, as Dawes made his face to shine upon me, "much as I appreciate the Court's confidence and Mister Mapes's somewhat delayed but still welcome apology, I really must ask that I be excused. I have a major case before the federal court tomorrow, and I really need the time for preparation."

"The federal court," Dawes said sarcastically. There are some state court judges who resent the federal court, partly because they think the federal judges think themselves better than the state ones (as they do) and partly because federal judges make more money than they do. "The federal court, Mister Kennedy, is junior to the Great Trial Court of Massachusetts by a fair number of years." Judge Dawes is a history buff, and will regale you with the past if you give him an opening.

"I'm aware of that, Your Honor," I said, learning some resignation. He would let me spend all day there, arguing why I should not have to spend all day there, if I gave him the invitation.

"This would be the *Schwartz* case, would it?" Dawes said with some malice.

"Yes, Your Honor," I said, wanting to yell at him that Lou Schwartz was important and this chickenshit vaudeville routine with Harry Mapes was not.

"A most intriguing fellow, Mister Schwartz," Dawes said maliciously.

I shrugged. "I've known Lou for a long time, Your Honor," I said. "To me he's a good friend whom I have known for many years, and now he's in big trouble. From which, I'm sorry to say, I couldn't seem to get him out."

"You're too hard on yourself, Mister Kennedy," Judge Dawes said. "From what I read and hear, Mister Schwartz was pretty fortunate to have escaped as long as he did without somebody coming after him." That was Mr. Schwartz's idea too, but I saw no need to give Luther Dawes that welcome news.

"Most of us would have to make that statement, Judge," I said, "if we were strictly honest with ourselves."

Judge Dawes's face got red. "Speak for yourself, Mister Kennedy," he said. He rearranged some papers on his desk. "As far as I'm concerned, I feel quite ready to put him in a different category from where most of us belong." He gave me the full magisterial frown which is supposed to strike terror into the hearts of all lawyers who have not managed to have themselves appointed judges. I did not say anything. "Up yours" is not deemed a decorous address to a sitting judge. He waited for a moment to see if I would say something like that, which would activate his contempt powers and give him a real excuse to harass me, but I am older now and calculate the costs of outbursts which will demonstrate my courage and integrity but otherwise accomplish very little. I did not say anything.

"At any rate, Mister Kennedy," he said, when he was convinced that he hadn't succeeded yet in baiting me into saying something he could make sure I regretted, "federal court and good friend in it notwithstanding, I don't think that it's too much for this court to ask of you to represent Mister Mapes here today, and I am going to so order. You said you wanted a conference in the next case?"

"Yes, Your Honor," I said, *"Mackin."*

"Both down for second call, Mister Clerk," Dawes said with satisfaction. "The *Mackin* and the *Mapes* cases, both with Mister Kennedy." Which meant that my insurance man at 11:40 a.m. was right back down at the bottom of the same list where he'd brought up the rear when court opened at 10:15 a.m., and that I now had the additional amusement of Harry Mapes to keep me there in Dedham into the forenoon. "Mister Mapes," Judge Dawes said, having accomplished the ruination of my day but still not quite content, "I told you you would need either a good lawyer or a smart one, and I've got you Mister Kennedy. You can decide which he is, after you have talked to him." Then Judge Dawes grinned at me, and ordered the morning recess.

3

"I DID not get out of that damned courthouse until ten of four," I told Mack when I got home that night, very late and still in my mind unprepared to give Lou Schwartz a fitting burst of eloquence at sentencing next day. "That goddamned Dawes kept me tied up there from first light until sundown with his goddamned foolishness. Grandstanding and playing to the gallery, that jerk, and we all have to stand around and be the audience." I made a double vodka martini.

"Well," Mack said, somewhat absently—she'd had a hard day on the job herself but she was doing all she could to listen to me while she charred a steak—"at least all that time you spent should've made old David understand why you cost so much."

"That little toad," I said. David Mackin had hoovered us for thousands to insure Mack would be a rich widow if I checked out, back when we were young and stupid. Then he seemed to reason from our quiet payment of his bills that we were heaven-sent soft touches. He braced Mack one night at some damned function to contribute a full thousand to one of his enthusiasms, and had grown indignant when she said we wouldn't do it. He told her it was our Christian duty, and she asked him where it said in the creed that we had to help him get his picture in the society pages. He got huffy about that, and they both said some more things. Then when he came to see me, having clocked a .13 on the Breathalyzer, noticeably over the .10 cheerfulness the Commonwealth allows the thirsty driver, he was stunned when I demanded three thousand dollars to defend him. "Three grand, Jerry?" he said. "It takes me years to earn that kind of money in commissions from a client."

"Nuts," I said. "It takes you six weeks of telephone calls and weekly visits to badger new, young daddies into buying more coverage than they can afford. After that it's just collection, and the company does that for you, in the first two years. So, don't give me that routine. Besides, what I do's like fixing TVs—what counts is not how long I spend turning screws and humming, but knowing which one is the right one when I open up the set. Three thousand dollars, in advance. That is what the freight is."

"That little shit," Mack said. "He wasn't pleased, I take it?"

"He was extremely displeased," I said, "and he made no secret of it. In the first place, it annoyed him that his case took the whole day. Had to keep going to the pay phone, canceling appointments left and right."

"He didn't expect something like that?" she said. "Hasn't David ever been to court before?"

"Insurance men and judges," I said, "have a lot in common. Both breeds think they outrank all other living beings, including each other. David thinks that everyone, including Judge Dawes and all those around him, should come to a screeching halt when David Mackin's case is on the calendar. I think he was a little miffed that they were hearing other matters today, if you want the truth. And Judge Dawes, of course, takes it as an insult if a lawyer lets it slip he might have some commitments in another court. Judge Dawes thinks you and your client have spent your whole lives preparing for the joy of seeing him, and he doesn't want you to miss out on the slightest bit of it.

"We got in there," I said, "and the first thing that Judge Dawes did was make it extremely clear that if I refused to be appointed to get Harry Mapes his rights, I was not going to have much success in making sure Defendant Mackin enjoyed all of his. David, who was out three grand, of course didn't see it that way. David doesn't go to court enough to know what's going on there, when there is something going on. He got the notion I was taking time out from his global problem to fool around with Mapes's case for nothing."

"Couldn't you explain it to him?" Mack said practically.

"Explain something to David Mackin?" I said. "Are you kidding, lover? By the time three-thirty rolled past, and friend David had been stood up and humiliated right out there in public, told he had to go to school and given a stern lecture about drunken driving from the abstemious Judge Dawes, who does not look like a temperance worker to these bleary eyes, he was long past any point of explanations, even if he had one. And you should've seen his face afterwards when I reminded him he'd turned his license in. We're standing out there on the sidewalk, colder than a witch's tit, and he's just gotten through telling me off for neglecting his case so I could be Mapes's lawyer, and I see him starting for his Thunderbird.

"I looked at him and what he's doing, and he's fishing his keys from his pocket, and I said to my disgruntled client, David Mackin, C.L.U.: 'Just what the hell do you think you're about to do?' And he looked at me and did not call me an asshole, but would clearly have liked to, and he said: 'Well, if it's all right with you, Attorney Kennedy, I thought I'd go back to my office and see if I can salvage one or two late-afternoon appointments from this wasted day.'

" 'David, David,' I said feelingly, 'it always warms my heart to see a conscientious professional going to the service of his clients. That is not what concerns me. What concerns me is how you are going to it.'

" 'Well, Jerry,' he said, 'since my office is in Canton, and I am here in Dedham, I thought I would get into my car and drive to it, you know? Or would you suggest that I flap my arms and avoid the traffic on One-twenty-eight?' "

"My, my," Mack said, "a little sarcasm from our unctuous buddy. I wouldn't've thought he had it in him, nasty cracks like that."

"He hides his light under a bushel," I said. "David's always doing that. 'Well,' I said, 'that would be better, probably, than driving your car anyway. You haven't got a license.'

"He stood there and gaped at me," I said. "Here's the silly, arrogant son of a bitch, got himself plastered, drove his car into the bushes, racked it all up and it's a wonder he didn't cut himself up pretty good at the same time, makes a fool of himself when they give him the breath test, and then he spends an entire day in court which ends with him being yelled at and fined and having to turn his license in, and he comes out of the courthouse and he's all set to drive himself to work. 'The hell do you mean?' he says. 'My car's right there. I've got to get to the office, for Christ sake.'

" 'Your license is in there,' I said. 'Remember? They took it away from you about twenty minutes ago. Said you can't have it back until after you pay this year's taxes, David.'

" 'Well,' he said, 'how am I supposed to get there, then? And what about my car?' So I had to explain to him, slowly and distinctly, that he'd have to call two people to come and meet him, one of them to drive his car home and put it away until the swallows come back to Capistrano. 'Shouldn't be driving those old relics around out in the snow anyway,' I said. 'Isn't good for them, all that salt and shit up under the rocker panels.' And then I turn around to leave him fuming on the sidewalk, and there is my prize client, Harry Mapes, talking to the television people."

"Just what is this guy Mapes's claim to fame?" Mack said. "Is he another one of Nunzio's dancing teachers?"

"Nah," I said. "Harry is a senior citizen these days, and Harry has responsibilities."

Those responsibilities, as Harry confided them to me in our attorney-client conference in a corner of the Norfolk County Law Library, were what he was counting on to get him right back on the street in Judge Luther Dawes's session. Not my wizardry with facts. Not my wisdom in the law. Not my spellbinding oratory. Harry did not want much of anything from me, in fact, not when you got right down to it. He hunched toward me on his wooden chair, cramped into a corner near a window next to mine, set off from the other library visitors by sheets of plywood, two-by-fours, gypsum wallboard, and some bags of nails the carpenters were using to remodel the old place, and gave me a dose of truth along with the worst breath I've drawn at close range in a very long time. "No," he said cordially, "I don't really need you, Counselor. The judge seemed to want to hook you for my case, and it don't matter none to me, if you know what I mean, so what the hell, I figure, right? Let Judge Dawes have his fun with Kennedy; maybe that makes him a little friendlier to me."

"You're the shrewd one, aren't you, Harry?" I said.

"Hey, Counselor, all right?" he said. "Don't take this personal. It's not like I did something to you, or anything like that. You think I had some idea you'd be in here today with your little fairy prince, I decided I'd come in and get you for my lawyer?"

"David's not a fairy," I said.

"Whatever," Harry said, and shrugged. "He looks like one to me. One night in the slammer and he will to other guys. Bet on it. Have more stuff up his ass than he dreamed was in the world."

"I've got other things to do," I said. "Get to the point, Harry."

Harry did get to the point. And what he planned to present was in my estimation just about what he claimed it was: a relatively fresh pitch which might get somewhere with a judge like Dawes. And if it didn't, what had Harry lost? He had no legal defense, and there was no fact question. When we went back to court after our ham sandwiches and bitter coffee at the noon recess, my presentation in behalf of Harry was to say: "May it please the Court. The defendant will admit to sufficient facts to warrant a guilty finding, and desires to be heard in allocution on his own behalf by this honorable Court."

Judge Dawes looked most suspicious. He thought I was trying to get out of something. "This is all that you propose to do for this man, Mister Kennedy?" he said. "This is your idea of full legal representation, for a man who's facing a felony conviction?" That had an ominous ring to it.

"May it please the Court," I said. "In the limited amount of time that this Court has allowed me to confer with my defendant, I have satisfied myself that there was no legal impairment that attached to his arrest. Neither is there any ground, other than the frivolous, on which I can object to the evidence that the Commonwealth informs me it will offer. The best that I can project for Mister Mapes is this Court's leniency, should this Court be moved to exercise it. To invoke that, there is the necessity to overcome the obvious inferences about him which his record of convictions raises rather forcefully. That requires, or would require, rather closer knowledge of his current circumstances than I can pretend to have had time to have acquired for presentation to you. Mister Mapes, though, is a seasoned courtroom veteran in his own right and behalf. He has told me what he plans to say to you. I think it is telling, that it's germane, and that it presents a strong claim for tempering your justice with mercy in this instance. I've advised him to present it. He has taken my advice. Therefore, with the Court's permission, I will sit down and let him do it." Which rhetoric, spread out over the record of the hearing, would nicely spike any plans that Luther Dawes had to cite me to the Board of Bar Overseers for failure to accord a full defense to an indigent defendant; I had just thrown any defects in that proceeding on him, who had given me too little time to prepare. As I said to Mack that night, it's too bad that we don't spend as much time in court looking out for people's welfare and getting justice done as we do trying to catch one another in embarrassing positions, working out old grudges and inventing new ones, while we play at practicing the law.

"I must say I'm surprised, Mister Mapes," Dawes said. He riffled Mapes's thick record as he spoke. "Your history wouldn't seem to leave a lot of leeway to a judge at sentencing."

"I realize that, Your Honor," Mapes said, shifting into that familiar old con's tone of sorrow mixed with anger, regret leavened with determination to do better, chagrin that so many bad companions have led him astray so often. "I realize that you've got your responsibilities. But the thing of it is, and this is what I want to say to you, I also got responsibilities, you know?" He was well into the imploring mode now, developed early in his long career, polished before parole boards and honed to a fine edge to probation officers and rookie reporters on the lookout for a human-interest column that might lead to a cushy job if some bleeding heart should read it. When you start your career while Babe Ruth was in his prime, and make it outlast all of Carl Yastrzemski's years as the successor to Ted Williams, you do gain a certain skillfulness at making the old pitches. Harry sounds like the original victim of society's oppression, and I have to admit that he's very good.

"Responsibilities?" the judge said, arching up those crowd-pleasing eyebrows in that stagey double take they so love for the evening news. He made another show of leafing through Harry's record. "I must say, Mister Mapes, and I assure you that I've read your extensive record carefully and with extreme attention, responsibilities were one thing that did not leap out at me." He let the cover fall on the record and fixed Harry with that glare softened by amusement that he thinks looks good on TV. "Care to enlighten us on them?"

Harry resettled his thin shoulders inside the seedy blue suit that he keeps for such charades, along with the white broadcloth shirt with the sixteen-inch collar that looks like a drape around his fifteen-inch neck. ("Makes it look like you've lost a lot of weight lately, Jerry," he told me, the first time I had a chance to catch his act up close. He winked at me. "Makes them think that you've been sick, and they feel sorry for you. Curley pulled it when they let him out of Danbury. Got himself a pardon from President Truman, the old bastard. Works every time.") He frowned and moistened his lips. He was building the suspense. He looked up at Judge Dawes pleadingly, perhaps the slightest suggestion of tears forming in his eyes. "It's Amanda, Judge," he said.

"Amanda?" the judge said, activating the facial muscles that communicated the refusal to be taken in. "I read pretty carefully when I go through these reports, Mister Mapes," he said. "I don't recall the name of anyone like that in all the reading that I've had to do for your case. Have you been married again since the probation people talked to you the last time?" Harry has been married four times. He went through the third and fourth ceremonies without the formality of divorcing the second wife, but that fact didn't come to light until she thoughtfully saved the Commonwealth the bother of going through a messy bigamy prosecution by dying of cancer at the age of fifty-four. Then Harry brought the still-existing marriage to light by claiming benefits due the surviving widower under her pension plan with the Colter Welting Co.—by then he had divorced wives III and IV, or been divorced by them, so he was technically eligible, and as far as I know, he collected. "You didn't take a fifth wife for yourself, did you, since the last time you had one of these chats with a judge?" Dawes knows that the TV people prefer to have the background titters in the courtroom tapes explained by someone who knows the reason for them, and that if he does that when he is that someone, he gets more air time for himself.

"No, no, Your Honor," Harry said obsequiously, "not another wife. I've learned my lesson in that line, at least. I can say that. No, Amanda is my dog." He paused at that point and looked simultaneously sheepish and forlorn, so that someone reacting quickly to the foolishness of a man claiming his dog as a dependent to exempt him from a jail term would feel ashamed almost immediately for laughing at a lonesome old man who had only a dog for his companion. Harry would not bring up his regular patronage of twenty-dollar whores bolstering their household allowances with a little daytime hooking in the truck-stop bars between Boston and the Cape; no need of spoiling carefully constructed images. The spectators giggled tentatively at what he had said, and the judge looked magisterial and stern, displeased at any laughter that he had not instigated. "She's just a poor lost stray like I am, Judge," Harry said earnestly, driving the point home for those jerks who had missed it. "I seen her at the pound and it was her eyes that did it. I hadda take her in and see if I could give her a good home."

"Didn't I just see something quite a lot like this on television?" Mack said when I was telling her about it. She had, and I told her so. The week that Harry was arrested on the charge that Luther Dawes was having so much fun with, there had been a heartrending story on the TV about a paralyzed veteran pensioner ordered out of subsidized public housing for keeping a dog in violation of the no-pets rule. He had showed up for his hearing in a wheelchair, with all the cameramen tipped off, and said he couldn't move it by himself because his arms were weak. He showed the people how his mutt pulled him around the house, and outdoors to his car, by a rope which hitched the dog to the wheelchair. That prompted a good deal of ridicule for the housing managers: the board ordered them to let the man keep his dog and his small apartment. Mapes had gotten the idea for his dog from that sideshow, and he admitted it to me. "I got twenty priors," he said in the law library. "I'm old now and that's in my favor, but I am still young enough to get caught in somebody else's house, and that sort of goes against me. Unless I go in there with something a whole lot better than I promise them again I won't do it anymore, they're not gonna let me out. The hell do I say this time, huh? 'I finally learned my lesson just by getting grabbed, Your Honor'? 'And a result you should let me go again'? They're not gonna buy that, Jerry, and we're both old enough to know it. Telling them I'm going straight now, that just isn't gonna do it. I got to have something a little different they can hang their hat on this time, and I figure that the dog is gonna be enough."

I told him I doubted it. "Maybe you're right," he said. "Maybe you're right. But what else have I got? My heart's all right. I ain't got cancer. Haven't pissed blood since I cut down on the booze. Nothing wrong with the lungs. Blood pressure's okay. Haven't got no family that'll even speak to me, let alone they got to have me on the street to support them. Shit, I don't even know where most of them are even living. But I figure, dogs are good. Almost everybody likes a dog, doesn't want it to get hurt. All these rest homes, getting dogs, that just shows you what I mean. Gives the old bastards something to think about besides how they wet the bed all the time. So, I go in there and I talk about the dog, tell the judge I'll bring her in if he wants to see her. Maybe then he lets me off, couple hundred hours down the VA Hospital, emptying the bedpans, reading stories to the patients, and that way I get to stay home with my dog and I don't go away again. This guy, you know, they're not on piecework here. He don't get better marks from Boston, where the head judge watches him, the more guys that he sends away to jail. All he needs where I'm concerned is something he can hang his hat on, and I'm betting that the dog'll be enough."

Judge Dawes received that pitch about the dog as though he'd spent his whole career apprenticed at the Old Vic. Harry could've improved the judge's part only if he'd somehow managed to locate a homeless child instead of just a dog. Which is some reassurance that the orphanages must be still enforcing some sort of minimum requirements, or else Harry would have had a kid, I'm sure. "A dog?" the judge said, all but rupturing his facial muscles. "You ... are you suggesting that I shouldn't punish you because you have a dog?"

It was as though the two of them had been bucking for a series. Harry let the judge enjoy his full audience reaction, and the claque performed impeccably. Then he launched into a summary of his long career of stealing things from people's houses, getting put in jail for it, then doing it again—by the time he started his wrap-up he was speaking in a hush. "I know what I am, Judge," he said. "I know what Amanda is. We are both getting old, and both of us have spent most of our lives in one lockup or another, except it was not her fault that she did and it was my fault I did.

"If I go away again," Harry said earnestly, "Amanda gets locked up again, and this will probably be her last time. They will put her to sleep. It could be my last time too, Your Honor, and I have to think of that. Jail hasn't done me no real good, and it could kill Amanda. So, what I am asking is, let me do some of that community service thing that they have got these days, and let me stay at home with my dog, and I will behave myself." He paused and snuffled once or twice, not at all convincing if you knew the old faker and were sitting close enough to see his eyes were dry, but most likely quite affecting from, say, twenty feet away, or on the other side of a television camera. "She's," he said, catching his voice for the merest instant, "she is all I got now, Judge, and I am all she's got. Can you give us two old dogs a break we maybe don't deserve?"

Old curs would've been more like it. But that, given Luther Dawes's fondness for publicity—and, to give Harry his due, the reasonable logic of the argument the old thief had just presented—was immaterial. Dawes had just been offered the jurist's equivalent of the lead part in *King Lear*, and he was not about to turn it down. He went into the thoughtful judge's pondering mode, the one which announces everything in a deeper baritone reserved for new decisions in the great traditions of Solomon and Moses, the measured delivery of a man about to temper stern justice with tender mercy. "You argue most persuasively, Mister Mapes," he said. Most likely receiving vibrations of my hidden disdain for his posturing, he then gave me what he hoped was a sardonic glance. "Far more persuasively, I might say, than a good many of the lawyers whom I have appear before me. Wouldn't you agree, Mister Kennedy?"

I cleared my throat to answer, and to let the courtroom tittering, caused by Dawes at my expense, die down before I spoke—I know a few tricks too, when it comes to courtroom inspiration of pity and fear in the onlookers. "I'd be surprised if he did not, Your Honor," I said. "He's been in court lots more than many of us, after all, and there are times like this one when he gets a more respectful hearing than we do." That drew a few *oohs* and *ahhs* and a little gasp from the sycophants, who thought correctly that I had been too sarcastic but did not perceive that Dawes had waived his right to hold me in contempt by provoking it in the first place. Furthermore, there wasn't any chance that I would hurt my client by getting Dawes pissed off at me; I had my deal for Mackin with the DA, and the judge had already made it clear that he was going to do Harry a favor and make sure at the same time that I got no credit for it.

Dawes frowned, this time because he was annoyed and not for some effect. He said: "I'll, ah, let that remark pass this time, Mister Kennedy, except to remind you that this is still a court of law." He paused again, expectantly, to see if I'd be fool enough to make some further crack about it sometimes being hard to tell, but I've been matching wits with the Luther Daweses of this world for over twenty years now, and I don't fall for sucker traps like that. I kept my big mouth shut.

"As for you, Mister Mapes," he said, all business now that I had spoiled his little minstrel show, "there's much in what you say." And then he ordered Harry to complete two thousand hours of volunteer work, ten times what Harry'd had in mind, at the school for the retarded during the next year, which would keep the old felon busy full-time, fifty weeks to come, hit him with two years to be served in minimum-security MCI Norfolk, and suspended that term on condition that he complete all his volunteer work.

"Too bad we got home too late to see if it was on the news," my wife, the former Joan McManus, said as she put the steaks and baked potatoes on the dinette table.

"Yeah," I said, "I know. That would improve my mood for sure, to see it again in instant replay." I got up from the table as she sat down at her place.

"Where're you going?" she said.

"To get another drink," I said, rattling the ice cubes in the otherwise empty glass.

"Which would be what, your third?" she said.

"My second, if we're keeping score all of a sudden in this joint," I said.

"Meaning: your fourth, along with your third," she said. "I assume you're drinking doubles."

"Jesus," I said, "what is this? You'd like it better, maybe, if I had a beer or something?"

"I'd prefer it," she said. "Even more, I'd prefer it if you had a beer when you got home, instead of those moonrakers that you've gotten into the habit of stoking up with lately, the minute you walk in the door."

I continued toward the liquor cabinet. "All right," I said, "I'll mark it down on my calendar. Tomorrow, right after Lou Schwartz goes to jail, I'll turn myself in down at the Washingtonian and have them dry me out."

"Jerry," she said, "let me up. That's not what I'm saying and you know it."

I mixed another drink. "Okay," I said, "I stand corrected. Somehow I seem to have gotten the impression I was being nagged about my drinking. My mistake." I brought the drink back to the table and sat down again.

"Diane's getting through," she said. She hacked at the steak as though it had done something to her too. Her lips were tight and she was scowling at the plate. Mack moved from residential real estate sales into corporate parcel planning at her office just as Jimmy Carter's recession had begun to erode business confidence, and what had looked like a promotion to more responsibility and considerably more money at first seemed more like a decision to commit financial suicide. Because she alone in the corporate division did not depend on her earnings to support her family—the three other women were divorced and had long since earned their way out of eligibility for alimony under the new rehabilitative state statute which cuts it off as soon as the ex-wife proves she can support herself, and the two men were sole breadwinners for their broods—she had been able to weather the high interest rates and general despair of the business world. That left her pretty much in control of the department when things started to improve, but it also left her managing the whole division, and Mack wasn't that good an administrator. She didn't like to ride herd on subordinates, or make it clear to those who were not working out that they had better start thinking about finding new jobs elsewhere; when she had been forced to fire one completely disorganized young man, caught using his company charge cards to entertain delighted young ladies whom he'd met in shopping-plaza singles bars, it wore her out for weeks.

"Well," I said, "that should be good news. Did Diane get the idea all by her lonesome, or did you have to suggest it to her?"

"I suggested it," Mack said. "I've got to start being tougher with those people, and I know it. I called her in to my cubicle this morning and I sat her down and said: 'Diane, here are the facts. You told Red Teasdale that the Hoadley Family Trust would give him an easement from the road to the Siding Acreage. Red put a binder on the Siding Acreage on the strength of what you said. Dennis Farina, that prick, found out from the railroad lawyers what Red Teasdale had gone and done, in perfect innocence. Dennis told his partner, and his partner is Bill Walsh. Bill Walsh isn't a bad guy, but Bill Walsh has a duty to his clients in the Hoadley Family Trust to make sure that they get top dollar for whatever they may sell. Now the Hoadleys want at least ten thousand dollars, and they're saying they want twenty, for an easement to the Siding Acreage. Red has got twenty thousand dollars down on that against a final cost of seventy. Which happens to be all that Red can see his way clear to financing, just for purchasing raw land. You knew that and I knew that when we told Red to bind the Siding, which means Red is now in a position to lose twenty earnest money if he doesn't deal with Walsh, and at least ten more if he does.'

"You know what she said to me?" Mack said. "She batted those big violet eyes of hers and fiddled with the pencils in my desk tray, and told me Red could find the extra ten grand if he wanted. 'If Red Teasdale really was that serious,' she said, 'he could find that Hoadley money without any trouble.'

" 'Diane,' I said, being very calm, not letting her see for a minute I would kill her if I could, 'what Red could do if he wanted is no business of ours. He told us right from the giddyap what he was willing to put into acquisition of the Siding property. Seventy was his top figure, which the client gets to pick. If you'd kept your big mouth shut, he could have made his pitch to the Hoadleys about how their land would be enhanced by what he plans to do with the Siding piece, and they would have gone for it. Now they're locked in to a figure, and they'll think he wants to cheat them. And that means he'll come to us and say we should make things right. And we'll end up splitting with Red what he pays to buy off Bill Walsh and the Hoadley family, which will most likely be five thousand bucks off our piece. Ace and Roy won't like it when I tell them that. Our share of that action came to fourteen thousand dollars. Your loose lip has cost us more than a third of that.'

"She didn't care at all," Mack said, stabbing the steak. "The little fool's on her draw and her commission plus, and it won't mean a hundred dollars out of her pay envelope. She just stood there and she shrugged and made that little shoulder motion that she does, and gave that injured 'I'm sorry' she uses when she's not sorry at all. So, and until then I don't think that I'd really made my mind up, I said: 'Diane, this is the fourth time that something like this's happened when you were involved in something fairly sensitive. I think the time has come when I've just got to tell you that this isn't working out.'

" 'Does that mean that I'm fired?' she said. 'It means that you're going to be,' I said. And I told her she's got three weeks to find another job."

"Why three?" I said.

"Why not?" Mack said. "I want her out of there before the first of March, that's why. I could've made it four, I guess, or two, as far as that goes. I didn't really plan it out, if you want the truth. I just decided that I've had it with her and I don't care any longer if her husband used to beat her and he's not seeing their kids. I'm fed up with her, and that's all that there is to it. She's gotten to the point where she's more trouble than she's worth."

"I hate sounding like a broken record," I said, "but I've got to take the chance. You ought to give some thought to telling Roy you want to get back into sales. This management crap does not agree with you."

"Like that steak doesn't with you?" she said, pointing toward my plate with her fork.

"Joan," I said, which I call her very infrequently because she does not enjoy thinking of herself as another Joan Kennedy and long since became tired of explaining that we're no kin to those Kennedys, "it's not my fault you had a bad day too, all right? So don't sit there and blame me for it, if it's all the same to you. I had a full ration of joy myself today, and if I want to unwind and enjoy a couple drinks before I actually begin eating, that should not be something that would piss you off at me. All I said was that you don't like running things, and maybe you should say so and stop doing it."

"Jerry," she said, "listen to me. Let me say it once again. Heather is grown up now. I have some abilities. I am good at what I do, and I can make good money at it. We can do things with that money when she's graduated, things that we've been putting off, or never even thought about." Mack has the first of those things that we never even thought about, a Mercedes station wagon, leased by the company, of course, but leased by the company for her—we not only didn't think about Mercedes station wagons; I never in my wildest dreams imagined that she wanted one. "I want those things, Jerry," she said, "and this is how to do it. Two or three major development projects and I'll be flying high. I don't want to get there and then turn around and notice that I've got a problem with you that I don't know how to deal with. Or one that nobody else knows how to deal with either."

"Can it, Mack," I said, the steak growing colder by the minute. "You've got no problem with me, except maybe that I tell you things that you don't want to hear."

"Do you think that, Jerry?" she said, looking very worried. "Sometimes I get this horrible feeling that everything's just coming apart all around me, and I don't know what to do about it. I see it happening, and it seems like I just stand there helplessly and I don't know what to do."

I hate that stricken look she gets sometimes. It's one of many things in this life that I don't handle well. I put the drink down and began to cut at the cold meat. "Look," I said, "I'm down. I know I shouldn't get like this when I draw somebody like Dawes and he makes me an unexpected present of somebody like Mapes, and I get the pleasure of seeing myself treated as some kind of a volunteer that the two of them called up from the audience to be the stiff in their magic show. The lady that gets sawed in half, and all she has to do is smile.

"I'm a trial lawyer, Mack," I said. "That's all I am, and I know that, and I'll most likely never be anything more than that."

"You might be a judge someday, if you wanted," she said.

"Unlikely," I said, "and anyway, I don't want. I like being a trial lawyer. It's what I always wanted to do, and be, and I'm good at it now.

I've been at it a long time, I'm at home in the courtrooms, and I'm a man who knows his business. Not some kind of a well-dressed bystander that you give a few lines to when you decide you're Judge Dawes, by God, and you're going to stage a public entertainment in your courtroom today. Some kind of an asshole."

"I see," she said.

"I hope so," I said. "This charade that we all went through today? That was supposed to be a sentencing procedure. But if that is what it was, then that's what everybody should get. Everybody that gets caught doing something that's against the law, but didn't hurt another person doing it, should get to stand up on his hind legs in the courtroom and draw Luther Dawes to put on something right straight out of Dickens. Let them all delight the crowds, and then go home to frolic with their dogs and praise the kindly judges so the evening news'll have an upbeat story to go with the body counts from wherever it is that we've got the Marines standing guard tonight.

"The trouble is, Mack," I said, feeling sorry for myself, "most of the time it is not like this. Tomorrow, for example, it is not going to be like that. When Judge Maguire comes out and sits down on his ass in federal court and puts the boots to Louis Schwartz, it is not going to be like that. It is going to be a bad day and a sad one, and a guy I like who's not a bad man either, when you come right down to it, nowhere near as bad a man as Harry Mapes has been for all his worthless life, is going to the can. If an old fraud and a thief like Harry Mapes gets off today on his twenty-first or twenty-second offense, Louis Schwartz for damned sure ought not to go away on his first one."

"But," she said, ever practical, "you'd have to say the cases aren't the same."

"I would," I said, "I certainly would."

"And the one you had today," she said, "you didn't have any choice about taking."

"None," I said.

"Whereas the one tomorrow," she said, "well, that's one you ought not to have taken."

"Even though I might actually like to say that I agree with that," I said, "I am not going to do it." I put a big piece of meat in my mouth and chawed away at it, trying to smile with my bulging mouth.

"No," she said, "because if you do, I will say: 'I told you so.'"

"Uh-huh," I said.

"As in fact," she said, "I did. Tell you so, I mean."

"Yes," I said, still stubborn, "that you did. But you did not have a good reason."

"Intuition," Mack said sulkily.

"That is not reason," I said, "let alone good reason."

She waited a while. Then she said: "I didn't know the reason then. Now I do know. Can I say it?"

"Sure," I said, "why not? When did you start pulling punches with me, kid?"

"Oh," she said, "geez, I don't know. It's just that, you thought you were moving up, Jerry, when you took Lou Schwartz on."

"He's easily the biggest case I ever had," I said.

"To other people, maybe," she said, "sure. But not to your clients that you've helped so much. Not to Teddy. Not even to me and Heather, you know? You thought you were going to get Lou off, Jerry."

"No, I didn't," I said. "I knew it was a tough case. I said I'd probably lose."

"Yeah," she said, "but you didn't believe it. You sound different when you're saying something that you really think, and something you just hope maybe you can get somebody else to think. You convinced yourself that you could win this loser, Jerry, and you never do that. Ever. And you did it because if he wasn't sick, that big faker Frank Macdonald would have had it, and that makes it big time in your eyes." I did not say anything.

"Jerry," she said, "I know you like Lou, all right? And that you're sorry that you lost. And so am I, all right? But you lost more than he did in this thing, Jerry, and that makes me feel bad."

"I lost more?" I said. "Lou's going to the can, not me."

"I know," she said, "I know. But your sentence is worse. You're starting to act scared."

4

"COUNSELOR," Lou Schwartz said to me in the morning, "I saw you on television last night." I had seen me on TV late the night before also, and I had not liked it one bit better than I had expected to. Mack and I had sat there in the living room, friends again allied against a regularly unfair world, and right after that fool weatherman finished his capers on the screen like some overgrown and deranged schoolboy, capable at any moment of unzipping his pants and displaying with a storm of giggles what I'm sure he'd call his *wee-wee*, and the sports announcer had guffawed and snickered out the scores, Harry and the judge's show came on for the last laugh. I appeared in the minor role of the uncomfortable scold.

"Yes, sir," Lou said, his white teeth perfect in his winter tan, his expensive hairpiece meticulously fitted to his remaining fringe, "I thought you were pretty good."

"Screw you," I said, "you bastard."

"That is later, Jerry," Lou said, "and the judge, Maguire, does that. You got the potential for an entire new career there, Attorney Kennedy, unless I miss my guess and of course I never do."

"Uh-huh," I said. "To which I could say, I suppose, that if you never miss your guess, how was it Judge Maguire became involved in this?"

"Jerry, Jerry," Lou said, "let me have my fun. Is that a nice thing to be saying to a man on Toothbrush Day?" I had explained that usage to Lou many years ago, when he first started being my accountant. Toothbrush Day is the day when defendants who have lost appear in court for sentencing and know that they are going. Those who are prudent show up with their dental tools and supplies of prescription drugs, because they do not get to go home and pack a bag after sentence is pronounced.

"I suppose not," I said.

"So there I was," he said, "in bed, bare-ass like a fuckin' snake between my satin sheets, my body all rubbed down with some expensive stuff Joanna gets to make me smell good, and I am all relaxed from the Jacuzzi, right? Joanna is removing her peignoir and getting ready to do some amazing things to me, and we have got plans that are going to mean that I am coming in here with my eyes all bloodshot today, because no man should go to prison horny. And I am lying there with this enormous hard-on poking up the sheets, and damned if I do not get shown this picture of my learned counsel.

" 'Look,' I says to Joanna, 'there is my learned counsel.' 'Where?' says Joanna, like I mean you're in the room. Right about then she has got the peignoir down around her ankles, if you know what I mean, and if you had've really been there, Jerry, I mean to tell you, you would have seen something that you would remember." Lou met Joanna in Las Vegas, where she was a showgirl. He likes to remind people that she is a very well-built lady, a fact which he seems to believe reflects credit upon him. "Did I ever tell you, Jerry, about Joanna's bush?" He had, many times. Each time he began by asking whether he had told me before, and each time told me again without waiting for an answer. "Joanna has got her bush shaped like a heart," he said, always with the same juicy delight. "She has them do it that way when she goes in for her bikini wax." That disclosure is always followed by a brief, lewd pause, during which Lou seems to expect whomever he has listening to join in a moment of lascivious tribute to Joanna's genitals. Lou is not the only man I know who does this sort of thing and therefore he is not the only one who regularly makes me wonder whether he is wholly sane, but I try to remember that I most likely do things that baffle him too, and he puts up with me.

"Anyway," Lou said, "I get her straightened out, Joanna, I mean, that you are on the television, not right in the bedroom, and so before we get down to the real entertainment for the evening, we watch your performance."

"You were thrilled, I'm sure," I said.

"Actually, Jerry," Lou said, "your part didn't seem that big, you know? Joanna thought you did all right, and so did I, as far as what you had to do went, but—and I said this to her—it sort of seemed like the judge and that guy you had were sort of working that thing out between themselves."

"I was at something of a handicap," I said. "I never met the goddamned dog."

"Hey," Lou said, "I didn't mean . . . I was just saying, you know? Besides, I'm probably too friendly with you anyway to judge something like that. I see someone I know on television and he looks lots fatter'n I think of him as being. That and the eyes, you know? Guys right off the street, guys like you and me that don't go on TV all the time, it seems like you're always looking shifty. The people that're on it, they can look right at you, it seems like, so you look at the TV set and they look back at you. But somebody like you, you know, you're always looking around, like you're nervous and you're looking for some way to get out of there."

"I am nervous," I said. "Every time I forget and I look up toward that camera, all I want to do is make it so I didn't do it, you know? So I didn't look at it. I always feel just like it caught me doing something. Picking my nose, maybe, or hustling my balls. Like the baseball players that they're always catching on the on-deck circle, got their hands down in their jocks, moving their balls around."

"Yeah," Lou said, "but all the same, I still thought you were good. Even though I am so close to you."

That had been Mack's reason for opposing my decision to take on defending Lou. She had said I was too close to him to represent him properly. "It's just what you've always said yourself," she said to me. "You said it about Frank Macdonald when he took Paul Sweeney's case. Long before that case was tried, months before Frank had that heart attack, that first one that he had right afterwards, you said Frank should duck that case. 'He's too close to the guy,' you said. 'He'll get himself all tied up in his own knots about it, and he won't be able to get far enough away from the fact it's his friend that's in the dock to act like his lawyer when he gets in court.'"

"I was younger then," I told Mack. "I was new at this. Teddy Franklin, for example—he'd just come to me. When I represented Teddy then, he was not a friend of mine. He was just another guy, someone who hired me. Now? I've been doing Teddy's work for more years than either one of us really likes to think about. I know him as well as I know anybody, except you and Heather. Are you telling me now I should quit representing Teddy 'cause I've gotten so I know him so well? Good Christ, woman, how could a man build a practice if he started firing every client that he really got to know? Every year'd be your rookie season, if you started doing that."

"That's not what I mean," she said. "Teddy and you're not the same thing as you and Lou'll be. Teddy's street goes one way: he gets into trouble, stealing Cadillacs. You get Teddy out of trouble, and he steals more Cadillacs. That's not what you used to tell me you were going to do, when we lived on pasta for three years of law school fun and games, all that noble oratory about principles and stuff, but it is what you are doing and it seems to make you happy.

"Lou is different," she said. "Lou is someone that you're Teddy to. You had trouble with your taxes; Frank said Lou would get you out."

"Keep me out," I said. "I didn't have the trouble, if you're bringing that stuff up. Frank just said that I was going to, and I should get Lou to prevent it. Which I did, and which Lou did."

"Same thing, from my point of view," Mack said. "That arrangement was: Lou works for Jerry, and it worked out pretty well. Now you're changing things. Now Jerry works for Lou, and we're going to see how that works."

"I can agree with that," I said. "I don't have trouble with that. Lou has done good work for me, and kept me out of trouble. Now Lou's in the gravy. I'll see if I can get him out. Nothing wrong with that, my love. That is what I do. Do that sort of thing for lots of people."

"Who you can do that stuff for," she said. "That's another thing about Lou's case that stinks. You are going into it to get him out of it. You've told me yourself that you can't get him out of it. It's precisely the same thing that Frank had with Paul Sweeney. It wasn't bad enough it was his father's partner. It wasn't bad enough he absolutely had to win it. No, it was also a hopeless case, one no one could win. Which meant Frank had to have a miracle. Absolutely had to have a miracle.

"You've told me all I need to hear about needing miracles, my love," she said. "You said you'd never get yourself in a position where you started looking for one, 'cause miracles don't happen anymore, and lawyers that take cases where they have to look for them are on their way to heart attacks instead. 'I always enjoy my lunch,' you've always told me. 'Even on Toothbrush Day, my client goes away, and I close up my briefcase and go locate Coop for lunch.' And now, after all those years of being sensible, you're going to tell Lou Schwartz you're going to represent him. It doesn't make sense, Jerry," she said. "It makes no sense at all."

"Of course it does," I'd said. "It all makes perfect sense. It's something that I have to do, something I wish I didn't. The only problem with the sense it makes is that I wish it didn't."

"Television," I said to Lou that morning, "is not something that you don't judge somebody on just because you know him. Television's something you forgive somebody for, if it's something you know, if it happened to him and he couldn't help it, all right?"

"I still think you have got some promise there," Lou said.

"We'll talk about that someday when there's nothing else to do," I said. "Today we've got other business." I described to him the main points that I'd touch upon in court. They did not amount to much. I would tell the judge that Lou reserved his right to an appeal. He could also reserve at the same time his seat on the Space Shuttle, for all the potential good it promised him. Grounds for an appeal become apparent on the day the judge creates them, doing something stupid in presiding at the trial, cause for much rejoicing that same night back in the office for the cherished fail-safe they give the defendant just in case the jury doesn't come back cheerful toward him. We had had no such rejoicing during *U.S.* v. *Schwartz.* Judge Maguire did not accept chances to do stupid things. The prosecutor, Michael Dunn, had given him a couple opportunities, offering evidence that might have poisoned the proceedings, put Lou in a good position to petition for reversal and remand for a new trial, set me up to play upon the government's reduced enthusiasm for staging the whole show again, raised the possibility of dealing for suspended punishment. Judge Maguire had firmly refused those temptations, politely but with assurance upholding the objections that I made against my will, knowing that he'd exclude what Dunn offered if I didn't object and thus tainted the appeal by my own silence. Judge Maguire did not take risks, any more than he accepted invitations. Lou's conviction therefore was as clean as the Pope's conscience. If he appealed, as he could, Judge Maguire would let him out until the First Circuit decided. Its decision would be that the trial was fair and Lou must turn himself in.

"Which if I go through all of that," Lou said, "means that first I pay you some more money, and I get to wait for summer. Then I lose on the appeal, and all of a sudden I am sitting in my box at Saratoga next August, me and Joanna picking veal out of our teeth and having some light table wines, perhaps, and a couple U.S. marshals show up and say: 'Skip the third race, Lou. They set a place at dinner for you down at Danbury tonight.'"

"That's about it," I said to him.

"Then: no, thanks, then," Lou said. "I think I don't want to do that, if it's all the same to you." He managed about half a grin. He patted the breast pocket of his pewter-colored suit, cheap worsted stuff that didn't come from Lou's customary wardrobe. A clear-plastic toothbrush container with a fluorescent-pink toothbrush inside protruded from it. "See?" he said. "I'm all prepared. Just like you and Frank were always saying." He shot the jacket and shirt cuffs over his left wrist, displaying a new Timex watch. "The Corum's in the safe-deposit box," he said with satisfaction. Lou always wore a Corum gold-piece wristwatch rimmed with diamonds that had cost about ten thousand dollars in Zurich years ago; it went well with his Ultrasuede suits and his Bally loafers, though the gems did tend to snag the cuffs of his silk shirts. "Not letting those hard guys rip me off, no sirree," he said. "Might be a couple days before the word gets down there, how I am a pal of Nunzio's. Don't want to get myself off on the wrong foot, cause anybody to do something he might regret later."

"There aren't any hard guys down at Danbury," I said. "Don't make this enforced vacation any worse than it's really going to be. Danbury is the place where they send the well-behaved guys."

"Bullshit," Lou said, shaking his head, "not if they're sending me there." Lou liked to pretend he was as tough as the other men that worked for Nunzio, those who did the things that protected Nunzio's varied business interests and insured the profits that he hired Lou to conceal. Which employment was what had attracted the government's attention to Lou in the first place. Lou could count on Nunzio's protection while he was doing time, but he wasn't likely to require it. Still, if it made him feel better to make believe like that, I could see no reason to deny him that small pleasure. "That's why I got this suit," he said, almost gleefully. "One-ten off the rack. Hard-finish worsted, just like all those cheap Yankee bastards wear that they inherited from their grandfathers and've still got soup and vegetables all over them from six or seven years ago. Still, though, not all that bad, you know? Doesn't quite have the drape you get with the seven-hundred-dollar models up at Louis', the Vietnamese tailors sneaking all around you, pushing pins in at your ankles and hiking up your crotch, but for going to the can, right? I hear we all dress pretty much alike in there anyway, once they get us deloused and everything." He patted his head. "Hope they don't work it like the Marines do," he said, "with the hair, I mean. If they're gonna mow this, they could ruin a four-thousand-dollar investment here."

"You seem to be taking this extremely well," I said.

He looked at me critically. "Yeah," he said, "I guess I am. At least if you're any indication of how other folks're taking it."

I saw no reason in trying to blow smoke at him. A feature of our friendship, not to mention the *sine qua non* of our professional relationship, has been candor. That was true from the beginning, when he was the provider and I was the customer. "I know about you lawyers," he had said to me back then. "How you're always saying, the first thing you tell somebody when you're gonna represent him is: don't lie to me, you stupid bastard. So I get to say that to you, without thinking about how maybe I might hurt your tender feelings, all right? Do not lie to me. You lie to me and I am helpless. And anyway, you lie to me and you're not really lying to me anyway—you're lying to yourself because you don't like the idea, paying so much taxes, and you think if you can tell yourself a little story, and then tell that same story to me, then I will tell it to the government and that'll do it for you.

"It won't," Lou said then. "I am not gonna let you get away with it, because if I go along with you, and that is what we file, then my cock goes into the blender right along with yours, and that don't appeal to me, you know? So, no bullshit, Counselor." And that is how we have done business ever since.

"Hey," I said to him on sentencing day, "it's not that I especially enjoy the idea of putting you in the position where you're giving sympathy to me, when it should be the other way around. But, no, I can't say that I'm taking this too well at all."

"Good Christ, man," Lou said, feigning some dismay, "I hope you're not gonna tell me this'll spoil your lunch. They'll be ashamed of you at Locke's if you start to act like that."

"You got the wrong guy," I said. "That is Frank that does that." Frank Macdonald's legend includes the story of a client whom he disliked very much, suffering through the fellow's complaints and harassments right through disposition of his case. Which included a long jail term. The client stood there at the bar as Frank closed up his briefcase, and he leered at Frank. "All right, wise guy," he's supposed to have said, "now what do we do?" "It's very simple," Frank claimed to have said. "You go with these gentlemen who have the handcuffs here. I go by myself to the Locke Ober Cafe, where since this is Thursday they will have the roast beef hash."

"Not anymore, Frank doesn't," Lou said, looking sad. I could not think of anything to say, and so for a while we both just sat there, miserable.

5

WHEN I started as a trial lawyer, more than twenty years ago, Frank Macdonald ruled the roost. He was not by any means the only top-flight defense lawyer in the city, let alone New England, as was sometimes widely assumed, or the whole Republic, as his more fawning friends would now and then allege when they had imbibed a lot of his booze at some celebration after a big case he'd won. Knowledgeable, envious, disapproving members of the trial bar frequently disparaged him, saying he was too young to deserve such a reputation, making snide remarks about his name in all the papers, asking whether anyone who drank as much as Frank did could deliver what he promised to a desperate client. But the public, from which clients come, did not hear those reservations. Where the public was concerned, Frank Macdonald was the king.

Now it all seems to have happened such a long, long time ago. My friends that I graduated with have gone from short hair into long hair, and we're looking toward no hair, older now than Frank was then when it seemed like no day went by without some news he made. Down in Austin a grand jury went amok with a young prosecutor, and the nation was astonished one night when two prominent Texas politicians were indicted with the clear prediction that a U.S. senator was next. Rich oilmen were worried and there was a great commotion. Two days later, Frank Macdonald stepped out of a jet at Love Field down near Dallas and delivered a few salvos of his own. The next several weeks were hectic, with him swaggering on television, making brash statements to reporters from *The New York Times*, heckling from Texas those who were sharpshooting him at home. Frank got a Not Guilty for an ex-governor, collapsing the entire circus down around the prosecutor's ears. It was said afterwards that the oilmen had spent more renting Frank than they had disbursed to purchase the politicians outright, and when Frank heard that he grinned and said: "No comment."

The police in Santa Barbara grabbed a fellow whom they said was the Surfing Beach Killer, and charged him with fourteen dissecting murders of young, blond, runaway beach bums. His family declared he didn't do it, and hocked a mansion on the Pacific Coast Highway to hire Frank to back them up—Frank got an acquittal. The United States Army convened a court-martial in North Carolina for the prosecution of a Green Beret noncom whom they said took entirely too much pleasure in his work in Vietnam, and Frank beat that one too. The worst result he had in those years was the Brattleboro Baby Baker, which involved a bedraggled young girl up in Vermont whose illegitimate infant daughter had somehow turned up in a commercial bakery oven with a finished batch of brownies; Frank had to content himself with getting her committed to the booby hatch for life, innocent by reason of insanity.

On the brighter side of forty, Frank Macdonald then looked like a man who had spent his later teen-aged years setting rushing records for the USC Trojans, without the assistance of a good offensive line. He had in fact spent those years as a cooperative student at Northeastern University, alternating ten-week class terms with part-time employment as a private detective. By rights, from the way he strutted, his twenties ought to have included thirty missions as a Navy fighter pilot, before he was mustered out to make a law review record at the Yale Law School. In fact, Frank had been judged unfit for military service, exempted by what lingered from a childhood case of polio; his tailors cut the suits so that his arm brace didn't show. He had financed his legal training at the Suffolk Law School, nights, doggedly collecting information on the wanderings of errant husbands whose displeased wives had hired divorce lawyers who in turn hired Frank. Frank had all the glamor that a sane man could have wished, and he'd earned every bit of it. But as he announced himself, it all came from his legal work: "I buckle all my swashes in the courtroom."

Mack and my classmates' wives did not like Frank Macdonald. Roger Kidd's snotty bride, Polly, sniffed that Frank was "recent." Mack told me that Polly Kidd was right about him, and said furthermore that he was "juvenile." I said Polly Kidd had been created by a taxidermist and had never gotten over the disappointment she felt when she discovered that Americans could no longer purchase slaves. I said "juvenile" was the term used by first wives to explain the motives of successful men who had taken second wives. Mack said I only had it partly right—it was for successful men who had married second wives and then cheated on them.

Frank Macdonald did not care what our wives thought of him. He believed his style in the courtroom—go in at ramming speed and dare anyone to stop him—should work just as well outside of it. "And besides," he would tell you, "it's the only one I've got." When he was on a roll, as he was in those exciting years, that style worked just fine. Frank would have been a fool to tamper with it, and he didn't.

That manner led to the belief that Frank had an ego which would fit onto Mount Rushmore only if they removed Washington. That was somewhat misleading, if you knew the man. It was true that he regarded himself as the lion of the Boston defense bar. But it is also true that every member of the Boston trial bar regards himself as its lion, if only in the privacy of his own shower stall. Frank's self-esteem was more noticeable because there were quite a few people outside the bar association who agreed with him, and took upon themselves the burden of extolling him—all he had to do was nod every now and then, which he was of course quite glad to do, and he began to seem like an egomaniac.

He seemed completely devoid of jealousy. He may have reigned over everyone who would allow it, but he did it generously. A rookie who attracted some modest attention by his trial of an obscure case which the knowledgeable—who quite frequently know very little—had regarded as a blowout for the prosecution, a sure loser that should be pleaded out at any cost, could expect a warm note of congratulations for a valiant effort, and an invitation to have lunch with Frank if he managed to win the impossible thing. Frank would go out of his way to deflect public praise of himself by mentioning the new star in his radio and television appearances, and if there was a codefendant drifting around without his own counsel in one of Frank's big cases, Frank would recommend someone who had started to do well.

I suppose a critical person would say that Frank patronized us. That he was paternal and condescending, and that he kept his grip on the press by making sure that any newcomer in the public eye arrived there under his sponsorship. Mack said he made potential rivals into toadies, and there was an edge in her voice which conveyed her apprehension that he was performing that transformation upon me. "He's seducing you," she said when I challenged her on that.

"Not me," I said. "I haven't got big tits."

"No," she said, "that is true, but you do have a brain. You and several other people that Frank has identified. You're a threat to him, Jerry, in your own sweet way." I scoffed at that. "You are," she said, "and he agrees with me, although he'd never say it. He buys you drinks and tells you stories, picks up all the checks. You all sit around and laugh at all his jokes, and anybody looking at you, seeing you like that, would think, if he didn't know you and he had to hire a lawyer: 'What the hell, they're all alike, all Frank Macdonald's boys. I might as well hire Frank Macdonald, go for the head man himself. Not even bother with one of his altar boys.' You're letting him control the business, when he entertains you. You're letting him say how fast you'll progress, and how far, too, now that I think of it. He takes you under his wing, and it flatters you, and you accept his management. So that is where you stay, under his wing, in his shadow, never showing on your own, always Frank's assistant."

"It's fun," I said then, "and the money's pretty good." It was that too, the money. Second counsel on a Frank Macdonald trial made a lot more than some unvouched-for unknown who was running his own case. Those clients that he had to distribute among us paid fees without question that we couldn't get elsewhere. I remember the first time that he called me to take a drunk-driving case, some selectman out in Bellingham who saw his whole life ending. "Charge him eighteen hundred," Frank said, "or don't take the stinking case." "Eighteen hundred?" I said. "God. I think I'm giving guys the shaft when I quote seven-fifty." "And that's why they complain when they have to pay you that," Frank said. "Eighteen hundred, on the table, no work done for less," and so that was what I charged. The selectman was convicted, as I knew he'd be and as I'm sure Frank had anticipated when he bumped the case to me, but I did manage to save the poor guy's license—this was a good many years before Mothers Against Drunk Drivers began to get driving-under treated like a crucifying offense—and his world therefore didn't end. He therefore decided I was the new Clarence

Darrow, if not quite the younger Frank Macdonald, and he sent me several other clients who paid similar tariffs. "I would not have gotten that first case without Frank Macdonald," I told Mack. "I would not have gotten that fee without Frank telling me to charge it, or the later cases which also paid big fees. Frank Macdonald made them think I'm worth a lot of money, and once they have paid it, no matter how the case turns out, they think I am worth it."

"Uh-uh," she said, "no way. What they're afraid of is they'll lose their licenses. They don't know you'd save them for half what they're paying you, or that you're doing it by playing hardball with every case because you actually like to try cases. They think you're putting the fix in, and that's why you cost so much. That you're probably charging them eight hundred for yourself, and palming a grand off to the judge and the DAs. And that you're too smart to tell them that flat out."

"Oh, bullshit," I said. "They never got that kind of an idea from me."

"I'm sure they didn't," she said. "They got it from Frank. If you ask me, that's how Frank gets most of his great cases. Some poor desperate soul, scared half out of his wits, sees that he's in big trouble, or maybe his kid is. And the first thing that they think of is: 'Who's that guy up in Boston that saved that crook in Texas? That goddamned Green Beret that burned up all the huts? Why, Frank Macdonald did that.' And they call him up and hire him because they think he will win, and that he'll do anything he has to, to make sure they get off. They don't hire Frank because they didn't do it and he'll prove they're innocent. They hire Frank Macdonald because they are *guilty* and they think that he'll rig it."

"That isn't so," I said. "Frank doesn't rig a thing. It's just that it's so damned unusual to find someone today who really likes to try. The prosecutors don't know what to make of him. Frank wins half the cases he wins because the stupid bastard who got the indictment never dreamed that the defendant would decide to go to trial. And then all of a sudden, the guy not only wants his trial but he's got Frank Macdonald standing there with all his white teeth showing, ready and entirely willing to do that very thing. They blow their lunches when that happens, and Frank knows they will. He also knows that that is what I do. 'You say my client's guilty, and he did something you can prove? Okay, my friend, let's see how good you are.' That's why Frank wins, and why I win, and why he sends cases to me. And that's the only reason."

"That's not what the people think," she said. "They think he's corrupt, and when they see you out and raising hell with him, or even just *hear* you've been doing that, that is what they think about you too. That you are corrupt."

"Jesus," Lou said, that bad morning, "he was something, though, Frank was, before all his wheels came off."

"Frank Macdonald," I said, "was the best I ever saw."

"The best any of us saw," Lou said.

"He'd've tried your case," I said, "things might have been much different."

Lou gave me a sharp glance. "You, ah," he said slowly, "you don't mean that, I assume."

"Mean it?" I said. "Sure I do. Frank might've walked you on this. Would've been a different case, different case entirely."

"You think you lost this thing," Lou said.

"Well," I said, "yes, I do. That's my name on the appearance slip, the one in the court. Says right there, in black and white, that I was your attorney. That file says you were convicted, unless I'm mistaken."

"You know, Jerry," Lou said slowly, "I'm a big boy now."

"I was aware of that," I said.

"Jerry," Lou said, "think about it. Be realistic, all right? For thirty years, almost, I've been doing what I do."

"I understand that," I said.

"You know what that is," he said. "You've known it for fifteen of them."

"Ever since Frank sent me to you," I said. "Was that fifteen years ago?"

"This coming April," Lou said, nodding, "fifteen happy years. Looked it up in my files, just the other week—I was showing them to Mendel, the nephew that I mentioned, getting set for this time off."

"Right," I said.

"That's a long time," Lou said, "in my line of work. Thirty years, I mean, the kind of thing I do."

"Are you telling me," I said, "you're looking forward to this? Like it's some kind of vacation? I thought you preferred Las Vegas, somehow, that or maybe San Juan."

"San Juan is dead now," he said, somewhat impatiently. "Been that way for years. Jerry, did you ever think about it, what I must be doing?" I just looked at him. "I'll answer my own question," Lou said, "you did not. You know what you are, Kennedy, you hopelessly nice guy? You're innocent, is what you are, a hopeless innocent. Just like Frank said you were. You haven't changed a bit."

"Frank Macdonald said that?" I said, feeling very stupid.

Lou Schwartz nodded at me, grinning like a horse. "Fifteen years ago," he said, "Frank told me that about you. 'Do his taxes, Lou,' he said. 'Keep the bastards honest. And if you can, while you're working with him, see if you can teach him some things, will ya? This kid's a sitting duck. He doesn't even know it.' "

6

I LEARNED at the beginning not to ask too many questions. When a client came to me, one I did not know, I asked whether he had money. Not: how he found me. During my sixth year in practice, I represented Joseph Vaster, a structural engineer with the Levitable Corporation. His responsibilities consisted of traveling around the world inspecting large buildings—hospitals, assembly plants for heavy machinery, entire college campuses, whole sections of new cities—which the company had constructed for foreign governments or other enormous international corporations. His job was to go to Basutoland and determine whether all the work contracted by Levitable for the new Ministry of Agriculture, say, had been done properly, so that when his firm turned it over to the provincial governor, or whoever was in charge that day, the roof would not fall in on all the happy local workers. "You sound like you must have been just about everywhere," I said, the day I met him in my office. "I guess I have," he said, "but most of the places I have been nobody in his right mind would ever want to go to."

Joseph Vaster was in his early fifties that year, married, no children, with a three-bedroom house in Tulsa, Oklahoma. His hobbies were golf and studies of the Crusades. "When I finish a job in the Middle East, or some place like that," he told me rather shyly, "I sometimes have Beatrice meet me there and I take some of my vacation, and we trace the routes that the Crusaders took, where they stopped and the castles and the monasteries that they visited." His particular hero was Richard the Lion-Hearted. He expected to complete his retracing of all of Richard's journeys within the next couple years, a project which his indictment by a special grand jury sitting in and for the County of Suffolk, Massachusetts, seemed to place in some jeopardy.

I saw no reason to stress that possibility to Joseph. In the first place, he was certainly intelligent enough to have perceived it for himself. In the second place, he was the sort of man who was appropriately married to a woman named Beatrice, and not the kind of man at all to whom one mentioned potential unpleasantness. Heather, six that year, had a babysitter named Gwennie who was fourteen and a freshman at Thayer Academy; Gwennie's word that year for dull persons was *dreeb*, which meant that Heather's word that year for people who bored her was also *dreeb*. The night that she encountered Joseph in my office, an unusual visit for her because I keep my family affairs quite apart from my legal practice and my questionable clients, she told me and Mack that he was a full dreeb, a judgment which we assessed as pretty much correct. Heather was always an insightful child, and very outspoken in her views—we took her to the Enchanted Village and to visit Santa that night, as we had the two or three years previously, and she made it evident that we could abandon that tradition anytime we might find it convenient, noting that the mechanical chickens were going bald around the area where the eggs came out, and that Santa had had something which smelled very much like pizza for his dinner. Heather was always partial to reality, if there was a choice in how to look at things.

Joseph Vaster wasn't. He admitted his experience, surviving coups and revolutions in most of the unstable countries of Central America and Africa, had not prepared him for the surprise that he had received in Massachusetts. "People shooting at me," he said, "I could understand. I was there, a total stranger, when they started shooting. Everybody who was there at that time would get shot at. If you had some brains, you would take cover and start making plans to get out. It was nothing personal.

"This, though," he said, fingering the paper that accused him of conspiring to pay bribes to a notorious crook in the state bureaucracy who had finally gotten nabbed and started squealing, "this seems to be quite different. This is very personal. This says that I schemed with someone

I've never met, to do things I never dreamed of, and paid money I never saw to somebody I never heard of until I read this paper. How could something like this happen?"

The explanation, as we lawyers like to say, was not far to seek. Levitable had been engaged by the Commonwealth to construct a huge depot for heavy equipment storage and maintenance required by the National Guard, precisely because of its global reputation for experience in that line of work. The smell of money attracted the grafters the way that little pieces of fish draw much bigger fish who are hungry, and cash started changing hands at a modest but nevertheless illegal rate. Joseph Vaster's innocent duties for the company had brought him to Massachusetts to inspect the new structure, four or five times. He stayed at the Parker House, close by Beacon Hill, and in the ordinary course of things was introduced to some nice-appearing gentlemen who were stealing money. They found him attractive, not because he knew a lot about the Crusades and could expound on them for hours, or because he was a sophisticated traveler who knew much about the world, but because he had an expense account which he could use to buy them drinks. They returned his kindnesses with tickets to the ball games they had cadged from lobbyists, and claims which they made boastfully to others of misdeeds that never happened. Joseph Vaster was a pawn, in other words, indicted by a sloppy prosecutor for offenses that he had not committed.

"Your trouble is," I said to him, "that Ranger Damon thinks they did. He really thinks they happened. And Ranger is a strong witness, whose own hide's on the line. We've got to go in there and prove that Ranger isn't telling the truth, when he sincerely thinks he is. We've got to do it by showing that those transactions never occurred. Proving negatives is damned hard, Joe, very hard indeed. Proving someone's wrong when he says that the horse was black is fairly easy, if you've got the horse. You just get the animal to stand still in the pasture, and you bring the jury out. They look at him. 'He's white,' they say, 'and this witness is lying. Leave the accused be set free.' But when there isn't any horse, then what do you do? Take the jury out to the field, say: 'Where is the horse?' They will just say: 'The accused stole the horse as well. Throw him in the can.' I don't mean to be gloomy, Joseph, and I don't mean we can't win. All I'm saying is that this is liable to be tricky, and you'll have to bear with me."

Joseph did bear with me, and so did Levitable. Fine company, that outfit, very protective of its men. It paid Joseph's legal fees, which were considerable. For those fees it got four days of the most intensive cross-examination that this advocate had ever put on up to that time—or since, for that matter. I made Ranger Damon recount all his days from birth, about, had him boasting of his heroic career as an Army commando during World War II, going on at great length and in tedious detail about all the honorable service he had given to his country and his Commonwealth until he fell amongst thieves on the Cardiff Depot project. For three full days, to the consternation of more senior lawyers whose clients still awaited trial on Ranger's testimony, I cajoled and prodded that stool pigeon into recitations which established beyond anybody's doubt that he could remember faultlessly the precise number and exact location of the freckles on the mother's breasts that nursed him. And virtually every detail of every event that had happened to him since: where those events had occurred, who else had attended them, and what they were wearing at the time those events happened. Often, even, what he'd smelled when things were going on. And then, on the fourth day, without the Court's permission, which I really should have gotten, I instructed Joseph Vaster to sit with the spectators when he came to court that morning, and covered it with the bailiff, who might have sounded an alarm when trial began with no defendant sitting at the bar, by whispering that Joseph had a bad case of the trots and should sit near the door in case he needed hasty exit. That arranged, I stood up as though resuming the line of questioning I'd interrupted when we recessed the previous afternoon, paused in the middle of my question, looked down irritatedly at my yellow pad, and let the witness show off once more his great memory, by having him spring in to remind me of what we'd been discussing.

"Now, Mister Damon," I said, "let me ask you this: What does Joseph Vaster look like?" And the witness didn't know.

He panicked. The color left his face and came back in a rush. He looked desperately at the defendant's chair, and there was no one there. He knew Vaster had to be around that courtroom someplace. He scanned the whole room as though he had just learned that it harbored an assassin with a contract out on him. He could not pick Vaster out. He did all the things that lawyers dream about. He licked his lips. He rubbed his fingers and his thumbs together nervously. He sweated just a little. He tried to speak and couldn't. I stood there silently, that question on fire in the air, for what seemed like an hour. When I rescued him, the point I made to judge and jury was already made. "You don't know, do you?" I said. And Ranger Damon, who had very little choice by then, said quite softly: "No, I guess I don't."

"I have no further questions of this witness," I said, and sat down. The prosecutor tried to rehabilitate him, but it was a perfunctory job, forty minutes or so of a losing struggle to remind the jury that old Ranger had met many people in his brief career as a corrupter, none of which in any way addressed the fact that he could not remember someone whom he had not in fact seen. The jury had the case for one hour after lunch, coming back at three o'clock to acquit Joseph Vaster.

"You were magnificent," he said to me when he had been told by the clerk that he was free to go without day. "You're right," I said, "and lucky too. I was extremely lucky." I did not tell Joseph Vaster, then or ever, that my strategy had been based upon my six-year-old daughter's appraisal of him as a hopeless dreeb, someone who so much resembled everybody else that no one who had not in fact done business with him would ever recall him later, someone so ordinary that one who in fact might have had dealings with him might not recall him either.

Neither did I emphasize to the reporters or the courthouse trial buffs who congratulated me outside the considerable advantage I had enjoyed in the Joseph Vaster case, one that the defense lawyer almost never has: my virtual certainty that the man was really innocent. Almost all of my work, and the work done by my colleagues, is based on the safe assurance that our clients did it. Laymen and the press believe that those who are accused of crimes in fact committed them, and that the police don't go around arresting people for no reason, and for the most part they are right. The only reason that they ever admire us is that the interval between indictment and trial cools off any passions that the defendant's act aroused, and unless he is a monster he is on his way to victim status himself by the time the evidence appears. He is one man and the government's against him, and most reasonably kindly people can feel sorry for a poor bastard in that position. Underdogs get sympathy, even if they did it. Underdogs who get off are seen to have been reprieved from an undeserved doom. Lawyers who spring them are extolled as champions, men who battled heavy odds, all by themselves, and won. I was willing to endure that reputation.

That evening, Joseph Vaster caught a plane back home to Tulsa. Gwennie got special permission to work on a school night. Mack came into town and met me at my office. We left that seedy lair and went to dinner at Locke Ober, just the two of us. We had a fine table by the window in the Men's Cafe on the first floor and we had the waiters crowd it with Bollinger Brut and lobsters Savannah. We sat there beaming at each other over the feast and exchanging small improvements and embellishments of our delighted dreams by means of that telepathy that comes when first love matures into something cherished that will last a long and reliable time. I had been happy before with her, and I have been happy since, but I have never in those times been happier, and I don't believe that she has either.

Into that magical evening, along with our dessert of strawberries Romanoff, came Frank Macdonald in the first expansive stages of his own intoxication. I knew him, of course, but Mack had not had more than a brief word with him at bar association lash-ups and that sort of thing. She did not welcome his intrusion that night, nor has she ever since.

7

"WHAT YOU two have got to understand now," Frank said that night, dragging a chair over to our table and joining us without an invitation or any suggestion on Mack's part that he might be welcome, "is that from now on you have got to be very, very careful. I mean: *extremely* careful, Jerry, you know? And you too, Joanie," he admonished her, wagging a forefinger in her face. "You also have to understand that. And help him, all right? Jerry has to be very, very careful." Frank claimed he kept his motor going on Jack Daniel's whiskey; it was bucking a little that night, and he burped little pauses into his homily.

Mack was impatient with him. Champagne did not make her more reticent than she was when sober, and she was not exactly introverted then. "He's careful enough as it is, I think," she said. "Most of the time, at least. Buying houses, going places, having some fun in this life before you have to hire a practical nurse to go with you on your trips? Jerry's very careful. As a matter of fact, the only thing I can see that Jerry hasn't been careful about all the time is sometimes when he's choosing friends."

Frank was not too oiled to miss that. He sat back in his chair and grinned at her. "But you do all you can, I bet, Joanie," he said, "to help him out when you see him making a mistake like that. Am I right on that, dear lady?"

"I try to be," she said, deliberately prim. She played with her napkin and arched her left eyebrow. "I think that's part of what goes into a good marriage." She gave Frank the old level gaze. "Wouldn't you say that, Frank? That a wife telling her husband when she thinks he's doing something that's a big mistake, that that's part of a good marriage? And that he should listen to her?"

Frank laughed and finessed her. "Gee, Mrs. Kennedy," he said, "I don't really know. I haven't had that much experience in that line, you know? Both of my wives, well, they never had that much to say about what I was doing. And what they did have to say was almost always wrong, which meant I didn't always listen to it. I guess what I think is that people shouldn't run their mouths about stuff that they don't know squat about. And that includes wives."

"I see," she said.

"Now, a thing like this," Frank said, jerking the chair up close to the table and putting his elbows onto it, "this is something I am an expert on. What is going to happen to you if you are a lawyer and you win a case like Jerry's." The waiter brought three snifters of a very old cognac.

"I think I'd like some coffee," Mack said as the waiter served them to us. "Some black coffee to go with this."

"Very sensible," Frank said. "Bring some for all of us."

"And the car keys, Jerry," she said, "if you're planning to drink yours."

I did not like that. If Frank hadn't been there, she would not have said it. If Frank hadn't been there, of course, neither would the cognac. If the cognac had been there, though, and Frank Macdonald hadn't, I would have in all likelihood handed them over without being asked. It was Frank's presence which made things so complicated.

Frank was amused by this. He nodded and he smiled. "Now on that,

Jerry," he said paternally, "Joanie's probably an expert. If she thinks you're getting smashed, then you probably are. I think you should do what she says on that, my friend. Which will mean that you and I can have a few more drinks, and everybody wins."

Everybody wins. That was Frank's motto. He would tell prosecutors at the outset of their cases, with the juries listening, that no one except the two of them understood what trials were. "My opponent here," he'd say, making his opening, "is not acting in bad faith. The judge up there on the bench—he wants only justice done. I am not in this case to confuse or to mislead you. We are all here for the truth.

"The truth, Mister Foreman," he'd say, "is an elusive thing. You ladies and you gentlemen, sworn to ascertain it, must have known in your hearts, as you took that oath, how hard your task would be. We spend our lives in search of truth, and know we seldom find it. Our churches, they are monuments to that long, unceasing search. And yet we are all in this room, seeking just that very thing, with a man's life riding on our success in this mission.

"If we find it, just this time, then we will have won. If we are brave enough, and if we have the patience, then we can together learn what really happened to this man. And if we cannot learn, my friends, know with certainty, then as the judge will tell you at the closing of this case, we—you—must be brave enough to say we do not know. And if we have that courage, you, I, and all of us, then everybody in this room will leave it having won."

"I don't know about that everybody winning," Mack said. "I don't think you've had the pleasure, seeing Jerry throwing up. Him on his knees there, in the bathroom, with his head down in the flush? I have seen that and I've heard that, and it doesn't look like victory to me."

Frank looked at me with mock astonishment. "Jerry Kennedy?" he said. Then he looked back at her. "My pal, Jerry Kennedy?" he said. "He gets drunk and throws up? You must be kidding me, my dear."

"Not very often, Frank," she said, "not very many times. Generally, only after he's been out with you. Drinking your Jack Daniel's and telling a lot of stories. Then he comes home in the bag, so I wonder how he got there, and I know that the next morning I will have two things to do: Go out to the garage and look at the car, see if he hit anything when he was coming home. And listen to him throwing up, spilling his poor guts again. That's what I mean about how sometimes he's not careful.

But most of the time he is, and he is also good." She beamed at me like some damned nun. I did not give up the keys.

"Well, then," Frank said, "we agree on this. Being careful's good. And that is what he has to be now, now that Vaster's out. Because now he is conspicuous, just like I have been."

"Does this mean," Mack said, "I should see a divorce lawyer?"

Frank pretended that he thought her remark funny. Frank made it apparent that he was pretending. Then he cut his laugh off in the middle and looked at her ruefully. "Look," he said, "you don't like me, and I guess that's all right. Lots of people dislike me. Maybe they've got something. But at least listen to me, all right? Hear what I have got to say. Because I'm not a bad guy, really, and I know a few things that could maybe help you, kid." That intimidated her, which was not what I'd had in mind when I brought her there that night, to have dinner with me in the warm glow of that old saloon and be happy because all of the hard work we'd shared had started to pay off. I wished Frank had been on trial in Buffalo that night.

"What he's done," Frank said to her, "is make the cops dislike him. When this started, all this hoopla with the Cardiff Depot cases, all the cops and prosecutors were like kids with brand-new toys. Christmas-candy morning for them, all they ever wanted. Reporters dancing all around, people making speeches. The taxpayers up in arms, let's go hang the bastards. And they got all those indictments, and they felt like goddamned *kings*. 'Look at all the rotten bastards we have caught,' they said. 'Now you all sit back and watch, while we try the scum.'

"Now along comes Jerry," he said, looking back at me. "Jerry's guy is innocent, or so old Jerry says. 'That is what they all say,' all the cops reply. 'Bring him in and we will show that Joseph Vaster's guilty.' So old Jerry brings him in. And he is innocent.

"The cops, Joanie," Frank said, "don't think that's the reason. They do not think Vaster got off because Vaster's innocent. To think that, they'd have to admit that they made a big mistake. They would have to say to themselves: 'Maybe Damon's lying. Maybe Ranger Damon's telling stories to us, huh? Saying things that aren't true, just to save his own pink ass?' Cops and DAs avoid thoughts like that. Which of course mean that they have to think it was their mistake. The cops think the prosecutor blew the goddamned case. 'The asshole didn't try it right, and that is why we lost it.' The prosecutors say to themselves: 'Stupid donkey cops. Haven't got the brains to see if Damon did know Vaster. What is this crap they are giving us? And is this the only one? Just how many guys did Damon lie about?'

"They can only think like this," Frank said, drinking some cognac, "when they're away from each other. Cops with cops can think like that, DAs with DAs. Get them together and they can't afford that kind of nasty criticism. Got to come up with some other explanation, how come Joseph Vaster got a walk from the jury." Frank poked me on the shoulder with his index finger. "And here is their goddamned reason," he said with malevolence, "Jerry goddamned Kennedy. 'He pulled a fast one on us. That bastard Kennedy's the one, made Ranger Damon look bad. Now everybody Damon mentions is gonna claim he made it up, and some of them may get their juries to think maybe Damon did. So other guys will get off, and that's Kennedy's fault too.'

"You see what that means for your husband, Joan?" he said. "That means he is not a good guy where the cops are concerned, not anymore, at least. It means they will start watching him now, see what he is doing. And if they can catch him doing something funny, they will be after him like he was raping babies."

"They can't do that," Mack said, but she looked troubled. "He hasn't done anything. Except be a lawyer, doing what good lawyers are supposed to do." She took a small sip of her brandy, but that was one more sip than she had planned to take.

"Doesn't matter," Frank said. "Doesn't matter in the slightest. What they will do now is make Jerry Kennedy their hobby. One of their little hobbies, that is—they've got lots of us. When a cop cannot incarcerate" (he pronounced it *incasherate*) "the bad guy because of the bad guy's smart-mouth lawyer, he will spend the rest of his life doing his level best to incarcerate the smart-mouth lawyer. I'm telling you, I'm telling both of you, it's how those bastards live."

"For what?" I said, trying to choose short words that did not have *sh* sounds in them, because I'd been sipping my cognac too, and I still had those car keys, along with the growing awareness that I ought to give them up. "I haven't taken any bribes, or given any either. I don't hold any office where somebody would bribe me, or get it into his head to say he did either. There's no way anybody can set me up that I know of, make me look like I am crooked, and I'm letting Mack drive home tonight so they can't scoop me there." I thought that was pretty neat, saving face like that as I turned the keys over and she shoved her snifter toward me. "Thank you," I said, taking it. "I do not chase women. I don't bother little boys. I don't accept extremely good deals on fine cars or big appliances that appear to be brand-new but for some reason or another are for sale off the backs of trucks. Everything we've got we can afford, at least since you started shunting a few fat cases my way, Frank, and as long as I can borrow five or six down at the bank for ninety days until the next client pays up.

"So," I said, "if they come after me, there's nothing they can get. I don't do anything. This case is the first time anybody outside of the clerk's office has paid any attention to me."

"True," Frank said, "all true. True up to now. But now, my friend, you're famous, and the president of the East Weymouth Rotary's not as well known as you are."

This was of course something that I wished to believe. "Really?" I said stupidly. "You really think so, Frank?"

"Oh, for heaven's sake, Jerry," Mack said, "stop acting like a fool."

"No, no," Frank said, waving her off, speaking solemnly, "he is. He really is about to become very widely known. This Vaster thing's the breakthrough case for Jerry Kennedy. Just like Sergeant Kinderhall there, or the Texas stuff." Mack first gaped, then started laughing. Frank shook his head. "Uh-uh," he said, "it's true. As sure as I am sitting here, it is. They are going to come looking for you now, and further-more, I tell you, they are going to find what they are looking for."

"They are not," I said righteously. "I already told you; I don't do anything."

"Yes," Frank said grimly, nodding a few more times, "yes, you do, you fresh little bastard. You pay income taxes."

"Of course I pay my income taxes," I said. "Only a damned fool doesn't pay his income taxes. If I didn't do that, pay my taxes, then I would be doing something, like you said. Not doing something that I should be doing. That would be doing something."

"You're pretty drunk, aren't you?" Mack said.

"I think I must be, now that you mention it," I said.

Frank ignored that side conversation. "And when you pay your in-come taxes," he said, "you do them yourself."

"Myself?" I said.

"You make out the forms," he said. "Figure up deductions. Calculate exemptions. Make sure that you include all your two-bit fees and that stuff."

"Sure," I said. "Why not? I'm a goddamned member of the bar, am I not? You think I don't know enough to fill out a Ten-forty? Couple Schedule Ds and that crap? Course I do."

"No," Frank said, "I don't. I think you don't know enough *not* to fill out your Ten-forty and your goddamned schedules. Because what you are, Jerry, is, you're precisely the variety of guy that tax collectors know is cheating on his taxes. When they wake up with upset stomachs in the wee small hours of the morning, they know it's because some tax-evading bastard like you is staying up, scheming to avoid paying his fair share of all the taxes that make this republic strong and great."

"Look, Frank," I said, blinking at the light reflecting off his diamond ring, "I am not avoiding doing that. I am already paying my share and the shares of several other guys I never even met, I think, of all those goddamned taxes that do all those goddamned things. I think I bought about ten or a dozen new jeeps for the Marine Corps last year, and from what I can see going out this year on my goddamned estimated taxes, the Navy is expecting me to buy them a new carrier. I can prove that I pay all my taxes."

"Uh-huh," he said. "How?"

"By showing them my books and records," I said with assurance. "My faithful secretary, Gretchen, who except for her frequent pauses for cheeseburgers, Cokes, and Snickers bars, gives her entire attention to my work and no time whatsoever making reservations for me to keep speaking dates in Jackson Hole, Wyoming, unlike other lawyers' secretaries I could name. She puts down in black and white every damned dime that I take in and all the dimes that go out. Which most of the time, I regret to say, there is not very many dimes' difference between."

"Let me ask you something, Jerry," Frank said. "While you and Gretchen are displaying all these books and complete records, every parking receipt and your Master Charge copies, explaining to the nervous, worried, and very suspicious agent that eight bucks for postage in a single week is really not a lot of money in this inflationary day and age, who is going to be counseling the troubled clients flocking to your office?"

"I don't know," I said. "I didn't think of that."

"Right," Frank said. "And—paying no attention to the interesting question of how many people who have been arrested will feel com-

fortable sitting around in an office crawling with guys that are obviously agents of some kind or another, which my own guess is: not very
many—who is going to reimburse you and pay Gretchen for the hours
that you spend in pleasant conversation with the IRS examiner who
can't believe you actually spend all of eight bucks every week on
stamps?"

"I see your point," I said.

"Good," Frank said. "That is some progress, then. There may be
hope yet for the unenlightened. What you have got to do, and do it
right away, is hire a man to do your taxes and put his name on the line
where it says who prepared them. Then, when the nervous little men
decide that it is time to find out just how you, Jerry Kennedy, have been
evading your taxes—not whether you have been evading them, but
how—and start their rapping on your door, you will open it politely,
just a crack, and say: 'Uh-uh, Mister Agent, I did not prepare it. Talk to
my accountant.'"

"Okay," I said, "and who is this guy that's my accountant, that I
don't even know yet?"

"Louis Schwartz," Frank Macdonald said firmly. "I will have him get
in touch with you."

"When Frank had me call you," Lou said that morning in my office
while Judge Maguire brooded in the federal courthouse over how Louis
Schwartz would spend the next few years of his life, the only question
really being just how many of them Lou would have to survive well out
of the fast lane that he found so exhilarating, "I had gotten enough out
of him to know that you were naïve."

"Thanks a lot, Lou," I said. "I guess I'm grateful for that, anyway."

"My pleasure," he said. "The classy part Frank didn't think to mention. Or if he did say something about how you were also classy, maybe
I overlooked it. But you are also that." He hurried on before I could
make any response to that further observation.

"I thought about that," Lou said, "coming over here this morning,
thinking about how this is going to be a very fine day for Michael Dunn
and all his IRS weasels and how two classy guys like us ought not to
have to help them have it, and it occurs to me that I should tell you
something, okay? Which is that being innocent and classy, sort of, is a
bad combination."

"I don't follow," I said.

"Well," Lou said, "it is dangerous. I am going away now. You will not have me to talk to or make sure that you don't do something stupid. Keep you out of trouble, as I have been doing. You are the kind of guy who does not spend all his time thinking up ways to do bad things to other people. Because you have class. You assume that they don't, because you are innocent. This is okay when I'm here. I always assume that somebody's getting set to screw you, and so I take care of that department. But now I am out of action. Michael Dunn has not got what he wants, that being Nunzio. Dunn and his little weasels are now thinking about you. You are next on their shit list."

"Did he say what you should do to get off of that list?" Mack said when I told her that night.

"That's what I asked him," I said. " 'Okay, wise guy, what should I do? Hire Bert Magazu?'

" 'You can't afford Bert Magazu,' he said to me," I said. " 'That's true,' I said, 'I can't.' 'And you don't need Bert, not just yet.' "

"Thank God for that," Mack said. "We can't."

" 'What you should do,' Lou said to me, 'is hire my nephew, Mendel.' "

"Are you going to?" Mack said.

"No," I said, "I'm not."

Just as Lou Schwartz had deduced when he advised me that morning. "I do not believe you, Jerry. You say you will do that, that you will get in touch with Mendel. But when I am gone away, before lunch this afternoon, you will start making up excuses. And by tonight, when I'm gone, they will be enough for you. You don't listen to your friends."

8

"YOUR HONOR," I said as I stood before Maguire down in the federal courthouse that morning to make my emotional appeal for compassion for Louis Schwartz, "as the Court is probably aware, this is a particularly difficult appearance for me. The defendant is my friend, as well as my client."

Maguire frowned at me. That remark was a veiled attempt to make the day's activity a little troublesome for him, and he recognized it for that. He had been for almost thirty years one of the most quietly competent trial lawyers in New England, the sort of circumspect, discreet, understated counsel whom counselors who disapproved of Frank Macdonald cited as the fellow who deserved Frank's public reputation. From Edmund Maguire's point of view, that was hard praise to bear; for the last third of his career trying cases, Frank Macdonald was his partner. Judge Maguire knew all about the difficulty caused by friends in law. Escaping from a merger of the firm he'd joined from law school with another where he would have been submerged into a huge and thriving trial department, Edmund Maguire had formed a new office with Macdonald in the expectation that Frank's contacts in the probate specialties would bring in clients they would both need to survive the first few years. To his dismay and astonishment, Frank had soon outstripped him by accepting cases from such as Nunzio Dinapola, and maintaining close friendships the likes of Louis Schwartz.

Caught in the consequences of his own lack of foresight, Edmund Maguire had behaved with the best dignity he could. "Frank is the rainmaker," I heard Edmund say one night at the annual meeting of the Massachusetts Bar Association, down at Chatham Bars Inn on the Cape, looking like the sort of serenely distinguished fellow the old white wooden hotel had been put up to shelter. "Frank brings in all the money, or most of it, anyway. And he's kind enough to field virtually all the phone calls and inquiries from the press," he said with a small smile of slyness, tacitly acknowledging that Frank provoked most of them. "I have to appreciate the service he provides. Still, it does seem only fair that he should get the adulation, while I get the judgeship."

"Frank got that guy his job," Lou'd said to me, back on the morning when he was arraigned, his first awareness that the judge who would be trying him was Frank Macdonald's partner. I told Lou I doubted that. Maguire had been nominated by Gerald R. Ford to the bench, on the strong advice of a good many Boston lawyers who knew politicians and liked Edmund J. Maguire. He had been fully accessible to people prominent in both parties who had required shrewd counsel, all of his career, and he'd never been active in either of them. He was a perfect selection for an interim, appointed President to make, a lawyer's lawyer who had beaten almost everyone who had opposed him in the courts, without offending any except those who had offended everybody else. Frank while semi-sloshed one night in the Last Hurrah, downstairs at the Parker House where he was buying drinks, had declared that Maguire was cruel to animals. "He has to be," Frank said. "The only way that any man could go through what we go through with the clients and the judges, and the clerks and the damned juries, without drinking up an ulcer or having a nice nervous breakdown, is by going home at night and kicking the living shit out of his cat. I am telling you," Frank said, "that if the SPCA ever gets the goods on Ed Maguire, it'll make what the poor dagos at the track do, doping horses, look like a goddamned garden party by comparison."

"Frank told me he got the judgeship for Maguire there," Lou said stubbornly. "Frank said that himself. Said he did it to get rid of him, stop all of his goddamned preaching. Said one of the things that Maguire preached about was me. Me and Nunzio." I told Lou that while it was the same Maguire, I was not apprehensive about having him preside, and that Frank had said a lot of things, at one time or another. I said there was not a fairer judge in Boston, or any other city I have ever visited.

"Fair is not what bothers me," Lou said. "Not whether he is fair to other guys, I mean."

"Well," I said, "fair's all I can promise you. If you want a judge who will bag the prosecutor's case for you, I might agree it would be nice, but it's not available. They got rid of all the judges who did that, took care of the guys they took a liking to, long before I ever got my ticket to appear in front of them."

Lou looked like he did not wholly believe that. "Okay, Jerry," he said, "but what still bothers me, all right? Is this guy Maguire here, is he gonna think that being fair to me means maybe putting it to me a little extra, on account of how he knows I did work for the Boss and always did, and he don't approve of that? Frank used to tell me things, you know, before he got sick."

I told Lou that Ed Maguire's distaste for him and Nunzio as clients had nothing to do with them as human beings. "Ed," I said, "the way I get it, always wanted to build up a practice representing hospitals, insurance carriers, corporations with big antitrust problems to try. When he went into practice with Frank, Frank just out of school, he thought Frank would bring in the divorce work, with maybe a small sideline on the criminal side, and that would pay the rent for them. Pretty soon he noticed all the hoods there in the files, and not many little matters from Ford and General Motors when their steering gears let go. That was what he didn't like, losing the kind of business that he lost because Frank was getting known for representing ax murderers. If he even thought about you, he most likely thought you were a nice guy. It was the people he saw staying away because you were coming around—that was what bothered him."

My opening remark had flushed up all that history. Judge Maguire let me understand that he would disregard it, only if there wasn't going to be another one like it. "The Court, Counselor," he said, without showing he was ruffled, "assumes that in every case involving disposition, defense counsel finds his duty quite unpleasant. Nevertheless, it is one which the terms of your employment by your client require you to discharge. You may therefore proceed."

"Thank you, Your Honor," I said, embarrassed to have asked for that rebuke.

"Unless, that is," the judge said, smiling a little to show that I was not to take the whole matter too seriously, "the particular difficulty for you in this case is that this client too has a dog about which he feels very strongly." That drew a mannerly laugh in the courtroom, but I didn't resent it as I had the obedient audience reaction Luther Dawes had milked in Dedham. People watch television, whether I like it or not, and more of them would vaguely recognize my name as that of the lawyer with the client with the dog than would ever know me as the lawyer who had done good work for hundreds of less colorful poor bastards.

I made a bit of business about glancing back at Lou Schwartz with a look that inquired whether he proposed to invoke his dog as a dependent needing him at liberty to ensure its survival, and he was resourceful enough to manage a limp grin and a shake of the head. "No, ah, Your Honor," I said, turning back to Maguire, "he assures me that he doesn't. This is a straight case of a first offender whose record would not seem to me to warrant incarceration for this infraction, even without the close personal knowledge that I've gained of him over many years of professional dealings having nothing to do with this case.

"As the probation report makes extremely clear, Your Honor," I said, knowing I was dealing with the echoes of Mike Dunn's request for five years to be served, based upon Dunn's strong belief that only Lou stood between him and the IRS in their determination to destroy the Mafia in these United States, "the defendant is a man in his middle fifties." I felt Lou cringe a little behind me when I said that, making him a liar with his lovely third wife sitting there, out in open court. "His record is un-blemished in a profession of trust for just over thirty years. Louis Schwartz until this prosecution had never been arrested, let alone ac-cused of serious crime." I did not have much force in my voice for this warm-up to the plea. The fact that the defendant has a clean record might mean that he's very honest; then again, it could mean he was very lucky, or quite clever, or did not encounter a truly tempting op-portunity until he took the one that got him in the glue for the first time. Mean-tempered judges have been known to interrupt the speech about no priors with gruff remarks that it's too bad the defendant didn't persist longer in his habits of clean living.

"My personal acquaintance with the defendant, Your Honor," I said, quite aware that almost no one gets less time because somebody says something at disposition, unless it's Harry Mapes and he draws Luther Dawes to say it to, "convinces me that he has never done an act against the law for any gain to him. And the evidence in his case that the gov-ernment presented, Judge, corroborates that fact. Louis Schwartz is an accountant. He prepared tax returns. Those returns were for someone who was not called in this case, let alone charged with an offense. Mis-ter Schwartz's testimony, which he gave on the stand"—always a sign of nerves, when the lawyer emphasizes that the witness testified from the same goddamned place that all witnesses occupy—"went unshaken when the government concluded its examination of him. It remains un-contradicted here today. Louis Schwartz wrote down numbers that he got from his client. He interpreted those figures according to his under-standing of the tax laws. If he was mistaken in those interpretations, of which there has been absolutely no showing, then there is a case for a civil proceeding to correct those errors and collect more taxes. But to charge him criminally, as the government has done, because he is not in a position to say whether the sources of income reported on those tax returns were truthfully detailed, that is unprecedented."

"Well, for Christ sake," Lou said when I told him how shaky our ground was, "of course it is, goddamnit. You think Nunzio is going to tell me to put down the barbut games? You think I would ask him where he got the money? You think I would like him to have me killed? Of course it is lies." I am never at my best or fully comfortable on premises that tremble under me. Mildly disappointed clients have suggested that this problem is the reason why I never did achieve the eminence that Frank predicted for me, the night he got me plastered in Locke Ober and commanded me to seek out Louis Schwartz. Cadillac Teddy Franklin, whom I have kept out of jail for twelve or thirteen years now, against very heavy odds, admitted once that he was always just a little bit concerned when I rose to get him loose on some fragile technicality which the arresting officer had neglected when he brought Teddy in. "It's not your line of bullshit, Jerry," Teddy told me worriedly. "Your brand of stuff is just as good as anybody else's. It's the way you act when you stand up to sling it, you know? Like you're getting ready to put something over on the judge and everybody else, blow some smoke right up their ass and make them do something that you don't think anybody in his right mind ought to do. I've got to say, even though it's always worked, at least when you've been representing me, it does make me a little nervous. I can see why other guys would get somebody else. You are only really good when you really mean it."

Teddy hit it on the head. I do feel somewhat flustered when the circumstances require me to dance around the fringes of the matter, putting on a show that wouldn't convince me if I were watching it. When I said Lou Schwartz had jotted down some numbers that he got from Nunzio Dinapola, that of course was true. Lou's problem was that the numbers he got from Nunzio, and the sources he wrote down for the money those numbers represented, were not altogether true, and Lou knew that when he wrote them down on the tax form. The government that prints the tax forms furnishes a place to be signed by the man who prepares them, if it is someone other than the taxpayer. There is a printed legend over that line for the preparer's signature. It recites that he believes those numbers and the other information he has entered on the form to be true and accurate, to the best of his information. That was where Lou Schwartz had signed the forms. The government had not experienced much trouble in proving to the satisfaction of the jury, beyond a reasonable doubt, that Lou Schwartz had not believed those numbers and that information to be true and accurate when he signed the form that certified he did. Furthermore, while what I said when I said Lou made no commission for that signature, while that was also true, the fact was that his willingness to sign such false certificates was a big part of what got him most of his wages in the first place. It was more or less as though I had claimed that a call girl on a corporation payroll, receiving no bonus for delighting some horny major customer of the company, must have acted out of love.

Judge Maguire elevated his left eyebrow to suggest he had a little trouble with that protestation of Lou's innocence. "Well, Counselor," the judge said, interrupting, "isn't that precisely what the law's intended to prevent, and punish when it does occur? That some accountant like your client, getting figures from *his* client, shouldn't just proceed to write them down, without first making sure they are correct? Satisfying himself that they are? And in this case, really, Mister Kennedy, the evidence is pretty overwhelming that he didn't make that effort. Isn't it?"

It wasn't only in that case, not by any means, and Ed Maguire knew it just as well as I. "What did Frank Macdonald tell you about me?" Lou asked the very first time that we talked.

"He said you are the best," I said, thinking that was safe enough.

"Huh," Lou said to me, "Frank's getting just the slightest bit conservative in his old age, I'd say. What I am actually's far and away the best there is. There is not only no one who is better—there's nobody who is even close. Does that say something to you, Counselor?"

"That Frank was understating things, but he was right?" I said.

"No," Lou said relentlessly, "that you cannot afford me."

"Well," I said defensively, "I mentioned that to Frank and what he said was that I could not afford not to afford you. I said I still wasn't sure, a man in my position, making what I'm making now at least, needed somebody that came recommended quite as highly as you did. And he said that I shouldn't worry about it, because in the first place you would save me lots of money that I don't need to be paying out in taxes, and in the second place you are deductible yourself. Which means when I pay you a buck, I am out about six bits."

Lou created a long pause. "Uh-huh," he said. I could hear him sucking his teeth on the other end of the line. "H and R Block is what Frank should've sent you to, for Christ sake. Most guys I do work for, when they pay me a buck it is one that costs them fifty cents or less."

"I'm not in that bracket," I said, getting annoyed. "I never said I was, and if that's the way it is, forget Frank said to call me."

"Calm down," Lou said, "all right? Frank thinks you're going to be a heavy hitter and not just someday, either. Pretty soon. He told me you are a good guy who should not get himself in a box the way Frank did when he struck gold like he did and all of a sudden it looked like the taxes were gonna destroy him. Frank's first big year, you know what I hadda do? I hadda put him in a busted-out restaurant, which I had a strong suspicion might be gonna burn down shortly afterwards, and did, or he would've gotten ruined on the taxes. This is cutting it close. It is better when the guy that does the taxes gets a little advance notice of what he will be up against. Makes a few recommendations of things you can do so they are all set up for when the big bucks start to roll in. It cuts down on the excitement, and that's always good for us guys that deal with numbers. Understood?"

I told him I still was not at all sure I was ever going to see the day when the big bucks came in. "It don't hurt in any case to be prepared," he said, treating the question as one that had been settled. "What you do is come and see me, and we will have a look at this thing. And no smart remarks about the office, all right? Someday you will understand why it is smart for me to fight with rats and freeze my ass off in the winter when the wind comes in from Portugal and this whole building shakes, but right now I am kind of busy and I haven't got time to explain."

On the morning of his sentencing, Lou said: "Now, for example, you take that building which you always give me so much shit about." I told him I'd be happy to accept title to China Wharf, the old granite warehouse on the waterfront that Lou Schwartz had rescued, for very little money, from the demolition crews eyeing it in the early sixties. *"Now,"* he said, "sure you would. Then, most likely, you would not have. The point is that I got that property for eighteen grand, net. Not because I was smart, or not just because I was smart, but because I also happened to have eighteen grand that I could risk on it. I wasn't in a position where I had to look at that old relic every day and see that it was what I owned instead of a decent house for my family, or taking vacations, or stuff like that. I had the money. And because I had eighteen K then, I have got something that is probably worth about four, five mill today. And it's not the only thing I've got today that is worth a lot of money, on account of how I had what was for a kid just starting out when I did a real shitload of money. Let's face it, Jerry, all right? I had that money because I was willing to do things for Nunzio that maybe somebody else who knew exactly the same things I did would not have the balls to do.

"So," he said, "my thinking is that if you got what you have got because for thirty years or so you have been saying that you have the balls to take the risks that make you lots of money, and you finally take one of those small risks and lose, well, you are in a position where you should show a little class. A little dignity."

I made a phony display of having something in my throat when Judge Maguire asked me whether Lou Schwartz had in fact done, and then been proven to have done, exactly what the law on tax preparers forbids. I suppose that did not meet Lou's standards of dignity, but when I want a little time to think, I take it. "Your Honor," I said, knowing that Maguire knew all the stalling tactics too, from his long years of practice, "the law is often far from clear on what it asks of people. The one that Mister Schwartz has been accused of violating was most likely meant by Congress to protect the revenue." *Protect the revenue*'s a shorthand phrase that means: make sure the government gets every dime it asks for. "There is no allegation in the case, or any proof either, that the Treasury of the United States was in any way depleted, or took in less than it should have, as a result of anything that Mister Schwartz did or failed to do."

Mike Dunn made a gesture at rising from his chair at the prosecutor's table when he heard that. In the privacy of his office, Dunn would be cordial and candid, forthright enough to admit that he was going after Lou because Lou wouldn't give him Nunzio. In the courtroom, he was less open about things. Out where he could be seen by the public, Dunn wanted all his armor polished, the white plume in his helmet nice and bushy, the banners that proclaimed him the guardian of America unfurled and snapping in the breeze. He was willing to do with an indictment what the cops used to do with truncheons in the back rooms of the precinct houses before the Supreme Court decided citizens have rights, but he was not about to let me say what he was doing, not without a protest.

Judge Maguire, on the other hand, was a man of the world. He had spent a lot of years in the same offices with Frank Macdonald, maybe not always agreeing with some of the performances his partner put on, but unavoidably convinced just the same that every client had the right to a defense. "You can remain seated, Mister U.S. Attorney," Maguire said serenely. "This is Mister Kennedy's time at bat. You have already had yours, and he didn't interrupt you."

"I was only going to say, Your Honor," Dunn said, subsiding in the chair and making quite a large mistake as he did so, "that I was under no duty whatsoever to prove anything about lost revenues."

Maguire looked as Mount St. Helen's must have looked about three seconds before it erupted. He has more decorum in his character than the entire Court of St. James's musters when all of the Queen's ministers convene, so he did not blow up, but because he so controls himself, it isn't necessary. "I knew, Mister Dunn, what you were going to say when I told you to sit down without saying it. You chose to interpret that as an invitation to do precisely the opposite of what I said I wanted done. Now I am telling you to sit down and keep still until you're called upon to speak in these proceedings. See that you do it." He gave Dunn a six- or seven-hundred-watt glare and then turned back to me, "Your point is taken, Mister Kennedy, despite the interruption. The Court, imposing sentence, will be mindful of the fact that Mister Dunn neither alleged nor educed evidence to prove that the Treasury was defrauded in any way by Mister Schwartz's acts."

It looked like a victory, but wasn't. Maguire and I might just as well have agreed that New England's weather's very changeable, for all the good that our agreement would do Louis Schwartz. I had to make a little progress from where we stood, there on that common ground, and I saw no ready means of doing so.

"That being the case, Judge," I said, "the Court and this defendant are left talking about punishment for a crime which did not injure anybody. The government was not harmed in the slightest, except by whatever the cost was of prosecuting Mister Schwartz for this offense. The taxpayer in the case did not complain, which means if he was injured at all, we must speculate upon the nature and the extent of the harm, and this Court's not allowed to do that. There isn't any measure which the Court can order taken by the defendant to make whole the party injured by his action, because as far as we know, no party was injured."

Maguire showed some impatience. "It's a technical offense, Counselor," he said. "We all understand that."

"Precisely, Judge," I said, "and in thinking about it, what I decided I would recommend to this Court is that it consider a punishment of equally technical nature. The defendant having been convicted of a major crime, his accounting certificate, if he does not appeal, will be automatically suspended until he has had a hearing on whether it should be permanently revoked. This serves to punish him, by barring him from the work that has been his livelihood. It serves to assure that the offense will not be repeated, because Mister Schwartz cannot repeat the crime if he cannot serve as an accountant. If punishment's intended to deter others by example, certainly this ought to have a sobering effect upon any other accountant who's considering prohibited conduct when making out tax returns for his clients. And since it will cost the taxpayers nothing to support Mister Schwartz if he is not imprisoned, there's a nice symmetry between the loss brought about by his offense, which is none, and the price of correcting him for its commission, also none.

"I therefore respectfully request the Court," I said, "to suspend any term of incarceration which it may impose, after hearing what I deem to be the government's somewhat exaggerated view of the gravity of this offense, for a term of probation. Say, perhaps, five years. During which time, if it please the Court, the defendant would not be allowed to hold himself out as an accountant, here in Massachusetts or in any other part of the United States. If the Court thinks that some immediate punishment is nevertheless warranted, I would respectfully request that a small fine be imposed. Except for other purposes of revenge upon Mister Schwartz, to which Mister Dunn has rather vaguely alluded in his remarks to the Court, none of which is properly considered by the Court in fixing punishment for the offense which is before it, I can see no other disposition which would serve the requirements of justice adequately." I then thanked the Court for its attention and sat down. Maguire asked Lou if he had anything to say. Lou considered for a moment and replied that he thought I had put before the judge all that he would have wished to. Judge Maguire thanked all of us, and sentenced Lou to spend two years in custody, remanding him to that of the U.S. marshal forthwith, and recessing the Court.

"There are times," I said to my dear wife that night, as I prepared a martini, "when this is a truly shitty way to make a living."

9

"IT IS ALSO," Cooper said morosely a couple of days later, when I repeated that breathtaking insight to him over lunch at Jake Wirth's, "a shitty living sometimes too." Cooper's office has a party wall with mine, and we use it the same way that African tribesmen use hollow trees, beating on it as a means of communication. This could be a problem if either of us had attracted a genteel clientele, the sort of cultivated, aging ladies and cultured gentlemen who employ my classmate Roger Kidd to manage their trust holdings, but Coop gets most of his business from people that he met doing twenty years' hard time as an FBI agent, and nothing much startles my array of pimps, car thieves, drug smugglers, and the like. Cooper had been having a genuinely rotten winter, coming on the heels of a full calendar year that would have depressed St. Francis of Assisi, and it did not surprise me when he said he had been stiffed by a third client in as many months.

"Mind you," he said painfully to me, trying to chew very carefully around his root canal work and meeting stiff resistance from the meat in Jake's goulash—I'd advised him not to have it, given the condition of his mouth, and he'd told me to mind my own business and leave him one of his few remaining enjoyments in life, even if it did hurt him to have it—"this should not surprise me. This is one of Peter's friends, just as screwed up as Pete is." Cooper suspended chewing, not from pain that was in his mouth, and stared sadly off toward the old wooden phone booth inside Jake's, as though he'd begun to wonder if some answers might be in it.

I did not intrude on that silence. Peter Cooper's youngest child, seventeen and totally messed up. He withdrew from Archbishop Cleary High School in the middle of his freshman year, one step ahead of the principal's assurance that he would be thrown out if he didn't. Peter was a casualty, and a well-chosen one, of solid rumors which alleged that hashish could be obtained within walking distance of the Pembroke campus. He marked time for one term in the Silver Lake High School, managing to stay out of trouble but not to accumulate sufficient credits to qualify him as a sophomore when he entered the Lang School in Middleboro the next fall. Repeating freshman year appeared to bore young Peter, and he cut a lot of classes. That free time he occupied with making new connections. Soon he was right back in business, but not for very long—the Lang School was run by some very tough young teachers who had learned drug rehabilitation the hard way, and they knew all the subterfuges Peter sought to employ. They also believed that the best cure for young lawbreakers was a good stiff dose of prosecution. That in turn provided me with an unwanted opportunity to get to know young Peter a lot better, inasmuch as Cooper could hardly represent his own kid dispassionately—"What I would like to do for him," he told me furiously, "is put my fingers up his nose and yank his goddamned face off, but his mother wouldn't like that and she's probably been through enough"—and was not in a position to retain any of the Boston lawyers who specialize in drug busts and drive Rolls-Royces to their court dates as proof of their acumen. "Fine business," Cooper said, "when not even lawyers can afford to hire good lawyers."

"Thanks very much," I said, pretending to be hurt.

"Oh, Jesus Christ," Coop said, "I didn't mean that, Jerry. That you aren't good, for Christ sake. What I meant was, I kind of assumed that you wouldn't charge me." Then he looked wounded and afraid. "Maybe I shouldn't've assumed that, huh?"

"Now look, for Christ sake, Cooper," I said, "I was joking, all right? I know what you mean." And I went forth to retrieve Peter from the penitentiary. I got the kid an SS, the suspension being on condition that he find another school and make some serious improvements in his approach to life's problems. Cooper got him into the school at Bald Mountain, a charming rural refuge out near Pittsfield which the sullen youthful inmates have termed Buchenwald. This fact comes out in the papers when the school's administrators are compelled to make one of their fairly regular appearances before the State Board of Concerned Persons, or whatever all those agencies are being called this week, to comment on widespread reports that they beat their charges and reward intransigence with solitary confinements; thus far at least, they have managed to convince their listeners that those are rank falsehoods.

Whatever it was that they did to Peter, it was enough to keep him out of circulation for the probation period required by the suspension of the sentence. Therefore, when he at last succeeded at escaping that previous November, AWOL from what should have been his junior year of high school but in fact knowing only a part of what the average sophomore's learned, he was clear of court at least. Having no real appetite for representing him again in that environment, I agreed to Cooper's request that I go and look for him—he had told his father they were through and quits, which Cooper said made him feel good when he was signing checks. "Checks, I might add," Cooper said, "which if I hadn't written them to Cleary, Lang, and Bald, would have financed a long winter in the Caribbean, in my very own small house." I went out in the Advent cold and found the kid where Coop's snitch said I would, standing on a corner in South Weymouth, wearing a thin leather jacket and a pair of surgeon's wash pants with a pair of worn black loafers and no other clothing, shivering and twitching in the sharp December wind, plotting how to sneak into the pharmacy at South Shore Hospital. Peter's nose was running fiercely when he got into my car, which I took as some evidence that he had been using it for something besides breathing and draining sinus cavities; the kid spent Christmas and the month of January getting better in a hospital in Maine to which Cooper had committed him "until at least Flag Day. At a cost equal to that of the small powerboat which I now can't afford, to go with the small villa in St. Thomas that I can't afford either.

"You would really like Marshall," Coop said with bitterness. "Marshall is the sort of lad which makes a man in our line really regret that our Founding Fathers were so damned picky about searches and seizures. I got Marshall off on a damned luggage charge, over at the airport, because some adolescent cop got eager when he spotted the punk and he didn't bring the dog around to smell the goddamned bag. Just waited until Marshall grabbed it and then he goes and he grabs Marshall. I suppress four pounds of good grass, give or take a kilo, at the bargain rate of one grand, and the little prick goes free. Went free like a goddamned bird, is what the bastard did. Stiffed me and took off for Aspen. Probably out there this minute, getting a blow job from some coke-crazed petroleum heiress, while he thinks about his next big score coming in on a light plane from Peru."

"Most likely," I said, having my own troubles with the stringy beef in gravy, even though my teeth were supposedly quite sound—Cooper calls periodontal disease "the sickle-cell anemia of affluent white males crowding fifty," and challenges all comers to locate an impoverished man with it in a dental surgeon's office.

"And if he is," Coop said, "I am the one to blame. It's my fault that he's circulating, getting rich importing dope, while I sit here in Boston with my thumb right up my ass. You know what our trouble is?"

"Specifically?" I said.

"Of course, specifically," he said. "This is supposed to be the prime rib of our lives. Our kids're pretty much grown, and we've tried to raise them right. We haven't wrecked our health as yet, and our wives aren't fat. We know what we are doing when we come into the office, and our clients can trust us. We've learned what is important, and we've learned to skip the rest. With my pension and retainers, plus what walks in through the door, I can gross a hundred thirty, and count on it every year. This should be the best year that I've ever seen on earth, and instead I'm going nuts. What we need, at least I do, is some kind of escape hatch. Some way I can duck out from this monster I've created." He paused then and snickered, and his face looked sort of worn. "All the work I put in," he said, "all those years in school. Get the degree in accounting. Join the Bureau and work hard. Go to law school nights and Sundays, which was how it really seemed. Overtime on cases, and more of it on the books. Finally make it to retirement, with my ducks all in a row. No more taking orders, or reporting in on time. No more sweat about a transfer, next year in Anchorage. Everything worked out right, just the way I planned. And I haven't got a damned thing, when I think about it. Nothing except problems that I can't solve for myself, and the only thing I can think of is to cry on your damned shoulder." He gave me a beseeching look. "Karen says that I sound cheap when I bitch about Pete's bills. I guess probably I do. She says it sounds like I don't love the kid. I tell her it isn't that, that I'm just frustrated, but I can't say that I'm sure. I say that what bothers me is that it's just a waste. All the great ideas we had, all the fun we missed. We thought we were just deferring it, and now it's just vanishing. We're just pissing it away, on those damned private treatment centers for people who have made themselves the way they are, and will not stop doing it either.

"Peter doesn't improve, Jerry, not a little bit. You know what that does to me, when he doesn't change? We blow all our money on him, and there's no progress. Nothing whatsoever happens that might make it seem worthwhile. Two months, three months, six months later, we drive out to see him, and you know how he greets us? Snarling. Calls me an old asshole. Says his mother's an old nag. Calls his sisters whores and cunts. Just sneers at all of us." He looked at me glumly. "You're a dumb shit if you're interested, if that matters to you."

"Thanks for the message," I said, wishing I could help Coop.

"Gratitude is always nice," he said with great resentment. "What is this shit, Jerry, that we've gotten ourselves into?" He looked like he might cry, right into his goulash that his sore mouth wouldn't accept. "Can you tell me that? Who arranged it this way, so that just as soon as you get something, some damned other thing just happens and yanks it all away from you?"

I did not have the answer for that when Coop asked for it at lunch. I still had not produced it when I got home that night. It was a little after seven when I pulled into our street—Kevin Road in Braintree Highlands, first left off Mary Anne, go too far and you'll wind up on David or Patricia; "Thank God," Mack said when we bought the place, "the developer's first son was not named Dick"—and there were lights on in all the other houses down along the street. All ours had for illumination was the forty-watt bulb in the end-table lamp next to the picture window in the living room; it was plugged into a timer which each afternoon around 4:45 snapped into action as the most pitiable deterrent to burglary that a sane man could devise.

I stopped the car in the driveway and sat there looking at the place. It was still a small garrison colonial, the upper story painted barn red with six white shutters flanking the three windows on the front, the first story painted white with four maroon shutters, two at the casement window of the dining room, two more idiotically framing the large picture window in the living room. The breezeway which connected the kitchen door to the one-car garage was no shorter than it had ever been, and the tiny white cupola on the garage roof was still in place where it had been for more than twenty years, refuge for a few hardy sparrows during nesting season. Nothing appeared to have changed, but somehow it looked shrunken. Almost as though Mack's weary words—"Oh, Jerry, for cripes' sakes, it's *small*"—had had an effect on it.

I remembered how handsome it had seemed, my first year out of law school when two quick referrals from Roger Kidd's firm, Kincaid, Bailey & Kincaid, had emboldened me not only to quit Culp & Hurley and set out on my own but also to announce to my then pregnant wife that we could start to think about a house of our very own. None of my classmates also lacking the foresight to be born rich had made enough progress to take such a step. I was very proud of myself that year, and very proud too of our house. I thought it was big then, and substantial too.

"Four bedrooms," the file flier at Southarbor Real Estate declared of my fine house. Southarbor, back when Mack was just a customer, was a lot smaller too, but it had gotten larger. We looked at Ace and Roy's small collection of listings in a three-desk basement office at the South Shore Shopping Plaza. It was next door to the ladies' room, and poorly sound-insulated; business was transacted to the sound of rushing waters. Today Ace and Roy administer eighteen thriving branches scattered from Braintree to Dennisport, operating out of their own brick office complex in a large development in Holbrook, and they lease Mercedes-Benzes for their top management ladies, whom they expect to arrive early and to remain very late.

"One and one-half baths," it said, the Xeroxed flier with the lousy reproduction of a Polaroid snapshot. "Full living room w/ frpl. Dining area. Spacious, modern kitchen w/ built-in disposal and dishwasher. Small area off kitchen cd. be used for den or study. Large, dry, unfinished full basement, w/ washer-dryer plumbing installed. Oil-fired forced hot water, economical to heat. Oversized one-car garage, w/ ample storage room. Breezeway cd. be made into screened-in porch for summer. One-third acre of high ground, tastefully landscaped. Asphalt drive and flagstone walkways. Large enclosed backyard, treed lot. View of country meadow." The best part was the last line. "Owner transferred, must sell now." "$26,500" had been crossed out: "$22,750." We got it for $21,500.

Mack thinks with a coat of paint, new tile in the kitchen, a set of new appliances which she could get at builder's rates, we could put it on the market for, say, "Eighty-eight. And probably get eighty or so, Jerry, if we wanted to sell fast. Housing's scarce now that the interest rates have dropped." Dropped: now that's a laugh. Mack was excited because banks were lending mortgage money at 12 or 13 percent plus points; we were dismayed when we learned that, the first years of our payments, almost six hundred dollars would be going for real estate taxes and for interest calculated at a steep 6.25 percent.

I took my foot off the brake and continued on up the driveway, the overhanging naked branches of the forsythia I'd planted as small shrubs along its westerly edge brushing against the right fender of my car and most likely scratching it. For years I have been pledging to cut those bushes back, and for years I've been failing to do it. Mack mentioned that when I decreed that first one home got the garage—she wanted it for her Mercedes, "which is lots more valuable than your damned Buick Regal."

"It certainly is," I said. "It's worth lots more to Ace and Roy, and to the people who've leased it to them. But my three-year-old Regal is worth more to me, and I say if I'm going to keep the ice off of some car, it'll be the one I own if I can get it home here first. Which there isn't much doubt in my mind that I'll be able to, goddamnit, four nights out of five." She said if I was that serious about preserving my car, I would prune the forsythias, and I said I would get to it next year.

The mailman had crammed the magazines into the small black metal box attached to the breezeway, chewing up the pages and rumpling as well all the first-class mail that he wadded up inside them. That was another reproach to my lack of follow-through. Faithfully each week throughout the colder weather, I complain that I would someday like to see what *Time* and *Newsweek* look like dry and smooth and even. Faithfully each time I gripe, Mack reminds me that the way to this paradise is to buy and install a larger mailbox. I carried the collection inside and dumped it on the chromium dinette table with the white Formica top that we brought home from the roadside furniture store on Route 1 in Dedham with the few dollars that we had remaining to us the day that we passed papers on the house. Twenty-nine ninety-five, as I recall, with four chrome chairs upholstered in white vinyl, long since relegated to the town dump and replaced with wooden ones. I switched on the overhead light and saw that the letters jammed inside the magazines included one from my daughter Heather, up at Dartmouth. I stood there in my overcoat, my hair probably sticking up, my damned briefcase in my hand, and my whole life tired out. In a while, less than an hour, Mack would come home touchy, still distracted by something she would think she could have finished if she had stayed just a little longer, and she would find me at that table, maybe with my coat still on. I would be having a martini and I would have read that letter, have it spread out there before me. It would not have brought bad news, but the mere fact that it brought news would remind me that the kid was grown up now, and I would have searched it for clues to changes in her life that I did not like. Mack would not ask which drink I was having. I would not ask what had kept her. I would tell her what she could see, that we had a letter. She would ask me what was in it, until she could sit down and read it. I would tell her what the kid said. She would smile wanly and kiss me, perhaps on the neck, which she would then rub and remind me that Heather was growing up. Later we would have some dinner, and then, feeling somewhat better, we'd sit in the living room and take greater risks with talking.

The thought crossed my mind that perhaps a small fire in the fireplace might make things a little better. Then I recalled that I never did get around to ordering firewood that previous autumn.

10

MACK ADMIRED the fire I'd built, when she got home, braced for trouble, right about eight-thirty. "Where'd you get the wood?" she said, finding me in my chair, reading shredded magazines by the light of the new seventy-five-watt bulb I had installed in the end-table lamp. She didn't even mention the martini I was sipping.

"Went next door," I said. "I asked the Coreys for some. Told them flat out I screwed up, forgot to order any. Jim Corey was very nice, said he understood. Told me to help myself to some. Had a beer with him."

"They are a nice young couple," Mack said, hanging up her coat. "They moved in last August, I think it was, while we were still down at the beach. They must think we're not very neighborly."

"My impression was," I said, "one of several, really, but my impression was they haven't thought about us much, or had the time to, you know?"

"I suppose not," Mack said absently, pouring white wine in the kitchen. "They've got two kids, have they?"

"Two extremely young kids," I said. "One's still in a high chair. Having some SpaghettiOs, throwing them around the kitchen, banging his spoon on his tray, having a grand time. Looked like strained carrots that he'd gotten in his hair, that blueberry stuff all down the front of him."

"Cobbler," Mack said, coming in, sitting down before the fire. "Nothing like it either, that stuff, that and the rice pudding. How old is the older one? Three or maybe four?"

"The one in the high chair is the older one," I said.

"Oh my God," Mack said.

"The younger one was in his crib, raising seven kinds of hell. Bottle wasn't the right temperature. Or maybe his pants were all full of shit. He was unhappy, anyway. Mummy's trying to cook dinner, Daddy's feeding older brother, this intruder comes in to beg firewood, and here's this young man and all his desires, totally ignored. He was really quite pissed off."

"Someday," Mack said, "and I realize I've been saying this for almost twenty years now, I should really write to Doctor Fitzmaurice and tell him that on further consideration I am not entirely sorry that we had to stop with one."

"A very nice gesture that would be, my love," I said, "were it not for the sad fact that Doctor Fitzmaurice has acquired staff privileges at a more celestial place."

"Oh yeah," Mack said, "I forgot."

"Alzheimer's disease," I said knowingly. "Don't give it a second thought, you can't remember things. There's nothing they can do about it, anyway."

"Oh shut up," she said. "How was your day, anyway?"

"Until I got home?" I said. "Or since then? You have got your god-damned choice."

"Which is likely to be worse?" she said.

"Not much to choose between them," I said. "One was dull and kind of sad, and I don't know what to do about it. The other one was sad and kind of upsetting. I don't know what to do about that either."

"Shall we start with mine, then," she said, "for a little change of pace?"

"Okay," I said, "I'm all ears. What misery did Diane invent for the company today?"

"Ah," Mack said, "Diane is moping. Just like she's been doing ever since I told her I was booting her ass out. Diane doesn't know it, but she's much less trouble that way. Which I'm not about to tell her because she'd stop doing it.

"The big news is something different. Are you ready for this?"

"I will brace myself," I said.

"I have it in mind," she said, "to buy a piece of land."

"That's an interesting concept," I said. "I thought you were selling land."

"I am," she said, "to other people, lots of other people. People who aren't any smarter than the two of us are, Jerry. Ordinary people who are building things, okay?"

"So far, so good," I said. "With the proviso, of course, that these people who have no more brains than we have do have something that we lack. Which is: lots more money."

"Not that much more," she said, "when you think about it. And if you really give it some thought, not as much in fact. It's just what they have is liquid. They can get their hands on it. What we have is tied up, and we can't use it for anything."

"I'm not sure I follow this," I said. Nor was I sure I wanted to, as far as that was concerned.

She leaned forward in her chair and clasped her hands before her. "Ace and Roy have got an option on the Commodore Islands. They are selling participations, shares of development rights, and I think we should buy a couple. Actually, what I really think is that we should buy five, but I can't see how we can afford to pass up two."

"Slow down here," I said. "The Commodore Islands. I do not know from them. Just what are these islands, and where are they located?"

"They're not really islands," she said, sitting back again. "What they are is high ground which is twelve feet above mean high water, so they look like islands when the tide is high. When it's low, they look like what they are, which is high ground that sticks up out of tidal marshes. There are seven of them, down near Marion, and five of them are buildable. The other two are smaller."

"This does not sound promising," I said. "What happens to these islands in a hurricane, for instance? Or another blizzard like we had in Seventy-eight? Does this 'mean high water' that they're twelve feet above include high water that is really mean? Or are they maybe ten or twelve feet *under* that kind of high water, so that what gets built on them will float, even if it wasn't meant to?"

"Those kinds of storms," she said, frowning, "are hundred-year storms, Jerry. Storms like that are very unusual. Almost any kind of coastal property fronting on a beach is going to be vulnerable to severe weather like that storm."

"This I know," I said. "I can recall very clearly finding pieces of the beachfront houses on our lawn down at Green Harbor, after that last one. The high-water mark was right at our front steps, which is a good four hundred yards and a big seawall from the usual location."

"Well, what I am saying," she said, "is that you don't plan for those things when you're laying out new projects. That is an assumed risk that the people who are involved in it just take into account."

"And buy a great deal of insurance," I said.

"Well," she said, "not actually. No more than a nominal amount."

"Sure," I said, "because insurance companies won't write insurance on that kind of property. They have got more sense than that, and more sense also than the people who think that since we had a big storm back in Nineteen seventy-eight, we are all set now until Two Thousand seventy-eight. Am I tracking this so far?"

She grinned at me. She fluttered her hand in the air. "*Mezza mezz'*," she said. "The whole theory is: you're building there to sell, all right? This is an investment that we would be making. We would be participants in these new condo complexes. We would not live in them. We would own so many units, as charter investors. When the buildings start to go up, Southarbor starts to advertise. By the time they're all constructed, they have all been sold. We have got our profits out. Everybody's happy."

"All of this assuming, of course, that the weather behaves," I said. "We finance the buildings we're not dumb enough to live in, because while we like the water we are not strong swimmers. What we hope for is the suckers buy those buildings from us before the next storm comes in, because that storm will remove those buildings from the land they're on."

"That's about it," she said, "yup. Buying for investment."

"I know guys who go to racetracks who say that about the ponies," I said. "Ace and Roy, I think, have bought some stuff they shouldn't. I would bet they bought it and then they tried to finance it, and the banks burst out laughing in their very startled faces."

"Money's still tight, Jerry," she said, "for recreational, second-home construction. Still very tight, and fairly high rates too."

"I'm sure it is." I said. "I'm also sure it can be had, if when the bank views the land they can see some probability that what's built on it will still be there when the mortgages have got five years to run. I bet that they can't even get government flood insurance on those parcels that you mention."

Mack began to look unhappy. "Jerry," she said, "Jerry, will you listen to me, lover? Beachfront land is very scarce. All of it's eroding. What's not built on's very poor, second-rate and crummy. These islands are in Marion, close to it, at least. It's a really lovely town. The view is out on Buzzards Bay, the Elizabeths and Martha's Vineyard. If you look west on a clear day you can see clear to Block Island."

"If you look south on a bad day," I said, "you can see a tidal wave."

She leaned forward again, pleading. "This'll go on advertising, and like hotcakes too, I'm sure. Close to boating, fine sailing. Good fishing and good swimming. No pollution. No Cape traffic, no fights with the bridges to cross that damned canal. Offer this one in New York, you'll sell it out by nightfall."

"Sell it on the wrong day," I say, "and it's gone by daybreak."

"Jerry," she said pleadingly, "those rich jerks can take the chance. "Won't you think about this? Please?"

"You wheedle well, Mack," I said. "I have always admired that."

"I know it," she said, smirking and smoothing her skirt on her thighs. "Dad always said the same thing." She became serious again. "But really, Jerry, all right? The participations are twenty grand apiece."

"Good God," I said, "that much? I was thinking: maybe five. Ten at the outside. But twenty big ones each? And you want to buy two of them? Forty thousand dollars? Jesus Christ, Mack, we can't do that. We don't have that kind of money. And didn't you say something about wanting five of them? A hundred thousand dollars? I'm glad I'm sitting down."

"Jerry," she said, "it's our chance. Ace and Roy have researched this thing. They know it will go. They've got all the permits for the access road, all the percolation tests, all the permits, all the zoning, everything they need. Do they say it's not a gamble? No, of course they don't. If we get another blizzard before they have gotten in and gotten out again, what they put into the project will float down to Stonington. But if they can get about four years more out of the interval before the next big blow, everyone who puts in twenty will pull somewhere in the neighborhood of one-eighty back again. Five of those investment units would be nine hundred thousand dollars, Jerry, all of it straight capital-gains taxes, seventy percent of eight hundred thousand dollars' profit free and clear to sock away." She looked as though she'd been wired for stereo. Her eyes sparkled and she could barely sit still in the chair.

"We don't have the money," I said.

"Yes, we do," she said. "We are sitting in it, and we have some more in Marshfield. If we sell this place, as we could easily, we could live in the beach house until the deal is finished. Then we'd have enough so that we could live anywhere we liked. Get ourselves a condo on Beacon Hill, if you like. Build ourselves a summer place that really would be something." She stood up suddenly and quivered for a moment. "This could make us, Jerry," she said, "make us rich and happy." She looked down on me and rumpled my gray hair. "We could both use that, my love, being rich and happy. I want you to think about it while I broil some lamb chops."

I did not think about it. It was a crackpot scheme. It was certainly dishonest. It was probably illegal. It would leave me in my old age, recluse in a beach house, busted out and disgraced as a paltry swindler who had tried to cheat some strangers and had been punished by God. I thought about my daughter instead, as though that would cheer me up. I had a third martini.

11

"THOSE KIDS next door," I said, gnawing on a lamb's bone, "paid ninety-one for that place."

"I know," Mack said, attacking her chop as though it had contained riches. "It's got central air."

"I didn't know that," I said. "How did you know that?"

"Kerry Jasper had the listing, off of MLS," she said. "Asked me if Twelve Kevin wasn't close to us. 'Sure it is,' I said, 'old Ten Kevin's right next door.' 'Classy neighborhood,' she said, told me the asking price. Which I thought was a little steep—they wanted ninety-four.

But then I looked at it and saw what was involved. Carrier. Big unit. You could cool a paint shop with it. Jenn-Air broilers, Lennox gas, built-in vacuum cleaner. Two-inch cut pile, wall to wall, all upstairs and down. Inlaid tile in the bathroom, darkroom in the basement. Full wine cellar, climate control—one of those big cabinets that cost about three grand. So, I could sort of see it, though I didn't think they'd get it. Jeff and Crystal Bates put too much money into that place, if you ask me, which they didn't. Should've sold it when he hit the pay dirt, built a new place of their own."

"She's probably doing that very thing right now," I said, "down in Florida."

"Uh-huh," Mack said, "she probably is, some beach-bum gigolo consulting. While Jeff and his newest bimbo scamper naked around his duplex on Com. Ave. and she takes care of all erection on the premises."

"Coarse talk," I said, starting another chop.

"True, though," she said, wiping her mouth. "Just as soon as those two kids were old enough to ship off to the prep school they could suddenly afford, the two adults, so called, in that house went absolutely nuts."

"That what you see for us," I said, "when Ace and Roy's scam pays off and we're rolling in the dough?"

"Uh-uh," she said, having some wine, "nothing that impressive. Just what I described to you, or something a lot like it. I'm not looking for a new man, and I still like our daughter. All I'm saying is this house is not right for us now. Back when we first bought it, Jerry, it was damned near perfect. Good thing too, I suppose, since we could barely afford it, but still that is what it was. This whole neighborhood was new, just like you and me. Bright-eyed, bushy-tailed, and fertile, getting somewhere fast. First the U-Haul trucks come in, never stay too long. Young couples buying their first houses don't have furniture, and they can't afford movers. After that, the diaper service, then the ice-cream trucks.

"A few years go by," Mack said, reaching for her second chop. "One guy makes a few bucks and gets pissed off at the crabgrass, so he hires some fine lawn service. His pal right next door to him gets lucky in the market, and he gets a Cadillac. For a while things are unsettled, people getting too big for their houses at the same time as their britches. Then the smart ones start to move out. The less smart ones stay behind, but act like they moved up, like the Bateses. Then in time they move out too. How do you think Ace and Roy, and people in their business, stay in business all those years when nobody's building houses? Selling the same houses that they sold before, that's how, marking time with new commissions on the same old properties. That's why it's so boring, selling residential stuff. Getting worked up for the eighth time over that damned in-ground sprinkler, it could drive a body nuts."

"We had a note from Heather today," I said between bites.

"Indeed," Mack said, lowering the bone that she was working on. "Now that's an interesting transition, I must say, Jeremiah. Is there some connection here I should know about?"

"Yes," I said, "I think there is. I didn't like the letter."

"Give me the quick gist of it, so I can get oriented," she said. "Is our darling daughter going into real estate, following in Mother's footsteps, for the glamor and prestige?"

"Not to mention the Mercedes," I said, "but: no, not that I know about. What it is, is that she isn't coming home for spring break, as I thought she was."

"This surprises you?" she said, arching her left eyebrow.

"Sort of, yes, it does," I said. "Back at Christmas when I saw her, maybe for an hour, she more or less suggested to me that she'd need the break for research. At the library." Heather has a double major, modern languages and government. We both warned her, when she took it, she would have to work like hell. She said she would not mind that, and her grades say that she hasn't. But it's still very demanding, and by rights it should cut into her free time to play. "What she said was that she'd have to spend the whole vacation at the BPL, and we talked about how she could ride in with me on no-court days and save on the damned parking."

"And you arranged all this," Mack said, "while she packed to go skiing."

"Yeah," I said, "we did." Heather's boyfriend, Charlie, comes from a wealthy family. I would call them wealthy, at least. Charlie's father is a lawyer, so's to have something to do. To have something he can say that he is doing, would be more like it. He's a partner in a big firm down in Washington, but he seems to spend most of his time in its branch in LA. Charlie's mother lives in Palm Beach in the wintertime, and comes north to Chatham in the summer. Sometimes Charlie lives with Daddy, down in Great Falls, Virginia. Sometimes Charlie bunks with Mum, and plays tennis the whole summer, which was what the lad was doing when he first met Heather—she was working at the time, lifeguard at the Beach Club down in Harwich Port. One of the Lloyd family houses is at Steamboat Springs. Charlie had invited Heather to go skiing out there over New Year's, gave her plane tickets for Christmas. Heather spent a week with us, dropping in between parties—she still has a lot of friends from Fontbonne around Braintree—and then took off Christmas Day for the powder in the Rockies. I did not approve of this, and that had not mattered. Heather was nineteen years old, doing well in school, and she had her mother on her side as well. "Now she writes home and she never mentions all the research she told me about at Christmas. Says if it's okay with us, she'll go West with Charlie just as soon as classes break, have a week of neat spring skiing, then go visit Dad in Palm Desert for a week or so of tennis. I assume that Charlie's paying for the plane rides in all this, because Heather didn't ask for money."

"And even though you wouldn't give it to her," Mack said, "you don't like that part either."

"That's correct," I said. "I don't like that part either. That kid isn't twenty yet. Charlie's just a junior. I know times've changed and all, but I can't say I like it. Back when I was growing up . . ."

". . . milking three cows before school every morning, walking five miles through the snow with your tattered green book bag," Mack said, grinning at me through the lamb grease.

". . . couples who behaved like that were at least close to getting married. Or else the girl who was involved was considered a loose woman, and the guy was keeping her. And I look at what she's doing, and I assume that they are fucking, and it bothers me, Mack. It really bothers me."

She stopped grinning at me. She put her hand out for mine and clenched it tightly for a while. "Jerry," she said softly, "try to be objective."

"Objective?" I said. "Damnit, I am being objective. I am looking at my only child's behavior and I see it plain and clear. I see it for just what it is, and it's something I don't like. Then I look at what I'm doing, and I don't like that much either. I am tolerating this stuff. I'm condoning it. We've got this silent agreement, where she refrains from coming right out and telling me she's screwing him, and I keep quiet and don't ask her because that's part of the deal. If I ask her, she will tell me, and then neither one of us will know what the hell to do.

"Shit," I said, "you know? This shits. If I'd been doing something like this, and my father'd found out, I don't know what he would've done."

"I do," Mack said, nodding fast, "he would've slapped you on the back. 'That's my stud son there, young Jerry,' old Tom would've said. Bragged about you to his pals down at the Navy Yard. 'You should see this piece of tail that my kid's knocking off. Jesus, what a knockout. Tits on this kid that'd make you faint to grab 'em.'"

"He would not've," I said, getting mad, and fast. "My father was a weekly communicant, for God's sake. Tom wouldn't even let us swear when we were growing up."

"I know, I know," she said wearily. "Treasurer of the Holy Name, fourth-degree Knight of Columbus, every month he made a vigil at St. Coleman's Church in Brockton—I know all of that stuff, Jerry, and I also knew old Tom. I saw how he looked at me, remember, what was in his eyes. He looked like an appraiser, Jerry, when he looked at me."

"You're dead wrong, Mack," I said, "goddamnit. He was a good family man. If I'd've done what Heather's doing, old Tom would've killed me."

"If you'd've been Heather," she said, "then I agree, he might've. I did not say that he would've bragged about his daughter. Absolutely not, he wouldn't. That would've been quite different. Chances are, if you'd been her, and he found out about it, he would have thrown you out of the house, and maybe slapped you silly."

"Oh," I said, "this is great. A little women's lib shit, just to make me feel lots better."

"Call it what you want to, Jerry," Mack said, letting go my hand. She got up with her wineglass and went toward the refrigerator. "Double standard, women's lib, anything you want. Fact of the matter is that you know I am right."

"It doesn't matter if you're right," I said to her. "What difference does that make to me when I try to figure this out? I got myself into this, letting my training slide. Go to church when I feel like it, ignore most of it. Bring my kid up with some notion, she decides what's right. Now she's doing something that I know damned well is wrong, and I can't say something to her?"

"No," Mack said, pouring wine, "you can't say anything. Because it is just like you said, how we brought her up. We raised her to look at things and make her own decisions. We told her she'd take the consequences. She took what we told her at full face value. She has thought about friend Charlie and decided that she loves him. If she loves him, she sleeps with him. Charlie seems to like this all right, and from what I see, he loves her back. Heather's lucky too, of course, because her doting parents sent her to a rich kids' school. Therefore, when she fell in love, she fell in love with money. Consequently, loving Charlie's quite a lot of fun. In addition to the sex." She put the wine back in the refrigerator and came back toward the table. "I must say, Jerry, what she's doing—it doesn't sound too bad. Even for an old girl like your devoted wife. If you're going to lose your virtue, springtime in the Rockies does sound like an inviting place to do it."

"Bullshit," I said, "bullshit. Heather's virtue is long gone. That much we can agree on. That went bye-bye down at Harwich, or wherever they were last summer when she made up her mind to put out."

Mack studied me as though I had been one of several horses entered in a long race which she had in mind to bet. "Ah, Jerry, my love," she said, "I'm not sure how to break this to you, but I think you're off a little."

"Off a little," I said, getting up with glass in hand, "off a little, am I?"

"Have some wine," she said. "It's kinder to your liver."

"I will have some ice and vodka," I said, going for the freezer. "That is kinder to my soul, which right now is sore beset."

"Have some vodka, then," she said. "One more probably won't hurt you."

"Just how am I off a little, as you so delicately put it?" I said, digging into the freezer bin where the ice-maker dumps the cubes so that they can promptly freeze together into one damned solid mass. "Do you want to tell me that?"

"No," she said, "I don't, not when you come right down to it. But I suppose I will. My guess would be that when you say that Heather became a fallen woman sometime late last summer, you are off by a good year. A little more than that, actually."

I wrenched some ice loose and put a chunk of it into my glass. I slammed the freezer door shut. I went to the liquor cabinet and took the jug of vodka out. I anointed the ice liberally. All the while my brain was running like one of those old punch-card computers, sifting through the names of Heather's boyfriends I recalled, wishing I'd paid more attention to the endless parade of them. "Andrew," I said viciously, taking a pull of booze. "That little bastard Andrew with the brand-new denim jeep. That snot-nosed little shitbag that I listened to all summer, how safe parachuting was. And all the time he's telling me I should let Heather jump, I'm sitting there like a damned fool and thinking he means out of airplanes, and he really meant into bed. I hope somebody tangles his goddamned ripcord for him, that little con artist."

Mack sat looking pensively at me. "I'm afraid so, Jerry," she said. "It was either him or Toby."

"Toby," I said, "nah. Not that little piece of shit. Mickey Rooney will play Toby in the movie of that summer. He was one of Heather's toys. She said that herself. Told me she went out with Toby so that he would stay around. Uh-uh," I said, "not Toby."

"I won't argue with you," Mack said as I returned to the table. "I don't think it really matters."

"No, of course it doesn't," I said. "Not which one it was, goddamnit. She was putting out for the beach, for Christ sake? Doesn't matter one damned bit."

"Let me ask you something," Mack said, "and keep in mind: I know the answer. Were we married when we first made love? In that furnished room you had?"

"No, my darling, we were not," I said impatiently. "As you said, you know the answer, and you also know the rest. That you were the first for me, and you were just as green. And you were also twenty-two, not some damned teen-aged virgin. And we knew where we were going, we had some experience. From the first night that I met you, I knew I was going to marry you, and you knew the very same damned thing, and we were both right. So that is not the same thing that you're asking me about. It is not the same damned thing at all."

Mack sighed through a smile. "You men," she said, "you're so easy."

"Easy," I said, "men are easy? That's not what bothers me, if you mean Charlie's easy. It's Heather being easy—that's what got me upset."

She took my hand again. "Jerry," she said, "it's seduction. Do you understand that? That is what it's always been, nothing but seduction. You thought that you got me drunk, talked me into bed? The drinks helped, I will admit, at the Spinnaker. After dinner, with the wine, at the Olde Cape Cod House. But they just made me feel even better about something I'd decided I was going to do anyway. I wanted you, all right? You wanted me, I could tell that, and I really wanted you. So that made everything quite nice, and I went to bed with you, and it was dynamite and we kept doing it and we've been doing it ever since. And, oh yeah, somewhere along the way we went to church and got married, so that made it all right, and here we are today. You are being righteous because this kid that we made, doing it, is probably out doing it herself."

"Except that," I said obstinately, "she is not going to marry Charlie, and they're not in love like we were. What she's doing's fucking Charlie, and I still don't like it, Mack."

"You would like it better," Mack said, "if Charlie Lloyd was like Jim Corey?"

"The young guy next door?" I said. "No, I can't say that I would."

"Well," Mack said, "that's the alternative. Jim Corey's two years older than you were when you seduced me. His wife's just turned twenty-one. A little more than a year older than your daughter, that kid is, the mother of two screaming brats with carrots in their hair. Is that what you want for Heather? Something like those kids've got?"

"How do you know all this?" I said, stalling for some time because that wasn't what I wanted for our shining daughter.

"Kerry Jasper," Mack said. "Kerry told me when those two kids, with two kids of their own, laid out ninety-one for that place back last fall. I guess the wife was too young to sign the mortgage papers or some other damned thing. 'Can you beat that?' Kerry said. 'Two kids they've got already, and a thirty-year mortgage, she looks like she's been in combat and he's borrowed his ass blind, and she's barely old enough to get a legal drink. Honest to God, Mack,' she said, 'and we thought we had it rough.' She also had a few smart cracks to make about how we must be the senior citizens of Fertile Hill now, which did not make me like our house better, but we'll let those pass for now."

"Holy shit," I said.

"Holy shit, agreed," Mack said. "We did it without getting caught, and we thought it was great. Heather's not about to get caught, and she's having a great time. How about, you write her back, send her a nice letter. Tell her how Lou went to jail, and the guy with the dog. Let the kid know that you love her and you're glad she's having fun. Charlie is a nice kid, Jerry. You might think of that."

"There is that, I suppose," I said, thinking of Peter Cooper. "I will do my level best."

12

THE REST of February slouched through, slushy, raw, and apparently uneventful. I suppose that should have been something to feel grateful about, but I was not in any mood for gratitude. I took on four new clients, which would have been cause for wild rejoicing when I first went into practice on my own, and collected eleven thousand dollars in retainers from them without feeling my pulse quicken. Part of the reason I was so blasé, of course, was that when I first went into practice on my own, eleven thousand dollars would have kept me and the office running for a good six months or so; now, if I draw four of it as salary, the remaining seven will keep the operation afloat for maybe two months, at the most. I tried to distract Cooper from another litany of woe about his oral surgery by registering a bitter complaint at what inflation had done to the legal profession, and that didn't work either.

"Lemme ask you this," he said through swollen tissues, "when that eleven grand would run things for a good half year or so, how much would you have been charging those four perpetrators you just took on?"

"I dunno," I said. "There wasn't that much drug stuff then, and two of these are druggies." The third was a child molester who perhaps was not the best choice that the Colebrook Unified School District might have made as the driver of its bus for junior high school students. "The baby-fucker," I said, "probably about the same as now—five grand, minimum. He wouldn't've had any more then than he could raise last week by getting his wife to agree to hock their house again. So, even though the case is worth ten or eleven, easy, it was take the five or bump it out, and I'm not in a position yet where I can kiss off five grand. Smelly little item, though. I wished I could have done that."

"Shit," Cooper said, "don't give me that routine. You tell me Jerry Kennedy is getting finicky, I'll tell you that the Red Sox are a shoo-in in the Series. You'd defend Adolf Hitler if he came in with the cash."

"You wound my feelings, Cooper," I said, "saying things like that. I am an officer of the bar of Massachusetts, sworn to provide competent defense to all whom I represent. I have no choice in the matter."

"Right," Cooper said. "The druggies. Call them same as drunks. They aren't, of course—drunks are sometimes sane. But say they are. Six hundred apiece, in the good old days?"

"About that, yeah," I said. "Might've upped to eight on one of them. He was visiting a pal at the Marriott when the cops came in with a small warrant and grabbed him for good measure. Classy fellow like that could afford a little extra."

"And you got them for what this year?" Coop said.

"The Marriott guy," I said, "two grand and very reasonable. The other one's a cheapo, half a pound of marijuana. One big one for him, but it's probably a plea, not much heavy lifting for his resolute attorney."

"And the fourth gentleman?" Coop said. "What was his assessment, in those happy days gone by?"

"Hard to say," I said. "His estranged wife says he beats her. He's the first one that I've had, in my whole career. Probably a grand."

"But in these post-OPEC times," Coop said, "you shucked him for a full three, for your total of eleven on four files that were worth two-thirds of that back when JFK was around."

"You know something, Coop," I said. "You are good with figures. How about you do my taxes for me this year, now that my vaunted courtroom skills've put my tax accountant into durance vile?"

"You still mourning that one?" Coop said. "Jesus Christ, man, quit it, will ya?"

"Never mind that," I said, "I am serious."

"I got one for you, then," Coop said, "go pound sand."

"Hey," I said, "what is this? You won't do my taxes, bastard, after all I've done for you?" I was only half joking, if the joke made half.

"You know my damned situation," Cooper said savagely. "Got this medieval torturer at work inside my mouth. Got that goddamned kid of mine in the booby hatch. No vacation. Wife's distraught, practice shot to hell, savings down the drain. You think what I need just now's a free accounting sideline? I think you're the bastard."

I was not going to let him up. "Cooper," I said, "have a heart. I know you've got troubles. But let's keep in mind, my friend, I helped you out with them. Now my friend Lou is in jail, and I need some help. Everybody tells me: 'Don't do your own taxes.' Okay, I listen to that, but they still have to get done. It's not like it was something that would take you a full week. I've got damned good records, man. Gretchen sees to that. If you like, I'll have her add them, give you all the figures. I can promise you, those figures are correct. All the receipts, canceled checks, everything you'd need."

"Jerry," Coop said, "back off some. Why would I need them? All receipts and those canceled checks—why would I need them? You have Gretchen do the numbers, I just fill them in? What do I care what you've got, if you've got the stuff."

"Well, Jesus, Coop," I said, "if I get audited. That's the only time you'd need them."

Cooper nodded several times. "That is what I mean. If they audit you, as they will, then I would need them. Because I'm the guy who, after all, signed your tax returns. And that means that instead of you, I get to entertain them. Jerry, damnit, understand, I can't afford to do that. In the first place, as you know, I am too distracted. If you had all your own buttons, you would see that anyway. You would not want me to be the guy on your taxes, because I most likely wouldn't do them right. And if by some miracle, I did do them right, I would not be able to defend what I did to a field examiner." He looked at me pleadingly. "Jerry," he said, "okay? Try to understand me. I am turning cases down, work that I could handle. If it's complicated stuff, lots of ledgers, many books, I am sending that stuff out. I know I can't concentrate, I can't give my full attention. I don't want to take something, something I know I can't handle, mess it up and then get sued, lose my goddamned ticket. Can't you just see that?"

"Yeah," I said, "I can. I should've thought of that."

"Which doesn't mean," Coop said, "that I don't appreciate your problem. Doesn't Kincaid do that stuff, your pal Roger Kidd?"

"That is not the answer, Coop," I said immediately. "I've already had that thought, and rejected it. Kincaid, Bailey and Kincaid is not my kind of law firm. Or to put it more correctly, I'm not their sort of client."

"I don't understand," Coop said, looking puzzled. "You're their kind of lawyer, seems like, all the stuff they send you."

I sloughed the question with an answer that was true, but not correct.

"I'm their kind of lawyer, Coop," I said, "in exactly the same way that the Spanish-speaking fat ladies with the kerchiefs on their heads are their kind of cleaning ladies, all right? Every night on their way home from those quiet offices in the Beacon Hill town house, Kincaid, Bailey and Kincaid, Roger Kidd and all them quiet, dignified fellers see the Puerto Rican women dumping out the ashtrays and emptying the wastebaskets, and on those rare occasions when they think about them at all, they think: 'Those spics are our kind of charwomen.'

"I do the same sort of service for them," I said. "I take the occasional grubbiness of which even their fine clients are from time to time guilty off their manicured hands before anything gets soiled. I am a garbage-man, and I am very useful. Something like the guy from the pumping service that cleans out the septic tanks at their beach houses in the early summer. 'Not a goddamned client, for Christ sake, are you crazy, man?' "

"I see," Cooper said. "Wouldn't want them patronizing me either, now that you put it that way."

That in fact was close to the damned truth, but not for the reason I had given Cooper. The chief reason that I didn't want to go to Roger Kidd, and ask him for that favor, was that I did not want to tell him how much money I was making. How little, actually. I made less than Cooper made, though he didn't know it. Of course, I didn't have his pension, which was thirty grand or so and increased every time the cost of living went up, and that helped him a lot, but the fact of the matter was that Lou Schwartz had been right: I didn't make enough to purchase the sort of protection that the way in which I make it seemed to demand. The first year that Lou went through my business expenses, he was genuinely appalled.

"Kennedy, you asshole," he said, waving records at me, "where the hell're your bills from the goddamned sweepers?" I thought he meant something like the cleaning ladies. "Included with the building rent," I said stupidly. "Not *them*," Lou said, exasperated, "not the goddamned janitors. The electronic surveillance guys, the ones that sweep your office. Get the bugs out, you know? Find the taps? Make sure that what is private stays that way, you jerk?"

"I don't have any," I said, very sheepishly. "The kind of business that I do, I didn't think I'd need it."

"Jerry," Lou said, "start paying attention. What you think's not important. It's what other people think. First you got the people, all right? Come in here and hire you. They sit down and tell you things that they've been doing. Some of those things are illegal. That is why they're here. Cops and people like that would be interested, see? Your clients should know that cops are not listening. You should be making sure of this, having people come in at least once a month or so, check your phone lines, stuff like that, keep things confidential."

I told Lou I doubted that the cops would bug a lawyer's office. This was before Watergate. I mentioned the Constitution and the laws against such searches. "You got any idea," Lou said, "just how silly you sound, standing there and saying that shit like you really meant it?" I did have some idea, and my face got red. "Yes," Lou said, "of course you have. You do learn after all. I will send my man around. You will let him in. Be nice to him, Counselor, 'cause he's coming every month."

"Lou," I said, "what does he cost?"

"For a little shithole like this," Lou said, "eighty dollars." He saw me starting to speak and he held up his right hand. "Don't tell me you can't afford it. I have seen your records. On what is in them, coming in and going out, you are absolutely right. My guy Joey, with his meters and his magic boxes? You cannot afford this guy. The dough isn't there.

"Nevertheless, Jeremiah," Lou said very gravely, "you will pay for Joey and you'll do it every month. Keep in mind what Frank told you, why I'm talking to you. It is now important to you to make sure that your Uncle does not hear what you say when you talk on the telephone. To make absolutely sure the FBI is not tuned in when some careless fellow that has hired you gets the idea in his head that he would like to tell everything he's done and a few things that he's planning. And in return for you doing this, my friend, I will not tell Frank or, God save your ass, Nunzio all the dumb things you've been doing or how you have just assured me that the cops do not bug lawyers. That will be our little secret. Frank thinks you are a smart boy, all right? Frank thinks he can judge character. It would kill Frank to find out what an asshole you have been."

"Lou," I said, "for heaven's sake, keep in mind what I am doing. I am representing pimps, and guys who drink too much. I have one guy who's a car thief. Last month, an arsonist. My clients don't know Nunzio, not personally at least. They think the FBI's a television show, with Efrem Zimbalist. Joe Vaster was a freak for me, the client I don't get.

Frank thinks I'm headed for big things? That's great. I hope he's right. But in the meantime, till I get them, deal with what I am."

"Listen to me," Lou said. "Just hear what I have to say. This past year you took in under forty thousand dollars. That is chickenshit. In this pigpen, it's enough, if your girl keeps working free. You could live off what you kept. Pretty shitty living, of course, but still a place to sleep." Mack was not working then, Heather being still young. I had paid Gretchen a full seven thousand dollars, including benefits. The rent came to less than six grand. The furniture was Dr. Carey's, taken as my fee for representing him when he got caught peddling narcotics prescriptions; it had been in no better shape than Doctor Carey was at the time, and the use I had allowed my rough clients to give it had not made it any better, but it did have the great attractiveness of being wholly free. Given all that scrimping, I had netted twenty-three, after I had paid the phone bill and kept my car filled with gas. That was more than our house cost, so I was doing well. Or thought I was, at least.

"The whole point of me being here," Lou said that day to me, "is that so far this year, thanks in large part to Levitable, you are earning at the rate of almost seventy. Your expenses haven't gone up, not too much at least. I would suggest that they should, some new furniture and stuff, because what you don't spend you will pay in taxes, but that's strictly up to you. If Frank's right, though, then you'll have to pay. If he's not, you won't." I would naturally decide to have it both ways at once: assume that Frank's prediction was right, but make no improvements in my office. What I did was buy the beach house, down at Green Harbor. Which, as Lou would remind me, was not at all deductible as business overhead, and did not do a thing to make my offices look better. "You could run a tire store in this dump," Lou said, "if you could get cars in the goddamned elevators. Wheel alignments, front-end jobs, new mufflers and snow tires. You should get some calendars from Snap-On Tools and Monroe Shocks. Give out free lollipops."

In the years since then, my income had improved. I grossed just under $108,000 the year before Lou went away. My overhead was up greatly too, of course, over $40,000, and so were the damned taxes, even more. I had nothing but my office overhead and my personal exemption to knock off my net income—the accountant at Southarbor who convinced Mack to file individually had also persuaded her that she had to claim all the real estate interest charges and local taxes on her return, since both houses had always been in her name sole, in case I got sued—and I found myself able to threaten real tears when I thought about what I was going to have to pay to Uncle Sam. Keeping Dartmouth nourished and sheltering what few pre-tax dollars I could with my two retirement plans left me with very little sporty money after netting almost $70,000, a fact which I found astonishing. That net, to Roger Kidd, would be cause for pity, and I didn't want that from him. Polly Kidd's trust fund alone annually coughed out more than that.

"Besides," I said to Coop that day, "Kincaid, Bailey and the other gentlemen don't do what I probably need done. Their work's all with old, respectable money, capital gains, convertible debentures, estate taxes. Lives in being, perpetuities, *en ventre sa mère*—all the shit that I ignored when I was back in law school. What in Jesus' name do I care about springing uses and divestments, all that fancy crap? What I need is someone cute, someone to reduce my taxes without getting me in jail."

"Well, I couldn't help you there, then," Coop said. "Though I'm surprised that Lou couldn't."

"Oh," I said, "Lou tried. Year after year, he told me I should start buying up stuff that I could sell and take losses. 'Investment, Jerry,' Lou said. 'You should have investments.'

" 'Lou,' I said, 'investments? What the hell do I invest? Losses? Gains're what I need. You have got things backwards, I think. All the money that I get, I use to pay taxes.' "

"You know something?" Coop said, looking speculative. "Given the box that you are in, you should see Bert Magazu."

"Huh," I said, "Bert Magazu. You know that I'd really like to? See Bert Magazu? And not just because I need tax help, although I could certainly use some. No, so's I could be one of the few guys that could claim to have laid eyes on him. Ever since I started practice, I've been hearing that. 'Bert Magazu, Bert Magazu, see Magazu on taxes.' It sounds like a chant to me, a goddamned football cheer. But I have never seen this guy, and even more than that, I can't say that I know a single soul that has. I'm not even really sure Bert Magazu exists."

"Oh," Cooper said, "put that aside. Bert Magazu exists."

"I'm impressed," I said. "You mean you've actually seen him?

"Well," Cooper said, "not that, of course, not actually seen him. 'Shake the hand that shook the hand . . . ?' No, I can't claim that much. But I did something almost as good. I investigated him."

"Now," I said, "that's interesting. What did the celebrated Magazu commit that made the Bureau curious? I'm surprised he would be that crude, get the FBI on him."

"Jerry," Cooper said, "they never told us that. Word came down from SOG, Seat of Government: 'Hoover wants this guy looked into.' So we started looking. I can assure you, he exists, very much exists. Formidable gentleman, Bertram Magazu."

"Twelve-quart brain and stuff like that? X-ray vision?" I said. "Leaps tall buildings without bounding? Knows the Code by heart?"

"Not exactly," Coop said, "but still pretty impressive. U. of Chicago bachelor's degree when he was about fifteen. Ph.D. in mathematics before he was twenty. Four more years at Cambridge, comparative law. One year at Yale Law School, enough for an LL.M. Turned down more big jobs in Washington than I dreamed had been invented. A good deal of contact, of course, with the Iron Curtain, most of it through Switzerland, some of it through Belgium. International scholar in ichthyology, which I looked up and found out that it means he knows his fish. Never been married, no known other evil habits. Admitted to practice in about sixteen different states, with some sort of connection to the bar at Lincoln's Inn. Very interesting fellow, but not much to hook him on. I think J. Edgar must've been a little disappointed. But he definitely exists."

"And he costs a lot of money," I said.

"Lots and lots of money," Coop said. "Sees only those few clients that come recommended to him, *after* he decides that they look interesting to him."

"Now," I said, "I know he's smart. That's the kind of practice I should have. No more people, bother children. And no damned drooling druggies. No clients with dogs, retained or appointed. No new car thieves allowed on these premises. Advertise in *Barron's* and the *Wall Street* goddamned *Journal*: 'Practice Limited to the Better Class of Felons.'"

" 'Persons name of Louis Schwartz need not bother to apply,' " Coop said.

"Right," I said, "that too. Too nerve-racking, damnit. Too discouraging. Only, of course, till next week, when I get him out."

"Motion to reduce?" Coop said, looking sympathetic.

"Yeah," I said, "a motion to reduce. Next to a motion for a new trial, the least likely to succeed. And of course Judge Edmund Maguire is merest putty in my hands, and will grant it instantly—which, if I were you, I might not believe that."

"Put it this way," Coop said, working his sore jaw, "I don't think, until I see it, I will put big money on it."

"Yeah," I said, "big money."

13

MY PRACTICE is repetitive, after twenty years. Half of what it repeats, from my clients' mouths and mine, can be reduced to those two short words: "Big money, Mister Kennedy, he promised me big money." The other half, or roughly that, is people who have created their own troubles with some kind of intoxicants, either because they did not get their big money or because they in fact did. Harry Mapes gets in the shit, in his golden years, because, old and slowed down, and never really bright, he decides that one big score will get him some big money. David Mackin, C.L.U., makes big money in his view; he decides that therefore he can do just what he pleases with his vintage Thunderbird, and he gets humiliated. Lou Schwartz went in for big money, what he got for hiding bigger dough of Nunzio's. Two new druggies looked to me just like the ones before them: the one with half a pound of reasonably good grass had planned to peddle it to his classmates at the Berklee College of Music, his anticipated profits being equal to the price of a short trip to LA, which for him was still big money. The other one, from the hotel, was moving up to cocaine; hashish no longer seemed to him to offer big returns. For me, in my middle age, child molesters and wife-beaters are a welcome change, people who did evil things because of warped passions that did not involve money. And, of course, I meet them all because I'm out for their money.

I try to avoid those facts or thinking about them too much. A ragtag parade of young men, mostly, between eighteen and twenty-six, finds its way through my door to the desk where Gretchen sits, and I listen to their troubles. Some are sullen, some are defiant, repeaters are tired or embarrassed, and we try to treat them as though they were individuals. It is better when we succeed, and they and their cases permit this: clients like Lou Schwartz bring on emotional upsets and make me appreciate somewhat long stretches of rank dullness.

"That Schwartz case doesn't go away," Gretchen said sympathetically, giving me routine reminders of my next day's schedule in the late gray afternoon in early March. "He did, but the case does not."

"Ahh," I said, "goddamnit, Gretchen, what else can I do? Maguire should've listened to me at the sentencing. Lou was only in there because Dunn had the hots for Nunzio. I like Ed Maguire just fine, but he should not've done that. Putting Lou Schwartz in the can was making himself part of the prosecution. Mike Dunn couldn't do it without Judge Maguire's assistance, so he nailed Lou on a technical and Maguire joined up. Judges shouldn't do that."

"Right," she said sarcastically, "you've got a point there, Jerry. Is that what you've got in mind, say to Maguire in the morning: 'Resign from the U.S. Attorney's Office, Judge, all right? It don't look good on you?' "

"That's not what I'm going to say," I said. "That's what I will mean, though, and old Ed Maguire will know it. No, what I'll do is go in there and beg for twenty minutes. Give him the old song and dance about substantial justice. 'Lou's experienced the shock of real incarceration, which all by itself has a real punitive effect. Just by putting him in, Judge, you have punished him. He's been in there for a while now, going on a month. On what you have given him, he expects to do almost nine months more. I'm not saying: "Let him out," although that is what I would like. All I'm saying is: "Reduce." Cut his term in half. Make it one year, to be served. Let him out in August. That will give him some hope now, when he really needs it. It won't minimize the crime, or thwart the prosecution. All it will do is improve the prisoner's state of mind.' "

"Then you could add," Gretchen said, " 'And it will let him catch the last half of the Saratoga meeting.' "

"I'm not sure Judge Maguire would find that totally persuasive," I said. "It is true, of course, and that's exactly what he'd do if Maguire did what I am asking, but I really don't see any purpose to be served by stating it."

"You have talked to Mike Dunn on this?" she said. "That pompous little stuffed shirt?" Gretchen is a partisan, after all these years. When she began with me, back when I was starting out, she was a trim young grass widow with two kids to raise, and she disliked people who had been committing crimes. She came from a large and respectable blue-collar family, and she reserved the respect she gave for people who worked hard. She assumed that those who stole were not fond of hard work. Her elusive second husband had been that sort of man. He had scooted from his duties, first his job, then her. Punks and pimps and burglars, thieves and pushers, sly con men: to her in her younger days, those were worse versions of him. "What I respect," she said, "is someone you can trust. Somebody who works hard and does what he says he'll do. Not some bum who looks at you and decides that he'll get what he wants by feeding you some bullshit. I've got no respect for them."

Mack back then was not impressed by Gretchen's stern values. "Uh-huh," she said knowingly, "little flatterer. All that means is: she wants you. That's *her* line of bullshit. Load this naïve young attorney up with all this crap. Make him see how tough she is, loyal and devoted. Then if wifey gives him shit, move right in and pounce. I think I will watch this cutie, watch her very close."

I told Mack she was wrong then, as she surely was. Gretchen was impeccable in her behavior with me. Did her job at damned low wages, went home to her kids. Settled into habits which resolved the cutie issue—Gretchen liked to eat and drink, and she put on weight. Making her own living, and her own security, brought her an increase of ample confidence. She went out with passing men, lived with three or four. "Take no shit and dish none out," she claimed as her sole rule. In time she began to see something of that same code in operation in the activities of those customers of mine who did not set out to harm anybody physically, or steal from those who had not protected themselves from injury by theft. She grew to despise those who disparaged our clients along with prosecuting them. She became protective of her outlaw pals.

"Now this little turd up there in Essex," she exploded to me one fine morning—the day after an ambitious new district attorney up in Salem had made an extravagant statement to the press in which he not only disclosed the multi-count indictment of Cadillac Teddy Franklin and four other gentlemen, but singled Teddy out for special praise as "king-pin of the luxury-car theft network which had been operating in the

Northeast for the past seven or eight years"—"he ought to be im- peached."

"On what grounds, exactly?" I said. "It's true, isn't it? Except for the time involved. Probably closer to ten or eleven years, I'd say."

"He is making Teddy out to be a bad guy," Gretchen said, very righteously, "and Teddy isn't that. I know Teddy, keep in mind, known him quite a while. Teddy Franklin's a nice guy. Anyone would like him. Very polite, very pleasant, always asks me how my kids are. When he calls he always says I shouldn't bother you, in case there is someone with you, sitting in your office. Always pays his bills on time, when I send the bills out to him. If the rent is coming up, and we're just a little short, all I do is bill our Teddy, and I never have a problem. Buys his wife nice stuff too, I guess, very nice things for her. Takes her off on all those trips, always sending flowers."

"Buys his girlfriends nice things too," I said maliciously. "Dotty doesn't let him take them off on trips, but he's very attentive to them. Treats them very well indeed."

"Yeah," Gretchen said, somewhat defensively, "well, that doesn't change my mind. I don't say necessarily that has to mean something. If a man has girlfriends, and he's married at the same time, well, I don't know how his marriage is or what he gets at home. Maybe there's a reason for it, something I don't know about. And if he has them, I say, and he doesn't flaunt them at her, you know, and he always makes sure that they're taken care of and they know that he is married, well, that's not something I think is necessarily all bad."

"Gretchen," I said, faking surprise, "am I hearing this?" I was nee- dling her and she was getting red. She had had a brief spell of passion with a younger man who had told her a lot of things, and many of them turned out not to be entirely true. His wife called her up one night and identified those points on which he had failed to be quite candid.

"I know," she said, "I know. But that's what I am saying. Teddy doesn't make his girls think he is leaving Dot. Or that he's divorcing Dotty, and they should be patient. Teddy's out to get their pants off, and that's all he wants. He told me, he tells them that, right from the beginning. 'You would be surprised,' he said, 'how often that works.' 'No, I wouldn't,' I said back, 'it has worked with me.'"

"My goodness," I said, "and I am cold sober too."

"Doesn't matter," Gretchen said, "I don't care if you're shocked. All you goddamned men believe it's all your idea. Sometimes, you know, it is not. Sometimes we just want to get laid, and you could spare us all the bullshit. And that's what Teddy's doing, all right? Skipping all the crap. And if she does, then that's all right, and if she doesn't, okay.

"See, Jerry," Gretchen said, with some sarcasm of her own, "I don't know if you've ever thought about this, but somebody in my position, who happens to be a woman, all right? And if she wants to get laid, like the men are always doing, well, and she doesn't have her own man, she will maybe decide that it's all right if she borrows someone else's for the night. Or maybe for even just a few hours or so, okay? Because she needs something he has got, for a little while." She smirked at me. "And I always return it in perfectly good condition, Mister Kennedy, when I am finished with it."

I did not pursue that conversation any further. I decided it was better and much easier if I just agreed with Gretchen that the Essex County DA was a little turd. Gretchen was very gratified when I got Teddy off, although I must say that my part in the dismissal of his case had much less to do with my great legal skills than it did with the disappearance of the Commonwealth's chief witness, who has not turned up since then—one of Teddy's codefendants was said to be a bad man who could arrange that sort of thing.

Knowing how Gretchen felt about sanctimonious prosecutors, and sharing her uncomplimentary estimate of Michael Steven Dunn, I said I had spoken to him about Lou Schwartz's case.

"I was in the little bastard's office yesterday, in fact," I said. That was a misrepresentation of the gentleman in two respects. He was not little, standing about six, six-one, and weighing, I would guess, about one-eighty or one-ninety, and the walls of his office displayed a lot of evidence that his parentage had been of sterling regularity. There were many color pictures: himself and an older man whom I assumed to be his father, the two of them in tennis whites, posed confidently smiling at the net of some court that they had conquered; himself and the same older man, with a strikingly attractive, I believe the phrase is, older woman who wore a fine emerald necklace, seated at the table where Mumm's Cordon Rouge champagne had been served and fine crystal glittered on an unstained light blue tablecloth, some ocean visible through the tall windows which admitted the twilight behind him; himself and a lovely young woman, both of them in yellow slickers, cuddled in the cockpit of somebody's sailing vessel; himself and that same young woman, with a chubby toddler. That familial exhibit was relieved by his diplomas from Colgate University and the Cornell Law School, together with his certificates of admission to the Massachusetts and federal bars, and his commission as a federal prosecutor. Somehow he had made a shrine unto himself on the white walls above the metal cabinets and veneered furniture the government provides to its dedicated young crusaders, and he with his carefully trimmed long blond hair and his neat straw-colored moustache was its curator. I had two contradictory wishes: either that I should have worn a white shirt rather than the striped one I had on, with a dark blue suit instead of the rumpled gray one that I wore, or that I had not shaven for a day or two, or more, and used snuff or chewed tobacco so that I would also stink.

Mike Dunn was cordial to me. He got up when I was ushered in by a pale secretary who showed color in her cheeks when he asked her to bring us coffee, and he shook my septic hand. He smiled graciously and said: "I've looked over your new motion, and discussed it with the boss."

The way that Mike Dunn said that inspired a third futile wish: that I'd come up with a new client, someone besides Louis Schwartz. Dunn shook his head just once as he uttered those words. "I'll say this for you, Jerry: You don't give up, do you?"

"Mike," I said, and sat down in the wooden armchair offered, "come on now, okay? Just be reasonable. You know and I know, and my client knows, of course, that the man that you are after here is Nunzio Dinapola."

"Can't fool you, can they, Jerry?" Dunn said, somehow making his vinyl-upholstered swivel chair into a goddamned throne. "I bet you suspected that from Day One of this case."

"You have not got Nunzio, and you're not going to get him," I said, stating my beliefs as facts.

"No," Dunn said, "I haven't. Which is Louis Schwartz's fault."

"Mike," I said, "again, okay? Just try to be reasonable. That's all I am asking. You put Lou Schwartz in the can because he won't talk. Fair enough, though I don't like it, that's your privilege."

"One which Judge Maguire seems to have acknowledged," Dunn said, with a tight, small smile.

"Grudgingly," I said, "not with enthusiasm. He discounted you three years, remember, off of what you asked. Sixty percent discount from the and they manicured her nails. Took their coffee breaks in her room, made her tell them all her stories. Jenny told them how she grew up, little maid in Sweden. They thought she was goddamned Heidi, damn her old dirty soul. 'She's a *darling*, Mister Larson, just a perfect doll.' We'd bite through our lower lips, then go in and see her. There's the old bitch lying there, ribbons in her hair. Little white bed jacket on, ribbons all through that. Makeup on, a new home perm, they even got her teeth cleaned. I tell you, Jerry, and I mean this, I considered murder. Take the goddamned pillow there and suffocate her with it."

"Jesus, Gretchen," I said, "try to calm yourself."

"Yeah," she said. " 'Calm yourself. Don't take things so hard.' You know why those nurses loved her? Because they did what she wanted, and that's all they had to do. Or else what they did instead of what they ought to've been doing. Probably neglected all the others on her floor, just so they could pamper Jenny, make her laugh and smile.

"Now they send her home to us," Gretchen said grimly. "Well, home to her own home, but it amounts to the same thing. Jenny's the only one that lives there, in that Hyde Park complex. Two floors up on River Street, 'cross from the Star Market. Housing for the elderly, wheelchair ramps and all. Which means, of course, that everybody else inside that building's just as damned old as she is. Which in turn means they can't help her, change her bed and feed her. So that means that we hire a nurse or else move in with her. I would go to live with Dracula before I'd live with her.

"Nurses get days off," she said. "Jenny's one takes Thursdays. This being Wednesday night, of course, the tramp is leaving early. 'Oh, that's all right,' old Jenny says, when her new pal tells her this. 'Harold's wife is coming over. She'll take care of me.'

"You beat that?" Gretchen said. "The bitch. We hate each other's guts. She tried to get me out of his life from the first day that she met me. She bad-mouthed me, picked fights with me, did everything she could. And when that didn't work, and we got married anyway, did Jenny stop? She did not." Gretchen pondered for a moment. "Harold doesn't have a good word for his ex-wife," she said, "and at first I was glad of it. But I know Jenny better now than I did when I married Harold, and I have to wonder, really, what that old bag did to her. Maybe I would like Jean, if I ever met her. Maybe we would sit down and we'd find out that we had a lot in common besides Harold."

She sighed. "I dunno," she said, "it probably doesn't matter. One way or the other, that's the mess that I am in. This Thursday and next Thursday, and most Thursdays from now on, unless Harold gets a day off, which I doubt that he will do, I will not be coming in. If that's all right with you."

"Hell, Gretchen," I said, "course it is. You don't have much choice, do you?"

"None that I can see," she said. "None that I have noticed."

14

JUDGE MAGUIRE that next day took my motion under advisement, which meant that he would deny it in writing in a week, thus sparing me the obligation to compose my features around real disappointment out in public view in the courtroom. Gretchen the day afterwards came to the office with a large box which she plunked down on my desk. "Answering machine," she said, "bought out of petty cash. This thing will do everything except get you your cookies. Take your calls and talk to people, choice of three messages. Refer calls, postpone the calls, tell you who called when you call in and beep it. Damnedest thing I ever saw, almost as good as me. Probably a good thing that they didn't have them back then when I first started looking for a job. 'The hell do I need you for, Gretchen, when I've got this little gadget? What you want for one week here, I can own this thing for life. And it doesn't eat snacks at the desk either, so it's a whole lot neater and it doesn't attract roaches.'"

"I don't like these things," I said, "if you want my opinion. When I get one, I hang up, say I'll call the asshole later. Which I generally do not, and that's what my callers will do too. The ones that're thinking about hiring me, at least. The ones that're stuck with me might use it, I suppose."

"I know it," she said glumly, "but we had to think of something. I really regret this, Jerry."

"Shit," I said, "forget it. What the hell could you have done about it?"

"Maybe you should get somebody else," she said, down in the mouth utterly.

"She was faking it," Mack said when I told her about it. "Fishing for sympathy. 'Tell me that you love me, Jerry Kennedy.' Honest to God, and at her age too. Her pudgy age, I might add. She must be getting simple, for God's sake. Maybe you should take her up on it, and start looking for another secretary. Somebody who'd be thinking about the work in your office that needs doing instead of wallowing in self-pity all the time and getting you to agree with her."

"I did agree with her, for Christ sake," I said. " 'Harold and me,' she said, 'from the day we decided we're going to get married, we had an agreement. No kids. I had two from my second marriage, he didn't have any with Jean, and we both agreed that was enough. Me and Harold are still kids ourselves,' she told me. 'We are selfish. We admit it. We have both worked hard and we're going to enjoy it. That's why we bought the big Winnebago. That's the kind of thing you can do when you're working and you're not spending it on kids.' "

"You ask me," Mack said, "which you didn't, I would rather blow it on ten kids than spend it on a goddamned Winnebago."

"So would I," I said, "and that is not what I am saying. All I'm saying is that that is what we wanted, and that is what we did. They did not want big responsibilities, and so they didn't have them. Now, as she says, they've got this big motor home, and money in the bank, they're both reasonably smart and they are in good health, and where can they go in their Winnebago? 'Nowhere, is where, because the old bat broke her hip.' "

"That is not fair, Jerry," Gretchen said to me. "It is the way it is, goddamnit, and I can't make it different. But it isn't fair either. There is the old bitch at home with a big picture window. All she has to do is sit there and look out of it, and she can see the street. She can see the street is icy, cars skidding all over the place. But she also sees the market, right across that icy street. So she decides she would like a Boston cream pie from the frozen-food section over there, and she gets her damned coat on and goes out on all the ice. On a day when Bobby Orr would not go out because of ice, this old asshole, eighty-two, is out to buy a pie. Makes it to the market all right, God was on her side for that. Buys her goddamned frozen pie and starts back home again. God had another call come in, I guess, before she got there. Falls on her ass in the gutter. Breaks her goddamned hip.

"The old battle-ax," she said, "she couldn't break her head. Oh no, just puts her legs out of commission, making us feel guilty we won't do her shopping for her."

"They should do her shopping for her," Mack said righteously. "Poor old lady like that, housebound in the winter, where's her able-bodied son who should be getting pies for her? I can tell you, lover, when we're old and gray, Heather better come around to shop for you and me. She doesn't, after I am dead, I'll come back and haunt the kid."

"Better practice on your haunting," I said, "if you're serious on that. Heather'll be skiing moguls out in Utah someplace."

"Now where is she?" Gretchen said. "In a nursing home? Not on your life, Jerry, in a nursing home. She's got too much money for the ones with Medicare. She won't sign it over and let them take care of her, and if you think that she's springing for a private nursing home, you have got rocks in your head. Jenny is dirt cheap, is what old Jenny is. Her insurance pays for nursing, for a while at least. When the nurse gets her day off, she will use me, free."

"Why doesn't Harry do it?" Mack said innocently. "Harry could take off from work just as well as Gretchen. It's his mother, after all. I think he should do it."

"Harry is the foreman at the Magruder Bus Lines shop," I said. "Harry takes a day off and they dock his pay a lot."

"Leave him hire another nurse, then," Mack said practically. "He could do that easy, if he makes all that damned money."

"That's what I said to her," I said, "and she said he won't do that."

"Something that I never noticed, I guess, until now," Gretchen said resentfully over the phone machine box. "Harry and his mother have got certain things in common. They are both cheap, when you push them, and so they are pushing me. She's got all that money, must be a good hundred grand. She won't kick it over and go in the nursing home. Good old Harry, he won't make her, 'cause he thinks that dough is his. Figures she can't last forever, I'm not sure that I agree, so he'll use me like she wants and keep all that money safe. Which means that she drives me nuts—she shits the bed on purpose. Yelling at me, calling me, making me bring her things. I tell you, Jerry, and I mean it, between her and you, I would rather be here with you and your crazy clients on the worst day we have ever had than home with that old bitch."

"Well, then," Mack said, "it's herself she's got to blame. If she lets

Harry push her around, she should stop complaining. Or else she out-lives him and his damned old mother too, which means that she gets the money and she laughs at both of them. And at you at the same time, I might add while we're at it, unless you have docked her pay."

I had not cut Gretchen's pay for taking Thursdays off. In the first place, I had underpaid her for a lot of years. In the second place, I never paid extra for long hours, which she put in a great many of with-out making one complaint. In the third place, I didn't want to because it would have angered her. "For the love of God, Mack," I said, "are you serious?"

"Yes," she said, "I'm serious. I knew you hadn't done it. And as a re-sult I was right when I said she's laughing at you. You are paying her to care for Harry's mother. There's a sucker in this, Jerry, and you're sit-ting in his seat."

"My God, Mack," I said, "this is incredible."

"What is?" she said. "Being tough and that stuff? Heartless enough so I think she ought to get work for the pay you're handing out? Isn't that the way you've been telling me to act? Telling me to crack down on the jerks that work for me? Just being practical, Jerry, just being business-like. It's a cruel world out there and excuses just won't work.

"Besides," Mack said, smiling, "I am educating you. All these years you've gone on thinking men are tough. Women are much tougher, Jerry, and it's time you learned this. That's why Gretchen's doing this, moaning and groaning to you. She is smarter than you are, and she's blocking me. Sooner or later, she knew that you'd tell me. And she knew what I would say, so she got you softened up.

"I know you won't cut her salary," Mack said, grinning at me. "I know it just like she does, and I admire her for it. She plays dirty just like I do, and she did it sooner. Smart broad, Jerry, very smart. I'll beat her next time. What else happened to you today?"

"Oh shit," I said, "nothing very much. Guy from Frank Macdonald's office called me up with a petition, wanted me to sign it. If it was okay to say that I endorsed it. One of those damned things that don't mean much in the long run, but I said yeah and I asked him: 'How is Frank doing?'"

"Now there's a name out of the past," Mack said with no more grin. "How is the old lush, anyway? Still taking booze IV?"

"The kid didn't seem to know much," I said. "Or pretended that he didn't. Said Frank's in Sea Island, bought a condo there. Resting up on doctor's orders, getting ready for a trial."

"He say where the trial was?" Mack said.

"Yeah, more or less," I said. "Something, about New Mexico."

"You believe this?" Mack said.

"No," I said, "I don't. I think Frank is finished, if you want to know the truth. No one's seen or heard from him. He's just not around. What is it now, four years or so? He had that heart attack? Must be, at least, close to that. Sweeney's getting out. Jesus Christ, he got convicted and he's coming out in better shape than his damned lawyer is. Can you beat that, damnit, Mack? Little bastard kills a guy, gets convicted for it. The trial leaves his lawyer prostrate, absolutely good for nothing, washed up and discarded, and he comes out free as birdies with a big smile on his face. Still got all of Daddy's millions, no cause for worry there. And the guy that defends him might as well be dead."

"That what the petition was?" Mack said. "To get him out?"

"Nah," I said, "that's automatic. He did more than most. He got ten years and did four. Most do less than three. Would've had parole lots sooner if he wasn't so well known."

"Well known," Mack said, "and he did the job up brown. Killed the father, maimed the mother, left a poor kid paralyzed. That kind of thing, it seems to me, four years is not too much. Not enough, if you ask me. Should get life for that."

"Remind me to exclude you from all juries that I pick," I said, getting up to make a new drink. "You're too tough for me."

"Well," she said, "so what, then? What was the petition for?"

"Chickenshit," I said. "Ken Duhamel is retiring, mandatory seventy. From what Macdonald's kid said, word is Dawes wants his seat. Luther Dawes is quite ambitious. Wants to move up a notch. Not quite satisfied to sit in Superior. Lining up support for the Appeals Court, with the governor."

"You're supporting Luther Dawes?" Mack said, setting the table. "Never thought I'd hear you say that, after all you've said."

"Supporting him?" I said. "Good heavens, woman, no. The petition is against him. Says he's unfit for the job. Says he's rude and overbearing, lacks judicial temperament. What it really amounts to, though it doesn't ask it, is a strong suggestion to His Excellency that he should remove the bastard from the seat he's got already. Maybe make an apol-

ogy to the trial bar for that first mistake, and send him out to be hanged.
What I signed will not help Luther, not in any way."

"Is that such a good idea?" Mack said with some concern.

"I thought about that," I said, sitting down back at the table. "I
deliberated while he read it to me on the phone. It's pretty strong, no
doubt of that. Does not mince many words. Then again, it's true, what
it says. Luther isn't fit. He's got the raw ability, the native intelligence.
But if he tried a lot of cases before he went on the bench, he did it
where nobody noticed, and he didn't learn a lot. He got that robe on,
and presto, he became Caesar. Nothing but a goddamned showboat,
and he does lots of stupid things.

"So," I said, "I thought about it, while the kid was talking. Luther's
sure to hear about this. He's not going to like it. He will eat large
chunks of rug and paw the turf a lot. Smoke will come out of his nos-
trils, and he'll be breathing fire. But should that be his protection, that
he's got a temper? Since he'll get mad when he finds out, do I run and
hide? I've got my self-respect involved here, how I think things should
be done. I don't want to tell the other eighty guys who signed: 'Hey, not
me, fellas, 'cause I'm scared.' Which is what I would be doing if I said:
'Don't use my name.' I got no respect for Luther, but I do have some for
me."

"There are eighty other lawyers?" Mack said doubtfully.

"Somewhere in that neighborhood, from what Frank's kid said, at
least. How I feel about old Luther, it's no quirk of mine. He may have
some special dislike for me, but what I think of him is no unique position. There's a reason, you know, when a consensus like that appears. It
means the guy is really bad, and shouldn't be promoted."

"Of course," Mack said, "it also means, if he is not promoted, he will
be sitting there some fine day when you come in with a client. And he'll
most likely do the best he can to get even with the guy whose name was
on that list."

"True," I said, "I thought of that. It will not help that client. But I'll
move to disqualify him at the first sign of bias, and he knows I will do
that. So will everybody else, and he knows that as well. I don't think
that Luther will want the Appeals Court spitting all his cases back, ordering new trials because he was prejudiced."

"I thought you said he isn't dumb," she said, still somewhat worried.

"I did," I said, "and he isn't. He's a grandstander."

"Well, then," she said, "won't he do it so that the Appeals Court can't see it? Jab you, knife you, hurt your case, but not so it looks too bad?"

"He could," I said, "yes, he could, if he had more patience. If he starts that, though, I'll see it, and I'll smoke him out. Get him so mad he'll explode, and put it on the record. Not too pleasant for my client, not much fun for me, but still, in the long run, effective, and that's what I'm after."

"You and eighty other guys," she said, still unconvinced.

"Around that number," I said. "Eighty, more or less."

"Coop sign?" she said.

"Good Christ, no," I said. "Look, I love the guy and all. He is my best friend. But don't get the idea from that, we're in the same league. Coop is just as old as I am, a little older, in fact. Difference is, not as a lawyer. There he's half my age. Coop tries very few court cases, and they're mostly small. His work's in financial planning, corporate security. Stopping all the hired help from cleaning out the treasury by reprogramming the computer. He's not a real trial lawyer."

"Which means," Mack said thoughtfully, "he never ran with Frank."

"It means that partly, yeah," I said. "He was in the Bureau then. That's what I mean: he is new. New at my game, at least. Nobody would ask old Coop to get on that petition. His name would be meaningless to the governor."

"Yours, of course, is not," she said, smiling at me wryly.

"That's right," I said, "it is not. Absolutely right."

Mack sighed elaborately and put up her hands. "Got to keep in mind, I guess, I'm married to a star. A sucker and a star."

15

REAL SPRINGTIME came in March that year, with crocuses and mud. I patrolled our property, which did not take very long. Two fence posts had rotted out; two rails looked bad also. The dogwoods in the back and front appeared to have survived. I made a mental note to have the roof in the back looked at; some of the asphalt shingles there were showing signs of curling. I detoured one day on my way home from the Cape, pulling into the yard of the house down at Green Harbor and glancing around for damage. I saw nothing from the outside which would have warranted alarm, and I didn't have the time to go inside and check things out—experience has taught me not to do that, anyway, because there is always something that could wait if you'd let it, and will ruin a good suit of clothes when you refuse to do that.

Gretchen and I adjusted to her new working schedule. She claimed that she came in around 7:45, on the four days she was working, and that enabled her to keep up with five days of work in four. I encountered no delays in getting pleadings out, or dealing with the other foolishness that is required, and I was not about to test her truthfulness myself by coming in at 7:30 to await her arrival.

My clients behaved as my clients always have, accepting quite serenely news that should have stunned them into deep depressions, getting desperate and panicky about annoying trivia.

David Mackin, C.L.U., called twice about his confiscated driver's license. The first time he was whiny, reciting the inconvenience of being dependent upon others for his transportation and inquiring whether there was some provision for license suspensions which resembled time off for good behavior granted to incarcerated persons whose deportment had been pleasant. I told him there was not and said the only document which controlled ninety-day suspensions was the calendar, and that mine said his had about sixty days to go. David volunteered his personal opinion that this was not fair or just. I conceded that he might be right, but it didn't matter. That conversation took up twenty minutes of my day and did not entertain me or augment my fee from David.

Two weeks or so later, David called again. This time he was peremptory, and uttered some veiled threats. He had attended a dinner dance in honor of a wholesale liquor merchant whose generous largesse had financed acquisition of several shiploads of dried milk for starving babies in the Orient. The guest list for this affair included, as such lists often do, several prominent attorneys who were willing to provide, free, gratis, and for nothing, heartening advice to non-clients who had retained other lawyers. David had learned from one such barrister that persons who have lost their driver's licenses can in certain circumstances apply for mitigation of their punishment by claiming to the court that they must drive between their homes and jobs if they are to continue to earn their livelihoods. David pointed out that his home and offices were separated by several miles, too great a distance for him to walk, and that his work could include emergencies. Such as when the pigeon starts to waver, I thought. He ordered me to obtain mitigation for him, and implied that my failure to request it at his court appearance amounted to incompetence of counsel.

I reminded David that his wife lived in the same house that he used as a residence. I called to his attention that the papers which incorporated his office listed her, correctly, as the treasurer and business agent of the company, and that her duties as such required her attendance each day during business hours at the offices where he performed his services. Therefore in his case there was no necessity that he drive himself between the place he laid down his head and those places where he poked around inside of other people's, and for that reason no court would allow him to drive his car between those separate locations. As for the emergencies, I said, if they happened in the daytime he would be on duty to receive them, and that those occurring after dark would not be deemed sufficient to permit him to drive then. I asked him in passing just how many such red alerts he encountered in the average year, and he said: "Not very many, but there's no need to inform the judge of that. Or of the fact that my wife works with me."

I told David it had always been my rule not to tell lies to judges, even or especially to those whom I disliked. I said that rule in my eyes required that I not stand silently when I had facts which if made known to the Court would prevent it from taking some action out of ignorance which it would not have countenanced if it had been informed. David said he thought that was a shortsighted way of looking at things, and that if he'd known I felt that way, he would not have hired me. "Shortsighted from your viewpoint, maybe," I said rather rudely. "Intelligent from mine, though, when it's how I make my living. As for wishing that you hadn't hired me, David, there we can agree." That agreeable exchange took over half an hour, and I billed him one hundred dollars for it. He did not remit his payment for that charge, as I did not expect he would, but he didn't call me again either. I considered that a payment in kind, and I was content with it.

My druggie with the half a pound of marijuana jumped bail. Without any trouble, really, I had gotten him released on one thousand dollars' personal recognizance, inasmuch as he had no record of prior offenses and a good record of attendance at school. Apparently he found some money to make up for what he'd lost in his business venture with the grass that had been seized, and had picked up his synthesizer and his amplifiers and just taken off for parts unknown. The judge was perplexed by this behavior because there was no chance whatsoever that he would have jugged the kid if he'd come in, and I was just as baffled as the judge was. "What do I say, Judge?" I said. "Youth is mercurial?"

"Youth is stupid's more like it," the judge said testily. "If he calls you, Counselor, tell him he's a jerk. Tell him also, when we catch him, as we always do, I am going to put him in the can for doing this."

"Only, of course, if he's convicted, Judge," I said primly.

"Oh, shut up, Jerry," the judge said, snorting at me. "You know damned well that they've got him, and now so do I. Those remarks will be off the record, stenographer."

Sometime during that month, Harry Mapes embarked upon a new and lawful career. I did not see the unveiling, or three subsequent performances, but I heard from others with the time for daytime TV that he had become a regular on an afternoon talk show. Sort of a consulting felon, as they described it to me. The whole thing got underway when Channel 8 began a series on means which the ordinary citizen could take to reduce crime. Apparently their logic told them they should have a criminal around, to provide his expertise on what would work and what would not, and they naturally thought of Harry, who was telegenic too. Harry was a big success, on camera with his dog. Gretchen watched him one Thursday, while nursing Harold's mother, and she said that he looked like he'd been acting all his life.

"He has, Gretchen," I said, "fifty years and more, I'd say. He just never got his big break until the dog joined in the act."

"He is really good," she said. "The dog's not bad either. Little black-and-white mutt, like the one on the record labels. 'His Master's Voice,' you know? Harold's mother tired herself out yelling at me the whole morning. You know what the old bitch does, just to torment me? She yells at me: 'Gretchen, Gretchen, will you come in here?' I am washing clothes or something, sheets and pillowcases that she's pissed all over 'cause she won't ask for the bedpan so I have to stop the machine. Like I really wanted, you know, hear what she is saying. 'What do you want,

Jenny?' I say. 'Something I can bring you?' See, when I go to her bedroom, I go right through her damned kitchen. She wants juice or something, case she's running out of piss, I can pour it on the way through
and I'm finished with one trip.

"That is not the way she wants it," Gretchen said, "the bitch. 'I want
you to come in here, Gretchen. Just come in here, please.' I start the
machine again, put down what I'm doing. Go through the damned
kitchen into the room where she is. 'Thank you, Gretchen,' she says,
getting her way like she wants it. 'I would like just this much juice.
Apple juice, I think.' " Gretchen held her thumb and forefinger about
two inches apart. " 'Jenny,' I say, 'for Christ sake, why do you do this?
Why don't you just say, when you call me: "Bring me a little apple
juice"? What's the point of making me walk in past the fridge, find out
that you want a little, go back out the fridge, get the juice and back in
here, then back out past the fridge? What does this accomplish, huh?
I'm trying to do things.' 'You bring me too much,' she says, 'and I can't
drink it all. Then it gets warm and it sits there, and you pour it out.
That is wasting juice, Gretchen, and I don't like that. I was brought up
to conserve things. You should try it sometime. You and Harold, spending money, like it's going out of style. If you waste things, mark my
words, someday you won't have any.'

"So," Gretchen said, "she falls asleep, snoring like a bastard. Sounds
like someone's got a snow thrower working in there, but it's music to
my ears. Means I can sit down a while, get a load off my poor feet. Pour
myself a glass of wine, turn the TV on, real soft. There is Harry Mapes
there, with his little dog. He could be on Johnny Carson. He is really
good."

Harry's first assignment was a ten-part series on ways to encourage
thieves to go and rob other people's goods. That was not the way they
put it, but it was what they clearly meant. I made some inquiries after
Gretchen's report.

"Karen most likely saw it," Cooper said to me. "That's all the poor
woman does, since Peter went to shit. Sit at home and watch TV, turn
her mind to lard."

She had indeed seen it, and remembered most of it. Harry Mapes
stuck in her mind as a very entertaining man.

"Karen says this first week," Cooper said, reporting, "it was apparently about how to avoid crime in general. Like you should not pick

dark alleys for your regular route home, if you have a nice watch and you dress like you have some dough."

"Sounds reasonable to me," I said, eating knockwurst and potato salad served warm at Jakey Wirth's. "Most likely muggers hide out in such dimly lit surroundings."

"That was the gist of it," Coop said, sloshing dark beer on his sore gums. "Also recommended against flashing a big roll. And not just in hard guys' bars either. Says the hookers and the nice crooks watch for assholes in nice places, try to gyp them themselves or to set them up outside."

"My, my," I said, "imagine that. Who would have dreamed such things? This is an evil world, my friend, when you stop and think about it."

"Certainly is," Coop said, gingerly chewing ham. "Said that ladies should hold on to their handbags when they are shopping, and ought not to leave their cash in grocery carts."

"Some larcenous shopper in the dog-food aisle with them might get it into his head to lift all their grocery money," I contributed.

"I assume so," Coop said. "Anyway, next week is his real specialty. How to foil housebreakers and make burglars gnash their teeth."

"I must try to catch a little," I said, drinking beer. "Now that Mack is working, our place is a sitting duck."

"All your Old Masters, no doubt," Coop said, wincing as he chewed.

"Not to mention," I said, "all my Krugerrands."

The day that I took lunch late at the Beacon Inn, three other sheepish men my age were in there drinking gin. I assume it was gin, at least; it may have been vodka or schnapps—I doubt that it was water. I knew two of them from courts; the third one looked familiar. Like me, they wore business suits, but seemed to have no business. Protocols in such cases dictate no recognitions. Those still in the bars at four in the afternoon are not there to confer. That is why the lights are dim, and the bartenders quiet. That is why the talk shows shimmer on the sets behind the bar—those inanities are furnished to capture inquiring eyes and discourage conversations.

Harry did indeed have his dog on the show with him. His subject was home security, and he had lots of ideas. "Dead bolts are very safe," he said, "but only if you throw them. You got dead bolts and they're not on, they're no good at all."

This revelation appeared to delight the young man who was presenting Harry to the TV audience. His face became wreathed in smiles, and all of his hair glistened. "I suppose too," he said, "that would apply to chain locks too."

"All locks," Harry said expansively, grinning. "Everything that we discuss, you come right down to it. Timers on your lights and all, buzzers, bells, and alarms: anything you put in will be useless if you don't use it."

"So, then," the young man said, "the first rule ought to be: pay attention to your property, and how you're going to guard it."

"Uh-huh," Harry said, "but with one exception." He leaned forward in his chair and patted his damned dog. "You get one of these devices and you've always got protection."

"Your dog, you mean," Hairdo said, lest anyone mistake it for a giraffe or something.

"Right," Harry said, approving his sharp wits, "my dog. A dog is the best device for protecting your own home." Also not a bad device for staying out of jail, I thought maliciously. "My dog here, Amanda, she is very good protection. Not because she bites, or anything like that. And not because she looks like she might actually be a Doberman or something like that, out of uniform."

"No, indeed," Hairdo agreed, chuckling lavishly. "I'm sure that we'd all agree, Amanda does not look fierce."

"What she does look, though, is *loud*," Harry confided. "Furthermore, she acts like that, in case anyone might wonder. Someone watching my house, say, he is going to see her. 'Guy has got a dog in there,' is what he will think. 'Wonder if that dog would bark, someone tried to get in.'

"Well," Harry said heartily, "he won't have to wonder long. All he needs to do is stand there, wait till somebody comes. Gas man, light man, plumber, might even be a friend: doesn't matter who it is that comes to my door. Amanda here will hear them and she'll start right in to bark. Show the people how you bark, Amanda, old girl," he said. I prayed that she wouldn't bark, but she was just as big a ham as Harry was, and let out three small yips. Harry gave her something that he took out of his pocket. He patted the dog on the head and smiled at her.

"Say," Hairdo said, "that's pretty good. Right on duty, huh?"

"Just like the old Coast Guard," Harry said approvingly. "All prepared, never sleeping, that's what Amanda is. I am sleeping, eating dinner, probably got the TV on—none of that will matter. Somebody shows up at my house, my good dog will let me know."

"Retired people, such as me," he said, without specifying what it was he claimed to have retired from, "we need this kind of dog. Not too big for us to manage, when we take it for a walk. Doesn't need much exercise, which of course we can't give them. Doesn't eat a whole lot either, which matters on a pension. And you know something else, Jack, huh? They don't cost anything. Dogs like my dog you get free, down at your local pound. Angell Memorial if you live in the city, your local pounds outside. All of them got lots of dogs, lot like my Amanda." A series of phone numbers for dog pounds began to roll in white letters along the bottom of the screen.

"That's a good point that you make," Hairdo said very gravely. "For you fellow seniors like our friend Harry Mapes, this could be important for you, how to get a dog. Shut-ins, those without their own cars, anyone like that. Give some thought to what our expert, Harry Mapes, says. He's retired too, like you are, although probably you didn't do what he did, in your working years. But he knows the problems, knows whereof he speaks. People get a little hard of hearing—am I right on that, Harry?"

"Absolutely," Harry said, "no use pretending that it doesn't happen, 'cause it does and we know that. Hard of hearing, sleeping more, don't go out too much. Well, if you get a nice dog, you'll have a companion. Plus your own full-time protector that you can count on. Costs a lot less than alarms, does the job even better. Plus which, you can pat it, which you can't do with an alarm."

"*Right,*" Hairdo said delightedly, and just about exploded. "We'll run those numbers by again now once more for you dog-needers." He thought that was pretty good, and grinned at his own wit. "And don't go away now either, 'cause we'll be right back."

"Did you see him?" Gretchen said when I got back to the office.

"Yes, I did," I said. "I nearly threw up, actually."

"Oh," she said, "sorry to hear that. These won't help you much."

She handed me two message slips, those goddamned little pink squares. Sometime it would be interesting to poll the entire country and see whether anybody has ever gotten good news scrawled on one of those damned slips. I would bet a large sum against that. People who have good news say that they will call you back, wanting if they can to share your glee and jubilation. People who have bad news plan their calls to catch you out. That way they can falsify regrets to message-takers, leaving their stinking turds in strangers' hands, and avoid hearing you complain when your fond hopes are dashed.

The first was from the Clerk's Office in federal court. It was a small courtesy, to ease the blow which had been mailed—Maguire had denied my motion to reduce Lou Schwartz's term of imprisonment. "Ah, shit," I said, and wadded it up, "piss on this whole shitty racket."

"You expected it," she said.

"I know, I know," I said, "I did. I still don't like it, though." The other was from Teddy Franklin. It had an unfamiliar number and she'd marked it *urgent*. "Oh-oh," I said, "where is Teddy? Who's got him in irons now?"

"Sharon," she said, "his hometown. I would've called you with it, but I didn't know where you were."

"Sharon?" I said. "Christ sake, what's he done in Sharon? Beat up Dorothy or something? Set his house on fire? Jesus H. Christ, get him for me. Here we go again."

16

HEATHER WAS on the phone from Utah that night when I got home late from Sharon and Stoughton. Mack gave me the phone, a perfunctory hello kiss, and a look of irritation and admonition all at once. "Here's your father now," she said, and ducked off toward the stove.

"Yeah," I said, my coat still on, "how are you, darling daughter?"

"Ooh," she said, from far away, "all tingly and warm, and glad to hear your voice."

"I just got in," I said, rather stupidly. "Teddy's in the shit again. I got him out of jail."

"Teddy Franklin?" Heather said, with bells in her voice and laugh. I heard her explain the reference to somebody near her out there in the snow. "Teddy's one of my dad's droller clients—he just steals Cadillacs." There was a baritone chuckle in reply to her. "What did Teddy do this time?" Heather said to me.

"Oh," I said, "nothing major, unless you dislike jail. Punched a cop right in the mouth. Cop did not like this. Swore out a complaint against him, locked him in a cell."

"Teddy must've been pissed off," Heather sympathized.

Teddy had been pissed off, in fact, which I was getting also, while I talked to my jet-set daughter, tingling out there in the snowfields far away. "Yeah," I said shortly, "he was, but he'll get over that. There's been a lot of pissed-off going around this part of the country lately. Don't see why Teddy Franklin should have immunity."

"You been having a bad day, Dad?" she said, solicitous. Solicitude is easy, when you're two thousand miles away.

"You could say that, yeah," I said. "Judge Maguire denied my motion to let Lou Schwartz out today," I said. "One of my wealthier clients who got bagged in a cocaine bust down at the Marriott called me up this morning to request his fee back. Seems he cut a deal himself with the government. Going to turn fink and turn in his friends instead of letting me keep two grand." I had begun to regret telling her that story from the instant that I started it. Two grand to Charlie Lloyd and his ilk was walking-around money. All I was accomplishing, by telling her these things, was a reminder to her that her father was a small-time mouthpiece.

"Are you going to give it back?" Heather said with concern.

"Of course I won't give it back," I said with some sarcasm. "I don't offer refunds, and besides, I think I've spent it. But enough of what I'm doing. What has your day held?"

"Oh," she said luxuriously, "deep powder and warm sun. Twelve or fourteen great runs, and we're having fondue now. Charlie found this great white wine, from Chile, isn't it?" The baritone within earshot confirmed it was Chilean. "It's really very nice, Dad," Heather said languorously, "and it's inexpensive too. You and Mother ought to try it. It's really very nice."

Being touted on cheap wines did not improve my mood. "Do they give you a brown paper bag with it?" I said. "I have to have a paper bag, you know, when I stuff the *Globe* into my pants and sit on the Common drinking."

Heather's not insensitive, even at a distance. Mack does not miss very much, and she was a lot closer. My wife stood hissing at me over swordfish frying. My daughter let some seconds pass, while she decided what to say next. "You're in kind of a bad mood yourself, I'd have to say," she said.

"Most perceptive of you, Heather," I said. "Yes, I am. I was looking forward to some time with you this month. You led me to expect it when you came home over Christmas." Once again I was regretting something I had started. This would do no good at all, and might do some real harm. I was not about to discuss what was really on my mind. She was not about to come back, looking penitent. Mack was getting mad at me, and all this was for nothing.

"Well," Heather said, "that's really too bad, Daddy. I didn't realize how much you were counting on it. Would you like me to fly home, take a plane tomorrow? Then I could go with you again, like when I was a little girl. Go into your office and play with all the paper clips. See if Gretchen might let me answer the telephone. I might even do some typing, like I used to do. Have you give me some dictation, write a couple letters. You'd pretend to send them out, put stamps on them and everything. Except the stamps would be Christmas seals, but I wouldn't notice that, and you really wouldn't file all those misspellings and bad margins. Wouldn't that be fun, Daddy, playing like we used to? That would really be a ball, a whole barrel of laughs."

I took inventory while she cleaned my clock for me. I concluded that I did feel perverse enough to keep it up. "Actually, no," I said, "now that you put it that way. In those terms, Heather, I can see I wasn't thinking clearly. It is a lot better idea that you went out West to ski. Drop us a line now and then, if the spirit moves you. Let us know how things are going, where you'll be next year. Maybe when tuition's due, board and room and that stuff. Those would be good times to file your regular reports."

"Ohh," she said, "this really sucks. You think I need this noise? You think I called up just for this, to get my ass reamed out?"

"Ahh," I said, "how do I know? I thought you were bored. But since you put the question, no, I don't think you called for this. But do I think you need it? Yeah, I guess I do think that. I'm doing it a little late, I suppose, but tough shit. Better late than never."

"Let me talk to Mother, Dad," she said in a tight voice.

"That will be my pleasure, dear," I said, and handed the phone to Mack.

She took it from me like a cop relieving a suspect of his gun, glaring at me while the fish sizzled. I went into the living room, dropping my briefcase on the chair and taking off my coat. "Oh, for Christ sake," I heard Mack say, followed by: "Oh, *Jesus*." I decided that while I really wanted to make myself a drink from the cabinet in the kitchen, I would be better off if I went to the bathroom first. It was quiet in there and there was some peace, and I washed my hands afterwards as though I had been a surgeon, or perhaps Lady Macbeth, trying to make the lather outlast the conversation in the kitchen.

I did not succeed, not that it mattered. I got a full gargoyle's glare when I went back out there, apparently in the middle of some detailed complaint from Heather. "He's just back out here now," Mack said, "going for the booze." She paused and looked away from me, while the fish got burned. "Look," she said, "I don't know, no. If I did, I would've told you. Sometimes they just act like this. All of them do, Heather. Charlie will, and your dad does. They get obnoxious sometimes. Maybe it's his time of the month, you know? That might be it. Maybe it's male menopause, hormones slowing down. All I can tell you is: it's common. Every woman learns that. Just when we think that we know them, they do something crazy. Just like that damned gun of his that he likes to carry sometimes. That night at the beach house when he shot it at that punk? If we hadn't been there, Heather, he would've killed him, probably. And then wonder afterwards why he was in so much trouble."

I poured about four ounces of Smirnoff into a glass, made it clear that I would nudge my wife away from the refrigerator if she did not move, as she did, and sat down at the dinner table with my anodyne for the day. Mack said with a snicker: "Yeah, tell me all about it. Think of what I've got to do, now he's in this state. I'm in the same house with him, which as you know isn't big." She paused once more and smiled slightly. "You just do that, kid," she said, her voice very soft. "Have a good time and enjoy yourself, and don't worry about this. This is my job, and I'll do it. Trust me, okay? Will you?" Apparently she would, because Mack hung up the phone.

"Satisfied?" she said to me, nodding toward the fish.

"I'm not that crazy about swordfish," I said with some belligerence.

"As you ought to know by now. Any fish but lobster gives me a touch of runs."

"That shouldn't be surprising," Mack said, "since you're such an ass-hole sometimes. Be nice if you could afford a lobster every time we have fish."

"We could afford a lobster," I said. "All you had to do was get one. Could've gotten two, in fact, what you paid for that fish you've ruined."

"What is it with you?" she said. "What's the matter with you? Two of your client pals act up, you think that you've got to? This some kind of ritual that you're all going through? Come home here about two hours late, I've got no idea where you are. All I know, you could be drunk, in some bar someplace."

"I don't do that, and you know it," I said immediately. "So you can lay off all that righteous shit and start thinking about what you've been doing. That is what I think."

"What I've been doing?" she said, in great injury. "What is this, the best defense, some of your damned courtroom shit? You know the house rules on that, Learned Counselor. No fair ringing those little changes in on me, Jeremiah."

"Just hear what I have to say," I said, "goddamnit, Mack. I'll depend on your sense of fairness, which I admit I'm not sure's a hot idea at this point, anyway. See if you don't think I'm right. No matter how much it may pain you to listen for a change."

She glowered at me. The fish began to smoke in the skillet. "Turn the damned fish off," I said. "I can't tell whether that smell is dinner burn-ing up or all the insulation on your own wiring that's smoking." She turned the burner off. "First thing," I said, "where I was, and how come you didn't know. When I left the office it was getting close to five. All I knew when I left there was where my first stop was. That was Sharon and the police, where my client was. They were holding him on charges. He would therefore need bail made. Sharon's in the Stoughton District. Where the clerk was, I did not know. All I knew was where he wasn't, after five p.m. He would not be sitting in the Stoughton District Court. Therefore, if I couldn't find him, I would be coming back to Boston. Which thing I had to do, that determined when I'd get home. All I knew was: I'd be late. Not where I would be, doing it."

"Therefore," I said as she started to speak, "now just listen to me. Therefore I had Gretchen put a call in to your office. Leave word with you that I'd be late. Be here when I got here."

"I'll bet Gretchen never called," she said spitefully. "Probably got her coat on the second you were gone."

"Bullshit," I said, "there you're wrong. Gretchen did call you. You were not in your office. I know this because I called in when I knew where I'd be going. Gretchen said your office said you were out on the road. You would get the message when you came back to the office. They knew you were coming back because you left your car there."

"I was out with Ace and Ricky," Mack said defiantly. "We went down to the Persian Slipper for a couple of cold beers."

"Wonderful," I said, "how nice. You are out in some damned bar, drinking with two guys. I am on the road. You get home for once before me, I become the villain. You know what your problem is, speaking of hormones? You're not married anymore. You just do as you please. I'm supposed to be here nights, with the home fires blazing."

"One night," she said, "one fire. That's domesticity? Don't give me that crap, Jerry, I can still remember."

"I didn't say I did it," I said, "just that I'm supposed to. If you'd gone back to your office, after the cocktail hour, you would have received my message. You would've known that I'd be late, and no fish would've burned."

"I went back inside the office," Mack said angrily. "I checked my desk and the board. There were no messages."

"Don't blame me for that," I said. "That is not my fault. And don't blame Gretchen for it either. She did what she was supposed to."

"I'm not blaming you," Mack said, "or shrewd little Gretchen either. Shrewd *big* Gretchen either, since that's what she has become. I am blaming shit-ass Diane, who's supposed to watch the phone."

"Now," I said, "that's interesting. Shit-ass little Diane. Might this be the same Diane you fired in February?"

"Yes, it is," Mack said dejectedly. "Which is probably the explanation why I got no messages."

"May I ask," I said, "what happened? How come she's still there? You cast her out into the storm, with oaths and imprecations, tell her she's gone by March. March arrives and she's still there, how can this have happened? Don't Ace and Roy trust you to run your division? Did somebody overrule you? Degrade your authority?"

"That is why I went out," she said, "with Ace and Ricky tonight. Roy said Diane could stay on, in residential stuff. Roy did not tell anyone, except Diane of course. Diane just sits there and smiles, just like you're suggesting. Ace says I should bear with it, wait for time to take its toll. I told Ace I think it's crap, and he says it doesn't matter."

"Roy," I said, "uh-huh. Is this what it looks like?"

"I think so," Mack said, fatigued, "that is what I think. Roy and Diane have got something going on the side. That's why Diane doesn't work, and why she's not worried when she screws up someone's deal. No one's going to fire her if Roy's getting in her shorts. I tried it and she's still there, so I assume he is."

"Did Ace verify that?" I said.

"Not in so many words," she said, "but for all intents and purposes, he might as well have, yeah. He said he has talked to Roy and made all of my arguments. Roy says Diane can sell houses, and she's staying on. Ace and Roy are equal partners. They can overrule each other. Roy's got Ace at stalemate on this, so it's her or me. I'm not keeping Roy's pipes clean, so that means it is her. If I care to make an issue of it, which I don't think that I do, I will be gone and she stays, and that's the end of it. Since I like what I am doing, otherwise at least, I am not making an issue. Which is what Ace said. 'Don't try to reform the world. You haven't got time, Mack. Finish your drink and we'll leave. Get in your Mercedes. Go home and get yourself some rest. Don't take things so hard. Roy gets over these things in the normal course of things. Give it some time and she'll leave. Just you wait and see.'

"So," Mack said, "that's what I did. And you weren't here. I was practically beside myself, what that bitch did to me. What I wanted was a shoulder, someone I could trust. Someone I could talk to about how goddamned women suck. All this bullshit you hear, Jerry, liberated women. They get in an office and it's just like it's always been. All else fails, just drop your pants, someone will be hungry. Talent, hard work, brains, and all: those are very nice. But if things start to unravel, they will all fall back on that. Once they get themselves in trouble, they start putting out. And, because you are such assholes, that will always work. Do the trick, you might say. Funny, isn't it?" She did not laugh, though, not so I could hear it. She just looked forlorn, and if I hadn't been pissed off myself, I would've gone and hugged her.

Which shows you how smart I am, pressing an advantage. "Uh-huh," I said, "Ace and Roy. The two real estate geniuses. These are the two guys that you want to sell our house for, because they've got this grand scheme which is sure to make us rich. Were you really serious, that

Commodore Islands project? Jesus Christ, am I glad that we're not involved in that. It's illegal, it's dishonest, and it's run by a pair of sharpies that can't keep their cocks out of the cash register."

Mack flared up again as though she hadn't lost. "Oh, blow it out your barracks bag, for Christ sake, will ya, Jerry? You lost your big chance on that the first night that I told you. I could see from your expression there was no hope in that line. You'd prefer to stay here in this tiny little house. Saving every goddamned dollar we can get our grubby hands on, getting interest from the banks that doesn't offset inflation, paying taxes on the earnings after we get screwed. In the summer, our beach house, just like Newport, right? It's no better than this place, and nowhere near as sturdy.

"But, okay, I understand. There's no way I can change you. This is what you want, I guess, and this is what you've got. If I want you, I accept that. Just like Heather has to accept all the crap you hand her. But don't think we're happy, Jerry, either one of us."

"Noted," I said, returning to the liquor cabinet and pouring another generous helping of what was obviously going to be my dinner that night. "On that happy note, at least, we are unanimous."

17

I WATCHED the late news that night on the living-room TV, for two major reasons. The first was that I hoped Channel 8 had either ignored Teddy's police dust-up or prejudiced his case. Given a choice, I would take disregard, but since I might not have my wishes granted in that as in many other things, I wished to monitor what they might have done instead. The other reason was that Mack had stomped upstairs right after the incinerated swordfish had made a seven-dollar snack for the garbage disposal, and I did not feature lying next to her in bed, watching the news next to her wrath on the small bedroom TV. My plan was to sit downstairs and tap the Smirnoff bottle until I heard the upstairs set shut up, which would mean she had also. Our house may not be as small as Mack believed it had become, but it is superb as an acoustical design.

If Teddy had been covered, it would have been a fluke. His case had arisen out of circumstances which by rights ought not have gotten him involved. The police in Framingham had conducted an investigation of a stolen-car ring, apparently in operation for a fairly long time out there. Its membership, quite loosely knit, supplied the Midnight Auto Parts concern so popular with people who dislike paying list price for their automobile repairs. What they did was steal cars, which they then dismantled, selling seats and wheels and front ends, transmissions and engines, from the cut-up cars. What they did, in short, had no connection whatsoever to what Teddy Franklin does, which is steal Cadillacs and only Cadillacs for resale with new numbers and fresh paint of different color somewhere else in the Northeast.

That distinction had eluded Sergeant Earl Glennon. He was young and eager and he disliked Teddy Franklin. This was not because he had met Teddy Franklin. It was because he had heard a lot about him, how he's never gotten nailed, and this angered Sergeant Glennon to the point of losing judgment. He decided that if cars were being stolen, and the commerce was ambitious, Teddy Franklin must be involved and should not be left out when the suspects were corralled. The fact that Teddy had not spoken on the wiretaps, or been named by the informers, or been seen at any time engaged in helping those thieves, did not concern Sergeant Glennon.

Glennon therefore in the early afternoon, even though he was off duty, drove to Teddy's house in Sharon. For that purpose he used, as he had a right to do, his pale green unmarked cruiser. Attired in civilian clothes, tweed sport coat and tan raincoat, he parked that four-door sedan right in front of Teddy's home. He took his portable red flashing light out of the glove compartment and put it on the dashboard, in plain view beneath the mirror. He kept his engine running, so exhaust vapors could be seen, and thus maintained the battery charge while using his radio.

Teddy lives in a nice neighborhood. The low-slung, large ranch houses are set on acre lots. The normal traffic in that area, on weekday afternoons, is limited to school buses, Ford Country Squires, Volvo station wagons, and the odd Riviera. Those cars do not come to a halt out in front of houses; they proceed on into the driveways as the automatic garage doors crank open before them. Consequently, Sergeant Glennon and his pale green unmarked cruiser were conspicuous parked outside of Teddy's house. This was as he had intended, in his eagerness.

Teddy, as his luck would have it, wasn't working that day. He had spent the entire morning in his large kitchen. One of his many interests, shared with his lovely wife, is what he considers to be gourmet cookery. They have an enormous kitchen, well equipped with gadgetry. Teddy told me he'd been making stock from marrow bones, working from that toward a fine sauce bordelaise. "At the same time," Teddy told me, "I was making pastries, a nice meringue vacherin to go with raspberries I bought."

It is still not clear to me just how Teddy learned of Sergeant Glennon's car outside. Somehow the telephone played a small part in this. Either an observant neighbor called to inform Teddy, or else Teddy, making his own call about some other matter, passed before the picture window in his living room and spotted it himself. Either way, he was not puzzled as to what was in that car, or what kind of car it was. Who the cop was, where he came from, what had brought him there: these were details that he lacked, and did not feel he needed. " 'What is this shit?' I say, when I see the fucker," Teddy told me when I met him at the jail. "How come I have got a cop parked there outside my house? Here I am in my own house, minding my own business. Got my raspberries and bones, got my recipes. Made a nice lunch for myself, some veal alla marsala. Glass of red wine, ordinary, nice piece of French bread. This is against the law? Why is my place staked out when there's nothing going on?

"It pissed me off, Counselor," Teddy said as he emerged from his cell at the Sharon police station. "Fucking damned Gestapo asshole, staking out my fucking house right in broad fucking daylight. He's got no right to do that. Make me look like I am Wanted, on the run or something, front of all my neighbors."

Teddy had a point there, which I could have argued. That is what I told him as I led him out of jail. "Trouble is," I said, "you didn't let me do it, haul the guy before some judge and argue harassment. Instead you go out the door, big hair across your ass, and the instant that you grabbed that guy, you lost my argument. He was not on your property. That street's a public way. Anyone can use it and it's not posted *No Parking*. What you did's not arguable, from any point of view. You accosted someone and he says you battered him. That's against the law, Teddy, and there is no doubt about it."

The clerk-magistrate in Stoughton was Don DiGuglielmo. He was pushing seventy and had heard most excuses. The Sharon cops found him at home, having an early dinner. When they gave me the telephone, I said I'd bring Teddy there, saving Don a trip back down to the District Court. "No, you won't, Jerry," he said, "not on your life, you won't. Back when I was young, I did that, held bail hearings in my house. Did it about five times, I think, before I got a lulu. Your guy doesn't like what I say, he may bust things up. Better it's the county's stuff that gets all bashed, than mine." In the basement of the courthouse, one Sharon cop there for the rules of custody, Teddy pleaded Not Guilty and was released on personal recognizance, trial to be held three weeks later, if he wanted one. "And," Don said to Teddy, closing up his books, "try not to punch anyone, between now and then, like this complaint says you did." Then he looked at it more closely. "Framingham?" he said. "What is this guy Glennon doing down here, anyway, in from Framingham?" That set Teddy steaming again, and I had to lead him out.

Channel 8 did cover it, and got it wrong of course. They had shaky tapes they'd made with their damned minicams. "Channel Eight's Jim Voorhies was right on the scene for this, as you'll notice watching films he made at the time of the arrests." The announcer was quite smug about this, since he hadn't gotten jostled. "Some of those arrested, it seems, didn't want their picture taken by our On the Spot News Team." Teddy's face was not among them, but his name was mentioned. "In what Framingham police said was a related case, Edmund Franklin, thirty-eight, was arrested at his comfortable home in Sharon Heights. Franklin was released on bail in Stoughton District Court, charged with attacking Sergeant Earl Glennon of Framingham in connection with the raids." That gave me another reason to watch television late: just as soon as Teddy finished eating the rug, if he had watched the news himself, he would be on the phone to me. If by some chance he had missed his moment of fame on Channel 8, some devoted pal would be on the phone to him, which would mean that Teddy's call to me would be a little later.

Waiting for Teddy's call with another serving of vodka, I was therefore able to hear Channel 8's disclosure that the governor had nominated Ann Tobin Belvedere, Esquire, of New Bedford, to the seat on the Appeals Court being vacated by the retirement of Associate Justice Kenneth Duhamel. There was a snippet of tape showing the governor and Attorney Belvedere beaming at each other, while the announcer's voice recited the blessings bestowed on the appointment by the Massachusetts Women Lawyers Association and the Judicial Nominating Committee. Mrs. Belvedere's credentials were said to include twelve years of sterling work as a defender of the rights of minor children in the probate courts, and two stints as a lecturer at the BU Law School. I had never heard of her, of course, inasmuch as I would sooner shave my balls with a serrated steak knife than accept a divorce case, and she apparently had had no appetite for the kind of work I do. Nevertheless, I applauded the governor's selection because her name wasn't Luther Dawes, and that meant Luther too was having a bad day.

For that vindictiveness I was immediately punished. Sitting there half in the wrapper, on the outs with my good wife, my stuffed effigy in the hands of my devoted daughter being tortured with hatpins out in Utah, waiting for a dispatch from my best client, who would be screaming his hysteria, I was treated to a thoughtful background piece by Channel 8's so-called Legal Specialist, Jack Rowley. Rowley has lost most of the red hair from his dome and the goatee which he grew to make up for it came in white. He looks like an earnest billygoat, but not as intelligent. Those of us who practice law have learned to dread his appearances. He gets things wrong; he misstates law; he buggers up the facts. A favorite device of his is to suggest that some decision of the State Supreme Judicial Court or the Supreme Court of the United States has thrown all precedent into confusion. This is taken by our clients as a new version of the Gospels, and we spend the next weeks trying to restore them to the real world.

Rowley confided to his viewers that the appointment of Belvedere was something of a shock. He said while she was qualified, and backed by women's groups, she had not been the front-runner for the seat on the Appeals Court. "Informed speculation," he said, meaning of course: his, "was that the governor until last week leaned to another choice: Judge Luther Dawes, of the Superior Court." Behind Rowley's right shoulder, the face of Dawes appeared. "Dawes, of course, is better known to the public at least." Rowley was on firm ground there, Channel 8 having given Dawes more air time than its traffic copter. "He's experienced in trial law, after many years of practice, and he's spent the last six of them presiding in the chief trial court of this Commonwealth. As one seasoned observer put it, when it was learned he was a candidate for the Duhamel seat: 'Dawes is strongly qualified, unimpeachably credentialed. It would be a big surprise if Judge Dawes didn't get it.' " My guess was that Luther Dawes was that seasoned observer and the big surprise was his.

"Surprise or not," Rowley said, "Dawes was not selected. Analysts of the system admit that they are puzzled. As one told me today: 'This is hard to figure. Nothing against Belvedere—she is a fine attorney. But even with the help this will give the governor among women's groups, it's hard to see how he could bypass Dawes for this unknown.'

"Late this afternoon," Rowley pontificated, "some hint of the reason surfaced with reports of opposition to the Dawes appointment. Eighteen members of the organized trial bar are said to have joined in a petition which declared Dawes unfit for the Appeals Court vacancy. Thus far, at least, the governor's press secretary has refused to comment on this report, but he will not deny it.

"We'll be watching for developments in this continuing controversy," Rowley said, having just created it. "And we'll bring them to you as they happen."

I realized, as Rowley's face dissolved into a commercial for Subaru cars, that I had been holding my breath while the nincompoop was talking. Therefore I heard Mack's feet hit the floor upstairs as she got out of bed to turn off the bedroom television set. Then I heard her walking out into the hall upstairs, stopping at the landing. "Jerry," she called, "you awake?"

I perceived no point in lying. "Yeah," I said, "I'm still awake. More or less, I guess."

"Were you watching Channel Eight?" she inquired innocently.

"Yes, I was," I said.

"Did you hear what Rowley said, or are you too drunk for that?"

"I heard every goddamned word," I said with bitterness.

"Eighteen lawyers, Jerry?" she said. "Eighteen lawyers was it, who went way out on the limb and stuck the knife in Luther Dawes?"

"That was what he said," I said, "eighteen members of the organized trial bar."

"Do you think, Jerry," she said, "that you were one of those? That that was the same petition that you signed for Frank Macdonald?"

"That is my suspicion, Mack," I said, clearing my throat.

"Well," she said sarcastically, "don't you think that is funny? That there were eighteen of you, when you thought there were eighty?"

"Actually, no, I don't," I said, taking my lumps. "I think that it's kind of awkward, since you mention it."

"Do you think that you misunderstood him, Jerry?" she said silkily.

"No, I don't think so," I said. "I think he said 'eighty.' "

"Still, if you were drunk or something," she mused on the stairs. " 'Eighty' does sound something like 'eighteen' does, I suppose."

"I was not drunk, Mack," I said, praying for Teddy's call. "I had no wax in my ears, and I was not distracted. Frank Macdonald's kid said 'eighty,' eighty goddamned lawyers. Maybe he said that's how many they were calling, and I thought he said: 'had signed.' That I concede could have happened, but not that he said 'eighteen.' "

"Luther Dawes is going to fight this," she said with satisfaction.

"No," I said, "you're wrong there. You're a day behind the times. Luther Dawes *is* fighting this. He's already started."

"Luther Dawes is going to hurt you, that is what I think," she said.

"You are partly right there," I said. "I'm not arguing. Luther Dawes will try to hurt me. He will do his very best. Me and everybody else whose name is on that list."

"Well," she said, "all but one. All but Frank Macdonald. Frank Macdonald's down in Georgia, isn't he, my dear? Judge Dawes can't do much to him. But since he can't get the instigator, he will have more time for you. Wouldn't you say that was right, Jeremiah dear?"

"Yes, I would," I said, "my dear. I think that is clearly right. I think that Judge Luther Dawes is hot after my tail. And furthermore, I want to say, it's nice to know you're with me in this hour of travail. Really makes me feel much better, knowing I have you."

That got me a long silence from the second floor. Teddy's phone call cut it off, at 11:40. "Counselor," he screamed at me, "did you see Channel Eight?"

"Yes, I did, you asshole," I replied to him. "When the hell do you think that you might decide to grow up, and stop getting yourself into shitty scrapes like this, you jerk?"

18

ON THE theory that it's best to know in detail what is bearing down on you, if your plans are to include any hope at all of escape, I made my first official act of the next morning a visit to the law offices of Frank Macdonald at One Center Plaza, opposite the Boston City Hall. My guess was that this gave me one more appearance on those premises for the year than could at that point have been claimed by its proprietor, but then I had a strong reason to go there, and he probably did not. What I wanted was to see that document I had endorsed before its transformation into a pact for suicide, my acquaintance with it to that point being limited to what I could recall from when it was read aloud to me. I also wanted to know just how many other leaders of the trial bar had been similarly reckless, and who the hell they were.

Frank's offices have been in Center Plaza ever since I can remember, but that does not mean they've been static. Frank's more restless than I am, and tends to move around some. Fittingly enough, I guess, his offices do too. So while I took space down at 80 Bolyston over nineteen years ago, moved my stuff in, made my nest, and haven't budged an inch, Frank has occupied more suites than a five-hundred-dollar call girl. His digs move from floor to floor, and across corridors. One year he is at the top and looking toward the harbor. Two years later, you come back and someone's selling stock there. Frank is at the other end, looking at the courthouse from a window on the fourth floor. When I went to see him this time, knowing he wouldn't be there, Frank Macdonald's offices were stuffed onto the fifth floor, looking toward the river. They had gotten smaller than I recalled them as being, and the stuffed royal Bengal tiger, rearing, was no longer greeting guests. I met a new receptionist, whose name was Eloise. She did not know me from the next visitor she might get from Boston Edison, and had not felt the lack. I could forgive her ignorance; underneath a pound of makeup, as best I could judge, there was hiding a young girl who had been born about the same time that I started practicing. I asked whether Frank was in. "No," she said, "he isn't." This kid was no hypocrite; she didn't claim regret.

"Do you expect Frank?" I said.

"No," she said, "I don't."

"I see," I said. "Okay then, who else is around?"

"I am," she said, sensibly, "Judith is, and Mousie."

"Mousie," I said. "Mousie who?"

"Mousie Feeley," she said.

"What does Mousie Feeley do in this law office?" I said.

"He's one of the lawyers," she said. "Him and Bruce and Donna. Bruce is on trial in Fall River. Donna has a cold. Jacqueline's a paralegal, but she's at Social Law. Antoinette's a secretary—she thinks she caught cold from Donna. Jim's a secretary too, but he is on vacation."

"What does Judith do?" I said.

"Judith works for Mousie," she said. "She's his secretary."

"I see," I said, which I didn't, "okay, let's try this. Lawyer from here called me up, week or so ago. Had some sort of a petition against Luther Dawes's judgeship. Read it to me on the phone, asked if I would sign it. I said I would and he thanked me. That's the last I heard. Then on the late news last night, and in this morning's *Globe*, I see where Dawes got denied, and I'm curious. Was that petition the one that canned Dawes? Did my name go on it? And if so, could I see it?"

"Oh," Eloise said, "is that so."

"Yes," I said, "it is. Now, I don't know the name of the young man I talked to. I do know it wasn't *Mousie*, but that's all I know. Have you, maybe, got some idea, who that lawyer might be?"

"Uh-huh," she said, nodding once, "that would've been Mousie." She flicked her left hand toward the call director like a viper striking. "Mousie," she said into it, "someone here to see you." The speaker on the call director gabbled back at her. "He'll be right out," she said, nodding, "if you'll have a seat."

I was in the act of preparing to sit down when a young man emerged from the ficus trees behind her. He looked like a light heavyweight who'd punched instead of boxed. His left ear had been mauled a lot and his eyebrows were scarred. His upper lip had been split and stitched up unskillfully. His nose had been rebuilt at least once, and it looked like more than that. He had the head and body to have stood about five-nine, but since he seemed to have been born without a neck he was about three inches shy of that. "Mousie," Eloise said, bored, "this man was asking for you."

"Jerry Kennedy," I said, and stuck out my right hand.

"Ray Feeley," he said, shaking. "Nice to meet you, let me say. Frank thinks a lot of you."

We went back to Ray's small office through a narrow corridor—one of the reasons that I give for staying where I am is that the rents in the newer buildings are so high that everyone gets all cramped up by cutting passageways. I felt like some old handler following Carmen Basilio through the tunnels of a tank-town arena toward the ring where he'd demolish a kid like a young Chuck Davey. I made a stern mental note not to call him Mousie.

"Frank said you've got balls," he said, when we were all crammed in. "When I told him who signed up, and who waffled on me, Frank said when I got to your name that you never ducked."

"Yeah, well, that's nice," I said, taking it for praise. Naturally someone like Ray would think that a compliment, and I guess it was if you did not mind looking like he does. "The problem is, that I've got now, I don't know what I signed."

Ray looked troubled when I said that. "Is that so?" he said. He leaned toward me at the desk and his eyebrows began to come together as though they had been on gears.

"Not the gist of it," I said, "that wasn't what I meant. I know what the thrust of it was, and I'm not disowning it. Thing of it is, if I'm right, it looks like this may be heating up a little, and the thought has crossed my mind that I have never seen it. So, I would like to," I said, "if it isn't too much trouble."

"Oh," he said, "no trouble. Of course not." He pushed down his intercom and talked to Eloise. "Gimme that petition, when you've got a minute, okay? And also bring us coffee when you're coming in with that." Eloise apparently was used to such commands. The speaker chirped back at Feeley and he released the console button with a look of satisfaction. "Be right in with that," he said. "Something else that I can help you with, while we're waiting for it?"

"Yeah," I said, "there is, in fact. When you called me, I remember, you said: 'Eighty lawyers.' TV news I heard last night said there were eighteen lawyers. Am I getting wax in my ears, or is my memory fading?"

Ray grinned at me as he leaned back and pulled open the center drawer of his desk. One of his front teeth was chipped, a large triangular chunk out. He wore a red and white striped shirt, with a gold collar pin. His black patterned challis tie was snugged up tight against it. His suit was dark gray and his hair was razor cut, and yet everything about him called for a gray sweatshirt with a towel at the neck. "No cause for alarm, Jerry," he said, pulling a pad out. "When I called you, we had eighty. Eighty on our list. Take a look at this list, if you're interested," he said. "I'll have Eloise run that through the copier, so you can take it with you when we're finished talking here.

"As you'll see from that list," he said, "we got through eleven signers. See, as I told Frank when he called up with this idea, the problem that confronted us with derailing old Luther was pure and simple, as I told Frank, that we started way too late. 'Frank,' I said, when he called up, 'I get what you are saying. And even though I can't say that I know the old bastard, I'd have to agree with you, just hearing what you say.

" 'Thing of it is,' I told Frank, 'the governor's not waiting. You wanted to spike him, okay, you should've done it sooner. We'll have one bitch of a time, getting people lined up now.' "

Eloise came in with a sheaf of papers and a rattan tray with coffee. The cups were white Styrofoam. The sugar was in packets. The cream substitute was in a brown jar. There were two white plastic spoons. She put the cargo on the desk and started out again.

"Eloise," Ray Feeley said, "take that pad from Jerry. Xerox what's on the first four pages. Make sure it comes out clear." She took the pad out of my hands and disappeared with it.

"Well," he said, drinking black coffee, "you know how Frank is. Gets an idea in his head, that's all there is to it. Doesn't matter he's in Georgia, hasn't been around. Will not listen, when you tell him, you can't get the papers out. 'Never mind all that,' he said, 'how you circulate it. Call them on the telephone. Read what it says to them. All the ones with balls hate Luther, and they won't be scared to say so.'

"Jerry," he said as I stirred, watching the cornstarch swirl, "this was three nights, have you got this, before the decision. He's dictating eighty names, as fast as I can write them. I don't know these people myself. I'm supposed to call them. I don't have a draft petition. 'Make one up,' he says. 'Call me back and read it to me. Then when I get one approved, ship it to me Federal.' Tell you something, Jerry," Ray said, "and I mean this seriously. There are times when I think that those damned overnight delivery services were the worst thing that ever happened to Frank. Soon as they were working he could sit down in the sun, run his office up here from most any place he wanted. I see those damned ads on TV, I could strangle those guys. They got no idea, I'm sure, how he can nag us with them."

"Must run into money," I said, sipping the foul brew.

"Money?" Ray said. "Money? Let me tell you, money. Every night, I'm telling you, at least four pouches go out. At least one to him down there in Sea Island. One or two more to the courts where he's got cases pending. And then, more often than not, one to his publishers."

"Publishers," I said.

"Oh yeah, Frank's got two publishers. One for this new lawbook that he's writing with Dave Reed, fellow out at Hastings Law that does the hypnosis. Then there is the other one, that's doing Frank's memoirs. I think myself that's Corinne's idea, those memoirs. I think she is writing those, but they will claim they're his.

"Every morning," Feeley said, "two more packages come in. This is at a minimum, two more coming in. Some days we'll have six or seven. Once I think there were ten. We get bills from these people like you wouldn't believe. Last month what we paid them came to more than our damned rent.

"Frank thinks this is wonderful," he said. "He sits down there in the sun, plays a little tennis. Got his sailboard and his golf sticks, and his Dictaphone. Xerox machine in his basement, Corinne's got her computer. She's got NEXIS, LEXIS, God knows what she has got. 'Why the hell should I come home?' That's what he says to me. 'This is home where I am now. Why should I be cold?'

"What do you think I should tell him?" Feeley said to me. "Tell him that he's out of touch? People've forgotten? 'Who the hell is Frank Macdonald? Where the hell is he now?' You know something, Jerry, when I started calling people? Keep in mind, that list you saw, Frank gave me those names. These are people that he knows, people that he trusts. He knows how they think and all, what they think of Dawes. I get eleven people," he said, "who agreed to sign. That is out of thirty, Jerry, thirty-four I called.

"Two of the first ten names I called, from the list Frank gave me, Jerry, all right? That he just rattled off to me on the phone? Dead. You hear what I'm saying, Jerry, what I'm telling you, for Christ sake? I am sitting here, in this office, with this list in front of me that Frank Macdonald dictated, these are guys that he knows and they are guys that will go through on something for him if he asks them, and two of them are fucking *dead*.

"Two guys are suspended from practicing. They had their tickets lifted by the bar association. Which was pretty embarrassing that I'm calling them up on the phone to ask if they will sign up to hose down a goddamned judge, and they have been hosed down themselves, for Christ sake. The second one starts laughing at me, says maybe he should sign. 'After all,' he says, 'who should know better than a guy who's been suspended as unfit to practice law, who else should be fit to be a judge, huh? Tell me that.' Then he takes pity on me. 'Look,' he says, 'all right? Let me give you a hand here. Read off to me what you've got for names on that list. I will tell you who is disbarred or in prison, things like that.' 'Dead too, far as that goes,' I say. 'Tell if you come across here anyone that's dead.'

"There was one guy in the slammer," Feeley said, shaking his head. "Six or seven people out of the thirty-four there left Massachusetts and went someplace else. Seven guys have quit practicing entirely. Wouldn't know a judge if they fell over one, for Christ sake. 'Frank's a little out of date, I'd say,' this guy that was suspended says to me. 'I would agree with that,' I say, and thank him for his help.

"So," Feeley said, "by the time that I get through, calling thirty-four names out of the eighty that Frank gives me, I have got eleven names, and yours is one of them."

"I thought it was eighteen," I said. "The TV said 'eighteen.'"

"Bear with me, Jerry," Feeley said as Eloise returned with the pad and the photocopies she had made from it. "Gimme the pad, Eloise," Feeley said. "Give the copies to Mister Kennedy." Eloise did as she was told. "Are the copies nice and clear, Jerry?" Feeley said to me. I leafed through them hurriedly, four sheets of scribbled names, with checks and crosses on them. "Nice and clear," I said. "Good," Feeley said to me, "You can go now," to her.

Eloise nodded and smiled at him. She did a little curtsy. "Thank you, Mousie," she said.

"You're welcome, dear," he said. Eloise went out, shutting the door behind her. "Eloise thinks I am cute," he said, "so that is what she calls me."

"I see," I said, nodding sagely, thinking him an asshole but not about to say so.

"The first sheet you have," he said officiously, "should be the original, the one with eighty names. You will see that I checked off the ones that I did call. Or that I learned from other people were not good to call—dead or disbarred, stuff like that.

"The second sheet," he said, as I turned to it, "ought to be the names of the eleven people who signed up. Yours will be the third one, I think, right up near the top. The other ones of course will be familiar to you."

That was a slight overstatement, I saw to my dismay. Thin Freddie Collier's name was first, and Kennedy was fifth. Marjorie Caldwell of the Mass. Defenders was the sixth name on the list, and there were three others with the MD notation added. The second name on the list was Jason Lafayette, a young black lawyer out of Worcester whose chief client was the Lords of Reparations, a Marxist cell of maybe twenty young black men who had done time and were demanding damages for their incarceration. Morris Breen was the eleventh, which did not inspire me—Morris said his specialty was First Amendment cases, which meant he was on retainer to a string of topless joints and bookstores that aroused small towns into picketing and acts of vandalism. "Four besides mine are," I said. "Familiar to me, that is. Not what I would call exactly: 'leaders of the bar,' but I do recognize them."

"That's what I told Frank," he said, smiling at me grimly. " 'Frank,' I said, 'you won't like what I've got to tell you. We have got eleven names, and that's all we've got. Four of them are Mass. Defenders that I collared in a bar. One of them is Morris Breen—nice guy but sort of stinky. Then we have the Mau Mau, Jason, and Freddie Collier. Actually, all we have got is Jerry Kennedy. Jerry's tough and he goes through, but he is all alone. I told Jerry we had eighty. This means he's alone. What I think you'd better do is let him off the hook.' "

I did not believe a single word of that. Not the words he claimed to have said in describing me. I did not doubt he'd disparaged all the other suckers. But neither did I doubt for the merest, briefest instant that he'd also bad-mouthed me. If I had been Sugar Ray, I would have decked the bastard. Since I wasn't Sugar Ray, and I was fat as well, I kept my big mouth shut and paid out more rope to him.

"What did Frank say then?" I said, acting curious.

"Didn't faze him one damned bit," Feeley said jovially. " 'Ray,' he says, " 'you're right, you know, it isn't fair to Jair. Tell you what we do, all right? Now listen to me here.

" 'I've been to the governor,' Frank says, he's telling me. 'What he tells me he wants is some leaders of the bar. See, he's just as jumpy about Luther Dawes as I am. But, and this is what he tells me, he can't dump him for no reason. "Frank," he says, "you've got to give me," and he's pleading with me now, "give me some kind of a petition that I can use to hang my hat on."

" 'Now,' Frank tells me, 'he don't say: Massachusetts lawyers. All he wants from me is some names he can hang his hat on, all right? People that the average person, reading in the paper, he would look at these names and agree they are big lawyers.

" 'So,' Frank says, 'what I have done, while you are wasting time, I have been making some calls on my own from down here, see? And I have got some names to use, names that are really big. I have got sixteen of them, and those're what we'll use.'

"Now," Feeley said, pointing at me, "you should turn to the third sheet. And that one, as you will see, is the names I got from Frank. And those names, you won't argue with me, those are heavy hitters."

Feeley was right when he said that—those were famous lawyers. David Reed, professor, Hastings Law School, led the list. Jennings Mills of Florida, former chief of antitrust, U.S. Department of Justice; Millicent Janes Bell of the Texas Law School; Carl A. Green of San Francisco, master of products cases; Daniel J. Carmody of the LA Bar Association: every name on that third list was a celebrity. "Look at the eleventh name," Ray Feeley said with glee. "Cole B. Younger, Abilene. Don't you love that one? Lineal descendant of the famous brothers that robbed banks. You see *The Long Riders*, Jerry? James boys and the Younger brothers riding into Northfield, Minnesota, got these great-looking long coats on, the black hats and everything? Jesus Christ, old Luther sees that name on that list, he's gonna think he looks up in his courtroom someday and there they all are, coming in at him."

"Yeah," I said, "but there's a couple things about this just the same, you know? This list I'm looking at?"

"Like what?" Feeley said to me. "You got some problem with it? Hey, Jerry, these guys are not turkeys here. These are some of the most famous lawyers in the whole United States. I mean, you can't be saying that, can you?"

"Ray," I said, "listen to me. David Reed is not a member of the Massachusetts Bar. Duncan Reo of Cheyenne: I have heard of him. Everybody's heard of Duncan Reo and his big wide Stetson hat, how much money he has gotten from the evil people who build nuclear power plants. Duncan Reo's not a member of the Massachusetts Bar."

"Well," Feeley said, "of course they aren't. That's not the list of them. That's the list of guys that Frank called up himself. Got them to agree that Luther should be stopped."

"This list, Ray," I said, "has sixteen names on it. If I'm starting to get things a little straighter here, that is two short of the number that went to the governor. Is this the list that went to the governor? Or is there another list, that Frank had sent to him?"

"Yes," Feeley said, "there is. That's the next sheet of paper. The fourth sheet that you have there, under the one that you've got."

I looked at it. It was identical to the third sheet, except for the addition of two more names at the bottom. Number seventeen on that sheet was my name. Number eighteen was Frank Macdonald's. "This one, you mean," I said, and I held it up for him.

Feeley nodded, grinning at me. "That's the one I mean. Eighteen names on that list, Jerry, all opposed to Luther. And I think you'll have to admit, it's a pretty heavy list. Every one of those guys, and I am including you, stating that it's his conviction Luther Dawes ain't fit to serve."

"Two of whom," I said, "are members of the Mass. Bar, and actually know Luther."

"That's right," Feeley said, "you and Frank Macdonald."

"One of whom," I said, "is still in practice here."

"Well," Feeley said, "that's true, between the two of us. You know and I know, of course, that Frank doesn't get here much. But he is still in practice here, and still pays his bar dues. This is Frank Macdonald's home base, his home territory."

"Your name isn't on this, Ray," I said. "I don't see yours here."

"I'm admitted in Rhode Island," Feeley said, shrugging. "Got an application pending, up in New Hampshire. But no, I am not admitted in the Commonwealth."

"Which means, if I understand it," I said, "I am the point man."

"I don't get it," Feeley said. "What are you saying, Jerry?"

"Ray," I said, "the Judas goat. The stalking horse. The POW the troops make walk ahead of them through minefields. The Indian that went to work as a scout for the pony soldiers. The only enemy of Luther's that is where Luther can get at him. Of the eighteen guys that hate him, I'm the only one in sight. Frank Macdonald's never here. The rest have never been here. The Defenders and Freddie Collier, they didn't make the cut. I'm the only one with no pants on, out in the cold breeze."

"Jerry," Feeley said, "all right? I swear I didn't do this. All I did was what Frank said, calling me from Georgia. Got the names and wrote them down. Drafted the petition, and he dictated that to me. 'Just put down,' he says to me, 'what I'm telling you. "We, the undersigned trial lawyers, knowing the importance of judicial temperament, of decorum on the bench, mindful of the absolute necessity that persons elevated to positions of respect must act always in accordance with respect for those before them, having been advised by our colleagues in Massachusetts of the lack that has been demonstrated by Judge Luther Dawes of its trial court, respectfully advise Your Excellency that it is our strongly held view that he is not fit to serve as a member of the Court of Appeals of the Commonwealth." ' That was what he told me to write down, and that is what I wrote. And put the names on it and had it messengered to the State House."

I had referred to the second sheaf of papers that Eloise had given me along with lists of names, and found the damned petition as he recited it from memory. "You had it verbatim," I said, "that is very good."

"Always been a quick study," Ray Feeley said to me. "Photographic memory. It really helps me sometimes."

I stood up as he spoke because there was danger there. If I hit this shit, he'd kill me, and that wouldn't make things better. "Ray," I said, when I was standing, "I am leaving now. You tell Frank when he calls in next, I would like a word with him."

"Sure," Feeley said, "I will, Jerry. Anything else I can do?"

"Yeah," I said, "give me his number, down in Georgia there. Case he doesn't call me up, I may want to call him."

Feeley looked regretful at me. "Gee, I'm really sorry."

"You are sorry, Ray?" I said. "Why should you be sorry?"

"I can't give you Frank's number," he said, looking sorrowful. "Those're Frank's strict orders. We can't give his number out. Doctor's orders, and Corinne's, no incoming calls. Frank is trying to get better. Has to pace himself. Make sure he gets all his rest. Nothing unexpected."

"Is that so?" I said. "That bastard. Give him my love, then."

19

"COOP," I said, "I'm at a loss. I don't know what to do." We sat in his messy office. I had intruded on him right out of the elevator. I sat there in his client's chair, my overcoat still on. "I'm buffaloed, I really am. Feel like I'm paralyzed."

"Start at the beginning," he said, lighting a cigar. Cooper, only in his office, smokes Parodi twists. They are black, misshapen things, and they stink like hell. Therefore Cooper's office stinks. He claims that he likes it. "Other people don't," he concedes. "I can understand that. That means those who come to see me, at least for the second time, really think they need to see me, and won't stay very long."

"I'm not sure where that is," I said. "Everything's collapsing. My wife isn't speaking to me unless it's something nasty. My daughter's nominating me to succeed Dracula. I can't get Lou Schwartz out of jail like I would like to, and after all these years that I've been keeping Franklin out, unless I'm way off the mark, he is going in. Then this morning, I discover, I have been taken in. My old pal there, Frank Macdonald, he has hung me out to dry. I am telling you, Cooper, before I came in here? First I made sure in my own mind that you aren't mad at me too."

"Start with the wife and daughter thing," he said through a cloud of smoke. "As you know, I'm good at that stuff. Good at family matters. Got one kid in the loony bin, and my wife's headed there. I'm an expert on that stuff, help you a lot on that."

"How about," I said, "we start with the other stuff. Maguire denied my motion. Got the notice yesterday. I don't think that Lou was counting on it much. But then again, Coop, he's in jail. Things get different there. Want to draft my letter for me? Tell him he is ditched?"

"How much did old Lou pay you, just out of curiosity?" Coop said.

"Huh," I said, "that's funny, Coop, you should ask me that. That's the first thing Mack asked me when I got down on this case. 'Not that it matters, Jerry, I guess, since you took the case. But just how much did Lou pay you for all this worrying?' "

"It's a fair question, I think," Cooper said calmly. "You and I both know, like she does, that you took this one to heart. We're both at the age where that's no laughing matter. Men who take things to heart at our age really take them there. Then their hearts attack them, just like Frank Macdonald's did. Lay them right out on their backs, in the hospital. Those are the lucky ones, I guess, that make it even that far. The unlucky ones go on their backs on slabs."

"You are a cheery bastard," I said. "Seven thousand dollars."

"That's an interesting figure," Cooper said to me. "Ordinarily those cases, trials of that magnitude, I thought that you charged for them in multiples of five. Five grand, ten grand, fifteen grand: so on up the scale. You had, what, three weeks on that one? Fifteen days of trial? Plus all the hearings on it, motions for discovery? Six or seven of those too? Lou Schwartz got a bargain."

"Lou Schwartz gave me years of bargains, doing my damned taxes. He knew what I charged guys and he knew how I got the figures. Calculate what they had on them, how much they could raise. Hit them just as hard as I could without driving them away. I charged Lou Schwartz by the hour, just like he did me. I gave Lou Schwartz a good rate, just like he did me. Lou was doing my work for about thirty an hour. That is less than plumbers get, and they don't come when called. I told Lou when he came in, his tail's in the crack: 'This looks like a two-week trial. Plus the crap that goes before, hearings and conferences. That is three weeks, more or less, a hundred twenty hours. You've been giving me, I figure, fifty percent off. I will do the same for you: sixty bucks an hour. That is seven thousand, two. Call it seven grand.'

" 'That is why you're going broke,' Lou said. 'This is one time I'm glad you never listened to me.'

"So," I said, "the trial was three weeks, and the stuff before it? Two. Plus the motion afterwards, another couple of days. Five and one-half weeks of work, at my established rate? Fifty thousand, four. So, you want to tell me I gave myself a screwing, I might be inclined to say you were right, old pal. But then there're all those years when Lou was nice to me. Some things you do in this world, you don't always have a choice."

"I'm not saying 'choice,' " Coop said. "Not saying that at all. All I'm saying is, enough. You have done your job. You gave Lou a good defense. Worked your ass off for him. Didn't do much good, but that is what you did. Now he's in the pokey and you've got to kiss him off. You defended this guy, Jerry. You did not adopt him. Write him a nice letter and give him his walking papers. Or, if that won't let you sleep, drive down there and see him. But when you see him down there, kiss him off, all right? Tell him that you're finished and you've done all you can do. Then stick to it when you get back afterwards."

"Okay," I said, "one down and two to go. Let's take Teddy first, then go to Frank Macdonald."

"Uh-uh," Coop said, "not right now. Teddy's a lunchtime conference. We consult on him, remember? Which means that he buys my beer. Frank Macdonald never pays, although I hear he used to. Therefore, first the family matters, then to Frank Macdonald."

"Let's do Frank Macdonald first," I said, and told him why. "Mack thinks that he suckered me," I said when I was finished. "That is what I mean when I say there are times when she is speaking."

"When she's got you, and she's right, you mean," Coop said.

"That's about it," I said. "Why do they do that?"

"I don't know," he said, mashing the cigar out. "They all do it, though, without a single exception. Karen, for example, knows I'm as upset as she is about the way that Peter's screwed up everything he's touched. This kid, Jerry, has potential, quite a lot of it. Six-tens on his college boards, the math exam, I mean. Took them in his sophomore year, just for practice, okay? Five-eighty on the verbal part, five-ninety-five averaged. Eleven-ninety combined score, when nine-hundreds are pretty good. Not a bad ballplayer either—he could be a kicker. So here is this kid, pretty bright, decent athlete. Good possibility of scholarships, if he applies himself. No question he can go to school, since we can pay tuition. Well, until we started paying therapists instead.

"So," Cooper said, getting up and glaring, "what does this damned kid do with all of this? Pisses it away, of course—that is what he does.

"I did not advise him that he ought to do this, Jerry," Cooper said indignantly. "I did not sit the kid down and tell him to screw up. I did not say: 'Peter, fuck things up. Use a lot of dope yourself and retail it to others. Blow your mind out, wreck your health, get yourself arrested.

Drive your mother to distraction, waste all of our savings. Make me impose on my friends and cause me embarrassment. My life's been too orderly. I need excitement, Peter.'

"Maybe that was where I slipped up," Cooper said resentfully. "If I'd told him to screw up, he would not've done it. If I'd said: 'Scramble your brains,' he would be straight-arrow. The dim understanding that I've got of how he thinks, that might be the reason that he acts the way he does.

"Nevertheless," Cooper said, "I am getting blamed. Karen takes the attitude she always let me run things. Now that everything's screwed up, it must therefore be my fault. When I leave home in the morning, she is still asleep, and I don't leave that early. When I get home after work, she is glassy-eyed. And I don't get home all that late, as you know from my habits."

"Drinking, is she?" I said, trying to be sympathetic.

"I doubt it, Jerry," Cooper said, "though I did think of that. One of those housebound ladies that gets at the cooking sherry when her husband goes to work, spends her whole day getting sozzled, feeling sorry for herself? Then a little nap, around the cocktail hour. Put some perfume on and brush teeth so you're reasonably sober? It's a possibility, but I doubt that's what it is. Pills I also thought of, so I tossed the house one weekend. Nothing, Jerry, I could find, absolutely nothing. One vial of old sleeping pills she got six years ago, when her back was acting up and she was having cramps. Otherwise, if she is hiding that stuff, she knows what the Bureau teaches. This man couldn't find it, if she's got it in the house.

"No," he said, "it's worse than that. It's more like she's withdrawn. It's like this is something that she wasn't prepared for. Now it's hit her anyway, and she is paralyzed.

"She acts like a zombie, Jerry," Cooper said sorrowfully. "She functions, but she barely functions, you know what I mean. See, Karen, when you think about it, she's had an easy life. Her mother and her father were nice, ordinary people. He taught junior high school English, coached some basketball. Navy veteran, World War Two, father of two daughters. Once, I think, he got quite drunk, at some sailors' reunion. This was such an event that he never lived it down.

"She brought me home," Cooper said, "her own FBI man. This was back when Ike was President, and they thought I was grand. Steady income, sober young lad, polite and courteous. She went right from what they gave her into what I did.

"Karen is conventional," he said, shaking his head. "Everything she did in life was following the numbers. Had three children without trouble, husband always there. Nothing that she saw before this gave her any preparation. Now she's just bewildered, Jerry, absolutely baffled. I say she blames me for this, and is punishing me for it. Maybe that's not fair to her, doesn't give her credit. Maybe she's not talking because she doesn't know what to say.

"Either way," he said, "the result is the same. She won't go to see a doctor. Doesn't like the minister. She has got friends, but they're like her, totally unsavvy. If she did talk to them, they couldn't help her much.

"So," Cooper said, "she is in there, inside her own head, and I don't seem to be able to do anything for her. She always looks like she either just got finished crying or she's just about to start. She's got these big bags under her eyes, and she's got no energy. Just sort of mopes around the house all day while I am gone, and then mopes around all night after I get home. It's awful, Jerry, you know? Absolutely awful." He looked like he might cry himself.

"Jesus, Coop," I said, "I'm sorry. I wish I could help."

"I wish you could too," he said. "I wish I could help you. What is it with Frank Macdonald? Something about that Luther Dawes thing I saw on television?"

I gave him the rundown. "That is very nice," he said. "That was very nice of Frank, to do a thing like that. What a prince of a fellow, who would do that to his friend. Make you famous like that. What's the matter with that asshole? Has he lost his mind? What's he think this is, a game? Some goddamned volleyball we play? Jesus H. Christ, Jerry, did he really do that?"

"Yes," I said, "he really did that. Now what do I do?"

"Okay," Coop said, sitting down, "let's we think about that. You of course cannot deny it."

"Wouldn't if I could," I said.

"And, if you could deny it, then you'd be a liar. This would not help you with Luther, who would call you one at once. That would leave you like two kinds of a low-down, dirty skunk. No, better make that three. Backstabber, liar, coward. I don't think you want to do that."

"Then there is the Br'er Fox route," I said without hope. " 'Don't say nuffin', jes' lie low.' Wait till it blows over."

"Not this time, I think," Coop said. "Luther Dawes won't let it. I would say by noon today, dinner at the latest, somebody will have that list. Somebody who can read. They can't reach Frank—no one can. They don't know the others. You are in the phone book, Jerry. They will look for you. You will have to say something. 'No comment' will not do it."

"Why not?" I said. "Others do. All I have to say is that this was a private matter. I was asked to sign this thing as one of a number, on the understanding that it was a confidential letter to the governor. Take the high road and say that as far as I'm concerned, it still ought to be that, even if it isn't, and I don't propose to discuss it publicly."

"Pretty lame," Coop said.

"I know," I said, "but what else have I got? Do that and then hunker down. See how they take it. Luther wants to press the matter, leave him do just that. Maybe it dies down, no matter what he does. Then all I will have to do is try to duck his sessions."

"You're right," Cooper said, getting up again. "Come on now and get out of here. Let me practice law."

20

LOU EMERGED from the dormitory wing of the main building at Danbury with his left arm around the shoulders of a shorter, downcast black man. He spotted me across the visiting room, fairly crowded with small children who had come with their mothers to cheer up their confined daddies and were bored and restless to the point at which they would not remain seated on their molded plastic chairs, and by raising his left eyebrow and nodding his head once indicated that he would be with me in a minute. The children whined and tugged at their parents' garments, wheedling small change from them to purchase Coca-Cola, and Lou finished his urgent advice to the sad man who was with him. For this he received a small but hopeful smile, and the black man stood away from him as he made his way toward me. Lou looked like the expansive and proprietary host of a good restaurant, with those people all his guests.

"Jerry, Jerry," he said, "very nice to see you." He escorted me to two chairs near a window at the front, where we could look out upon the concrete patio. "Too bad," Lou said, "that you couldn't wait till spring. Willie there, that black guy? Tells me it's kind of nice there. Tables with umbrellas and they move the chairs outside. Almost like a country club, like someone's always saying."

"Willie's a new pal of yours?" I said, too innocently.

Lou first gave me an amused look. Then he started laughing. "What's the matter, Jerry?" he said. "Think I'm getting double-gaited?"

"Well," I said, "you must admit: you wouldn't be the first one. Lock you up in here like this, man who's completely healthy. It's been known to happen, Lou, tougher guys'n you are."

Lou shook his head and grinned at me. "Nah," he said, "not likely. My memory's too good, for one thing, and I've still got that. Joanna also claims, she says that I have still got her. Nah, Willie's an old pal of mine, over thirty years. Knew him in Havana, back before Castro came in." He stared fondly back across the room, where Willie stood beside the Coke machine, drinking dejectedly. "You might not think this today, seeing him like he is now, but Willie used to be one of the toughest guys I knew."

"What's he in for, Lou?" I said, making conversation.

"Ahh," Lou said, "chickenshit. Like everybody else. Finally got caught, just like me, too old to enjoy it. That guy's sixty-three years old, too old for this joint. He should be in Phoenix someplace, ready to retire. Instead some young bastard hooks him, perjury, I guess. Got him into the grand jury, asked him lots of questions. Case was quite a lot like mine, when you come down to it. Ask the guy what he can tell you about what someone else is doing. If he takes the Fifth Amendment, get him immunized. Then bring him back in again, ask him a few more times. Either he will lie and you will get him nailed for it, or else he will tell the truth and someone else will nail him. These cocksuckers that do this, they think it's funny. Take a man as old as he is, put him in that box. Naturally he's folding up, going down the tube. He'll be lucky if he makes it, two more years in here. And this isn't that bad either, as these places go. Man's wife comes down, and he's careful, he can get a piece of ass. Nothing like Atlanta, say, one of those fucking places."

Lou shook his head sorrowfully. "It's because you *can't* get out. That's what does it to you, that you do not have a choice. Maybe it's a lousy day, cold and wet and shitty. You were home and you looked out, you might not want to go out. But when you are home like that, you get to decide. Papers didn't come on time? Well, you'll go out and get them. Nothing on hand that you want to eat? Go and get something different. You are inside like this, you cannot make those decisions. Things that need attending to, you cannot attend to them. Makes you feel like you did when you were a little kid. Had to stay after school sometimes, because you sassed a teacher. Had to go up to your room, you gave some shit to your mother and she told your father on you. Takes your dignity away, that's what it does.

"Myself," Lou said, "I do all right, all things considered, that is. I look at what this kind of thing can do, somebody who's as tough as Willie used to be, and it kind of shapes me up, you know what I mean? I try to take it philosophically, all right? I am fifty-five years old. My third wife, the lovely Joanna, believes honestly that I am fifty-one, because that is what I was telling people I was meeting backstage at the Tropicana when we get introduced to each other, seven years ago—that I was forty-four then. Some of the honeys that I met since then will tell you I am about forty-nine these days, because I adjust my falsehoods as I get a little older. But the point is that I get away with this bullshit, because I still look all right and I do not let myself get all down in the damned dumps. Plus which, it is possible, honeys will believe just about anything you tell them if you can convince them first that you will give them two hundred dollars in exchange for certain oral pleasures, but I try not to think about that too much.

"So," Lou said, "already, before they put me in here like this, I have had a better life than most people that are like me, guys that come up from the ass-end of nowhere and don't even get to dream of if they live till they are eighty. You realize how many poor working stiffs there are out there, every week they're sneaking something out of the pay envelope, putting it into the credit union so that someday they surprise the dumpy wife with a crummy three-bill package deal out to Las Vegas there? See Tom Jones in person and blow every buck they have trying to shoot craps with guys that know what they are doing when they step up to those tables? People like that junior G-man Dunn that put me here? I bet he is making about thirty grand a year, and loaning back a chunk of that to his damned government, buying U.S. savings bonds that don't pay as much interest in a whole damned year as Nunzio's worst shylock could get for him in a week. He thinks that Capri's a car that Mercury makes, for Christ sake." I did not tell Lou that I thought Dunn was smarter than that; there was no point in disturbing his precarious good mood.

"There are thousands of those guys, Jerry," Lou said resentfully. "Guys in his job, IRS guys, all basically stupid. There are many of them that can add the figures up, and if you give them enough laws, they can get anybody. When I started out in this, Bernard Goldfine was the big crook, him and all the other assholes that gave bigger jerks warm coats. All these years it took them to run me into the damned ground. And then when they finally do it, this is all they get. I think this is a victory, and that is why I can help Willie, 'cause I know I really beat them."

"Well, Lou," I said, "that is fine, that you can look at it this way. But what I've got to tell you is, they still think they have won. Judge Maguire turned down my motion to reduce your sentence here. Mike Dunn says unless you talk, you are here till New Year's. That is what I have to tell you, and I wish it wasn't so."

Lou licked his lips and stared at me. He blinked a couple times. "Jerry," he said, "listen to me. Just once: listen to me."

"I am listening," I said.

"Good," he said, "that is good, because this is important. First thing is, you've got to stop this, taking things so hard. You think that you lost my case. You did not lose it. When I got indicted there, I was not surprised. I called Nunzio, right off. 'They are doing it,' he says. I went over to his place and talked about it with him. Nunzio is tactful—he don't ask if I will talk. I am diplomatic too—I don't ask him not to kill me. 'What will you do about this, Louis?' Nunzio asks me. 'Plead it, I guess,' I say back. 'What's the alternative?'

"Nunzio's disturbed at this. 'That does not sound right. We should have Frank in here on this. Tell us what to do.' I tell Nunzio that Frank is not in working order. 'Frank is very sick,' I say, 'since the Sweeney case.' 'He should not have tried that case,' Nunzio says to me. 'That was not a good enough case, that Frank should have tried it. Sweeney's kid was going away. Everyone knew that. Frank made himself sick with that. That was a waste of Frank.'

" 'Nevertheless, Nunzio, that is what Frank did. As a result, he is sick, and no help to us now.' 'We will call Frank,' Nunzio decides, so that's what we do. Frank comes on the speaker phone, and we all talk to him."

"Just out of curiosity," I said to Lou, "how did Nunzio get Frank?" Then I told him how Ray Feeley would not give his number out.

"Nunzio has numbers if they're numbers that he wants," Lou said. "If he wants your number, you had better give it to him. Otherwise he calls some guy who goes and wakes you up. Then you have to go with him to where Nunzio can talk. Why did you want Frank's phone? Something else bad happen?"

"Finish what you're telling me," I said. "One thing at a time."

"Frank is full of bullshit, of course, when we call him up. He will rip the needles out, come back home and try it. Nunzio does not like this. He tells Frank to stop it. 'You are too sick to try cases these days, Frank. You tell us what Lou should do. That is why we're calling. Lou's idea is that he admits it, goes to court and says he's guilty.'

"Frank of course does not like this," Lou said with distaste. "His idea always was, nobody ever pleads. This is not because he thinks that everyone can win. He said that was his idea, sure, but that was not the truth. The truth was, he liked to try. He really enjoyed it. Trying cases was Frank's fun. Made him feel alive. You know what I think, Jerry, explains why Frank drank?"

"He was a mick," I said, "a mick and a trial lawyer. All micks drink a quart a day. Trial lawyers drink two pints. That made half a gallon that Frank had to swallow daily."

"Uh-uh," Lou said, "wasn't that. Much more complicated. Frank went at the stuff because he wasn't trying cases. When he was just starting out, and nobody knew him, he was in court every day, and it was fun for him. Trouble is, he won a lot. Guys started ducking him. Toward the end there, before Sweeney's case, Frank was doing well if he got three big trials a year. One week, two weeks, maybe three sometimes—that left Frank with forty weeks and no fun whatsoever. His brain was still working, though, going like a bastard. So, to calm himself down some, he increased his drinking.

"Then the Sweeney case comes in. This is not a plea. No prosecutor in his right mind will put this punk on the street. What was his blood alcohol? Point twenty-six or something? Frank Macdonald's on the case? Who could give a shit? Jesus Christ could try this case and even he would lose it. So Frank takes the turkey in, and he loses it. Most guys would be able, they could handle this, losing a damned hopeless case that Jesus couldn't win. But Frank of course always believed that he could out-try Jesus. This was a big blow to him. It really made him sick.

"Nunzio lets Frank exhaust all of his bullshit. Then he tells Frank, no, he won't, get out of bed and try it. All Frank is to tell us is if he thinks I should plead. Frank says that he does not think so. Nunzio asks why. Frank says it will just encourage them if I do, Michael Dunn and them. They will get the idea that they can wreck old Nunzio by getting his guys one by one into the same box I am. First I don't talk, and I plead, and I go away. That is one good man he's lost—who will be the next one? 'Trying Lou's case won't stop this,' Frank tells Nunzio. 'All it will do really is cost them some time and money. But sometimes, if you get delays, that is good enough. Tie them up with trying Lou and maybe buy a year. Then and only then is Dunn free to take on another guy. Next year, perhaps, he takes out another guy. And maybe, if he's still around, a third guy after him.

" 'Point is,' Frank says, 'four's his limit. Five at the outside. Those guys generally leave after six or seven years. They don't get this kind of case until they've been there a couple, got themselves experience and think they know all the answers. So, you stall them, wait them out, make them turn square corners. And then maybe, when a new election's over, Michael Dunn is gone from there and you can start to rebuild. But if you start pleading guys, you raise his efficiency. He can try for more indictments, three or four guys at a time. And then you also have the risk, he gets one that's weak. I know all your guys look good, look like they'll stand up. But everybody looks like that, until somebody hits them. That is when you find out who is strong and who is not.'

"That is naturally what the Boss wants to hear," Lou said. "That is why he called Frank up, to hear him talk like that. He says he agrees with Frank, which I know isn't so. He asks Frank to recommend somebody he can hire to represent me. 'Should I get this Magazu?' Nunzio says like he's worried. 'He is the best man, I hear, for things with income tax.'

"That was all show," Lou said, "for my benefit. Nunzio wants me to know that expense is no object. He will get the best in town, to save my ass from jail. 'Magazu does not try cases,' Frank says. 'He's too fine for that, for getting down there in the pit and doing actual fighting. What you need for this job is someone who'll break a sweat. Dave Reed out in San Francisco, maybe, or his partner, Carl Green. Cole Younger there, from Abilene, he is also good. Any of those guys come in, they will do good work. Cost a lot of money, maybe, but they'll give you value for it.'

"At this point, I had enough, these guys discussing me. There I am, right in the shit, and they're trading me like hog futures or some other damned thing. All that Nunzio wants from me is that I should reassure him. If I don't plead, and I lose, as I know I am going to, he will go to sleep at night, knowing I'm not talking. Other guys that work for him will not start to get nervous, thinking I am pleading because he has turned me loose. This is quite important to me, reassuring him. If he still feels good about me, he will not kill me. When Nunzio gets nervous, Jerry, and he thinks you are the reason, he does something about you, so that he feels good again. When you work for Nunzio, you keep that stuff in mind.

" 'Look,' I say, 'can I say something? I'm the sitting duck here. I don't want some asshole flying in here, all right? Getting a whole bunch of money to put on some goddamned show. In the first place, if we do that, this guy will not *win*. He *will* make the judge mad, and he'll add something for that. I know these guys are your friends, Frank, and I don't like saying this, but what I need here's a trial lawyer, not some damned showboat.

" 'Furthermore,' I say to them, on the speaker phone, 'anybody that I get, I am going to pay him. He gets paid by Nunzio, they'll bring it out in court. I did this for Nunzio, that I won't talk about. Nunzio paid for my lawyer—is that why I still won't talk? This is just another way, make more trouble for us. I don't think I want to give them so much help in this.'

" 'Aw right,' Frank said, 'you're the client. Who you got in mind?'

" 'Jerry Kennedy,' I say. 'He's tough and I trust him. He will go in and try the case, and he will hate to lose it. But he will not ham it up, and he'll do a good job for me.' "

"Just out of curiosity," I said, interrupting, "what did Frank say when you said that? How did he react?"

Lou gave me half of a grin. "Don't be so anxious, Jerry," he said. "I will come to that. Nunzio went through the ceiling; that was the first thing."

"Nunzio objected to me?" I said, somewhat startled. "What the hell brought that on? I don't even know the guy."

"You don't know Nunzio, maybe," Lou said, "but Nunzio knows you. He's heard all he needs to hear, or thinks he needs to hear, at least, of Jerry Kennedy. Ever wonder why it was you don't get Mob cases? That thought ever cross your mind, why they don't come to see you? Nunzio don't like you, Jerry. He does not trust you. He thinks Irish guys all work for the police. Mike Dunn's name on my indictment? That did not surprise him. What would have surprised him, maybe, was if Mike's last name was dago, but as far as Nunzio's concerned, all Irish guys are either cops or really wish they were."

"Frank Macdonald's Irish," I said, "and he works for Nunzio."

"Frank was the first one he hired, and the only one. And you know what Frank did when he got on the payroll? Every single chance he got, he tells Nunzio he's right. Frank Macdonald always told him: 'Don't trust other Irish guys. I'm the only one that's right. All the rest are cops.' " Lou studied me and laughed a little. "See what I am saying? All those times you used to tell me what a great guy Frank is? I was practically choking. He was playing you. Keep you quiet, out of sight, badmouth you if he had to. But at the same time, make sure you think he likes you. That way, maybe, you'll be useful, and he'll still get all the money. And until he had that goddamned heart attack, you have got to admit, Jerry, it worked pretty well."

"Son of a bitch," I said.

"Yeah," Lou said, "he is. Anyway, I'm solid on it. You are who I want. 'This is my case, and my hide. This is my time I'll be doing. Jerry knows me, I know Jerry. I am comfortable with him. Jerry will not screw me when it comes time for the fee, and that means I can pay Jerry without going into hock. Jerry can stall off this thing as long as anybody else can. Jerry's reputation's good, and he doesn't piss off judges.' Oh, you would've been proud of me, how I fought for you. It was almost as good, Jerry, as the way you fought for me."

"Son of a bitch," I repeated.

"You were right the first time," Lou said. "Now do you see what I am saying? You did not lose my case, Jerry, and you should stop thinking that. What you did was all I asked, all any man could do. Play for time and cut your losses, do the best you can. Miracles I don't expect. I'm not a Catholic."

21

OFFICER DEMETRIOS AGORAS of the Framingham Police Department was six feet seven inches tall, and very lean. His complexion was swarthy and his nose was long and pointed. His black hair was cropped short. He had an expression of eagerness to cooperate on his shining face, and he leaned forward expectantly in the witness chair to receive each question. His voice was incongruously high-pitched for so big a man, and it was difficult to keep from thinking of him as a very large dachshund as he lurched and trembled, yapping out replies. Don Di-Guglielmo took advantage of the fact that the clerk in the Stoughton District Court need not face the witness from his chair; he turned so that Officer Agoras could not see his face, and put his hand over his mouth to muffle sounds he made. I sat at the defense table and I did not have Don's option. Furthermore, when he laughed, I could see his shoulders shaking. This made it extremely hard for me to keep a straight face as I looked at Agoras, which is something that I try to do out of respect for people.

Assistant District Attorney Virginia Dwyer Fogel was a very earnest lady who was about five months pregnant. She was not a large woman and her condition was evident. She told me in the hall outside, when we were introduced, that Dwyer was her maiden name, which she had retained when she married "James L. Fogel, Esquire. Or, as you may know him now, James L. Dwyer Fogel. He is with the Shattuck firm, Shattuck, Kilburney and Mead." I said that I did not know the young man, under either name. "We are having twins," she said, beaming behind her oversized, pink-tinted glasses and wrinkling her nose. "Amniocentesis, you know? Make sure everything's all right." She patted her large tummy then, to show me just where it was that everything was fine. "I think that when a woman reaches my stage in life, you know, you can't exercise too much care, to be sure of things like that. Jimmy thinks that too," she said, becoming informal. " 'That old biological clock there,' he says, 'must make sure it hasn't stopped.' "

Ms. Dwyer Fogel was just as methodical when she was on her feet in court. She had Agoras on the stand to authenticate some photographs. These were eight-by-ten glossies, done in living color, of the face of Sergeant Earl Glennon as it had appeared to Officer Agoras in the Framingham Union Hospital on the day when Teddy punched it, almost three full weeks ago. Sergeant Glennon was young too, just like Agoras was, and he had done some healing since he called at Teddy's home. His face in the courtroom that day was only slightly disfigured; the cut that Teddy's signet ring had made on his upper lip was still slightly puffy and an angry shade of red. There was therefore a good reason to produce the photographs. They showed the yellows, purples, blues, and the unstitched gaping flesh where Teddy's fist had struck. There was, in other words, no reason to exclude those pictures from the evidence at trial. As Judge Norma Redmond had said when the officer was called up to the stand and she found out what it was that Ms. Dwyer Fogel had in mind for him to do to entertain us, they were certainly admissible, and quite material. But before Judge Redmond had a chance to ask if I would stipulate to letting them come in, Ms. Dwyer Fogel declared that she wanted no favors.

"Mister Kennedy," she said, with a reproving smile for me, "is well known in Norfolk County for his attitude toward courts. He is very, well, *demanding* of the judges who sit here. I have no desire to inquire whether he objects. I will present all my evidence and avoid that controversy."

I had watched the judge quite carefully while all that was being said. She was on a temporary reassignment from the Boston Municipal Court, filling in for the incumbent pompous white presiding judge who was down in Florida. Knowing him, not knowing her, I had preferred her, sight unseen. Once I saw her, middle thirties and a black, I had liked her even better—I don't think that a black judge will always disbelieve white cops, as though some sort of prisoner of the ghetto legend in which honky cops are the bad guys; what I do think is that a young and black judge from the hard-ass BMC is a lot better choice for a defendant charged with striking a policeman and on trial for doing it in the white suburbs. Judge Redmond might not quite approve of someone bopping cops, but she would not be shocked to hear that someone actually had done it.

"Mister Kennedy?" Judge Redmond said, when Ms. Dwyer Fogel finished. "Have you anything to say, or should I be watching you?" She was smiling when she said that, and I liked her attitude.

"Your Honor, please," I said, getting to my feet, "I can't say that I was aware of my own fearsome reputation. But if the district attorney wants to present all of her evidence, and do it by the numbers, far be it from me to object to the procedure."

"Mister Kennedy," the prosecutor said as I resumed my seat, "may have forgotten his exchange last month with Judge Dawes, but I can assure my brother that Judge Dawes has not forgotten."

I was halfway to my feet again when the judge motioned me to sit. "Madam District Attorney," she said wearily, "put your case in, if you please?"

The trouble with that mild instruction was Ms. Dwyer Fogel's lack of grasp of rules of evidence. All that she had to do with her enormous dachshund was determine whether he had seen the subject of the photographs on the day when he took them. If he had the brains to say yes, then she had to show the pictures to him, and ask him to look at them. Then when he was finished she would ask him what they were. He would say that they were pictures he had taken that day, and that they depicted Sergeant Glennon, front and profile, as he looked that day, fairly and accurately representing what he'd seen with his own eyes. Ms. Dwyer Fogel would then offer them as Commonwealth's exhibits, and I would not object because I'd have no grounds to do so. Nor would I have questions upon cross-examination. Or, as Judge Redmond had suggested, Ms. Dwyer Fogel could have asked me, while we were out in the hall, if I'd agree that the photos were admissible. I would have inspected them and said I did agree. Officer Agoras could have gone home without speaking.

Since she had not asked me, and would not allow the judge to, she was now in a position to display her ignorance. She was under the impression that she had to qualify her witness. Apparently she had the notion that he had to be an expert to take color pictures of a man who had been walloped in the mouth. We were learning that Officer Agoras was a student at Northeastern University, in his second year of studies leading to a B.S. degree in law enforcement and criminal justice. He had

had some training for his duties as photographer for the police department, and we were hearing all of that. I was pleased by all of this, but I was also nervous—behind me I could hear my client fidgeting and snorting.

Every time that Teddy Franklin has a case come up for trial in District Court, he tries to get out of it. "I'm a very busy man," he began, when I got him on the phone late in the afternoon the day before his case was scheduled. "These things waste my time. I got orders to fill, right? Guys that I've made promises to, and they have made promises. It's coming up on summertime, spring's on the way, you know? This is my busy season now, from now till Labor Day. Guys that did well in the market, guys that got tax refunds coming, guys that got new honeys they are taking on vacation and they would like to impress. These are careful shoppers, Jerry, guys that come to me. I am a good businessman. I can't be disappointing them."

"You disappoint the Stoughton District Court tomorrow, Teddy," I said, "and the judge who is sitting there will put out a nice bench warrant for your ass. You know this, pal of mine."

"I should be down in Providence tomorrow, Jerry," Teddy said. "My contact down there tells me that place is alive with units right now. I got this kid I am teaching, that he just gets out of school? He is with me and things go right, I can make a nice quota. This is costing me good money, Counselor, hacking around like this with you in courtrooms all the time. I told you, when this come up, let's just get it over. You say that I'm gonna lose? Okay, I'll take your word. All I want is the street. I can take the bust. You're the one that's all upset that I might get convicted. That's your record interests you, you have kept me clean. All that it does from my point of view is cost me lots of money."

"Speaking of which subject," I said, "glad you mentioned that."

"The minute I said that," Teddy said, as though addressing these remarks to a third person on the line, "the very minute those words left my mouth, I knew I stuck my foot in it."

"Well, after all," I said, "it has been a while, Teddy. Lots of thoughtful and reliable professional advice going out over the phone lines, keeping you out on the street, free to do your business, pass the time of day with cops from Framingham, bang the wife when the urge comes upon you."

"Less and less of that, I notice," Teddy said morosely. "You had any of that difficulty, Counselor, way I've been having recently? Takes you all night to do what you used to spend all night doing? Have to fit a nap in in the afternoon before the sergeant major will salute in bed that night?" He sighed. "I tell you, Jerry, it's depressing. Old stud like I'm getting to be, used to have a hard-on when I woke up in the morning, I could pole-vault to the bathroom on my own horn there. Now? Shit. Limp as overcooked linguine."

"Nice try, Teddy," I said. "This is March and they've started sending me the cheery letters from up there in Hanover, telling me about the Father's Weekends in the fall when all the leaves are gold and crimson and the Big Green's playing Penn. Or whoever the Big Green's playing this year. Few months go by, then the one that's got the bill inside it for the old tuition. Got to keep track of these things, you're a parent like I am."

"Well," Teddy said resentfully, "I'm not."

"True," I said. "What you are is an old and valued client who knows he can depend on me for the very best in top-notch legal advice. And does. Regularly. And you have by your own admission, Teddy, been having one gangbusters winter, you should pardon the expression."

"This is true," he said. He sighed again. "I'll see what I can do."

"It will be appreciated," I said.

"Which gets me back to why we do this," he said. "This District Court bullshit tomorrow, all right? Why are we going through this shit? I started thinking about this when you called me yesterday. It's just another dogshit trial. We go through all the motions. It goes against us, we end up appealing. Why bother? You padding the goddamned bills on me, two trials instead of one?"

"Hey," I said, "none of that shit, buddy. You and I both know you get your legal work from me for the same reason that your customers buy Cadillacs from you: you want the best and you've found out a guy who gives it to you cheap. No bullshit about that now, Theodore."

"Yeah," he said grudgingly, "I know."

"Ordinarily," I said, "we go through the District Court trial with the steno there to take it down because it locks the cops into their testimony before the real hotshots in the DA's office get their paws on all the witnesses for the real game in Superior."

"Which is another expense, damnit," Teddy said. "Goddamned stenos, two dollars a page and about ten words on them."

"Cheap at half the price," I said. "This time, though, I've got another reason, okay?"

"Which is?" Teddy said.

"This is a blivit you have handed me this time," I said. "Your classic five-pound load of shit in your basic two-pound bag. I ain't gonna win this here contest for you, Teddy, without being extremely lucky. Much luckier than you or I has any realistic reason to expect. Especially the way things have been going for me lately."

"That fucker set me up," Teddy said. "He come out to my house to see if he could get me going. He did that on purpose."

"And you nicely obliged him," I said, "you blazing rustic asshole. I can't give you an exact date, Teddy, but I'm certain that I must've told you somewhere along the line that you cannot go through this world bashing cops. It isn't wise. It leads to arrests, court cases, days lost out of your thriving business, and in this case, I fear very strongly, to conviction."

"He set me up," Teddy said again in anguish.

"I know he did," I said, "and that is not a defense."

"You mean to tell me that a jury," Teddy said, "a jury will sit there and hear about how this guy drove all the way out to my house and jerked my chain for me until I belted him, and then they will convict me for doing the exact same thing that any one of them would do if they did that to him?"

"If they listen to the judge," I said, "they will. Because the judge is gonna tell them it don't matter if somebody calls you a cunt-lapper to your face. You still cannot hit him."

"It's your job," Teddy said, "to make damned sure they don't do that, listen to the judge say that to them."

"And it's not a job I'm sure I can pull off," I said. "Jurors aren't supposed to let attorneys tell them to ignore what judges say. Judges do not always react patiently when they hear lawyers start to propose that sort of thing to jurors. When, as, and if I try it, that judge may land on my defenseless head and make me shut my mouth. Then what do we do, Mister Franklin? Utter fervent prayers?"

"It isn't fair," he said, "a guy can do that to you and you can't do shit to him."

"No, it isn't, Teddy," I said, "but it is the law."

"Shit on the law too," he said.

"That too, perhaps," I said. "But be that as it may, this is the way we're doing it. I want this case tried in Stoughton, where we will not have a jury. See how this dud works out there, what punishment you get. That's the very worst that happens when we lose it there—the judge in the District Court puts a ceiling on how much the next judge can do to you. So that gives us an idea when it comes up in Superior, and that's worth some inconvenience. That seem reasonable to you, my friend? We'll be out before eleven, I can almost guarantee you, and that isn't much to ask."

It was ten minutes past eleven when the photographs came in. I did not have any questions and I did not object to them. Ms. Dwyer Fogel then called Sergeant Earl Glennon to the stand. Judge Redmond, looking at her watch, suggested to the prosecutor that she get right to the heart of things. Ms. Dwyer Fogel appeared somewhat rattled by this, but by eleven-thirty we were on "the day in question." After some preliminary fumbling, Ms. Dwyer Fogel started to get conversations in. That made it the sergeant's turn to irritate the judge. He said that the defendant "used an expletive, Your Honor, when he referred to my official vehicle." He further testified that Teddy "used an expletive when he referred to his own house, and again when he had reference to his neighbors, Your Honor." He was small, and pale and righteous; Teddy had offended him.

Judge Redmond leaned toward Glennon and she said politely: "Was it the same expletive each time he used one, Sergeant?"

"Uh, yes, ma'm," Sergeant Glennon said in confusion. "Your Honor, I mean." I could hear Teddy snarling behind me, and I shushed him from the corner of my mouth.

"Referring, perhaps," she said, very meekly, "to the act of sexual intercourse?"

This made Sergeant Glennon very worried, and his face showed his concern. "Uh," he said, looking quickly toward Dwyer Fogel for assistance and not getting any, "yes, ma'm. Your Honor, that is. Ma'm."

She leaned back in her chair. "I thought that was probably the one," she said. "Court will take defendant's alleged choice of words into consideration in evaluating the evidence."

Both the cop and the prosecutor appeared to be rattled by that statement. He sat silently in the witness box, fidgeting a little in his chair and looking very worried. Ms. Dwyer Fogel stood there in her power suit of tweed, the jacket cut the same way mine was and the skirt tailored to accommodate her family condition, absolutely motionless. Teddy exhaled loudly behind me and the judge folded her hands at her waist. It seemed as though the silence extended for several minutes. Finally the judge said encouragingly: "Madam District Attorney?"

That appeared to snap the prosecutor out of her reverie. "Yes, Your Honor?" she said brightly, like some little kid who had just been called on to recite but did not know which poem was expected.

"Well," Judge Redmond said, leaning forward again and resting her elbows on her desk so as to enable her to rest her chin in her hands, "I was wondering: have you some more questions?"

"Yes," Dwyer Fogel said, "I do."

"Good," the judge said. "Good. Why don't you ask them, then? My guess is that if Mister Kennedy here is as combative as you'd have the Court believe, he is charging Mister Franklin by the hour for this case. Why don't we try to finish it sometime today, if we can, shall we?"

"Uh," Dwyer Fogel said, blushing, "certainly, Your Honor." She turned back to Glennon as though she had been a robot. "Officer Agoras," she said, smiling, "please tell us what happened then." Glennon opened his mouth, plainly not sure what she wanted: she nodded at him and sat down at the prosecution table, finished for the day. The cop, with his mouth open, stared at her and then at me. Neither of us helped him and he looked to Judge Redmond. "My name is Glennon, Judge," he said, as though he were offended. "The first guy, that took the pictures, he was Officer Agoras."

"I remember him, Sergeant," the judge said, smiling at him. "Your name is Earl Glennon," she said, looking at her notes.

"Yes," he said, "that's what it is."

"It's all right," the judge said to him, smiling mercifully. "We all understand who you are. You may testify. Tell us what else happened that day, who said what and to whom, and what other things you noticed."

The cop licked his lips and began, without looking at the prosecutor. He kept his eyes down as he talked, because he was shutting them to visualize his report he was not allowed to read. He had memorized it very well; he might as well have read it. What he said was just as stilted as the written words had made it. His concluding recitation was his first sign of human response. "I informed the defendant that my presence at his house was that I was engaged in the performance of official duties, which consisted of a full, and complete, investigation my department is conducting relative to several persons and in connection with the theft of certain motor vehicles. And that I was then and there engaged in a lawful surveillance of his dwelling place, and that I would be the sole judge of when it was to terminate. And he punched me in the mouth." Sergeant Glennon's voice was much louder at the end of his statement than it had been when he started out. He nodded twice, vigorously, and then settled back in the witness chair, straightening his sport coat around him, most likely nearly as indignant at the memory of what had happened as he had been on the afternoon when it had occurred. Assistant District Attorney Dwyer Fogel remained seated and silent at her table. Judge Redmond made notes on her pad at the bench. Don DiGuglielmo composed his features and returned to his normal position, facing the attorneys in the courtroom.

The judge finished writing. She looked up expectantly at Dwyer Fogel and grinned at her. "I assume, Madam District Attorney," she said, "that you have no further questions?" Dwyer Fogel seemed surprised that she would ask, and replied in a startled tone: "No, Your Honor, nothing more." She did not make any pretense of standing when she said that, which the judge noted silently. She looked at me. "Mister Kennedy?" she said, very pleasantly. "Do you, perhaps, have some questions for Sergeant Glennon here?"

Not being pregnant, I stood up before I answered her. "Yes, Your Honor," I said, "quite a few of them, in fact."

Judge Redmond nodded, pursing her lips. "I rather thought you would," she said. She wrote something on her note pad while she said: "Proceed."

"Sergeant Glennon," I said, "that expletive you mentioned: was it 'fuck,' or some variant thereof, that you had reference to?"

Sergeant Glennon's face showed alarm immediately. He glanced involuntarily at the judge, moistening his lips. She was busy writing something else in her notes of the trial, and did not meet his gaze. He looked at the prosecutor, flustered. She was no help either, sitting back in her chair with her hands folded in her lap.

"You understand the question, sir?" I said.

"Yes," Glennon said, now very nervous.

"Please answer it then, Sergeant," the judge said, without looking up from her writing.

"Yes," Glennon said, his voice somewhat firmer, his jaw setting to show disapproval of these tactics.

"The word was 'fuck' or a variant thereof?" I said.

"*Yes*," he said, annoyed, "I just told you that."

"Just answer the questions, Sergeant," Judge Redmond said, now folding her hands and gazing at him benevolently.

"Yes, Your Honor," he said.

"You testified that my client used that word," I said.

"Several times," Glennon said.

"Right," I said.

"No need for any colloquy with the witness, Counselor," the judge said pleasantly.

"Sorry, Your Honor," I said. "I was getting to my question."

"Proceed more directly to your questions, please," she said, very pleasant.

"Yes, Your Honor," I said. "Did you use that word yourself, Sergeant, during that discussion on the day in question?"

The question threw him. Anyone watching his face could have seen the emotions chasing one another across it. Obviously he had bandied obscenities quite capably with Theodore that day outside Teddy's house. He knew how preposterous he would sound if he denied it. But at the same time he was apparently too inexperienced to know that his admission of his full part in the slanging match would not harm his case in the slightest. I keep forgetting how police departments have changed in the years since I started practice. The emphasis on computerized record-keeping and communications has been reflected in the recruiting and promotion policies of the departments. This kid had made sergeant without acquiring any street savvy at all. He looked desperately at the prosecutor for guidance. She gave him no help whatsoever, either because she realized the question was not objectionable or because she was too new at the game herself to understand that he was floundering.

I said nothing. The judge cleared her throat. "Sergeant Glennon," she said gently, "do you understand the question?"

He gave her a pleading look. He wet his lips. He nodded.

"Then answer it, please," she said. She was still the soul of nice.

"I," he said to me, "I don't remember."

Judge Redmond leaned far back in her chair and tapped her front teeth thoughtfully with the eraser end of her pencil. She gazed at Sergeant Glennon with what was obviously amused incredulity. "Sergeant Glennon," I said, "did you have any trouble recalling whether Teddy Franklin uttered the word 'fuck' in several forms that day, when you testified on direct?"

Now he became defiant. "No," he said, and clamped his jaw shut on the word.

"Stuck firmly in your mind, did it not?" I said.

"Yes, sir," he said.

"But as to whether *you* said 'fuck,' " I said, "that's lost in the mists of memory?"

"Sir?" he said, slightly innocent, trying to stall.

"You cannot now recall whether you personally uttered the horrid word?" I said.

He licked his lips. He pondered the question from every angle he could think of. "No," he said.

"Okay," I said, "moving right along here, Sergeant, do you have any present memory of whether you used any other profane or obscene words that day, in your conversation with my client?"

The assistant DA stood up. Judge Redmond did not give her a chance to object. "Yes," the judge said patiently, "that is a little broad, Counselor. Could you rephrase the question? Put it a little more specifically?"

"Certainly, Your Honor," I said. "Sergeant Glennon, did you call the defendant a 'shithead' on the day in question?"

"No," Glennon said, in visible anguish.

I feigned great surprise. " 'No,' Sergeant?" I said. "You answer here today, you wish this court to believe, you did not call Teddy Franklin 'shithead' on the day in question?"

Glennon became sulky. "I'm not sure," he said.

"Well, Sergeant," I said, "which is it? You didn't call him 'shithead,' or you're not sure now whether you might in fact have called him 'shithead'?" I can't say that I take a great deal of pride in my ability to tie an inexperienced witness into a bowline knot, but it is sort of fun and I had not been having much of that lately.

"I'm not sure," Glennon said, still sulky.

"You might have?" I said.

"It's possible," he said.

"All right, Sergeant," I said, "let me ask you this: do you have any present memory of what your purpose was in visiting my client's house that day?"

Between the instant when I started that question and the one in which I completed it, Judge Redmond decided to conclude the entertainment. She may have remembered an important engagement elsewhere. She may have grown bored. I may have displayed just a smidgeon's excess of sadistic satisfaction in mistreating Sergeant Glennon. She interrupted me. Her voice was suddenly fatigued. "Mister Kennedy," she said, "not that I wish to break your train of thought, but are you by any means proposing to defend this matter on the grounds of fighting words?"

The correct answer to that question was: Yes. My answer was: "Not in precisely those terms, no, Your Honor. What I am trying to establish is that the sergeant's visit to my client's home that day was without actual, colorable, official purpose, and that accordingly he stood as any other citizen vis-à-vis my client that day."

"Meaning," she said, showing me just a little smile of transient complicity, "that if Sergeant Glennon here had just gone over to Mister Franklin's house on his day off and parked his own car right in front of it, Mister Franklin would have had a right to punch him?"

"Not exactly, Your Honor," I said. "Sergeant Glennon's complaint states the charge as one of A. and B. *on a police officer.* If he was not in fact acting in his capacity as a police officer, then . . ."

". . . Mister Franklin punched a private citizen," she said. "Is that it, Mister Kennedy?"

"Well," I said, "the Constitution does provide that the defendant is entitled to precise information of the charges against him."

"Noted," she said, grinning. She wrote something on her notebook. "Except for that line, do you have any other questions on cross for this witness?"

"No," I said, and sat down. Teddy hissed behind me. I turned my head to the left and muttered: "Shut up, all right? Just shut up."

"Thank you, Mister Kennedy," the judge said. "Madam District Attorney," she said, "do you have anything further on redirect?"

Startled, the assistant DA made it halfway to a standing position before saying: "No, Your Honor." The judge smiled and nodded to her also. This was a very even-handed court indeed. "Thank you," Judge Redmond said. "Sergeant Glennon, you may step down." Utterly bewildered, the cop sought silent assistance from the prosecutor, then from me, then from the judge, got none and got off the witness stand. "Is that the Commonwealth's case?" the judge said. The prosecutor merely nodded. The judge nodded back. "Commonwealth rests," she said, writing in her book. She looked up at me. "Has the defense any evidence?"

I heard and felt Teddy coming out of his chair like a lion behind me. I heard him whisper: "Tell her *yes*, goddamnit, Jerry."

"No," I said blandly. "The defense rests, Your Honor."

Teddy sounded like a faulty boiler valve behind me. "What?" he said.

The judge smirked as she wrote in her book. "Defense also rests," she said tidily, leaning back to admire the succinct entries she had made. She folded her hands and looked at each of us benignly. "The case does seem fairly clear-cut to the Court," she said. "Does the defendant wish to be heard?"

"No, Your Honor," I said, Teddy sputtering and grumbling behind me. "I agree with the Court's interpretation of the facts. The case is plain. I see no need for argument."

"Thank you, Mister Kennedy," she said. She beamed down on Dwyer Fogel. "Commonwealth?" she said.

The assistant DA stood up and straightened the skirt of her executive-cut suit for powerful and pregnant ladies and said: "Yes, if it please the Court." .

"Court is not pleased," Judge Redmond said benignly.

Dwyer Fogel faltered. "I'm sorry?" she said, leaning forward as though she feared her hearing had deceived her.

"Your remark seemed to inquire whether the Court would be pleased to hear argument from the Commonwealth," the judge said. "I thought you wanted information. I supplied it."

"I don't understand," Dwyer Fogel said.

"I don't want any argument," the judge said pleasantly. "I will listen to one, if you insist on making it, because that is your right. But I don't think in this case that it's necessary for you to exercise that right. Do you?"

The prosecutor frowned. "Well," she said, as though this had been a very difficult question, "no. No, I guess I don't."

"So," the judge said brightly, "the Commonwealth will not argue either, then?"

"I guess not," Dwyer Fogel said, and sat down again.

"Good," the judge said, and she scanned her notebook. "Court finds that the defendant, Edmund Franklin"—she looked up and smiled at Teddy—"did assault and beat one Earl Glennon, at Sharon, and as otherwise stated in the complaint of said Earl Glennon, and that said Earl Glennon was then and there a police officer engaged in the performance of his official duties." She nodded. Don DiGuglielmo, in the chair in front of her, pondered what she said and nodded too. "Clerk agrees," the judge said, smiling. "Court finds the defendant guilty."

Behind me, Teddy exhaled very loudly and uttered "*fuck*" in a hoarse whisper which would have carried easily from the right-field stands at Fenway Park to the ears of the second baseman. The judge worked her mouth and said: "Court also finds that the defendant Franklin employed expletives when conversing with the complaining officer." She looked at me brightly. "Now," she said, "as counsel is aware, I am temporarily assigned to this court, and when I am on such assignment it's my policy to dispose of all matters expeditiously, if possible on the same day that they are heard. Therefore, unless counsel for the defendant objects, I will save everyone some time and inconvenience by disposing of this case right now, without bothering with the formality of a probation report."

"No objection, Your Honor," I said, Teddy seething behind me. As I resumed my seat I growled at Teddy: "Shut up, for Christ sake. I know what I'm doing."

"Yeah," Teddy whispered too loudly, "and so do I, you shit—putting me in the fucking can."

The judge, indulging herself in another partially hidden grin, turned her attention to the prosecutor. "Has the Commonwealth a recommendation?"

"Yes, Your Honor," the assistant DA said, standing up again. "This is not a minor offense. The defendant knew the victim was a police officer well before he hit him. The evidence is plain that the victim's status as a police officer not only failed to deter the defendant from assaulting him, but was a factor in the defendant's motive to do so."

The judge arched her eyebrows at that. "Are you saying, Madam District Attorney, that Mister Franklin has a program of punching cops?"

"No," the prosecutor said. "What I am saying is that Sergeant Glennon's position as a police officer was a factor in the conduct of the defendant."

"It certainly was," the judge said. "It was a good deal of the provocation here, the way I view the evidence."

"But fighting words, as the Court said," the prosecutor began, looking pained, "are . . ."

"Not a defense," the judge finished for her, smiling. "Which is a good thing for the Commonwealth's case here today, because if they were a defense, Mister Franklin's would be pretty nearly airtight."

The prosecutor's face got red. "Be that as it may, Judge," she said, "the Commonwealth still views this as a serious offense. We recommend a sentence of one year in the House of Correction, to be served."

The judge nodded. "Thank you," she said briskly, and at once turned to me. "Defendant?"

"Yes, Your Honor," I said. "If the Commonwealth's sole witness had not been a police officer, this would have been a charge of making an affray. Then, had another police officer observed the altercation, Glennon would have also been arrested, along with Mister Franklin." The judge rewarded me with that small smile again, but did not say anything. "Since Glennon is a cop, though, instead of putting up his dukes, he flashed his badge. So instead of having two men in the dock for making damned fools of themselves in an otherwise quiet residential neighborhood, where the first of them had gone in the first place with the obvious if not avowed intention to make some sort of trouble and the other one was sitting quietly in his own home, we have only the one who was minding his own business and not bothering anybody when the cause of this whole ruckus arrived on the scene. This does not seem entirely fair to me." The judge smiled again, but still offered no comment. "If this then had been the situation I described," I said, "Earl Glennon being merely a private citizen showing up at Mister Franklin's house with no discernible purpose whatsoever except to see if he could not stir something up, my guess is that the Court would probably impose a fine of fifty dollars or so upon each of the participants and take the opportunity to tell Glennon to stay away from Franklin's house and stop trying to stir up trouble. I realize you can't fine Sergeant Glennon, since he brought the charges instead of being named in them. Still, in the interests of substantial justice, I would ask that you impose upon my client no greater penalty than he would have incurred had his provocateur not enjoyed his advantage in the altercation." I sat down.

"Thank you, Mister Kennedy," she said. "The defendant also has the right to be heard personally before I pronounce sentence. Does the defendant wish to say anything?"

"Yes, Your Honor," Teddy said behind me, murderously, nearly overturning his chair as he rose from it, "what I got to say . . ."

"No, Your Honor," I said fast, rolling out of my chair and seizing Teddy's left arm, "he does not."

Teddy glared at me and then back at the judge. "Your Honor," he said very loudly, "I . . ."

"Thank you, Mister Kennedy," she said. "And you also, Mister Franklin." She went back to the notebook, as though reading from her entries. "The Court, having heard the evidence, and the defendant Franklin having been found guilty thereon, orders that the defendant pay a fine of one hundred dollars, plus a surfine of twenty-five dollars, and costs of fifty dollars, for a total of one hundred and seventy-five dollars, and that he stand committed in lieu thereof until said fine and costs shall be paid or the defendant shall file his notice of intention to appeal. Are you getting this, Mister Clerk?"

"Yes, Your Honor," DiGuglielmo said, scrambling to collect his paper and pen, along with his idle wits. "Got it all down, every word."

"I," Teddy said loudly, "I still . . ."

I tightened my grip on Teddy's arm. "Defendant will discharge the fines forthwith," I said.

Judge Redmond stood up. "Thank you, Mister Kennedy," she said ironically. Then she turned toward Dwyer Fogel. "And thank you also, Madam Prosecutor, if I may say so." Dwyer Fogel sat there like a rock and said nothing. "Court will be in recess," the judge said, shaking her head. "Time for luncheon, happy campers."

"Thank you, Your Honor," I said.

"You're welcome, Mister Kennedy," she said, on her way off the bench. "I must say, though, it's been a while since you've defended one of two guys in a fight, I think. We're generally charging lots more than fifty bucks or so for that sort of behavior these days."

"Inflation has hit everything," I said.

"Ain't it the truth, though?" she said, and left the bench.

22

TEDDY MADE me go to Lucy's, which I do not like. Lucy's is a vast restaurant in Weymouth which suggests by its appearance that redwood and glass if properly combined will gradually metastasize upon the land, creating a great looming structure which will shelter hundreds while they eat. Thousands, maybe, now that I think about it. Its owners started it about a dozen years ago, hacking the location out of lowland swamps along Route 53, paving what they cleared and filled and putting up what's now no more than the command center for the whole complex. I pass by the place infrequently, but every time I do, it seems that there are large machines demolishing more swamp, laying more asphalt, and constructing new foundations to expand the joint some more. The theory of its operators, which certainly seems to be correct, is that if you serve a lot of food at a low price, assuring those who purchase it that it is finest Greek cuisine, and if you prepare alcoholic beverages in pint-sized containers, you will end up paving everything from Providence to Portland. My objection is that everyone who eats there seems to arrive and remain in a state of uniform high glee, which makes the joint extremely noisy. I also don't believe that when you serve me a martini in a glass the same size as a pail, everything inside that glass is booze. And I dislike feta cheese, which Lucy's sprinkles upon everything except the drinks—I think feta cheese resembles patent brand-name bait for surefire correction of stubborn rodent infestations. Teddy likes the food and says it is authentic. It's the place that I don't like.

"Shit, no," I therefore said to Teddy when he proposed that we meet at Lucy's, as we lingered after his conviction just outside the Stoughton District Court. "I've got to get back to my office, for Christ sake. This is Thursday. Gretchen's out. I've got a machine taking my calls, and I'm probably getting lots of them, from friends of Luther Dawes."

"Weymouth's sort of on the way," Teddy said resentfully. It is sort of on the way to Quincy, where Teddy has colleagues in business that I do not wish to know.

"Weymouth isn't on the way to anything for me," I said, "except extreme depression." I was in an edgy mood, despite the fact that I considered the outcome in Teddy's case an eminently satisfactory one. "I still haven't done my taxes, and I'm running out of March."

"Oh, bullshit," Teddy said, "don't give me that shit. You're too smart to do your own taxes, Jerry. You have got to eat lunch anyway, you know, just like Aunt Jemima said. It won't hurt you very much to humor me for once."

"Watch that honky mouth," I said. "We went in there on what amounts to a motion to discover, only a much better one than any papers could be. And instead we come out with a very big favor. That black lady just did you a very big kindness, without leaving any tracks."

"That's what she thinks," Teddy said, "so I know you do too. I happen to believe she overcharged me some, but if you will have lunch with me, I'll pretend it's okay."

"No," I said, "not good enough. If it was lobster thermidor that you were offering, and not some crazed Greek's version of a pizza, I would make the trip. It is not and so I won't."

"How about," Teddy said, "a Greek pizza, and a beer, plus which I will pay you."

"Are you going to pay me lots?" I said.

Teddy nodded. "A generous amount, Counselor," he said. "All of it in cash too, I might add, since we are talking taxes." Teddy thinks I cheat.

In the restaurant, which I know Teddy likes just because it is so crowded and so noisy that it would take a super-sleuth to eavesdrop on a customer, he fished from his inside pocket a white envelope containing a thick wad of money. It was sealed. I compressed it and it did not give much. "There is quite a lot of stuff in here," I said. He nodded. "Is it all singles?" I said. He shook his head. "My, my," I said, and put it in my pocket. "Your kindness is greatly appreciated, Mister Franklin," I said.

He appraised me. "Jerry," he said, "I known you a long time, all right?" I agreed with that proposition. "You give me a certain amount of shit," he said, "and I give you a certain amount of shit."

"In that department," I said, "I would have to say I think we're about even."

"So do I," he said. "Now what I would like to do is say something, all right?"

"Always has been," I said.

"I am a little worried about you lately, my friend," he said to me. He had an anxious expression. "I don't mean nothing by this, you know? But like I say, I known you a long time, and I haven't seen you like this, all these years that you been getting me out of the shit."

"I've been a little distracted," I said. It did not surprise me that Teddy had noticed I was off my feed slightly, and I must say I was touched by his concern. But the reason for it was not one which I relished sharing with him. There is a natural flow in the relationship between an attorney and a client, and it dictates that the delivery of advice always be from the attorney, to the client, at least when legal matters are involved. I might seek Teddy's advice on how to hot-wire a Coupe de Ville, but not on how to write a codicil. "Had some things on my mind."

"Which I figured," Teddy said, as the waitress brought us preposterously large schooners of beer. He did not resume talking until she had gone away. "At first," he said, "at first I think it is maybe something about your kid there, you know?"

"No," I said immediately, "Heather is fine. Absolutely fine."

He inclined his head and arched his eyebrows. "Well," he said, "I know that now, and that is nice and I am glad to hear it. But it was a possibility there, you know? She is still one of them damned teen-agers, and you always say what a honey she is getting to be, and then there is the stuff with drugs and older guys and all that other shit there that kids can get involved in, and she was down in Harwich Port, where you couldn't watch her and everything, so you can understand why I thought that. It was a natural thing to think."

I had not told Teddy that my daughter had a summer job on the Cape. My family and my clients do not meet or socialize with one another. Frank Macdonald gave me that advice a long time ago. The clients of a criminal defense lawyer are almost always criminals. They come to you in that condition and they remain in it after you have represented them. Relationships between lawyers and clients can turn rancid very fast. It is not good for clients to have too ready an idea of precisely where you are most vulnerable. Teddy was as close to me as any client I have ever had, but I had not discussed my family with him except to cite tuition bills when it was time to extract some money from him. I now regretted that. "Harwich Port?" I said innocently.

Teddy is not stupid. He knows when he has given something away which it might have been wiser to keep to himself. "Yeah, down the Cape there," he said uncomfortably.

"Teddy," I said, "just for my own curiosity, how did you secure that information?"

He became nervous and rearranged his tableware. "Well," he said, "that hotel there. The Outer Shoals, is it?" It was. "There is this friend of Dotty's, Carol, and the two of them are buddies, and Carol and her husband, Bruno, they were down there for a couple weeks. He's got about eight camera stores and they are loaded." He paused to see if that would do it. I said nothing so that he would see it didn't. "So they can afford to stay there," Teddy said. I remained silent. "Goddamned place costs all outdoors," he said. I did not speak. "Dotty was after me, rent one of them cottages that they got there, and I said: 'Well, what is it?' And she tells me it is a living room that they have got a couch that makes into a bed, and a fireplace, and a bedroom with a couple more beds, and a private bath. And I ask her what this costs and she tells me and I say: 'Holy Jesus,' all right? It was a lot." He stopped again. He got no help. "But like I say," he said, "Bruno's rich and he can probably afford it." He drank beer. I waited him out. He put the beer down and folded his hands. He stared at me.

"Interesting, Teddy," I said. "Not responsive, though."

"He was out the pool one day," Teddy said. "Strikes up a conversation with her."

"What was this conversation about, Teddy?" I said.

Teddy actually blushed. "I dunno," he said. He raised the schooner again and drank deeply. He finished all the beer before he finished being embarrassed. He put the empty schooner down. "The hell is that waitress, goddamnit," he said, looking around with feigned impatience.

"I think you do know," I said. "I'm beginning to think I know too. Spill it."

"Well, Jesus, Jerry," he said, very red. "I mean, after all, you told me yourself she is becoming a very good-looking woman, didn't you?"

"No," I said, "I didn't."

"No, huh?" he said. He looked down and examined his clasped hands. "Shit," he said, "I wish I never'd gotten into this."

"I might agree with you there also," I said, "but you did and now there isn't any backing out of it."

"No," he said, "I guess not." He spotted the waitress and got her attention. He pointed to his schooner and held up his finger for another. She acknowledged his order. This seemed to make him feel better. He was able to look me in the eye. "Look," he said, "all right? Bruno and Carol, them two go places together, but they are not with each other necessarily when they go to them, if you know what I mean. What they do is, they go down there in Bruno's boat, which he has got a big cabin cruiser. Thirty, forty feet, I guess it must be. And they check in the hotel and they put the boat in the harbor there, and Carol mostly stays at the hotel and Bruno mostly stays onna boat, all right? And they get along all right, doing this, which according to what Carol tells Dotty they've been doing for some time."

"I see," I said.

"Jerry," he said, almost pleading with me, "you have got to understand, all right? It's different, see? I think it must be different or something when you don't have kids. Me and Dotty, you know? It's not like we always see eye to eye on everything, okay? And we got out to Vegas, or down the Cape there for the weekend, and like last winter when she dragged me all the way to Honolulu, all right? I do that. I go. And so does she. And it's okay if it is just the two of us. But if we meet some other couple that we kind of like, and that likes us too, as far as that goes, or if maybe I just meet some broad and Dotty meets a guy and they are not together, and that is also all right. It doesn't mean anything, I guess is what I'm saying. Like everybody should get all upset about it afterwards. We been married a long time, and we are not divorced. And it's the same kind of thing there with Carol and Bruno, I guess."

"Bruno, in other words," I said, "was trying to pick up my daughter."

"Well," Teddy said, "yeah. That's about it, I would have to say. She is a fine-looking piece of . . ."

"Don't finish that, Edmund," I said. "I don't know why it makes a difference, since I already know what you were going to say, but it really would be better if it didn't get out on the record, all right?"

"Bruno said she is really something to look at," Teddy said. "And he is all embarrassed when he's telling me this, okay? Because apparently he told her quite a lot about him while she was finally getting around to mentioning to him who she is and who her father is, and Bruno recognized your name from hearing me talk about you, naturally, and he says to me: 'Jesus Christ, Ted, huh? I don't know what the shit to do. One minute there I am, I think this chick's really going for me and I'm gonna have her out on *Shutterbug* as soon as I can find out when her days off are, and Carol's already off somewhere with some guy she met in the bar at the Bellbuoy, and I know for a fact that lifeguards don't work after dark? This is gonna be like fuckin' *beautiful*. And this kid is gorgeous. And then I finally find out her last name, and she lets it drop by way of no harm who her fuckin' father is, and I am right here in the shit up to my fuckin' *eyeballs*. This is Jerry Kennedy's kid here that I'm picking up?' He did not know what to do."

"Just what did he do," I said, "not knowing and all?"

"Well, for Christ sake," Teddy said, "the fuck you think he did? In the first place, Bruno thinks if he scores with this kid and *I* find out, I will probably kill him. And then he starts to think how he told her all this stuff about himself, plus which she can find out who he is just by looking at the hotel register and everything, and if she tells you about him, you'll do something worse'n only killing him."

"I see," I said.

"Yeah," Teddy said, very uncomfortable.

"Just for the record, Teddy," I said, "what is Bruno's last name?"

He gazed at me as the waitress caused a time-out by delivering his second beer. There were small droplets of sweat on his upper lip. "The pizza will be right out," she said comfortingly.

"Thank you," I said, not averting my stare from Teddy, and she went away.

"Counselor," he said, "if something happened, and I mean this, I would give it to you, all right? Even though I know that you would probably do something like what got me into court this morning there for doing what I did to that cop. Okay? Because even though I don't have kids, something like that and I think I could understand it good enough so I would see how you would feel, and I would give it to you.

"But in this case, Jerry," he said, "I'm not gonna do that. Because nothing happened. I admit that Bruno did all that he could to make it happen, and it wasn't his fault that your daughter there said something so he didn't do it after all. That I don't argue with you. But still, nothing happened. So, I'm not gonna give it to you."

"I see," I said.

"And, Jerry," Teddy said, "all right? It's not like I am telling you how you should be a father. Because I have seen enough of you and how you go about that so I don't think you need some advice from me, okay? That's never even been one. But, and I mean this, my friend, this kid of yours is twenty years old or so there, and Bruno ain't the canine dog patrol guy there. He don't pick up mutts. So if he is interested, and he was really interested, this is not the first time some guy has been hitting on her, and it won't be the last."

"I realize that," I said. I do realize that. The realization is located totally inside my head. In my guts there is no realizing done. That was where I had churned up a boiling hatred for Bruno, whose last name Teddy was withholding. There was enough rationality remaining in my head to make me think that Teddy's decision was probably correct.

"And furthermore," Teddy said, "you should be glad of that. Because if she was a dog and guys did not consider doing things with her, she would not be happy and like she apparently is now. Okay?"

"Teddy," I said, "you have an unexplored genius for making an unpleasant reality seem like cause for gratitude. You should've been a politician."

"Yeah," he said skeptically. The waitress brought the two small-sized pizzas we had ordered, each of them adequate to sustain a whole Greek coastal village for a day or so. Mine was plain, as I had ordered it, so that it looked pretty much like a cheese pizza you would get from a franchise pizza shop: bland, undistinguished, and unlikely to cause digestive uproars. Teddy's was heaped high with peppers, small fishes, chunks of sausage meat, onion slices, olive bits, and what seemed to be the ubiquitous feta cheese. Using both hands to convey a piece to his mouth, so that its freight would not cause the crust to buckle, he said: "You're out of your mind, not getting yours like this."

"No, thank you," I said, tearing off a slice of my serving. "If I want to see something like that, I don't have to come to this place. All I have to do is shine a flashlight down the disposal to see what jammed it up full this time. I have done that enough, and had to put my hands down in it, to know I never want to put it in my mouth."

Teddy bit and chewed enthusiastically. He shook his head from side to side to show that it was hot in his mouth. He somehow contrived to pour beer in on top of what he'd taken. He swallowed and grinned at me. " 'S great," he said. "You oughta try it." I shook my head in refusal. "So, anyway," he said, looking serious again while planning his next attack on the pizza, "that is how I know it's not your daughter in college that is eating at you, all right? Because I *know* she is all right, so that can't be it."

My pizza was also hot. I contented myself with moving the seething cheese around in my mouth fast enough to avoid searing my palate. I too poured beer in to reduce the temperature, as soon as I could manage. I did not say anything.

Teddy took that as encouragement to continue. "If it was Mack, I decide," he said, "that you would have mentioned. You don't go around telling your troubles to just anybody," he said, "and I know that. But if it was Mack, you would have said something. You did not say nothing. It could not be Mack.

"I think of money next," he said. "Everybody needs dough, don't care who he is. Some guys need more dough'n others, sure. Play the ponies, can't pick ball games, chasing ladies, you name it. You don't do them things. Still you could need dough. Everybody needs it. Then you come right out and ask me for some dough. I think: 'This is it. Jerry's on some rough days getting paid by guys. Me among them, when you think about it. Got the kid in school there up at Dartmouth, all that money flying out the goddamned window for that fancy school? Case of the shorts, that is all it is.'

"So," Teddy said, pulling off another generous chunk of pizza and arranging it in his mouth so he could still talk around it, "I decide I will do the right thing by Jerry. And I got to admit that I have been having a good winter, so it doesn't exactly leave me with no money to give you that envelope, all right? And you know what is in my envelopes, which is always nothing but big ones. So, you pinch it there and you don't know exactly how many of them you got in there, but you know it isn't five or ten of them. As a matter of fact, Jerry, it is eighty of them, got it? Eighty big ones in that envelope."

I was somewhat embarrassed now myself. It's easy to forget, when you have earned the money and your clients have not inconvenienced themselves too much to pay you immediately, that it comes out of their pockets too. They do not initial some pink voucher which is then bucked down to Accounts Payable to cause some gnome to start up a computer that prints you a check, not when they are the sort of clients that I have. What Teddy Franklin pays me he first has to acquire, by himself. When he gives it to me, he can't spend it on himself, and he knows where it went. It does not hurt to make some show of proper gratitude. This man takes risks to get what he pays me.

"I meant it when I said that I appreciated it, Teddy," I said. "You've been a good client for a lot of years now. The fact that we've been able to trust each other as we have, as long as we have, that means a lot to me. I ought to say so now and then."

"Ahh," he said, dismissing that with his hand as he basked in hearing it, "it's not like you didn't earn it, all right? And you didn't bug me for it either, which I happen to appreciate.

"But what I am saying," he said, "is: I watched you take that package. And I see you pinch it there. And I know you got a good idea of what is in it. And I can see that it don't solve your problem." He leaned back and yanked a new piece of pizza from his serving. He licked his fingers. He stared at me. "I don't mean you weren't glad to get it," he said. "Don't mean that at all. But I do know you can't fix what's on your mind with what is in that envelope. And I know there is something on your mind. Because you said it yourself: you have been distracted about something."

"Teddy," I said, "I am sorry. I thought I was concealing it better."

He used the traffic cop's stop gesture on me that I have used in his behalf so many times in court, when some witness is embarking on a long and unpermitted speech which we don't want the judge or jury to take in. "Don't get me wrong," he said. "I'm not, it's not like I didn't think you weren't doing good work. I seen you there this morning with that nigger lady there, and I'm not shitting you about this, all right? If you would've let me do what I wanted in there today, I would have screwed it up so bad nobody could've made it right again. And I know that. But even while I'm giving you a hard time there, that goddamned cop is up there with his expletives and all that shit, even while I'm getting mad, all right? I can see that you are playing this broad like she was a violin. And you are doing this at the same time when I am doing everything I can to ball you up in the process. Now," he said, gesturing with the pizza, "that is the work of a true artist, Jeremiah. Watching that and seeing how it goes on there, that is something which a man would tell his grandchildren, all right. I hear all this bullshit about how great Frank Macdonald and them guys, Ed Maguire there that used to be his partner, all of them. How great they were when they had their shit in order and they didn't drink themselves to death yet or decide they'd rather be the judge and just goof off all day, and I know they were good. But I tell you, my friend, and I mean this, all right? And I am saying this *after* I have had the pain of paying for it too, you ought to keep in mind. You are the best that there is. There is nobody in plain sight who is better on your side when you are in the shit than Jerry Kennedy. Nobody." He shoved the pizza into his mouth and bit off an enormous chunk. He talked with his mouth full of it, nodding at the same time and reaching for the beer. "I have told guys this," he said. "Lots of guys I have told it to."

"I know this," I said. I was really touched. Teddy has sent me a lot of business, and many people he's referred to me have told me afterwards how energetically he has promoted me. "I know it and I thank you."

He shook his head again, his cheeks bulging with that disgusting garbage he was eating. " 'S all right," he said. "Think nothing of it, all right? Just the truth, is all. And when you are distracted, like you say, and like I know you were today, it doesn't mean you haven't got your full mind on the job. That isn't what I mean.

"What I mean," he said, swallowing, "is that we been together a long time, all right? We're friends too, Jerry, see? You act like this and I say to myself: 'My friend is worried about something. When I am worried about something, I can tell him what it is and he will do something to help me. If I find out what it is, I can tell him what I know and then maybe I can help him.' So I try to do that, and as I just got finished telling you, I see I didn't succeed at it. I did not find out what's on your mind."

I did not say anything.

"Therefore," Teddy said, "you have got to tell me now. Because I did not find out, the ways I tried."

"Teddy," I said, trying to clear my throat of an obstruction which seemed suddenly to have sprung up in it.

"No," he said, shaking his head, "don't do that. Don't give me some song and dance now that it's private business and you will work it out. I know that it's private business. I know you haven't worked it out. You must therefore need some help for that, and if you could've found it, you would have. Which means you cannot find this help that you need. Maybe I can. Maybe I cannot, but I know some guys who can. Maybe I don't even know that, but the guys I know, they will know somebody.

You would help me, Jerry. It will hurt my feelings if you sit there and you won't let me help you. You will insult me if you do that, and you are not the type of guy that does that to his friends."

"I try not to be," I said.

"So," Teddy said, "since you're not that type of guy, and you're not saying anything, I have got to think that I am wrong, is that right? And that everything's okay with you, and nothing's out of whack. Because otherwise, as we agree, you would tell it to me."

"Yes," I said, "that's right."

That afternoon, for the first time, I heard of Malcolm Wainer.

23

MALCOLM WAINER entered my life by sticking his business card in the crack between the frame and the locked door into my office. This is a common practice which does not impress me much. It is popular among persons who wish to take just a few minutes of my valuable time, as they always put it, to explain to me how much I need complete sets of decisions by the Alaska Supreme Court, or other costly merchandise equally certain to cause me to wonder greatly, once I've used it for a while, how I ever managed to perform my work without it. People selling photographs in plastic driftwood frames; people selling stationery "just as good as what Shreve's sells"; people who want contributions for sick, tired, and wounded cops; people who intend to share their close friendship with Jesus; it is not just wealthy clients who arrive to find us out, and everyone thus disappointed always makes sure to return. Therefore my customary action, on receipt of calling cards, is to collect them and drop them onto Gretchen's desk blotter, on the off chance that there is one from someone she wants to see. I did notice, I admit, *Internal Revenue Service, Department of the Treasury*, on Malcolm Wainer's dropping, and those hateful words did cause me to make mental note of his name. But that was all I did, as I told Mack that night.

"Did it say that you should call him?" she said, looking worried.

"Might've," I said, "I'm not sure. That was not why I was there. I went back in town from lunch to get my calls off the machine. I did not haul my ass in there to spend what was left of my fool day calling up the IRS to ask for trouble, damnit. There were three calls from Jack Rowley on that goddamned magic box. First one was supercilious; the second one was snide. The third one sounded quite a lot like a small threat to me. 'This is my third try to reach you, Mister Kennedy. I am doing my best to give you a chance to comment. Judge Dawes and his supporters have been very candid with us. They claim his rejection was in large part due to you. If you do not wish to comment, that is your privilege. But if you do, you've got to call me, or I'll have to say you didn't.' "

"Oh my God," Mack said, "this too? I think I'll have some wine. I was thinking I'd go on a diet, but I'll wait another night."

"What you mean: 'this too'?" I said. "Ace started banging Diane too, did you find out?"

"No, no," Mack said, at the refrigerator, "I go second tonight. Start with what went on with you. Then we'll get to me."

"Rowley was straightforward," I said. "He has got Frank's list. He reads just as well as I do, if it's something that simple. He looked at all those eighteen names that dislike Luther Dawes, and so did Luther, I guess. Frank's and my name were familiar, or at least the most familiar. 'I called Frank Macdonald's office,' Rowley said when I called back. 'They told me he was not in, and they did not expect him. I asked where I could call him and they refused to tell me. I was able to reach David Reed and this Attorney Reo, as he's called, but neither of them seems to know much about the specifics of Judge Dawes's nomination. Mister Reo said he's never even been in Massachusetts, when we talked.' "

"What did you say?" Mack said, looking very worried.

"I gave him some lip," I said, feeling very tired. "Told him: far as I knew, that is probably the truth."

"Was that smart?" she said.

"No," I said, drinking vodka, "that was probably not smart. But his attitude annoyed me, you know? Attitude, and tone. Sounded like he'd caught me flashing on the Common. Here he'd called me, hadn't he? And I called him back. I admit, he called three times, and that probably irritated him. But am I supposed to sit there in my office all day, waiting for Jack Rowley's call? And where the hell does he get his authority, trying to bully me? Nothing but a law school dud that didn't pass the bar. Who the fuck does he think he is, sounding like a prosecutor?"

"He thinks he is someone with a television camera," she said. "One that he thinks he can use to make a fool of you."

"Well," I said, "he is that, and he's very likely right. But that does not mean I'll kowtow while he does it. 'All right,' he says, very prissy, 'then let's hear your statement on this. We have from the governor the statement that's in question. His office has declined comment on it beyond that it was influential in the governor's decision. Sixteen of the eighteen names are not from Massachusetts. Frank Macdonald can't be reached. What have you got to say on this?'

" 'On what?' I said. 'Where the listed people live? How the governor reacted? How come His Excellency won't comment? Statement about what, Mister Rowley, if you please?'

" 'Tell us,' he says, and he's getting mad by now, 'whether you in fact did sign the statement that the governor released.'

" 'Oh,' I said, 'just that? Well, that is pretty easy, and no cause to get upset. Yes, I did permit my name to be used on that statement.'

"He apparently believed this was a big admission. Really started boring in, now that he had that. 'And did you, in fact, Mister Kennedy, endorse the views in it?' 'That Judge Dawes is unfit, Mister Rowley? Yes, I did.' 'And do you in fact, Mister Kennedy, think that he's unfit?' 'You mean, Mister Rowley,' I said, 'am I going to back down now? No, I haven't changed my mind. I thought Luther Dawes was unfit for the place on the Appeals Court when I subscribed to that statement, and I doubt that he's improved much since it became public knowledge.'

"That sort of slowed him down," I said. "Wasn't what he wanted, or maybe what he expected? 'Mister Kennedy,' he said, 'let me ask you this: you seem like an unusually forthright person, with the courage of your convictions. I am doing a special report on the entire Dawes nomination, getting statements from him and a number of other people who are willing to adopt positions on this public issue. I wonder if you'd be willing to come by the studio. Sit down with us and say what you think about it, with the cameras running. Because so far in this whole investigation, you're the only person who's been willing to be quoted on his opposition to the judge.' "

"Dear sweet Jesus," Mack said, "what did you say, Jerry?"

"Told him that I wouldn't, naturally," I said. " 'I'm not a performer, Jack, and I have witnesses. Not that kind of a performer, at least, and I know it. I've got no objection to your quoting what I say. Go ahead and use it, for whatever it is worth. But go in to the studio and beat my gums about it? I don't think I want to do that, though I do appreciate you asking.'

"Then he starts to beg and plead," I said with some satisfaction. "Much crap about my civic duty, make sure all sides are heard. This is an important story. Has far-reaching implications. Is the governor a weakling? Was he swayed by women's groups? What does this say about the way that we select our judges? 'Nothing doing,' I say, 'I'm not going to get involved. When I signed that thing, I thought it was a confidential paper. My name would be one of several that opposed Judge Dawes's candidacy, and that's all I had in mind. If you're asking, I regret that the statement was made public. I don't think it should have been, but I wasn't asked.'

" 'Oh,' he says, and acts surprised, 'you didn't expect this? That your name would become public, with the other names?' 'No,' I said, 'I really didn't, and I'm sorry that it did. I regarded this as a purely private matter. I was making my opinion known to the governor. What influence it might have on him, that was up to him. If it had some, that was fine, and if it didn't, same thing. I had no desire to embarrass Judge Dawes publicly, and I am sorry that that has occurred. If it has occurred in fact.' And that was it," I said.

"Did Rowley say when this report would be on?" Mack said. "I think you should watch it."

"Yeah," I said, "tomorrow night. Starting at six o'clock. On the six o'clock news, I mean. Sometime during that." Then I told her about Teddy, his good trial and that he paid me. "On balance, I think," I said, "a passably good day. I've grossed nineteen K this month, and that is eating money. Haven't quite accomplished what I wanted for my clients, but I did come close with Teddy and Lou isn't mad at me. Now if my druggie friend turns up, gets hooked for jumping bail, I'll relieve him of another grand and make it an even twenty. Ten months out of twelve like this? I could stand that duty. This keeps up until October, I might buy one of those condo shares."

"Yeah," she said grimly, "that would be great, all right."

"Mack," I said, "for Christ sake, all right? Let me out of jail. I realize you're still pissed off, and so am I, for that matter. But isn't three days long enough to sniff at one another? Can't we at least pretend we're friends, even though I'm mad at Heather?"

She let out this great big sigh and shook her head a few times. "Jerry, Jerry," she said, "it's just not that simple.

"Heather's called me three times since you talked the other night. It was six a.m. out there when she called the first time, and you know just as well as I do how she hates to wake up early. Poor kid said she hadn't slept a single wink all night. She broke down a couple times while she was talking to me. 'What is it with Dad?' she said, time and time again. 'What's Dad doing, acting like this? Why does he hate me?' "

"I don't hate the kid, for Christ sake," I said. "What is all this crap? I'm not pissed off 'cause I hate her—I'm mad because I love her. Love her, and I'm upset at the way that she is living. Upset also at myself, because I don't know how to stop her. This is hatred, for God's sake? Something's backwards here, I think, and I don't think it's me."

Mack nodded two or three times and exhaled very loudly. "Jerry," she said, "spare me, all right? I know all you're going to say. I know also all the things that Heather's got to say. I have heard you on the subject and I've heard her on it too. I don't know what to tell the kid, and I don't know what to say to you. Until I think of something, I guess, that's how things will stand. But I will tell you, Jerry, it is perfect hell for me. When I'm home, you're sulking at me. Go to work, and she calls up. Day and night I'm getting it. I don't get any rest. I can't tell her you are wrong—I know you're sincere. I can't tell you she is wrong—that just isn't what I think." Mack put her head way back and closed her eyes for a moment. Then she brought it forward again, shaking it as her eyes opened. "I don't know what to do about this," she said like a puzzled child. She chewed at her lower lip. "I've thought about it and I've thought about it, and I've had three headaches which I think I will re-member always, if I live till I am ninety. But I have not come up with anything that I think might really help." She looked at me sadly. "This is coming out of my hide, Jerry. I hope you can understand that."

"Well," I said, ever the soul of Christian compassion, "that certainly takes the wind out of my sails. For several minutes there I was actually feeling reasonably good about the way things had been going. Little friction with the daughter, maybe, but I'm convinced I'm right on that, just as you have said. Little sand between the sheets of the old marriage bed, perhaps, but nothing that an oyster could make a decent pearl from. Made a little money; got a good result for Teddy: Lou Schwartz isn't pissed at me even though he's doing time: you got to forgive me, sweetheart, but I thought things were looking up. Must be getting overconfident, in my twilight years."

Mack just sat and stared at me. Her shoulders were slumping. She cleared her throat twice but did not dispel her huskiness. "Jerry," she said, "listen to me. I know this is hard for you, but you have got to listen."

"I am listening," I said.

"Francine came in from Accounting this morning," she said. "She had my records with her. This came as a surprise to me. We'd blocked out an hour next week for my taxes. Not much to do on them anyway, of course—we did all the scut work back in January, when I brought my estimated payments for last year up to the eighty percent requirement. Just a matter next week of going over the completed returns and signing about four more checks to cover everything. Painful as hell, maybe, but not complicated.

" 'Francine,' I said, 'what is this? You are coming in a week early to remind me that I'm getting murdered? This I knew.' "

"You are getting murdered?" I said. "*You* are getting murdered? You've got the real estate taxes and the mortgage interest on both houses to deduct, and you tell me that you are catching it in the throat? My heart goes out to you, Mack. It really, truly does."

"Jerry," she said levelly, "I asked you to listen. I do not have overhead, office, and salary to Gretchen that I can deduct. I am paying this year, for the year I just went through, almost thirty thousand dollars, once they add on that goddamned self-employment tax. I call that getting murdered. I bet you're not paying that much, and anyway, goddamnit, I thought we were partners."

"I don't know yet what I am paying," I said, but she didn't seem to hear me.

" 'Murdered,' Francine says, 'that is what they all say. You can say something from now on that is much worse than being murdered. You are being audited.' "

"Oh good Lord," I said.

" 'Oh good Lord' is right," she said. " 'Books and records, all receipts, anything that will support the statements you have made. Get them all together and get your ass down to our office.' That was Francine's tidy way of putting it. So, a week from Monday, I am going in to chat. I am not going to like this, Jerry. I'm sure it will cost me money."

"Is Francine going with you?" I said.

"Yes," Mack said, "of course. She prepared the damned return. She is on it, Jerry. You don't think I'd go in there by myself, do you, lover?"

"Look, Mack," I said, "no offense, but the sarcasm isn't needed. Is Francine a lawyer these days? Passed a bar exam?"

"You don't need it," she said. "I don't need it either. Francine's a tax accountant, Jerry. She has taken courses. She has her B.S. in this crap. She knows what she is doing."

"Okay, okay," I said, "pardon me for breathing. I think you'd be better off if you had a lawyer. Accountants are good with figures, putting things on paper. Lawyers are the ones that get trained to conduct negotiations. You should have a lawyer with you to protect your gorgeous ass."

"Uh-huh," she said, "sure I should. Why, does Lou Schwartz need company?"

We did not speak one word to each other for the rest of the evening.

24

TAX RETURNS and seedy clients are good resources to fall back on when you wake up on an April Fools' Day with a bad hangover and the rancid recollection of a mean fight with your wife. That is one advantage to the kind of practice I have: no matter how low-down and dirty I may feel, how dog-eared and stupid my soul is when I get to work, what I have to do in my job almost always brings me into contact with someone who is more discouraged than I've managed to become, or something that's so tedious and disagreeable that a good mood would be wasted on it. "Gretchen," I said when I arrived at the office, "pull the records for the past year and get me my tax returns. Might as well get that crap done before I have to."

Gretchen, looking somewhat startled, nodded toward the couch. "Mister Beal is waiting for you," she said. "He has an appointment. His case file is on your desk."

Calvin Beal was my client who was charged with beating his wife. For the merest instant I considered asking him for a few pointers, but I put that raw idea aside and told him to come in. He did not look any better than he had when I first saw him in the Quincy District Court, except for the fact that he was not wearing handcuffs. His file said that he was twenty-eight years old, and his appearance said that he was sneaky-dangerous. He was about five-ten or so and weighed about one-fifty. He had greasy black hair and a moustache that needed trimming. His eyes were very bloodshot and his clothes were not too clean: maroon plaid shirt without a necktie and a maroon sport coat with a silver thread in it, chino pants that were quite rumpled and a pair of work-man's boots. He looked like a small animal that had been hit a lot, and had turned vicious under all the punishment.

"Mister Beal," I said as I sat down at my desk, "no new troubles since we saw each other, down in District Court?" This was Calvin's maiden voyage through the mills of justice, which to me meant only that he had not been caught before, and not that he had led a life beyond reproach until this great misfortune. Rookies in the justice system sometimes fail to make connections; it does not occur to them to tell their lawyers if they've been arrested for some new crime since they were accused of the first one, and that information can have great importance. Further-more, the rookies often bloom into repeat offenders after they're first caught—the cops then recognize them and give them less latitude.

Beal thought about my question long enough to make me wonder if he was making up some lie. "No," he said, "I don't think so. Nothing you could help."

"Let me be the judge of that," I said paternally. "Sometimes there is something I can do, make things a little easier."

He turned his head a little, so that he could watch me from the cor-ners of his eyes. He tilted it as though he were a dog alert to determine whether it was going to get a scrap from the dinner table or a sharp cuff on the ear. He snuffled twice and swallowed. "I dunno," he said. "I doubt it. You were there that day the judge threw me out." The judge in the Quincy court had conditioned Beal's release on bail on his "un-dertaking not to return, and to remain away from, the marital domicile under any circumstances, or for any purposes, until this case shall be tried." Calvin had asked in a whiny voice if that meant he could not go home. The judge said it meant exactly that. I had tried to shush Calvin, seeing that as the first step in a possible effort on my part to intervene in the proceedings. Calvin had turned to me impatiently and said: "No, you shut up, Mister Kenefick." Then he addressed the judge indignantly and said that all his clothes were in the apartment in Hough's Neck where the police had arrested him on his wife's complaint, and that his three kids lived there. He patted the lapels of his maroon jacket and asked if the judge meant that he could not go home to get other clothes. The judge told him that indeed he could go home for his clothes, if that was what he chose to do, but that he would be arrested if he did so and would await his trial in jail. "You didn't," Beal said to me in my office, pronouncing *didn't* as *dint*, "you didn't do nothing for me then, it seemed like, so I could get my clothes or something. You didn't even try to do something then. You didn't say anything, or anything."

"In the first place, Calvin," I said, "you did not give me a chance. You were doing all the talking that day, on that issue. If you had been willing to let me do the talking on your side of things, I would have tried to secure the judge's permission for some member of your family, or a friend of yours, to call at your apartment for your clothes. The judge would not have been obliged to permit that, but he might have. That is, he might've if you hadn't first seen fit to piss him off. After you got through yelling at him, there was very little to be gained from having me address him."

"Well," Calvin said, "you didn't, though. You still didn't do anything."

"Calvin," I said, "this is a cruel world. Almost all the judges in it, when they get A. and B. cases, try to separate the defendants from the victims until everyone's cooled down. That's why it is best, if you want to batter someone, to pick someone who does not live in your house. Because if you decide to beat up someone in your house, you are very likely to be put out in the world without shelter or possessions until you've been tried. Where are you living? With your parents?" Calvin's parents lived in Randolph, where his father is a house painter. Calvin's father had called me, and paid me, when Calvin was arrested.

"No," Calvin said morosely, "not in with my parents. Me and Pops don't get along together too good."

"Well, then, Calvin," I said, "where have you been living? In a tree or something? It's been cold and we've had rain. You must've slept indoors."

"I was with Irene," he said. "Me and Irene, I was staying with her. At her place in Whitman."

Irene was a waitress at an Italian restaurant in Quincy, and the arguable cause for Calvin's awkward situation. Calvin had been working with his father on a small job of interior renovation at the restaurant, and had struck up an acquaintance with Irene. Calvin's wife, Janet, had caught wind of this new friendship and had objected to it. She had also disapproved of Calvin's late hours, which she suspected him of sharing with Irene. Janet was a short but still fairly large young woman, four years older than her husband and a good thirty pounds heavier than he was. She could holler pretty loud, from what Calvin told me, and she had been doing that the night he was accused of hitting her. "That may not have been the best idea you could have had," I said. "Staying with Irene."

"You mean," Calvin said, "because Janet don't like her?"

"Yes," I said, "I do. That's exactly what I mean."

"Well," Calvin said, "I don't care what Janet thinks. What are you anyway, on her side or something now? Janet's side, I mean? You gonna sit there and tell me I shouldn't see Irene?"

"Calvin," I said, "look, all right? I am your trial lawyer. Your criminal trial lawyer. All I want to do is try your case for the best result possible. The chief witness against you is your devoted wife, Janet. Janet got you riled enough so that you decided to deck Janet. Janet called the cops and got you clapped in irons. Janet's complaint was the reason that the judge threw you out of your own house. That judge and those cops you see as your enemies, they don't give a shit about you, Calvin, all right? Until Janet called them they did not even know you, and they didn't want to, either. It would be all right with them now if they could forget you. If when your trial date comes up the end of next week, they can tell each other that it's okay to forget you, they will be more than pleased to do that very thing.

"Janet is the key to that. Do you understand that, Calvin? If the two of us go in there next week and we find out that Janet has cooled off a little since you belted Janet, she might decide: 'What the hell—I'll let bygones go.' She would tell this to the cops, and then she'd tell the judge. The judge would give you a stern lecture and then he'd let you go. No convictions, no nice fines, no thirty days in jail. Wouldn't that be nice, Calvin, if all of those things happened?"

"I don't understand," Calvin said suspiciously. "How you going to do all this, make all that stuff happen?"

"I'm not, Calvin," I said. "I can't, as you've probably suspected. All I can do is hope that Janet, on her own, decides that that is the way to go. Then, if she acts like she might withdraw her complaint, I can go to work and see if maybe I can persuade the judge to let you go with a good tongue-lashing. Which is not what I would call a lot of fun, standing there and letting the judge chew you out, but easier to bear than a short stretch in the pokey.

"The thing of it is, Calvin," I said, "you living with Irene while you wait for this case to come up, that was not a hot idea. Janet . . . does she know where you are living?"

"How could she know?" Calvin said. "I didn't see Janet. I didn't talk to Janet. Judge said if I had something to do with Janet, he would put me in the can. So I didn't."

"Let me ask you something, Calvin," I said. "How did Janet find out you and Irene were sweeties in the first place?"

Calvin shrugged. "I dunno," he said. "I guess somebody must've told her or something. My mother, probably. Her and my mother get along good. It was probably my mother."

"How would your mother get the information?" I said. "She work on the painting crew with you and your old man?"

"Nah," Calvin said, contemptuous of me. "Pops would've told her there, I was getting some. Her and Pops don't get along that good themselves. He was always doing things, I was growing up. That would be something, me and Irene, Pops would say to her to jerk her chain some, he didn't have something else to do that night or something."

"I assume Pops knows where you've been living," I said.

"With Irene, you mean," he said.

"Yeah," I said, "with Irene, I mean. I assume your father knows that."

"Well," Calvin said, "yeah, I would say he does. Pops, I mean, I have been working, and he knows I don't sleep there. And he seen me come in with Irene when I get there in the morning and she's going to her other job there that she has, at the day-care center."

"Irene's a busy lady," I said.

"Yeah," Calvin said, "she does that. See, if she works there in the morning like that, she can leave her two kids there for the whole day, and they don't charge her nothing."

"Well," I said, "that would make a difference, of course."

"Yeah," Calvin said.

"So," I said, "we can conclude that your father knows where you are living, and that probably means that your mother also knows. Which means that, in all likelihood, Janet also knows."

"Yeah," Calvin said, pondering that. "I think that is right. Janet prolly knows where I am living now, I guess."

"And," I said, "since she was mad before about Irene, when she had much less reason, we can also assume that she's probably even madder now."

"Well," Calvin said, "yeah. Probably."

"Which means," I said, "that it isn't very likely that come Thursday morning, Janet will come in to District Court and say to the judge that she wants to let you off the hook there, would you say?"

"No," Calvin said, looking very puzzled, "now that you say it that way."

"Which means," I said, "that we'll have to make a choice then. Either we will go to trial, or you will plead guilty. Neither of which strategies looks very promising."

"I don't understand," he said.

"Calvin," I said, "listen up. Hitting your wife isn't the accepted thing these days. Used to be you belted her, and someone called the cops. They walked you around the block, one stayed and talked to her. Second time it happened, they might take you down to the station, but by morning it was okay and they let you go again.

"Now," I said, "it's a big scandal. Everyone's upset. Women's groups and newspapers, raising bloody murder. Crisis centers they can go to, all kinds of excitement. Battered wives are the new thing—very popular.

"Batterers are different, Calvin," I said patiently. "Guys who hit their wives now—they're not popular. People say mean things about them, call them nasty names. See them in the courthouse and they want to punish them. You are one of those outcasts. Do you understand me? Somebody that hits his wife, a defenseless woman."

"Yeah," Calvin said, looking very worried.

"Now they want your scalp," I said. "And now they often get it."

"Yeah," Calvin said. "You mean the newspapers and stuff."

"Correct," I said. "So, we must analyze this carefully, see what we can do."

"Yeah," Calvin said, crossing his legs and beginning to look interested.

"Okay," I said, "you are on the stand, up there telling the judge and the people in the courtroom why it was you hit her."

"You mean," Calvin said, "admit it? Get up there and say I did it, just like Janet says?"

"Well," I said, "didn't you?"

"Yeah," Calvin said, "I did. But so what, huh? I get up there, say I did it, they will do what you said. Come around and cut my balls off."

"Calvin," I said, "you'll be under oath. They will believe her. She had marks on her face when I saw her. They will definitely decide one of you is lying, and it will not be Janet that they will decide's the one."

"Well," he said, "then I lose. Why do I need you then, if I'm gonna lose? This why Pops paid you that money, I go in and say I did it? Shit, I'd've known that's what I do, I would've said: 'Forget it.' "

"Calvin," I said, "why did you hit Janet?"

"Because she was yelling at me, man," he said angrily. "I come home there, it was late, might've had a couple beers. I put in a long day, all right? Worked my damned ass off. Have a couple beers and then I finally get home, there is my big fat wife there, shooting her damned mouth off. I told her to shut up a few times, and that didn't do no good. Finally said to her: 'Janet, if you don't shut up, all right? I am gonna clout you.' And she didn't, and I did. Yelling all that stuff at me, telling all the neighbors. Keeping the kids up in their bedroom there, have them listen to her that I am fucking Irene. I said: 'Janet, you shut up. Or else I will clout you.' And then I went and when she wouldn't stop doing that to me, with the kids and the neighbors there, I hit her some and she deserved it." He stared at me defiantly.

"Calvin," I said, "did she make any effort to defend herself?"

"What?" he said.

"Defend herself," I said. "You know—put up her dukes, cover her face, try to kick you in the crotch. Run and hide, even. Anything, to stop you from being able to hit her."

"No," he said, "she didn't do that. She didn't do anything like that, try to kick me in the croagies or anything. No."

"Or run away?" I said. "She didn't try to get away from you either?"

"No," he said, "didn't do that either. Just stood there and she's yelling at me, she knows what I am doing, I am fucking this Irene, and I told her what I would do if she didn't cut it out, and she didn't and I hit her and knocked her on her ass. And she's lying there on the floor and she wipes at her mouth there, and she was bleeding a little, and she looks at her hand and she sees the blood and she looks up at me and says: 'Bastard, fucking bastard, you fucking this whore like that and you hit your own wife, bastard. Irene fucking bastard.' And she got up, she is getting up while she is saying this, and she stands there and she keeps on yelling it, and I hit her again and I knock her down again. And she does the same damned thing again. 'This whore is blowing you and your dirty cock in her mouth,' she says when she is getting up, and I hit her again and I knock her down again. And she crawls over to the phone and she says: 'You better get out of here, fucking Irene bastard, because I am calling the cops now.' And I kicked her in her big fat ass and she falls on her face on the floor, like, you know? And I say: 'You think I will leave you here with these kids by yourself, so that you can say these things to them about me, is this it?' And she calls the cops up and she tells them I am there and I won't leave, and as soon as she hangs up, she says: 'Fucking Irene bastard. Hey, you kids, you come out right now and see your father here, that is fucking Irene whore.' And I knocked her down again, right on her big fat ass, and that was where she was when the cops get there. And they take *me* away, like it was me that started it."

"Right," I said.

"Yeah," he said.

"She is bigger than you are, isn't she?" I said.

"Bigger?" Calvin said. He snorted. "Fat fucking broad. I'd kill her, she'd tried anything, and she knows that. That I would kill her. If she tried to hit my balls or something."

"Right," I said. "So, what she did instead of hurting you herself, or doing something that probably would've made you kill her, was get you arrested for screwing your Irene. And thrown out of the house."

"What do you mean?" he said.

"Didn't she?" I said. "She had to take a few good licks to get it done, of course, but basically what she did was get the cops to expel you from your own house and the judge to say you can't have your own clothes or see these kids you mentioned, because you were screwing Irene and she didn't like it. Isn't that about right? What she really did was get you arrested for screwing the waitress. And now she's probably going to get you put in jail for it, to boot, which will mean that you'll be broke and you won't be screwing Irene and when it comes time to divorce you, she will have you over the barrel, baby, as a convicted wife-beater."

"Yeah," he said, understanding and dismay showing on his features, "yeah. She did do that, didn't she? That cunt."

"No," I said, "she didn't. That is what she's doing, and she'll pull it off unless we're careful, but she hasn't done it yet."

"Well," he said, "if I can't lie, I mean, what can we do?"

"Calvin," I said, "listen to me. You are going to learn contrition. Contrition and humility. They're both good for the soul."

I stayed in the office that night until quarter of eleven, working on my taxes and assuring myself that when Mack called to ascertain my whereabouts, I would not yap at her. This enabled me to study some contrition on my own, because Mack didn't call. When I got home just before eleven-thirty, her car was in the garage and she had gone to bed.

25

COOPER CAME into my office without banging on the wall first, just as soon as I came in. He sat down in front of me as though he meant to stay. He looked at me the way that my father looked at me the morning after I arrived home drunk for the first time. "Good morning, Mister Cooper," I said. "Something I can help you with?"

Cooper snorted. "I doubt it," he said brusquely. "Offhand, I would have to say, you couldn't help a dog. You're really in the shit this time, wouldn't you agree?"

The mind does not operate with full efficiency after weekends like I'd had. I just assumed that he referred to what was going on with Mack.

How I thought he'd learned of it, I cannot imagine. "You could put it that way," I said. "You could argue that. Friday night I get home late, my wife is asleep. Saturday I get up early, while she's still asleep. Get my old clothes on and go out, spend the whole day at the beach. Nothing like a cold and rainy Saturday, rattling around all by yourself in a closed-up summer place."

Actually, I hadn't been entirely alone there. Mike Curran from across the street spotted my car in the driveway and a couple of lights burning in the dark gray flannel morning, and had come over to spend some time with me and mind somebody else's business. He could see something was eating me, and after a while he could see also, to his sorrow, that I was not about to tell him what it was. That made him believe he was justified invoking his superior years to tell me what to do. "You should go to confession," Mike said. "You should talk to a good priest. The sacrament of penance, Jerry—you should ask for the Lord's help." I think the world of old Mike, but I wasn't going to do it and I made that clear to him. That hurt his kindly feelings and made me feel even worse.

"Got home around dinner time," I told Cooper, "with a take-out pizza. Ate it by myself, of course—Mack wasn't there. Had a few more drinks than I really might've needed. Fell asleep or passed out in the chair before the news. Woke up around three o'clock, staggered up to bed. She was asleep of course. Woke up just before noon and it's her turn to be gone. Watched the basketball games, two of them, and I really don't like that sport. Went out and got Chinese food, which I really don't like either. Ate that by myself and watched some more TV. She comes home at nine o'clock—by then I'm curious. 'Where've you been?' I say. Natural curiosity. 'At the office,' she says, and she marches up to bed. She was still asleep this morning, or pretending that she was. Yeah, I'd say I am in the shit, and maybe something worse. I don't know how, see a way, I can get out of it."

"I see," Cooper said.

"I mean, Coop, I really don't see one," I said. "This is horrible. Man and woman live like this? It's just impossible. Sleep in the same bed like two bums in a mining town where hotel space is scarce? Don't sit down to eat together, don't have conversations? This is awful, Cooper, and I think I'm stuck with it. Guys like me, you know, in this mess, we're not set up to handle it. Guys like me don't get divorced or have affairs, or go out to pick up broads. Guys who do that, they have practice, years of getting ready. This the way I'm going to live? Work here and go home? I'm not sure that I can stand it. I may lose my mind."

"Jesus," Coop said, "I knew there was something wrong, but nothing quite this bad. What can I do, Jerry? Can you think of something?"

"Coop," I said, "I'm at my wits' end. You . . . what the hell can you do? What the hell can anybody actually do, is what I want to know? And don't tell me, for Christ sake, see a psychiatrist. Or go down to the rectory and see the goddamned priest. I've been through those things, right in my own head. All that anyone can tell me is, I've got to patch this up. But that I already know, before I go to see them. Question isn't whether I have got to get this fixed. Question is just what the hell I can do to fix it. And that is the shitty question I don't have the answer to."

Cooper asked what started it. "That is a good question," I said. "That is a real good one. I think it was several things, working all together. Lou Schwartz was the first one," I said, ticking him off on my fingers. "Mack was pissed I took his case. Said I shouldn't do it. Said I'd take the loss too hard, and then when I took the loss . . ."

". . . too hard," Cooper said.

". . . too hard," I said, "she got on me for that and I didn't think she should. Naturally, I told her that. Said it didn't matter. Didn't matter whether I should have defended Lou. I had to take the man's case when he asked me to, no matter how hard it might hurt to lose it. And she doesn't understand that.

"Then," I said, "for number second, I decided that she takes her job too seriously."

"Cripes," Cooper said, "you're bitching about that? If Karen could get her ass moving fast enough to get her out of the damned house and out really doing something, take her mind off the damned kid and get her out with people, I'd be doing cartwheels down the corridors in here."

"That's what you say now," I said. "Thinking: unmixed blessings. That's the way I looked at it, when Mack first went to work. Few more bucks in the old pot? That never did much harm. Something for the wife to do, 'stead of tatting doilies? When the issue first comes up, it looks absolutely golden. Then you start to find out that you're back in second place. And quite a ways back too, I might add, lots closer to what's in third place than to what's up there in first.

"With Mack what happened, I think, is she got obsessed with it. It was fine in the beginning, when she went out selling houses. But she got too good at that, I guess, or just too greedy, maybe, and she moved up in the office to administration work. Mack's not good at running things. She is too softhearted. Doesn't like to get on people, make them do as she says. They don't do it, therefore, and she comes home all pissed off. So I griped about that to her, and that pissed her off still more.

"Then, to make things interesting," I said, "there is number three. This is confidential, Coop, like everything I tell you. Heather's sleeping with her boyfriend, and her father doesn't like it. I made my views clear to Heather, and she got quite mad at me."

Cooper sat there grinning at me. "Uh-huh," he said, "well, that figures. Daddy's getting jealous. I had two girl children, Jerry. Both of them are married. One of them just made it to the minister in time, so our second grandchild was just slightly premature. This is normal, Jerry, and I can tell you that it passes. You'll get over it in time, that she's getting laid and all."

"Maybe that is true," I said. "Assume that it's normal. Just the same, if it's so normal, why can't I express it? If all fathers feel this way, why does saying it make me the bastard of the week?"

"Because that also is normal," Coop said. "Daddies all get righteous. Daughters get mad when they do. Then after some time goes by, all of them calm down and start acting reasonable."

"Yeah," I said, "but then Mack got the idea in her head she would act as Heather's lawyer, with me prosecuting. That leaves us without a judge, and that means: no decision. No decision means that we just go on snarling about it. And since Mack is on her side, that leaves me alone.

"This is not a lot of fun, Coop," I said, "when you get down to it. When I got home Friday night, the kid had sent a letter. It was open on the table, and I couldn't read it."

"Aw, that's silly, Jerry," Cooper said, "for Christ sake. You're the one that's acting childish, if you won't even read her letters."

"Really?" I said. "Listen to me. It was the address. On the envelope it said: 'Mrs. Joan Kennedy.' My name isn't Joan, Coop. It was not addressed to me. Therefore, since Mack did not invite me, I did not read it."

"I take it back," Coop said. "You are both being childish, both you and your daughter. And your wife is aiding and abetting, from the sound of it, which puts her in the jelly with the pair of you." He nodded. "Very neat, I must say, the way you all cooperate so heartily in making each other just as miserable as possible. Efficient too. Everybody pitches in, so nobody is left out."

"You think it's that simple," I said. "Just say: 'You're all being childish,' and that will be the end of it?"

"No, unfortunately," Cooper said, "I do not think that at all. Being childish is an underrated pastime. Everybody thinks it also means that since what's being done is childish, it is therefore simple. Generally, when larger people start acting childish, it is very complicated. Take my situation, all right? My son is getting close to the age at which he will become an adult, even if nothing he has done up till now and nothing he does in the short time that remains before he turns eighteen even remotely resembles adult behavior. I am already an adult, at least officially. But he has written me off, and I, equally rational, have done the same for him. This leaves us in a big fat mess, but that mess isn't simple."

"All right," I said, "most profound and all that, but it's rhetoric, that's all. What do I do, to correct it? Want to tell me that?"

Cooper frowned. "Look, Jerry," he said, "I was not prepared for this. I knew something had gone haywire in your life, but I thought it was just Lou Schwartz. Until the weekend, that is."

"Cooper," I said, "uh-uh, that is not enough from you. You came in here uninvited. You're a volunteer. You solicited my troubles. No fair ducking them."

"What I was prepared for, Jerry," he said dourly, "was what you've got exploding out there at Channel Eight."

"I don't follow," I said. "You mean this Jack Rowley thing?" Cooper nodded, very slowly. "That is not a problem," I said. "I gave him a statement. Told him freely that I signed the thing and that I still agreed with it. I said I was sorry that it had to become public, but publicly or privately, it was the way I felt."

"You did not see Rowley, I guess," Cooper said very slowly. "Friday night you didn't see him? Hear what he made of that?"

"Got home too late," I said, "and missed it. Not entirely on purpose. Well, it was on purpose, but the purpose wasn't to avoid seeing Rowley—it was to avoid seeing Mack."

Cooper nodded again, slowly. "Uh-huh," he said, "well, it's trouble.

Basically what Rowley did was put on a striptease. His version of this Dawes flap is that it was sabotage. Starts out with the buildup: Luther's a saint in shoes. Luther's got a lock on Judge Duhamel's seat. Then behind the scenes, like Luther's old King Duncan, someone sticks a knife in him, and Belvedere is picked. You know who's Macbeth in this, the way he's telling it. There's two guys in the part."

"Let me give it a wild guess: me and Frank Macdonald," I said. "Jack says that we did it?"

"Didn't come right out and say it," Cooper said reluctantly. "Didn't quite come out and say you two can make the governor drop trou anytime you want. Near as I can recall it, he said it was like this." Cooper dropped his voice into a loud baritone. " 'Eighteen trial attorneys made a very private protest to the governor. On the face of it, that sounds like quite a lot. But we have learned exclusively that sixteen of them don't know him. Only two of Judge Dawes's critics have appeared in his court. Only two of them are licensed to try Massachusetts cases. One of them is Frank Macdonald, noted trial attorney, whose practice has been chiefly outside the Commonwealth. The other—Jeremiah Kennedy, obscure Boston attorney, little known to laymen but with very strong connections.

"Tune in next week, starting Monday,' Rowley says. 'That's when I'll begin a series on the courts of Massachusetts. Judges and the Men Who Make Them—Just Who Really Decides?' "

" 'Obscure Boston attorney'?" I said. "That was rather snide of Jack. Mack says that I'm sleazy, but she gives me marks for class. 'Obscure'? What is this crap, huh? That's downright insulting."

" 'Little known' and 'obscure,' " Cooper said somewhat meanly. "Not only are you out of sight, nobody knows you either."

"Her last year in high school," I said, "Heather lobbied for a VCR, one of those TV recorders that will watch the boob tube for you. I knocked that idea down just as soon as it came up. She was plotting to record *General Hospital*, see that bullshit in the evening when I want to watch the game. Now I wish I hadn't done it. I could use that thing."

"If I can make a suggestion," Cooper said, "okay? I were you, I'd get my ass down to Jordan Marsh at lunch. Buy myself a portable and put it on your desk. If you're staying late enough so you miss what Jack says, you are going to regret it, I think, when the newspapers begin calling."

"Won't work in here," I said. "Steel-framing building. Eats the signal.

Tried that back in Sixty-seven during the World Series. It's like watching gulls in gravy."

"Want to go down to a bar, then?" Cooper said helpfully. "I'll go with you, if you like. Keep you company."

"Oh," I said, "big help you are. 'Let's go to a bar. Have a few pops, watch old Jack, start home around seven.' I get home and there is Mack, standing at the door. 'Where've you been, asshole?' she says. 'In a bar, dear,' I say. 'Watching me get made a fool of, on the television.' Whiskey stinking on my breath, spirit beat to shit: go home that way to the woman who's already pissed at me? Good thing you didn't go to med school, Cooper—that's all I've got to say. Your cure for a migraine headache would be the guillotine."

Cooper began laughing, which in turn cheered me up some. "All right, Jeremiah," he said, "how about lunch then, instead?"

"Lunch it is," I said. "Bring poultices and sympathy, and try to think of something."

26

GRETCHEN HAD gone shopping when I went to lunch with Coop. Those excursions never required less than three full hours. Therefore when I returned I did not expect her there. Coop detoured from the elevator to visit the men's room. I inhaled the tasty smell of disinfectant from the men's room—the landlord had been having trouble with his maintenance; the substitute cleaning crews believed that lots of pine-oil solution makes up for not scrubbing the commodes—and picked my way through the discarded cigarette pack cellophane and tinfoil from chewing gum down the hallway toward my office, taking my keys from my pocket to unlock the door to it. Fully half of the fluorescent light tubes in the corridor were burned out; I was therefore unable to see very well.

I could see, of course, that a man was standing squarely before my locked office door. He was under six feet tall, and he was wearing a raincoat. He had both hands gripping the handle of a Samsonite brief-case, which he held before him in the fig-leaf position. He was flexing his knees against it, so that it bounced rhythmically against his legs, and his mouth was pursed as though he just might whistle. He looked at me appraisingly, even insolently. As I got closer to him I thought I could see him smirk. "I thought he was a client," I told Mack that night, when we'd reached a thankful truce in that informal war we had been having. "Another shitty, scheming client, not too big a fee. What I had him fig-ured for was child-molesting or some other really sordid dirty work like that. Thought maybe my bus driver from the Colebrook Unified School District'd been recommending me to all his pervert friends. 'Shit,' I say to myself when I get a look at him, 'this guy coughs up four grand, it's the most I can expect.' Sort of sandy hair he had, not too well cut or recently. Glasses in black frames that didn't fit his ears or nose quite right, so they were sort of tilted when they sat there on his face. 'Maybe one of those guys,' I think, 'that spends all his life in some insurance company, working with the figures every day, nobody even notices him until some night he gets busted stealing women's underwear off back-yard clotheslines down around Fall River. Takes it home and sniffs the crotches, hides it in his closet. Cops arrest him and they search, he's got ten thousand panties, you know? Plus a couple hundred bras.'

"But that wasn't what he was," I told her. "He was from the IRS. Flashes me some kind of wallet that I assume bore him out. 'Malcolm Wainer, IRS,' he says, like it's what he always wanted. 'You'd be Mister Kennedy, that works out of this office?'

"Now," I said to Mack, relieved just to be talking, "keep in mind that I am on my way back from my lunch with Cooper, right? Cooper has been giving me his private prescription for the troubled soul, which is reasonable conversation and a good amount of beer."

"In other words," Mack said, "you were about half plastered."

"Cheerful," I said, "cheerful, and a little hopeful too. Thinking there was much in what my old friend Cooper said. That maybe what I cher-ish most in this world has not gone to shit and flinders because we were being stupid."

"Not," she said, "lover man, that we *weren't* being stupid."

"No no," I said, "not that. Just that maybe what we've got is durable enough, so it can survive periods like this one has been when we're being very stupid. So, my confidence is up a little and therefore so's my lip. And this jerk sees me coming toward the door that he is blocking, sorting out my key to it and got nobody with me, and he cleverly deduces that my name is Kennedy and I work out of the office that says *Kennedy* on it? 'No,' I say, 'of course I'm not. I am a burglar. I like to come in buildings when the folks are out to lunch. Try my keys out on their doors, steal their calculators. Yes, of course I'm Kennedy. Who the hell are you?'

" 'IRS, I said,' he said, getting a little testy. 'Have you got some problem with your hearing, may I ask?'

" 'No, I haven't, actually,' is what I say to him. 'Only problem I've got that I know about is getting in my office while you're blocking the door there.' Like I say, I'm confident. You are getting audited, but I'm not on that return. Only returns of mine that they've got are the ones that Lou did, and I know for a certainty there's nothing wrong with them. So what is this bird doing, keeping me from my own office?

" 'Oh, sorry,' he says, quite sarcastic, and he steps aside. 'I've been here so many times and found it closed,' he says, 'I guess I'm sort of surprised to see that there really is an Attorney Kennedy, and that he does work in this office.'

" 'Life's just full of little tweaks like that,' I say to him, opening the door. I let him in, turned on the lights and so forth, hung up my overcoat, led him into my office, offered him a chair, took my accustomed place behind my desk, and asked him what was on his mind.

" 'Oh,' he says coquettishly, 'I bet you can guess that, Attorney Kennedy.' "

"Was this guy a fag?" Mack said. "Is that what you're saying?"

"I'm putting him on a little too much," I said. "He wasn't delicate, or anything like that. What he was was nasty. Sneering, you know? Snide. And not very good at it, like he was new to all this power and still getting used to it. 'If you came here to play guessing games,' I said back to him, 'you've got more time than I have to fool around today. What is it you want to know, that's had you making this joint one of your regular stops?'

" 'You represented Louis Schwartz in the federal court,' he says, opening his briefcase and producing lots of papers that he looks at while he's talking like he thinks I'm going to lie, and he will haul out his own copy of my court appearance slip, wave it in my face and say, well, how do I explain that? And I will get all flustered and start begging for his mercy. These guys are beautiful. 'Uh-huh,' I say, eloquently, volunteering nothing. Let him know right from the outset, he gets name, rank, and serial number from me if he asks politely. After that, it's due process, the whole ball of wax.

"He gives me the beady eye," I said to Mack. "He wants me to see that he's used to this sort of reticence, shrewd types such as I. He's no rookie I may think I can buffalo, shifty tricks like I'm pretending to cooperate, admitting right off the bat that I represented Lou. 'Do you still represent him?' he says. Crafty little bastard. 'Far as I know,' I say. 'Haven't had a letter from him, firing me, at least.'

"Doesn't falter one iota," I told Mack. "Presses right on, undeterred. He is used to my type. This is how I'm going to play it, okay by this kid. 'Mister Schwartz is now in Danbury,' he says, watching me real closely to see how I react to this news. 'Uh-huh,' I say, very calmly. 'Federal correctional facility,' he says, just in case I was maybe trying to suggest that Lou'd gone down there for a gourmet dinner, or the place is a fat farm or something. 'Uh-huh,' I reply smartly, sticking with a winner."

"You," Mack said, "you don't seem to have contributed a whole lot in the course of this discussion so far, am I right in this?"

"Absolutely," I said. "So far Malcolm and I have agreed that Lou Schwartz got sent to Danbury while I was his lawyer, if not because I was his lawyer. And while we have concurred on each component building block of this negotiation, he has verified my answers from his sheaf of papers. Papers that he brought with him, for that very purpose."

"It seems a little pointless," Mack said.

"Yes indeed, it does," I said. "Until, that is, you recall what Lou was always saying, or maybe it was Frank Macdonald the night that we all got drunk in Locke's."

"I did not get drunk," she said absently. "You and Frank did. You got absolutely plowed. I was very well behaved, and I drove home that night."

"Uh-huh," I said.

"You're getting so you sort of like that little answer, don't you?" she said.

"Well," I said, "after all, so far as I know right this minute, it's served me pretty well in awkward conversational situations today, and I'm sort of inclined to stick with it until it fails me."

"Anyway," she said, "what was it Frank told you the night that you and he were drunk?"

"That the agents get paid for wasting your time as well as their own," I said. "Would you, back when you were on commission, or even now that you are on part salary, hang around outside somebody's locked office for close to a whole hour, waiting around just on the off chance that he might show up there before your quitting time arrived?"

"He didn't call first?" she said.

"If he did," I said, "the box refused to take his calls. We do get some dial tones on that, people hanging up, but unless that was what he did, no, he didn't call. He told me today's was his fourth visit to my office. His fourth visit, Mack, and it is not as though the eighth floor there at Eighty Boylston Street was right on his way home at night, near where he stops for milk. Once before, he left a card. Otherwise, he comes and goes, like some goddamned peeper. Lou says those guys get instructions, try to show up unexpected. Call ahead, make an appointment, you will get prepared. Maybe have your lawyer there, or your accountant, huh? Someone to advise you, tell you: 'Keep your big mouth shut'? That's not what they have in mind, they spring that first visit. What they want on that one is for you to blurt out something that you haven't thought about.

"Besides," I said, "what's it to him if I am not there? Five o'clock rolls around, and he goes back to the barn. Puts down in his file that he spent fifty minutes waiting outside my locked office door, didn't see me, left his card, returned to his base. Or whatever they call where they start out from and go back to—Ground Zero, maybe, all I know. From your point of view, he has wasted that time. But he still gets paid for it, in taxpayers' money. Nothing gets deducted from his paycheck for this period, fifty minutes he spent camped outside my office, plus the forty minutes total he spent going to and returning. He gets paid for that hour and a half just like he actually accomplished something for his government today. And he gets it without exercising all his little gray cells too, so he isn't overtired."

"I see," she said. "I don't think it makes sense, mind you, but I see."

"Malcolm now turns on the laser gaze," I said. "He pins me with the million-candlepower stare and challenges me to duck a rocket that he's just about to launch. 'We are investigating certain tax returns,' he says, like I might have been imagining he was out taking a census. 'We have reason to believe that Mister Schwartz was the preparer.' Which reason, of course, is his name and signature, right on the bottom of the first page, left-hand side, of those returns he mentioned. 'What we want is your permission to interrogate him about these materials.'

"This," I told Mack, "is where I begin to take matters just a little bit more seriously. 'Certain tax returns' can cover quite a lot of very interesting ground, especially when this guy tells me only that what these returns have in common is Lou's signature on them. Lou worked for a lot of people whom our government dislikes. This guy could be asking me if it's okay with yours truly if he and several other gentlemen just as well dressed as he is go down to Danbury and invite old Lou to comment on returns he made up for Nunzio and other moderately famous local people."

"Would Lou do that, anyway?" she said. "If this wimp went down there and told him you said it was all right for him to discuss what he did for Nunzio, do you think Lou would do it? Even if you did say it was all right?"

"No," I said, "of course he wouldn't. Lou would tell him to go shit in his hat if the guy arrived with authority from Jesus. Lou is not like a good many of my clients. He depends on me for legal advice, not to make up for the fact that God gave him the intelligence of a normal parakeet. Of course he wouldn't do that. What he would do, though, would be to ask permission to call counsel on the telephone, call me, fire me, and then get himself a new lawyer. Pronto. Making sure, in the process, that everybody in the Western Hemisphere got word of the fact almost at once that it is not a good idea to have Jerry Kennedy representing you these days because he just told his client it was perfectly all right to get all undressed in front of a posse of IRS agents. I realize that I can make a fool of myself if I want to, and I guess it is thoughtful of young Malcolm to volunteer his help in case I have decided I would like to destroy my reputation as a thinking adult human being, but all the same, thanks just the same. I'm not gonna do it. 'Well,' I said thoughtfully to Malcolm, keeping a straight face while I spoke, 'I'm afraid I'll have to disappoint you on that one.'

"Malcolm takes no chances," I said. " 'You're withholding your permission?' He says this as though he's shocked, like everyone that talks to him is always at the rough and ready to do just what he asks them for. This is something else Lou mentioned, long, long time ago. 'These guys play dumb, Jerry,' he said. 'Some of them don't have to work too hard to be convincing, but never mind that—it does work. They pretend they know you, and they thought you'd do as they say. Act like they inquired about you, and they didn't expect this.' And that was what friend Malcolm did when I said: 'No.' Like everyone'd told him I am really a nice guy. Patriotic American. Salt of the goddamned earth. He cannot believe his ears. 'Yes,' I said boldly, to his disbelieving face, 'I'm afraid I must refuse.'

"If he had been chewing Fleer's Double Bubble Gum," I told Mack, "he would most likely've swallowed his whole cud. 'Well,' he said, appalled at my attitude, 'may I ask why, then, Mister Kennedy?'

"I thought about saying yes and waiting for him to put the question formally, but something in my upbringing and training told me that it isn't wise to go too far when toying with an agent of the IRS."

"Well," Mack said, "I should hope not, certainly."

"Doesn't do to get them really pissed off," I said. "Little annoyed, maybe, because I was not going to give him what he came for. But totally bullshit at me, personally? That did not seem like a really good idea. So I say: 'Sure, and I will tell you. As you may be aware, Mister Schwartz was indicted only after he had made it very clear to everyone concerned, including, I believe, a Mister Avila from your agency, that . . .'

"'Mister Avila's been transferred,' my pal Mal said to me. 'He was transferred and promoted to head up our office in El Paso shortly after the first of this year.'

"Which of course would figure," I said, telling Mack about it. "That's another thing Lou told me, how that operation works. 'What you have to understand here, Jerry, is that these guys live on scalps. This little opus with me, here, nailing my ass to the wall, when it's over, they'll be gone, the agents on my case. Off to new and bigger things, their reward for knocking me off. Always remember, Jerry, when you're dealing with those bastards and they give you *mucho* bullshit that it's nothing personal, just a job they have to do, that is a flat fucking lie and you should not believe it. It is personal to them. It means their next promotions. It means money and more power, respect and choice assignments. This guy Avila here, this square-shooting gentle fellow, when he sees me he is looking at a couple GS grades, and maybe if he plays his cards right a long spell in warmer weather.'

" 'I was not aware that Mister Avila had been moved,' I said. 'At any rate, if you can reach him, down there in El Paso, he will confirm what I've said: no charges were brought against my client, Louis Schwartz, until he had made it clear he would refuse to discuss with the IRS any details of the tax forms he prepared for that one client.'

" 'Nunzio Dinapola,' pal Mal said very primly. He looked at some of his papers, just to make sure of the name.

"I was just as formal as he was," I said. " 'I believe that was his name. Therefore, as Mister Schwartz's lawyer, I would have to say that I think he's established, at considerable inconvenience to himself, that he does not intend to talk to you about the work he has done on any tax returns.'

" 'The questions we have,' Agent Wainer said, 'wouldn't necessarily pertain to returns prepared and filed in behalf of Taxpayer Dinapola. Nunzio Dinapola, that is.' And he pretended he had to get the name off his damned papers again.

" 'Be that as it may,' I said. 'Whosoever returns you may have in mind to ask him about, I cannot and I will not advise him to talk to you. I will in fact instruct him to do just the opposite. In point of fact, if you're concerned, it probably doesn't matter. I'm very much inclined to doubt he'd do so even if I did so advise him. If *anybody* so advised him, as far as that goes. But be that as it may, and for whatever it is worth, I will not so advise him. And therefore I cannot give you my permission to see him.'

"Malcolm looked very miffed," I said. " 'You realize, Mister Kennedy,' he said, 'that we can insist on seeing him, with or without your permission. That my repeated efforts to get in touch with you were intended as a courtesy. He is a federal prisoner.'

" 'Indeed I realize that,' I said. 'And of course I also realize that he can insist on having his attorney present at such time as you arrive, and that when everyone is sitting down and has his cup of coffee, little tin-foil ashtrays for the smokers who may be present, he can refuse to answer each and every question that you may put to him. And furthermore, Mister Wainer, given what has happened up to this point to my client in this case, whether I am the attorney or he gets another lawyer, I can guarantee you, bet you any sum you name, that that is what he will do too. That one is bulletproof.' "

"Are they really going to do this to poor Lou?" she said. "Go down there now that he's in jail and start hounding him some more?"

"Well," I said, "if I had to make a guess, that's what it would be."

"Is it that same Michael Dunn who's behind this?" she said.

"Behind it?" I said. "I don't know. In on it? For certain. He's got his little heart set on cutting a trophy head from the biggest gangster in the town, and he knows who that is. He thinks he's got the Godfather, and Lou's all that's stopping him. So he is going to give Lou another hosing now, and see how he reacts. See if the time he's done already's weakened him a little. Besides, they've got nothing else to do. Why not give old Lou another drubbing, just for old times' sake?"

"Well," she said, "that's what I mean. Don't they have something else to do?"

"Mack," I said, "there are thousands of these people. Malcolm here and Mister Avila, now in the West Texas town of El Paso, those're only two guys out of whole hordes of them. There are dozens more right here in Boston, standing around in office-building corridors, shifting from foot to foot and looking worried because nobody seems to be working. You think Michael Dunn and whoever else has got a hair across his ass for Nunzio, you think they can't find two or three more guys that aren't doing anything that's real important, if there's somebody else that should catch their eye as well? I don't think that, not at all."

"So," she said, "Lou's case starts out as a big pain in the ass which I know you are sure to lose before you even take it, and you take it and you lose it and the damned thing isn't over. What a colossal pain in the ass, Jerry, wouldn't you say? Really?"

I leaned over in the bed and kissed her. "Whatever you say, kiddo," I said. "Want to watch the evening news?"

She laughed a little, a nice change from the way things had been going. "Jerry," she said, hugging me, "have lunch with Coop more often."

27

"COMPARED TO a poke in the eye with a sharp stick," I said, when Cooper came into my office the first thing the next morning and asked my reaction to the Rowley Special Report: Our Judges—Who Decides?, "it wasn't bad at all. You're a better marriage counselor than you are a press consultant. Mack says you should give up law and practice that full-time."

Cooper at lunch the day before said that he had figured out my family problems. "This is good to hear," I said, drinking some dark beer. "Care to share your genius with me, since I'm buying lunch?"

"Nooners," he said very gravely. "Nooners is the answer."

"Nooners, for Christ sake?" I said. "Coop, I'm middle-aged. Mack is no spring chicken either, come right down to it. We're not a couple of hot-blooded adolescents, bunking in some motel for a quick roll in the hay, and we're not sneaking off with other people, cheating on each other. These problems that I have got, they're not with an affair. This is a goddamned marriage, damnit, almost twenty-three years old. Try to give it some respect, if you can manage that."

"Look," he said, "bear with me, Jerry. You don't understand. This is not some dizzy broad that's talking to you now. 'How to Put the Romance Back into Your Scruffy Marriage.' Mack and you are very close, and you always have been. Now you've got this disagreement, and it's scrambled both your brains. Trouble with the pair of you is that you never fight. Then along comes something, something fairly minor, and both of you are stunned to find out that you're not in synch. You'd've had ten years of fights, couple walkouts and a separation, maybe, you would see this argument for the piss-ant business that it is. But you've got nothing serious to make comparisons. You see that she differs with you, and you can't believe your eyes. 'What is this? Mack don't agree? Just what is this shit?' And you therefore get all mad, start acting like an asshole. At the same time she is seeing that you're really mad at her.

'Jerry's tacked off at me?' she thinks. 'Jerry Kennedy? Here is this bum that I cherish, he's got the balls to fight with me? I will show that little pisspot. I will fix his ass.'

"Maybe when this started," Coop said, "you had a real beef. But if you had a beef, which I doubt, it was not with Mack. Mack did not tell Heather: 'Go and fuck your brains out.' Mack did not do anything, which was the correct action. Maybe Heather should've known, don't make it so obvious. Let old Dad pretend what he likes, and don't rub it in. But Heather didn't know this, and she made it obvious. So obvious that you, Jerry, finally have to see it.

"Now," he said, "my own opinion, which you can disregard, is that you had no complaint. She is old enough. She is making a mistake? This is possible. When you're nineteen, pushing twenty, that goes with the turf. She has some rights in this matter, and mistakes is one of them. Either way, though, right or wrong, if you're mad it's at her. She's in Colorado, California, someplace, though, so you get mad at Mack. That was when you had your head fully up your ass.

"Now," he said, "you're lonesome, because Mack returned your fire. Therefore, tell her what you told me, that you're all upset. She will understand this because she already knows it. This does not mean that you get away without admitting it, but it does mean that admitting it should not be all that painful.

"I suggest you do this," he said, "in the goddamned bedroom. Call her up and tell her that she has to leave work early. Tell her to meet you, that you're coming home early and you really have to get right down to basics. Doesn't have to be a pretty goddamned speech, soft music in the background with the strolling troubadours. Get in bed and talk about this, let things take their course. Then when you both feel better, maybe you can work out Heather's business. Which will still be Heather's business, Jerry, after it's worked out, and my guess would be that you will still be really pissed at her. But that will be all right, I think, compared to what you've got. That looks and sounds like misery, and you have got to stop it."

I thought about what he said, and I went home and did it. "It worked just like you said, Coop," I said, "just like fucking magic, if I may coin a phrase. You've really got a knack for this stuff. I think Mack is right."

" 'Marriage counselor,' " he said. "Nah; it wouldn't work. Sooner or later I would get myself a client with a few more brains than you, and he or she would ask me how my own home life is doing. That would put me out of business, if that question should come up. Lemme stick to your problems. What was Mack's reaction to Jack Rowley's Show and Tell?"

"Horrified, of course," I said, "absolutely speechless. Thought he ruined my career, lynched my reputation. Thought I should sue him and his next of kin as well. Do something to make him stop, all that sort of thing."

"Be nice if you could," Coop said, "very nice indeed."

Rowley doesn't try to compete with TV's pretty boys. This is sensible of him, because he's fairly ugly. Nothing that's part of his face seems to fit in with the rest of it. His reddish hair is spiky and extremely thin on top; his head is noticeably bumpy and it's mottled here and there. His ears are prominent and large, with long and drooping lobes. His forehead's freckled and his eyebrows are patchy. His nose is longish and both squashed and bent. He has a cleft chin and the cleft is very deep; the lower part of his face therefore looks something like a miniature baby's arse, but with the wispy white goatee. His mouth is wide and his lips are narrow. His parents lost no money to the orthodontists of this world when his teeth came in.

Rowley does not try to compensate for his appearance with abundant charm. His approach to the camera is one of hostile tension. He hunches over his desk, his hands clenched in front of him. He speaks in a portentous voice, a sonorous baritone. He would have done well as a radio announcer during World War II, reporting bombing devastation on the hated enemy.

"Six weeks ago," Jack Rowley said, a large picture of Judge Luther Dawes in color on the screen behind him, "Superior Court Judge Luther Dawes looked like a shoo-in for promotion. Seeking the vacancy that opened on the Massachusetts Appeals Court when Justice Kenneth Duhamel retired, Dawes seemed to be everybody's favorite. But not quite everybody's, as we told you Friday night. Governor John Tierney, under heavy pressure, picked a woman for that place, Ann Tobin Belvedere." Pictures of Tierney and the lady from Bristol County flashed in Luther's place.

"Miz Belvedere is qualified," Rowley said. "She has a good track record in her chiefly probate practice, and she's endorsed by women's groups. But," said Rowley, frowning, as the pictures disappeared, "is she in fact *more* qualified than trial judge Luther Dawes? He had hundreds of trials in his years as an attorney, before his appointment to the bench six years ago. In those six years, Dawes has handled major felonies—murder, robbery and rape, complicated frauds. Much more demanding work, in most laymen's eyes, than the day-to-day divorce work that Miz Belvedere has done."

The camera angle changed on Rowley and he reacted slowly, as though he had been a mannequin installed upon a slow-moving turntable. "As we've told you," he said, "as we learned late Friday night, the governor based his decision on a private letter to him. That letter had the names of eighteen lawyers on it, all of them strongly opposed to Luther Dawes's nomination.

"That sounded like strong medicine," Rowley conceded sadly. "Eighteen prominent attorneys, all opposed to him? But we went further in the matter, dug down into it. We learned that sixteen of them were not from Massachusetts. Sixteen of the eighteen who opposed Judge Luther Dawes"—Luther's picture reappeared, looming over Rowley—"did not even know the man. Had not tried against him in his career as a lawyer. Had not been before him in his six years as a judge. Had no knowledge of him, except what they had been told. Only two men from this state would let their names be used. The governor gave in to them, and named Miz Belvedere.

"Who are these men?" Rowley pleaded to the camera. "Who gave them the power to select our judges for us? What is their claimed expertise? Do they have special knowledge? If so, what is that knowledge, and why won't they state it publicly? What is the reason behind their power over Governor John Tierney?" He straightened up in his chair and glared resolutely into the camera. "Stay with us, folks," he said. "I'll be back later in this broadcast with the first of five parts in our special report: Our Judges—Who Decides?"

After about twenty minutes of reports of government-funded construction projects, fires in three-deckers located in and around Boston, and complaints of racial discrimination by two Latino policemen from Lowell, along with what seemed like about ten commercials which appeared to offer white teeth, happy stomachs, clean armpits, and new cars free to anyone who'd like them, Rowley was on the screen again. He had moved while we were watching other things—now he was in a conversation pit of sorts, three swivel chairs upholstered in electric-blue tweed, with a circular coffee table in the center of the grouping. The light came up full on him; the people in the other chairs remained hidden in shadows.

"As recently as last week," Rowley said, "Judge Luther Dawes thought he had that vacancy on the Appeals Court of Massachusetts." The lights came up on the man seated in the middle, next to Rowley on the right. It was Luther Dawes himself, looking tensely cheerful in a gray pin-striped suit. White lettering popped up on the screen under his breastbone: *Judge Luther Dawes*. "He dresses well," Mack said. "He isn't a bad-looking man, when you get down to it."

"Frank Macdonald dressed well too," I said back to her, "but that cut no ice with you."

"That was different," she said. "Frank was using you."

"Oh," I said, "so that's the difference. Using me is not permitted. Harpooning my career is different."

"Shut up," Mack said pleasantly, as Rowley orated. "Well-informed State House observers were sure that he'd be appointed. Judge Dawes himself had made no calls, as that would be improper." I choked. Mack told me to shut up. "But other persons he knows did, and they said he was in.

"Judge Dawes," Rowley said, turning toward him slowly, "do you think you know what happened? Can you tell us what went wrong?"

Luther looked extremely solemn, as though giving this some thought. "Basically, I think I can, Jack," he said slowly and distinctly. "It was all political. Naturally, I have to guess, but I am well informed. I don't think there's any question but that I was sabotaged."

"Sabotaged," Rowley repeated, recoiling just a little. His expression showed he marveled, recommending that reaction to the people who were watching. "You mean, then, Judge, that you think you were attacked unfairly?"

Judge Dawes nodded, sad and sober, leaning forward in his chair. "Yes," he said, "I do think that. I am certain of it. I was the unknowing victim of a very small cabal. Not a large group, mind you, Jack," and he held up one hand. "Most of the trial bar, I must say, gave me full support. Full support and their endorsements, if you'll let me boast a little."

"And well you might boast, Judge," Jack said, beaming at the judge. Then he turned back to the camera and grew stern again. "Two men only, in this state, criticized the judge. Two men who found sixteen others, living far from here, undid Judge Luther Dawes's hopes of the Appeals Court appointment." He turned back to face Judge Dawes. "Who were these two men, Your Honor, who accomplished this?"

"One of them was Frank Macdonald," Dawes said with angry distaste. "He's been called 'flamboyant,' I guess, 'colorful' and 'bold.' But as far as I'm concerned, he's just another lawyer. In my court, I've made that clear. Everyone stands equal. Frank Macdonald or John Doe, all cases are tried fairly. Frank Macdonald, naturally, didn't like that attitude and sought revenge on me."

"What utter bullshit," I said. "The goddamned hypocrite. Frank has never tried a case before this bastard in his life. Frank hasn't even been here to try cases since old Luther got his robe."

"Shut up, please," Mack said again, patting me to calm me. "Judge Dawes has the floor tonight. You declined."

"He was the ringleader, then?" Rowley said to Luther. On the wall behind him came a picture of Macdonald. It was an old black-and-white still picture, catching him and freezing him as he lunged from a courthouse doorway, necktie starched out over his left shoulder and face contorted badly; his mouth was partly open and he looked like he was snarling. Just behind him was another figure, hat down over eyes and coat collar pulled up to his ears, looking very furtive. My guess was that the picture was from Frank's old days in Texas, when he and the world were both very young and he was slightly reckless.

"That he was," Dawes said. "Very dangerous man, I think, despite his reputation. Always has made it his practice to intimidate the judges. I was one who wouldn't buckle, wouldn't give in to his tactics." Dawes settled back courageously in his chair and folded his hands across his belly. "Consequently, Jack, he's always hated and opposed me. He was the ringleader in the effort to discredit me. The effort, I am sorry to say, that succeeded all too well."

"Judge," Rowley said then, leaning toward him, looking troubled, "I believe you said there was another man in this. Someone here in Massachusetts who was also part of this campaign to sabotage your chances. Could you name that man for us, perhaps tell us why he did it?"

Luther Dawes looked anguished. Anyone who watched him could see that what he had to say was something he regretted. He shook his head once, and nibbled at his lip. Deep frown lines showed on his forehead;

you could see this man has feelings. "Jack," he said, "the other man . . . I must say I was astonished. This is a trial lawyer who has practiced many years. Unlike Frank Macdonald, who is something of a showman, this man always tried his best to do a decent job. Never became widely known. Never had big cases. Name is not a household word, if you follow me. Most people who are watching us have probably never heard of him."

"You don't see why he'd do this to you? Is that what you're saying, Judge?" Rowley prompted sympathetically, since the judge was so upset.

Luther played it to the hilt. "At first, I didn't, Jack. At first, when they said: 'Jerry Kennedy,' my inclination was to think that this could not be true. But clearly, Jack, it was true. It was part of the cabal. Jeremiah Kennedy, an ordinary man. A decent man, from all accounts, who's always done his best."

Rowley shook his head in wonder at the perfidy of man. The perfidy of me, actually, since I was the one Dawes mentioned. Rowley turned back to the camera and I came up on the screen. I was in full color and I looked like a damned fool. I was rumpled, fat and nervous, and my beard showed through my skin. "Richard Nixon," I said, looking at me there. "Should've run for President, with that kind of a shadow."

"This is Jerry Kennedy," Rowley intoned at us. "Shown here in a recent case, before Judge Luther Dawes." The tape they made of me in that case froze me gesturing. I had my right forefinger aimed like a gun at someone. My big mouth was open and my hair was all mussed up. Shaving mornings, I'd ignored the jowl that I am getting. I could also think about a better barber too. And it was hard for me to deny, as I looked at me, that I had busted quite a few veins in my cheek and in my nose. Rum blossoms on the seedy bastard, I thought dispassionately. Must tuck a few back now and then, to get those whiskey burns.

"This would be the Mapes case?" Mack said, woebegone.

"Mapes or Mackin," I said. "It would have to be."

"Stay with us once again folks," Rowley said in a voice of doom. "We'll come back in the second segment of tonight's broadcast, and we'll tell you more then about Jerry Kennedy."

Rowley disappeared into an ad for the phone company, and I wheezed the air out of my lungs as I slumped in my chair. "Goodness, gracious," I said. "This isn't fun at all."

Mack patted me again. "You want a drink, kid?" she said comfortingly, starting to get up.

"Jesus Christ, Mack," I said, "I don't think I should. That old bum they're showing people, they say he is me. If that's true, I've had enough, wouldn't you say, kiddo?"

"Well," she said, "if you had told me, say, a month before you had your little screen test there, I might have made a small suggestion that you should cut down. But that guy that they're showing there, if he is really you, there isn't much that you can do now to make his poor face look better. And frankly, darling, looking at you where you're sitting now, I'd say you could use a drink, and I'd like one myself."

It took a small amount of courage, even with the vodka, to subject myself to viewing what they had to show me next. Rowley came back looking merciless and bold, his lips set and his face grim and his juices at the flood. I came back in freeze-frame also, right up there behind him, looking like I spent my nights huddled in some doorway on East Berkley Street in Boston, tugging on some cheap port wine and watching the sea serpents frolic inside my corroded brains. "Jerry Kennedy, Esquire," Rowley said in gloom. "Frequently appointed by the judges of our courts to represent the indigents who can't afford attorneys." He turned back to Dawes. "You appointed Kennedy yourself from time to time—isn't that so, Judge Dawes? What can you say about him?"

Dawes put his frown back on his face and repeated his small head shake. He nibbled once more at his lip and then steepled his fingers. Someone behind the cameras obviously didn't like that; you could see him get a signal, and he dropped them. He shifted slightly in his chair and cleared his throat at last. "Kennedy," he said, "I don't wish to harm the man. As you say, I did appoint him. Frequently, in fact."

"Liar," I said, "motherfucker. Goddamned hypocrite."

"Hush," Mack said, "at least let's hear this. Everybody else is."

"Lawyers," Dawes said, "when they are in private practice, very often seek such cases, ask for them, in fact. If they're in court anyway, with a fee-paid client, those appointments add to income, without causing them much work. Generally they're simple cases, often easily disposed of in the same day they're acquired. Kennedy was competent, as far as I knew, at least. Never heard complaints about him, except from other judges."

" 'Other judges,' you say," Rowley interjected. "Without naming them, Judge Dawes, can you tell us what they said?"

"Well, Jack," Dawes said, smiling sadly, "of course I wouldn't name them. But I'd say what they had to say was my reaction also. Kennedy's a lawyer like a lot of other lawyers. Knows the rules of evidence, good on the procedures. Not always thoroughly prepared, but then of course, who is? And he can be abrasive, sometimes. Hard to get along with. Seems to think he runs the place, the courtrooms, I mean. Never lived up, in his own mind, to his great potential. Pretty much acceptable, I guess I'd summarize it."

"But certainly, in your mind, Judge, not a bar leader," Rowley said to Dawes.

Dawes looked like he found that idea at least somewhat amusing, if not preposterous. "A leader of the bar?" he said. "Jerry Kennedy? No, indeed, he isn't that. Certainly not in my mind."

Rowley nodded when he got that and turned back to face the camera. "We have with us here tonight, somebody else who is well acquainted with Attorney Kennedy. Many of you out there," he said genially as the lights came up on the third member of the tableau, "will recognize WMNX-TV's consultant on crime and crime prevention, our own Harry Mapes."

Harry was wreathed in smiles. His face was ruddy and his white hair was nicely barbered. He wore a polyester green sport coat and a red and white striped shirt. "I'm surprised," I said to Mack, "he doesn't have his dog." She shushed me again.

"Harry," Rowley said to Mapes, "you know Attorney Kennedy."

"Yes, I do, Jack," Harry said, smiling and nodding, rocking slightly, most ingratiating. "Had him as my lawyer, Jack, three or four times, I believe. In my old career, of course." He grinned expansively. "Before the good Judge Dawes here made me finally see the light."

"And what was your impression, Harry," Rowley said, grinning also, "of Attorney Kennedy? Was he what you'd call, I guess, a really heavy hitter? Someone that you thought a standout in the Boston trial bar?"

Harry shook his head sadly, but he still kept his smile. "Ahh, Jack," he said, "that's sort of a tough one. Jerry Kennedy, I know, thinks he did right by me. If you were to ask him, how he thinks he did for me, I am sure he'd tell you that he did his level best.

"But, a standout is he, the trial lawyers I have known?" Harry shook his head regretfully. "He's not. And I have met a lot of lawyers, in my misbehaving days, Jack. I've seen dozens of them, right up close, seen them come and go. Kennedy is competent, just like the good judge says. But he's no heavy hitter, Jack, not in that league at all."

"Tell me, then, Harry," Rowley said, "how do you explain it? Here you are, a defendant, and this is what you think. Here is Judge Dawes on the bench, and that is what he thinks. Both of you agree, I think, that Kennedy's okay. But no more than okay, right?" The judge and Harry glanced at each other and then they both nodded. "Okay," Rowley said, "an ordinary guy." He swiveled back now to the camera, and the lights dropped down on his guests. "Be with us tomorrow night," Rowley pleaded to it. "Join us then when we explore just how this could have happened. Frank Macdonald's not around, no longer lives in Boston. Jerry Kennedy? A nice guy, but no Clarence Darrow. How could these two men derail Judge Dawes like this? We'll have answers for you in part two tomorrow night." As he spoke white letters crawled across the screen: "Special Report: Our Judges—Who Decides?"

"Wow," Mack said, sitting back in her chair and expelling all her breath. "That was pretty nasty, Jerry, I'm sorry to say."

"It really is remarkable," I said, agreeing with her. "I suppose I must have had a couple thousand clients. Maybe even more than that, if you count all the whores, eight and nine of them some mornings, Captain Midnight was still working and there was a Combat Zone."

"It seems like it must be at least that many," she said.

"Oh," I said, "well, 'seems like,' if you're going to go by that? If it's what it seems like, then I've had a couple million. Maybe even as many as the population of Manhattan, if it's what it seems like.

"Out of that collection," I said, "just one goes on TV. Just one of the thousands that I've represented hard gets himself a job in TV where he comments on my work. Is it Teddy Franklin, who is free because of me? Is it Joseph Vaster, who was saved by my quick wits? That stupid little bastard, that dumb shit Donald French, that I got off with three years when he could have been convicted of murdering a federal agent? All of those silly bastards that I saved their licenses? All the whores that I set free, or that faggot there, Teller, that I saved from evil fates?"

"Absolutely not," she said. "Not that I can see."

"No," I said, "of course it's not. It is Harry Mapes. Harry Mapes, the little shit, who never even paid me. Harry Mapes, who hates my guts, because I don't like perjury. Harry Mapes is the one that is up for Emmies this year. And is Harry satisfied, when he gets his shot at me? Is he content to say only that he doesn't like me? No indeed, not good old Harry, star of stage and screen. Legend-in-his-own-mind Harry, he will twist the knife. Suck up to old Luther there and crucify his lawyer. Who didn't want to be his lawyer when that bastard Luther named him."

"Your luck has not been good of late," Mack said thoughtfully. "You are not on a roll."

"This bastard Mapes there," Cooper said next day, "he really doesn't like you. And Rowley sounds like, if you ask me, he is out to wreck you."

"Which leaves an interesting question, Coop," I said. "What can I do to prevent this? Or at least reduce the damage? I think I've got to talk to Jack, get my position stated. I think what I've got to do is demand equal time."

"Jerry," Cooper said, "all right? Don't rush into this. I saw your picture last night there, and it did not look good. You go on that show with him, and he may murder you. It might even make things worse if he had you there. He would be a bum in court if you were up against him. TV is Jack Rowley's court. It's his woods like court is yours. You sure you want to tackle him where he feels at home?"

"Coop," I said, "I'm really not. I'm really sure I don't. But what I want and what there is are not the same thing this time. I have got to challenge this thing, hammer it myself. Unless you can think of something better, that is what I'm going to do."

28

MOUSIE FEELEY asked me if I thought he was attractive. "Actually, not very," I said, "but don't take that to heart. I have never been that interested in boys."

"Good," he said, "so call me Ray. Eloise can call me Mousie because she thinks I am cute. Unless you also think I'm cute, you don't get to do it. And if you do think I am cute, you should be examined."

"Fine," I said, "so listen to me. I have got to have Frank's number. I have got to reach him. I've got this guy coming in, and Frank's name will crop up. It's important that we talk before this guy comes in. Having you tell me that you will have Frank call me, that just will not do it, Ray, and that's why I'm impatient."

"Jerry," he said, "listen to me. I know you're upset. I saw that crap on Channel Eight and I would be also. But think of my position here, where I am sitting in this. You tell me that it is urgent, and I sympathize. If it were just up to me, I would give the number.

"Frank is my employer, Jerry," Feeley said. "Frank pays my wages, Jerry, and my Blue Cross and Blue Shield. Frank consequently thinks he has a right to tell me what I can and cannot do. If I do what he has told me not to do, all the sympathy I feel for you will not make any difference. Frank will tell me I should see you for my dough.

"This job is important to me, Mister Kennedy. I am old for a new lawyer, and I do not look like one. I look like I've been in fights, and lost a lot of them. Big firms don't hire guys like me, and little ones aren't hiring. I don't have much capital, so I can't start my own. I don't dare to piss off Frank, not for anybody. I get forty grand a year for doing what he says. That is what I'm gonna do, no matter what you say. You don't get his number from me. All calls come from him."

"All right," I said, "tell him this, and that it's important. Channel Eight is tap-dancing on my recumbent form. They have got that goddamned list that you and Frank made up. I have their guy coming in to take down my reactions. I don't want to shit on Frank while I'm doing this. This means I should talk to him, get his point of view. Also means that if I don't, he has to take his chances. Their guy's coming to my office at two o'clock today. I don't hear from Frank by then, I have got to wing it."

"Stand by to wing it, Jerry," he said. "Good luck in your mission."

"What does that mean, Ray?" I said. " 'Go and screw yourself'?"

Feeley sighed. "Uh-uh," he said, "not that in the slightest. Means that Frank won't call by then. There is just no chance. Six or seven, maybe, there would be an outside shot. But no chance whatsoever between now and two o'clock."

"Why is this, Ray?" I said. "He's out playing golf? Buzz him on the pager that he puts on with his pants. Hell do I care if it makes him blow a three-foot putt? You and he got me into this. I think he owes me."

"Jerry, Jerry, calm down," Ray said. "I don't know what he does. All I know is Corinne says he gets no interruptions. If it's golf, then it is golf. If it's swimming, swimming. Maybe it is therapy, he likes a long massage. Doesn't matter, though, to you, what the hell it is. No calls reach Frank until six, 'cause that is Corinne's rule. I do not tangle ass-holes with Corinne."

Nobody tangles assholes with Corinne. She became Frank's third wife off a dozen years or so as dean of admissions at Mills College, south of San Francisco, and she kept her skills in order. What she must have done to jittery parents of young ladies with feeble college board scores was perfect training for the tasks she'd undertaken when she agreed to assume management of Frank Macdonald's life. I had met her at a dinner, seven or eight years ago. I was jovial, I guess, and Corinne was not. I told her what great times Frank and I had had. She informed me that was over, "not good for Frank's health." I began to jabber that they weren't just my idea. "Oh, I'm sure of that," she said, sighing a silver sigh. "Frank's too outgoing for his own good, and he simply will not stop." She made me feel like a thirteen-year-old boy caught with his dick out and erect during algebra instruction.

"No, Ray," I said, "I'd imagine not. If Frank is paying salaries, it's because she is letting him. Okay, give the message then, and I am on my own."

"Damned shame," Mack said that night when I quoted that to her, "took you so long to get ready, make that big decision. You'd've dropped that bastard last year, or when I first told you to, you would not be in this shit now, even needing his help. Frank Macdonald and Jack Rowley. What a pair of jerks. Stay with one, you get the other, wind up streaming shit."

"Jack Rowley, kiddo," I said, "is an MCP."

"A chauvinist? I'm not surprised," she said with satisfaction. "If you had said pederast, that might have impressed me. But chauvinist? Of course he is—all wimps are chauvinists."

Jack Rowley had arrived promptly, right at two o'clock. He peered at me as though he was mildly disappointed. "Funny," he said when we shook hands, "I thought you looked different." I did not tell him the truth, that I did look different. Nothing like some good advice, if you listen to it. "Lighting's better, maybe," I said, "than in Dawes's court-room there."

"Could've fooled me," Rowley said. "Maybe the cameraman."

We had fooled him, Mack and I, starting the night before. "Okay," she said when I told her my idea. "This is risky, doing this, playing with his cameras. But maybe, if we plan it right, we can cut those risks. Ace and Roy are making ads for the cable TV. Some of what they can do for those ads, we should do for you." Therefore, after I saw Cooper that day, and conversed with Mousie, I had left my office and gone up to Copley Place. I spent half the morning in Marlene's Garden Bower. I was pummeled, oiled, and kneaded. I had my pores sealed. I was razor-clipped and tinted, blending in the gray. A young woman with some tweezers worked on my eyebrows. I sat under sun lamps and I had a manicure. "I'll feel like a goddamned fairy, Mack," I said when she proposed it.

"Yes," she said, "you probably will. I just wish that I could see it. But you will look like Cary Grant when they get through with you. Not like some old derelict in some story of the homeless."

"Look," I said, "I know you like her. She bought that big house from you, and you say she's all right. But just the same, Mack, at my age? Like a goddamned poodle? Sitting under a damned dryer? Having makeup put on? What if someone sees me there getting all that done? Wouldn't it be better if I went to Dotty? She does that same sort of stuff, and out there on Route One at least I'd have better odds that no clients might see me."

"You're getting soft, I think," she said. "Go to Dotty Franklin? In the first place, all she does is put blue tints in hair. Except for those ladies who are more discriminating—they get rose with blond highlights, and that's not what you need. Besides, when you mention clients, how would Teddy take that? She would tell him you'd been in, and he would lose his mind. 'My big lawyer, getting rinsed? Kennedy's gone soft.' No, Jeremiah, this one is my territory. Go and see Marlene like I say, put yourself in her hands. Wear your new gray suit there that you save for funerals. Have your shoes shined. Wear the shirt that Heather gave you Christmas. You're not really an old wino—you just look like one."

Rowley had two women with him, each loaded down with baggage. One of them lugged what looked to be two black saddlebags suspended from her shoulders; she carried a heavy silver-finish tripod. The other one had a portable TV camera and a large battery pack, slung from her left shoulder. She held a long canvas seabag in her right hand. They both looked very scruffy under all the stuff; L. L. Bean–type lace-up boots on one, and hiking boots on the other. Black jeans and gray whipcord trousers; nubby gray sweaters bagged out from much hard use; yellow slickers with hoods that plainly had not been used to protect their frizzy hair. They looked young and they looked sullen, and they looked around the reception area of my office with evident lack of approval. Rowley gestured toward them over his left shoulder. "Sadie," he said. "Vera." He did not explain which was which.

I stepped toward them and offered my right hand. "First thing to remember, Jerry," Mack had said to me, "no matter how pissed off you are, you are really a nice guy. And you want people to be aware of this. So act like it, all right? Be nice to whoever gets involved in this shooting match, and don't let on how really furious you are."

"Jerry Kennedy," I said, "pleased to meet you." Sadie and Vera stared at me. "Evidently they are not used to people making conversation with them," I told Mack that night. "These broads are men's equals, see? They are accustomed to be treated like shit in the same way that the men who do their jobs are treated." One of them, the one on my right with the camera and the seabag, dropped the bag on the floor with a clank and stuck out her paw to be shaken. "Hi," she said. The other one just stared at me as though I had been some form of marine life that interested her photographically. "I backed off," I told Mack. "What do I know, huh? Maybe in addition to being a female technician, she is also a deaf-mute that fills a quota handicapped employee's slot."

I retreated from them and turned to face Gretchen, who was watching all of this quite avidly. "My secretary," I said, "Gretchen Larson." Rowley, taking off his coat, grunted something. Sadie and Vera inspected Gretchen, said nothing, and looked to Rowley for instructions.

Rowley threw his coat over the chair. He pulled his trousers up tight to his crotch, hustled his balls irritatedly, and gazed around the space. "Kind of cramped," he said.

"We're not doing it here, Jack," I said firmly. "I thought we'd sit down in my private office where we can be sure of not being disturbed."

"Is that bigger?" he said.

"No," I said, "it's smaller."

Rowley winced and shook his head. He sucked at his teeth. "Cripes, Jair," he said, "I don't know. See, this is what I meant. You came to the studio, we're all set up for this. Lots of space, the studio cameras, engineering stuff. We can do this road stuff, but it's more for breaking news. Lights and all this junk we bring, they're just not as good. These kids, they are good and all, but they still need the room. There are limits, you know, Jair? To what we can do."

"Now," Mack had said the night before in bed, "you are always telling me about the courtroom camera. It makes you uneasy and you don't like looking at it."

"Right," I said, "I really don't. You want what I really wish, it wouldn't look at me. And if you saw the same show I did, now you know why I do."

"Okay," she said, "you're uneasy."

"Naturally," I said. "In the courtroom, I'm on display. I am a performer. I am playing to a judge. To a client also. To the jury, if there is one. Not to lookers-on. What the peanut gallery thinks, that does not concern me. Put that camera in there, it makes me damned nervous."

"So," she said, "what you need, then, is some concern for comfort. Where do you feel comfortable? Really comfortable?"

"Geez, Mack," I said, "I don't know. You're still good-looking but the drapes are kind of drab. Besides, would it look that good? Both of us in bed here with the blankets all pulled up?"

"That would be good," she said. "Channel Eight would go for that. And for the finale, we could copulate on the air. 'We're not saying: "Fuck you, Jack." We have got each other.' But they wouldn't go for that."

"Okay," I said, "then my office. That is my home turf. I will see Jack Rowley, but I'll see him in my office. Make a little ad for myself, while I am about it. People in the shit see that, they will know I'm cheap. Nothing fancy about me, nothing too expensive. Just what it takes to do the job. Come on down and see me."

"Jack," I said to Rowley as he measured my small space, "like I told you on the phone, you forced me into this. While you're here, or I am there, I'm not getting paid. Therefore, if you want the story, I have to ask you to come here."

"Yeah, I know, I know," he said, and clapped his hands. "Okay,

Sadie, Vera," he said, as though rousing two strong horses, "onward and upward here, to Jerry's private office."

"You should've seen their faces," I said, telling Mack about it that night. "The three of them looked like they had been put in jail. Much murmuring and back and forth, 'Jesus, I don't know.' 'Light there from that window stinks. Glass's really dirty.' 'Put that halo over there, see how that works out.'

" 'Look,' I said, 'I'm in the way. What about this, Jack? I'll be in the outer office, seeing the mail. You folks get set up in here, call me when you're ready.'

" 'I assume,' Jack says, looking at my desk, 'nothing in here's confidential, we might maybe see. Wouldn't want it in the pictures, anything like that.'

"Not much he wouldn't, I think," I said to Mack. "Guy looks like a great white shark, thinking about that. 'Absolutely not,' I say. 'Perfectly all right. Nothing out in view here's even partly confidential. Just as long as we can get this done today. Get the facts on my side out, that is what's important.'

"The hardest thing of dealing with those bastards, Mack," I said, "is not their assumption that you are extremely stupid. That is bad enough, of course, but what is really hard is keeping your face straight while they are doing it, you know? Like you really are so stupid that you believe all their crap.

"Rowley looks concerned. 'Well, Jair,' he says, and the two broads are smashing the equipment around like a couple ironworkers building some damned drawbridge or something, 'this of course does get back to what I told you when I first called you, and you refused to go on camera with me. And that is that, naturally, your side doesn't get presented at the same time as the positions of your opponents do. And the first three parts of my report, which will run through Wednesday night, those are already in the can, Jair. Taped, edited, voice-overed, commentary written, everything. So, what we're doing here today will naturally be part of the report, Jair, but part four, you know? Not until Thursday night.'

" 'Jack,' I said, 'this disturbs me, you know? I have no "opponents" here, as you describe Judge Dawes. Or Harry Mapes, as far as that goes. "Opponents" would be people whose positions I dispute. My purpose in this is merely to make sure that all the facts are represented in a straightforward manner. I know facts that they may not, and since they're talking, Jack, I think I have no choice but to bring those facts out.' "

Mack nodded. "That is good," she said. "Very reasonable."

"We begin," I said. "Sadie and Vera are slamming around, getting in each other's way, holding up light meters, saying 'Shit' under their breaths, and then finally we're all set. 'Mister Kennedy,' Jack says, very formal and official, 'Judge Dawes has charged that you are one of a cabal, a very small cabal, of lawyers who sabotaged his elevation to the Court of Appeals of Massachusetts. What is your reaction to that charge?'

"I lean forward earnestly and look right at Rowley. 'Jack,' I say, 'the judge is understandably upset, as I'm sure I would be too. He's disappointed, naturally, that he didn't get the job. And it's never very pleasant to learn that the people who have seen you work don't think your work is good.

" 'But, Jack,' I say, 'Judge Dawes's work has been mediocre at best. He's mercurial and arbitrary, when he's on the bench. A man like Harry Mapes may get a break from him, but that only means another poor guy can look forward to injustice. I didn't think Judge Dawes was fit for the promotion. I told that in confidence, to the governor. Now Judge Dawes is embarrassed, and I'm sorry for that. But we all have to have the courage of our views, I think, and I stand by what I said.'

"Jack does not think fast," I said, telling Mack about it. "Jack was evidently startled: I was not defensive. 'You say, Attorney Kennedy, your remarks were confidential? You did not intend that they would come to public notice?'

" 'I was astonished,' I said. 'It's a breach of protocol, if not one of ethics. We trial lawyers see the judges, watch them every day. Should we remain silent when their names come up for new jobs? If we think a man's unfit, who should know better? Do we bite our tongues and keep our information secret? Governors do not see judges. Governors don't know. I think governors deserve our advice on this, and I think we are obliged and duty-bound to see that they get it. Making it a public matter—that's a different thing. I regret the governor's action in that respect, Jack. I think it was a mistake, and it will haunt him later. Next time there's a vacancy, men and women in my job will think two or three times before they present their valid, relevant opinions on the candidates. And that is regrettable. Most regrettable.'

" 'So, then,' Jack says, 'when Judge Dawes said you conspired against him, that would be an error, you think, do you?'

" '*Conspiracy*?' I say, and I recoil in horror. '*Conspiracy* is a crime, Jack. A criminal offense. If Judge Dawes said that, I'd say he has proved my case. Is it to be a felony, to thwart his blind ambition? Or will he be satisfied with just a misdemeanor?'

"Now I lean forward once again, and fix him with my stare. 'This just illustrates my point, what I said about him. Judge Dawes misconstrues the law, in this case for himself. He thinks free speech about him is a criminal offense. I say that his thinking that proves that the words were right. He should not have been appointed to the Appeals Court. Whether he should sit where he is? I'll leave that to you.'

"Jack looks very troubled now. He is floundering. 'Mister Kennedy,' he says, 'what about this, then? Judge Dawes has made an allegation that you're linked with Frank Macdonald. He says you and Frank Macdonald have controlled the governor. He says that you did this as a naked show of power. One that will intimidate all of our other judges. He says that you've done this so that judges will obey you, and be careful with your clients lest you take revenge against them. What is your response to this?'

" 'Paranoia,' I said. 'I opposed Luther Dawes because I know him very well. He commits the judge's worst sin: he is unpredictable. One man, like your Mister Mapes, gets his walking papers. Another on the same day may be put away forever. And the one who goes to jail will go there for no better reason than a man like Harry Mapes has been released onto the street. That reason is the judge's mood, and how he feels about him.

" 'That sort of uncertainty is fatal to the process. That sort of capriciousness is frightening, in fact. It means that the punishment for an offense will depend upon the judge you have drawn. It means that it further depends on how his stomach feels. How his eggs were cooked that morning. Was he stuck in traffic? Some men, when His Honor's angry, get long prison terms. Others, when he's happy, escape punishment entirely.

" 'Luther Dawes in his career has been guilty of that kind of misbehavior. He is guilty regularly. He is guilty often. I think he's a bad judge. I think he would be worse if he were elevated to a higher court. That is not Judge Dawes's view, I am very sure. But it is my view—I expressed it. I am standing by it.'

"Rowley let the tape run while he gathered up his thoughts."

"They can edit that," Mack said. "Edit anything. They can cut your speech down to a tiny glimpse of you."

"They can," I said, "but I doubt they will. Jack's committed to a five-part series here. He is trying to make noise. I provided that. He gives me a good display, he can bring back Luther. Make himself look more important. More free fireworks.

" 'Mister Kennedy,' he says, 'you are a trial lawyer. You appear quite often in the Superior Courts.'

" 'This is true,' I said.

" 'Well,' Rowley said, 'since Judge Dawes sits on that court, and seems destined to remain there, is it not a possibility that you will have to appear before him again in the future?'

" 'It's a possibility,' I said. 'There are more than sixty people on that court, plus the judges of the District Courts who sit by designation. They rotate from court to court. But it's a possibility.'

" 'Well, then,' Rowley says, and you should have seen him, Mack— face looked like an old washboard, had so many furrows, 'having said what you have said, first to the governor and now to Channel Eight, don't you have to fear that Judge Dawes, if he sits on one of your cases, might, ah, well . . .'

" 'Get even with me, Jack?' I said. 'The very fact you ask that question shows you think I'm right. That's precisely what I've said, what bothers me about him. What's bothered me in his trial work, what troubled me when his name was proposed for the Court of Appeals. He is entirely capable of injuring a client of mine just to get revenge on me. And that question came to you, Jack, because you too have seen him up close and you've seen that side of him. And this campaign of his on TV, which you are promoting, is further proof of what I said: he isn't fit to serve.' "

"Pretty rough," Mack said, and whistled.

"There was more," I said. "Figure, if you're doing this, no good deed should go unpunished. Gave my old pal Mapes a shot, kicked him around some. If they use it, like you say, I have gotten even."

"Have you?" she said musingly. "Even with Macdonald?"

"Mack," I said, "the guy is sick. Have compassion on your friends."

29

CALVIN BEAL was late on Thursday in the Quincy District Court. He wore handcuffs and fresh bruises, and he was in custody. Disconsolate about the charges that he'd beaten up his wife, Calvin had gone drinking when he got through work on Wednesday. Irene, his new playmate, had quit early to be with him. They had gone to the Crossroads, a gin mill in South Weymouth. It attracts its regulars from a plastics factory which manufactures rubbish pails and other molded goods. Those regulars are young and tough and unskilled and they do not like newcomers. They especially did not like Calvin, once he'd gotten noisy. Irene didn't drink too well, but she drank a lot. Irene got noisy too. When one regular said something, she said something back. Calvin stood up to defend her challenged honor. That was when the fight broke out, around nine o'clock.

Patrolman James Lewis of the Weymouth police brought a list of charges. He began with those which he thought most important, working his way down to those which seemed more trivial. Calvin was accused of assault and battery by means of a dangerous weapon, to wit: a shod foot, on the person of a police officer, to wit: James Lewis. "This one," I said to Calvin, when we chatted that fine morning, sitting in a small room with a sheriff just outside, "what did you do? Pop the cop? Kick him in the ass?"

Calvin craned his neck as though he had some kinks in it. He looked like a cormorant, a greasy, ugly fishing bird that's never satisfied. "Nah," he said insolently, "kicked him in the balls. Tried to kick him in the grapes, at least. Not sure if I connected." He waggled his head in small circular motions and re-telescoped his neck. "I was pretty drunk, I guess," he said reflectively. "Don't remember too much, you know? About what went on."

"Okay," I said sarcastically, "having that in mind, let's just go through this stuff, see what we have got. 'Resisting arrest,' yes, of course—that would surely follow. Kick the nice cop in the crotch, he could take that view. 'Possession of controlled substance'—you had some marijuana?"

Calvin resettled his head once more on his dirty neck. "Must've slept wrong in the jail. My neck's stiff," he said. "Either that or someone hit me. Got me from behind." Calvin snorted and he shook his head again. "Dirty bastards, ten to one, they have to call the cops? And then when the cops get there, they arrest the one? Don't seem fair to me."

"I know it, Calvin," I said. "It's not fair at all. For some reason, though, it always works that way. Time and time again, you see it happen—give the cops a choice in these things, and they take the trouble-maker. Always going after the one guy who started it. Could be ten more, even twenty that he fought. Doesn't matter. Every time, they want the instigator."

Calvin snuffled sadly and he thought about all that. He nodded once or twice and said: "Well, I don't think it's right. They were gonna, take me in, just 'cause I was fighting, where are all those other guys? They were fighting me."

"They're included by implication, Calvin," I said. "This charge of making an affray—that refers to your opponents in the fight. Let's get back to the controlled substance, shall we? What did you have, pot?"

Calvin seemed to have trouble collecting his wits. "Uh," he said, "Irene. Irene had some grass, right? In her bra there, was where she had it. Some, uh, really righteous grass."

"Irene isn't charged, that I know about," I said. "If she is, I'm not interested. I don't represent Irene. I represent you, at least on the Janet matter."

"Well," Calvin said, "on the thing with Janet there, yeah. But you also, don't you have to, be my lawyer on this stuff that I got this morning too?"

"No," I said.

"*No?*" Calvin said. His eyes bugged fully open. "What is this shit: No? You telling me this, you're not my lawyer on this? My father give you three grand there, *Mister* Kennedy. Means, that means when you take that money there, you are gonna be my lawyer."

"For the Janet thing," I said, "as you succinctly put it. I am representing you on the case which is supposed to be tried here this morning.

For which you were supposed to be here and meet me at the coffee shop across the street at eight-thirty sharp."

"Well," Calvin said, "there was one guy there that didn't want to come, you know? That they had in the lockup there. And then the car, there was something wrong with it and it wouldn't start. So, and then they get him in the car there, and they get the jumpers and they get it started there. Fucking dumb cops can't do nothing. Guy there, he takes the jumper from the positive and he puts it on the negative, and then he's got the other jumper there and it's on the negative, and he's gonna hitch it up, the positive on our car, and I yell at him: 'You asshole,' I say, 'don't do that. Blow the fucking battery up, you fucking stupid ass-hole.' And then the guy that made the trouble when they put the cuffs on him, he gets all mad at me there, you know? And he says to me: 'You fuckin' asshole, tellin' him. Should've let him do it.' And I say: 'Fuckin' asshole? Who's the fuckin' asshole if the battery blows up and the fuckin' car's on fire, right?' " Calvin brayed heartily and shook his head in disbelief. "Fuckin' assholes," he said.

"Calvin," I said, "are you finished?"

"Huh?" he said. He focused on me. "Yeah, sure, I am finished," he said.

"Good," I said. "So listen to me. I represent you on the Janet thing. I will also stand up with you on these new charges this morning here, so that you can be arraigned on them. You will plead Not Guilty."

"Naturally," he said. He nodded vigorously. "Of course not. I would plead Not Guilty anyways. I didn't start it with those fuckers, that they just arrested me."

"My appearance slip will say that it's solely for the purposes of this arraignment, Calvin," I said. "No trial counsel, got it? No hearings and no pleadings and no bail reduction motions if they do not let you out. For the arraignment here this morning, I will represent you on the Crossroads charges here. Then I will see whether the Commonwealth wants to try the Janet thing today."

"We should try them both together," Calvin said thoughtfully. "Get that fat cunt Janet in here and those other fuckers too." He made a sweeping motion. "All of 'em. All over with. All at once. Same lawyer for the whole bunch."

"Calvin," I said, "wouldn't do it."

"No?" he said, regarding me with interest.

"No," I said. "No chance."

He guffawed at me. He shook his head. "You are something," he said. "Gotta hand it to you, Mister Kennedy. Telling me a thing like that, and you already took my money. Really something." Then his face closed like a door and he said: "Eat shit, fucker. You took three grand from my father. You are gonna do this. All of it, the Janet thing, and also from last night." He leaned toward me over the small table. "I know you, you cocksucker," he said, with a breath like a swamp. "I know all about you, what a big shit you think you are." He leaned back again and his lips curled righteously. "I seen you on TV there, talking about you. Judge there and the other guy, both of them know you. Monday night and Tuesday, they were talking about you. Big pals with the governor and how you're fixing cases." He leaned forward again, with his forearms on the table. "That don't cut no shit with me, Mister Kennedy. You think you know all this fucking shit and stuff like that? Well, you just remember something. You and me in here today, you got that dumb shit outside, and all these cops around. But you fuck me up, you bastard, and I'll come around for you. Maybe not this week or something, but I'll come around. Come around and see you sometime. Find out where you live. Give me any more of your shit. You'll find out, you fucker." Then he leaned back in his chair again, and grinned happily at me. "Grass was Irene's," he said. "She give some of it to me. I was saving it for later, and I put it in my pocket. They arrested me? They find it. That's all there was to it. Now, what else you want from me, *Mister* Kennedy?"

"Very little, actually," I said, and stood up to leave the room. "See you in the courtroom, Calvin. Stay as sweet as you are, always."

"So," I said to Mack that night, when she saw the gun, "I went back out in the courtroom and in time his case was called. The cases that he made last night, the ones for arraignment. I stood up on my hind legs and put it to the court. Judge Toner's hard of hearing, but he is cooperative. Slowly and distinctly, I got all my points across. Calvin had Not Guilty pleas entered for the fracas. Calvin's thing with Janet there, as he likes to put it, was continued sixty days, so he could be examined. I was granted leave to file a motion to withdraw. I wrote my motion out in longhand and I filed it. Judge Toner granted it at once, appointed Mass. Defenders. DA moved for a commitment, thirty days of observation. Mass. Defenders, Joanie Doyle, joined in DA's motion. Calvin's bail was upped to twenty, with recognizance."

"So, he's locked up—why the gun?" Mack was practical. She dislikes my .38, calls it "repulsive." I have told her many times that it's a work of art. One she may not like, perhaps, but Smith & Wesson's best. Anyway, I always argue, beauty's not important. What's important's what it does, what I need it for. "That is what's repulsive, my dear: Why I need the thing. You don't like that? I don't like that. It remains the fact.

"People have been known to get out," I said of Bridgewater. "It's secure and they are careful, but there are escapes. Calvin is ingenious, my love. He is also strong. He is young and he is reckless, and his brain has snapped. This young man is crowding thirty. Never had a record. All the years when kids get records, Calvin's nose was clean. Fifteen, eighteen, twenty-one—not even one arrest. Now he's twenty-eight and working, and he's dangerous. I don't know why this is, why this mangy dog got mean. Realized his wife was fat? Pissed off at his father? Irene makes him feel like Tarzan? Too much paint inhaled? Could be almost anything. Point is, he has gotten mean, and he might get out. If he's nuts like I believe, he could be out soon enough, without an escape. Joanie Doyle will do her job. She has got no choice. Doctors say he's daffy now, she'll plead insanity. Judge won't have much choice on that—he will have to grant it. Calvin isn't stupid. He behaves and he goes free. Free of Janet, free of cops, free to come see me.

"This could happen anytime, and I would never know it. They may say they'll notify me if they let him out. I did tell Toner, after all, he had threatened me. But someone always slips up there, letting people know. No one makes the call that's ordered, I will be defenseless. So, that's why the gun, Mack, so I'll have it if I need it. I paid two grand of the little bastard's fee back into the court. Let them hold it for him until they see if he's sane. If he is, then he will need it to get another lawyer. If he isn't, then he'll have it when he's finally discharged. Maybe he'll hate someone else when that fine day comes. Take his money and forget me, just as I will forget him."

"Interesting," she said, "that he saw the TV stuff."

"Interesting," I said, "just the stuff I wasn't in." Tuesday night's agenda on Jack Rowley's taped reports was Harry Mapes's detailed review of the whole justice system. Harry's range of course was great, with all his experience. He discussed trial judges from the early thirties on, serving up examples right into the present day. Luther Dawes was one of the best, Harry was convinced. "What I like about him, Jack," he said to Rowley, "is the way he takes the extra time to see what a man feels. Many judges, you know, Jack, they're all cut and dried. 'He did this? Then I'll do that,' and that's the end of it.

"All that does, Jack, and I know, is keep the cycle going. Guy does something? He goes in. He comes out again. Nothing's changed except he's worse, and he has gotten older. He's not sorry. He's not better. He's still got the same problems. Hasn't got a job, most times, so he can make a living. If he's got a family, he's got to get to know them. Most of them, the families, they're not sure they want that. Guy embarrassed them like he did, when he was in jail, he can be their father or their husband or their brother—they will still look at him from the corners of their eyes. 'Uncle John's a convict, there. Think he uses drugs? Been in there with all them bad guys—he must be one too.' You know what they do, Jack, when their relative comes out? Hide their money, like he would steal from them." Harry bobbed his head and did his best to look anguished. "Many guys have told me that, Jack, and you too, Judge Dawes, you know? Kind of thing that shames them, when their family don't trust them. Makes them feel like, you know, they got nothing to hope for. Families won't even trust them, who the hell else will? Guys go back to crime when that kind of thing starts to happen. Figure: 'Hell with it,' all right? 'I've been branded now.'

"Thing that Judge Dawes did with me that day gave me hope. Then, Jack, when I get the call here on the crime prevention show, that was the big break in my life. What I always needed." Harry smoothed his maroon jacket—he must have had a wardrobe there, at the TV station. "Made me think: 'I can do something. Besides be a bum.'

"Lawyers like this Kennedy," Harry cautioned all, "they don't like it when the judges do that stuff. Makes them look like you don't need them. Cuts into their fees. What the heck, am I right there? Sure, you know I am. I go into Judge Dawes's court, talk to him like I did. Tell him I've got a new reason, for another chance. Why do I need Kennedy? What's he gonna do? Judge hears what I've got to say, gives me a new chance. Kennedy's unnecessary, that is what he is. Naturally, when Judge Dawes here, looks like he'll get more power, guys like Kennedy get nervous. Think they'd better stop him."

"That's your explanation, then, for Kennedy's behavior?" Rowley said to Mapes. "He opposed Judge Dawes because he thinks he's bad for lawyers?"

Luther nodded just a little; he agreed with that. Harry crossed his legs and clasped his hands upon his knees. "Right, Jack," he said, "mostly that. Protecting their own business. Never mind the client's rights there, what happens to him. Long as all the lawyers make out, he is satisfied."

"Tomorrow night," Jack Rowley said, meaning Wednesday, "Judge Dawes will go into detail on the flaws in our system. What he's tried to do as judge, what still needs to be done. How that's dangerous for judges, to attempt reforms." Luther had performed as promised, at interminable length.

"Many social crusades," he said the next evening, "as good-hearted as they are, lead to problems in the courts which no one has expected. Drunken driving, for example—nobody likes that. Loss of lives on our highways, injuries and death? The harm's just incalculable, and we have to stop it.

"The way we have chosen," he said, "one big way, at least: we've passed new laws, gotten tough, put the drunks in jail. We did all this, really, without thinking matters through. Didn't pause to think that this would mean more trials. Under the old system, and it wasn't good enough, people charged with drunken driving mostly pleaded guilty. Went through some re-education, took some driving classes. Paid their court costs and went home. Took no time at all.

"Now they all want jury trials, since they're facing jail. Now we're lucky if we handle two a day. Our dockets are clogged up and our cases are backlogged. And lawyers who would charge five hundred now are getting five times that, because jail's involved.

"What we did, with our improvements," Judge Dawes said solemnly, "was make a market for the lawyers, in the middle class. We created for them a new, well-to-do, variety of criminal, you see? And men like Jerry Kennedy are getting rich on that. Naturally they take an interest in how judges are promoted. They want us obedient, somewhat scared of them. I am here to tell them that it isn't going to work."

Rowley that night followed his tape with a teaser for my segment. "Be with us tomorrow night," he said, looking solemn. "See what Attorney Kennedy's reaction to this is."

Rowley's anchorman looked eager, as though this was news to him. "You got Kennedy to talk, Jack?" he said respectfully.

Rowley nodded with assurance. "Yes, indeed, I did. And what he had to say, Bob, well, it isn't love and kisses."

"Real hard-hitting stuff, Jack?" Bob said breathlessly.

Rowley nodded once again. "Very much so, Bob. Jerry Kennedy does not like some of what he has been seeing, hearing what Judge Dawes and Harry Mapes have had to say, about him and his profession. Be with us tomorrow night: Kennedy replies."

"Well," Mack said on Thursday evening, "do they have TV in Bridgewater, so the inmates there can watch?"

"Sure they do, in the game room," I said. "Calvin sees tonight's performance, he will go right off the wall."

30

TEDDY CALLED me on Palm Sunday, when we got back from the beach, nicely grimy and fatigued from a long day at the house. "What's the matter, Jerry?" he said. "You were gone all day. Signing autographs or something, big celebrity?"

"No," I said, "I was in church, praying for your soul. Spent the whole day on my knees, seeking your salvation. 'God,' I said, 'look out for Teddy. You know how he is. Lovable but too impulsive, thinks I can protect him. Lead him from his reckless ways. Teach him to be good. Let him learn a legal skill. Home repairs would be good. I could give him work right now, he knows heating systems.'"

"Counselor, you're getting silly, now that you are famous. I reform and you are finished. Have you thought about that? Daughter in her fancy school there, houses at the beach? All that goes if I go straight. You really sure you want that?"

"You're right," I said, "I should have thought. I'd be lost without you."

"Damned right, Jerry," Teddy said. "Glad you're shaping up. Watch out what you pray for, pal. God can be a wise-ass. Next thing you know, you will get it, what you asked Him for. Then you will be up shit's creek, and you won't have a paddle. I go straight and you go broke. That don't sound like fun."

"I have always said this, Teddy: you can find the jugular."

"Unless maybe by then," he said, "you're in television."

"Not much chance of that," I said. "Money isn't good. Those guys love me when I'm free. They don't pay retainers."

"Yeah, yeah, I know," he said. "But you have got potential. You know the part that I liked best? It was Friday night. The part where you were giving it to the fucker with the dog. What's his name there? Harry something?"

"Harry Mapes," I said.

"That's the piece of shit," he said. "Fucking Harry Mapes. I see him on Monday, giving you the business? 'Who is this jerk?' I say. 'Why is he on this? Little ham-and-egger here, everybody knows him. He's like the bag ladies on the Common, or some other shit like that. Just because the guy's familiar, everybody knows him, now we're supposed to listen to him? That don't make no sense.' Then you come on Friday night, and what was it you call him? Something like the town dump?"

" 'Common nuisance,' " I said. I said Harry Mapes, and other people like him, were the prices paid by lawyers for their right to make a living. "If the law gave Harry Mapes the treatment he deserves," I had said to Jack Rowley, "after all these many years, it would treat him just as it does every other common nuisance. Someone gets caught operating a loud roadhouse, you know, there's a motion to abate it, put an end to the nuisance. People who keep cats, many, many, cats. Goats or chickens, horses, pigs—anything like that. Something that sets up a stink or makes a lot of noise—what you do with that stuff is abate it legally. Get an order. Shut it down. Put it out of business. You don't do what Eight has done, put it on television. You promote this broken-down old burglar as a social critic? Team him up with Judge Dawes there, as experts on justice? That's ridiculous, my friend. Just ridiculous."

"That's it," Teddy said to me, " 'a common nuisance.' Right. That Rowley guy there looked like you just set his tie on fire. Never seen anything like you before in his whole life. They had one shot of his face, it was when you were rolling through that stuff about how Dawes is fucking up the system, playing games with people, and I thought that bugger's eyes were gonna pop out of his head. Jesus, Jerry, I must say, it was beautiful."

"Thank you," I said graciously, "if I do say so."

243

"Hey," he said, "it isn't like, I was surprised, you know. Down at Lucy's there, that day, that was what I told you. Nobody can sling the shit like you can, when you believe it. You're a fuckin' killer, Jerry. I have always said that. All I'm saying now that's different, you're not in the right line. You missed your goddamned calling, Jerry, is what I am saying. You're gonna be a big goddamned celebrity from now on, is what I predict."

"Teddy," I said, "forgive me. What's this leading up to?"

"Jerry, Jerry," Teddy said, "is this any way to talk? Here I am, I call you up, tell you how great you are. And now all of a sudden you are getting jumpy on me?"

"Force of habit, Teddy," I said. "You'll have to forgive me. I get home on Sunday night, really need a shower. Phone rings and it's you who's calling, I just have to wonder: what is going on, my friend? Something out of whack?"

"Jerry," Teddy said, in a more concerned tone, "I admit, I do have this problem. Me and Dottie yesterday, get up pretty early. Take a plane from Logan and go down Atlantic City. Check on how our luck is running? Catch a couple shows? Just a little outing, Jerry, not spectacular."

"Yeah?" I said. "How was it, Edmund? Lose your shirt and your pants too, playing games of chance?"

"Not too bad, actually," Teddy said, "I lost about eight hundred. Would have been lots worse if Dottie hadn't quit roulette. That is not the problem, though, not why I am calling. What it was, we got back here, got back here tonight. And in the back door to the house, there's a piece of paper."

"*The Watchtower*, no doubt," I said, "urging you to repent. Give that eight hundred to Jehovah, 'cause He's really quite pissed off."

"Well, somebody is," Teddy said. "It was a subpoena. They want me to show up in front of the grand jury."

"Oh, shit," I said. "What county, Teddy? I'm assuming it's not federal."

"Middlesex," he said. "The East Cambridge Courthouse is where they want me to be. Thursday morning, ten a.m. Them against John Doe. Can they do this, Jerry, like this? Call me in like this? Just stick something in my door? That's all there is to it?"

"Uh-huh," I said, "yes, they can. Do it all the time. 'Last and usual abode,' they just leave it at your house. That is valid service, Teddy, if you don't show up. Just like it was in your hand, or your body was in theirs."

"Doesn't seem fair," Teddy said. "Spring it on you like this. And this 'John Doe' stuff, that too? That is legal also? This damned thing don't even tell me what it's all about. I go in there with my pants down and I don't even know what they are gonna ask me? How can I get your advice, if they can act like this? Pretend they're not even sure what guys they're going after. Maybe it is me they want. That is possible. This thing tells me nothing, Jerry, absolutely nothing."

"Teddy," I said, "calm down. It will tell you more than that. On the back of that thing there is someone's signature. Guy who served it signs his name. Read it to me, please."

"Lemme see here," Teddy said. "Looks like a kid's writing. *Oh*, now I got it, Jerry. It is signed by Glennon. 'Earl' and then looks like a 'J.' 'Earl J. Glennon.' Yup. 'Framingham Police Department. Earl J. Glennon, Sergeant.' What is it with this pisspot, want to tell me that? He forget, I was convicted, that shit case he brought? What's he gonna do, Jerry? Get me indicted now? Accuse me of killing him, he thinks I got off easy?"

"That's unlikely," I said. "Possible, I suppose—he could kill himself in such a way as to make somebody think you did it, have a pal of his arrest you, get you tried for it. But even though he's dedicated and he really doesn't like you, that is going pretty far, even for that kid. No, more likely it's the car-theft ring he had. He thinks you're part of it, Teddy, and he wants to get you for it. Especially since you belted him. He does not like you."

"*Bastard*," Teddy said. "I really need this shit? I am not involved with that, those goddamned German sleds. None of it is what I do. None of it, Jerry. BMWs, Mercedes, Porsches, and that shit. I have not touched one of those things since I was a teen-ager. What's the matter with this asshole, he can't understand it? Get it through his goddamned head: I do Cadillacs."

"Maybe, Teddy," I said, "he thinks you could help him. Thinks you might know people, have some evidence for him."

"Well, shit, Jerry, I mean," Teddy said, "sure, I know some guys. But Jesus, huh? What is this, if I know some guys? I know lots of people, but so doesn't everybody? Doesn't mean they get subpoenaed, have to talk about them. I mean, this isn't right, you know? It just isn't right."

"Teddy," I said, "these guys that you know—do they include some people that are nervous about this?"

"Well," Teddy said, "I mean, you will hear certain things. That maybe this guy may be doing something, and if anybody hears of someone that would like to buy some stuff, he would be the man to see because he might have some. But, Jerry, all right? This is shit, selling parts of cars. You got guys that do it and they are completely different. This is not your operation where somebody wants a car. Like say they want a Biarritz, white with red upholstery—somebody would say: 'Call up Teddy,' and I would hear about it. And I would know the kind of thing, and I would think about it. And if everything was right, I would say: 'Okay. I can get that unit for you. No sweat. See you Tuesday.' And that would be the end of it until I see him Tuesday. Give the guy what he has asked for, tell him where it is. 'This here's the ignition key. That one's for the trunk.' And whether numbers need to be changed. All that kind of thing.

"But, Jerry," he said, "that is easy. If a man knows what he's doing, it is like a piece of cake. In and out in half a day, no loose ends and stuff. These guys out in Framingham, they got inventory. They got fenders, they got doors, they are selling engines. Dashboards, the Recaro seats, various kinds of wheels. Molded wheels and then the forged ones—those're always breaking and they cost four hundred new. You know what you need for this, you are selling parts? You have got a junkyard, baby, and a goddamned warehouse too. You are not, you can't be, mobile. You can't come and go. Some guy watches me, all right? He should not expect to find me in the same place more than once. What I do, there ain't no buildings, no phones you can tap. This time when I meet you, it might be in Attleboro—next time that we do some business, it could be in Worcester.

"Now," he said, "you see what I mean. I am not involved in this thing they are hot about. If I know some guys that are, it's because I know them. I know one guy on the Red Sox. He is a nice fellow. This mean, if he drops the throw, I should get an error? Or if somebody doesn't like him, I should piss on him? Uh-uh, Jerry. Not this trip. They are on their own. They don't hurt me, I don't hurt them. That's the way it works."

"Teddy," I said, "this is nice. It does not mean zilch. They have got the paper on you. That is all they need. You've been through this crap before. You know the whole drill. Thursday morning, ten a.m. I will meet you there. We will go in with your paper and I'll talk to the DA.

If the DA's rational, we'll be out by noon. 'Fifth Amendment,' I will say. He won't be surprised. If he's a prick, he will wait. Maybe right through Friday. If he's been around a while, we will go in first. You will give your name and stuff. He'll ask you three questions. Third one will be whether the next fifty will force you to plead the Fifth. You will say: 'Advice of counsel, I respectfully refuse to answer,' and so on through the whole routine. Then he'll let you out and decide what he wants to do next. He may decide to drop it or he may get immunity. Bring you back and make you talk, no risk of incrimination out of anything you say."

"What if he does that, then?" Teddy said with vast annoyance. "What do we do if he does that, that immunity bullshit?"

"We palaver, Teddy," I said, "and decide what you will do. Balance talking against jail, where you'll go if you do not. Could you talk against these guys, it came down to that? Or would that be suicidal? What's your thinking on that?"

"Shit," he said, "these dime-a-dance guys? They are not the weight. These guys all have steady jobs, work from nine to five. Got the wives and got the babies. This is moonlight stuff. Picking up a few stray bucks, use to pick up girls. Flash a big roll, mostly fives, in the joints along Route Nine. These're chickenshit, my friend, not the chicken salad. They decide they'd knock me off, they'd be dead by morning."

"Okay, then," I said, "there you are. So that is one option."

"What's an option? Talk?" he said. His voice was indignant. "Jerry, I don't talk, all right? Not for anybody. Not if it was ants and roaches they were looking to convict. I would not give the Pope any testimony, if it was Hitler he was after. Uh-uh, fuck that, none of that shit. Even for these bozos. Glennon wants them, let him get them. I'm not helping him."

"I stand corrected, Teddy," I said, "that is not one option. So if you get immunity, we are back to one. Balance it yourself. You don't talk, you go to jail. It is actually that simple.

"My guess is, though," I said, "that it will not come to that. This case that they're making here, you are a distraction. Only reason you're in it is that cop wants your ass. DA is obliging him, cutting him a piece. It is not a big piece and I'd bet it's the last one. What you know about this car ring, it's not worth much trouble. They don't need your testimony, so I kind of doubt they'll force it. This is Sergeant Glennon's picnic. He did this to you. This one they have let him have. I bet it's his last one."

"That fucking little snot-nosed kid," Teddy said furiously. "That goddamned kid, that fucking kid, I'd kill him if I could. Guys like you and me, us guys, you know what I'm saying. You and me, we got, we show maturity. You go into court like you do, no big fucking deal. It is something you've been doing, for a lot of years. You know what is going on, and you go in and do it. Don't go stomping in there, making some production of it. Just go in and do your job. Make your dough and get out.

"Same thing goes where I'm concerned. I'm professional. I know what I'm doing, like I maybe didn't always. Know the rules and know the people, what is going on. Do what I do and just do it. Don't get caught and if I do, then I know what happens. None of this horsing around. None of this dumb shit. But this goddamned kid here, he is screwing this all up. Him and all the others, all the other kids like him—they are half-assed little jerks. Playing cops and robbers and just wasting time, is all.

"And that is what I'm saying, Jerry. You know what I mean? I did not act like this when I was new at things. I known you a long time, and you didn't act like this. Not when I was looking, at least, and I always paid attention. So what the fuck is going on here, is what I would like to know. Are the people getting worse now? Or am I just getting old?"

"I think that is probably it," I said.

"Getting old, you mean," he said. "Thanks a bunch, you fucker. You are no young virgin either, when it comes to that."

"This I was aware of, Teddy," I said, laughing at him. "Had myself some sharp reminders at my summer place today. Seemed like everything I touched gave me twinges in the back. Turning on the water valves, simple things like that. I knew I was getting old. Never doubted it."

"Yeah," he said with satisfaction, combined with resentment, "but still, you know, you're sounding good. And you looked good on TV. You're, ah, doing okay now. Wouldn't you say that?" There was also a note of mild anxious concern in his voice. Teddy and I have been a team for a long time now, and he does not conceal his personal interest in my availability when he is in a jam.

"Yes," I said, "I mostly am. Did my taxes, got them paid, wife is talking to me."

"How about the daughter there?" Teddy said acutely. "Everything is copacetic with the Miss America?"

"Tolerable," I said, "merely tolerable. No outright hostilities, but things have been somewhat better. She'll be home, six weeks or so. That will work itself out. We've got history to work with—always liked each other."

"Well, then," Teddy said, "you are okay then. Better'n you were, at least, back in Stoughton there."

"Right, I am," I said. "No opposition there. And with you coming up in Cambridge, I'll be prosperous again. Must see what I can do to get that DA to stall you. Run up about a week of full days, yawning at the courthouse."

"Oh, you bastard," Teddy said. "Oh, you fucking bastard. If I didn't need you, Jerry, I would never call you."

The trouble with such evenings of comfortable contentment is that they do not occur except in periods of partial ignorance. Anyone who is always in command of all the facts knows better than to go off guard. I went back on the next day.

31

GRETCHEN GOT up from her desk when I came in the door. She threw "Good morning" at me like a street kid pegging rocks. I hung up my coat and said: "Something going on?" She said: "Uh-huh, Jerry, yessir-ree, there is plenty going on."

"Wonderful," I said, heading for my office. "Nothing like a thriving practice, all those many matters." *Many matters* has become an inside joke; they are invariably and unconvincingly cited by lawyers who are starving for persistent lack of cases, to explain their absence from the courts that are in session.

Gretchen took the client's chair opposite my desk. She had a fistful of pink message slips and a grim look on her face. "Jerry," she said as I sat down, "we have got some problems." She flourished all the messages as the phone rang again. I reached out to answer it. "Let it ring," she said. "All this stuff that I've got here, the machine took these. It can take another one. We have got to talk." I pulled my hand back. "Talk," I said. "Go to it."

"Jerry," she said, "the machine. When I'm out on Thursdays? You don't play it back, I take it, when you come in from someplace."

"No," I said, "not always, I don't. Why should I do that? In the first place, that is your job, yours or the machine's. You're supposed to screen my calls, throw out all the trash. I get back here, it is late, what's the point of it? I should get my dinner late, sit here and play back dial tones? I don't think so, Gretchen, old kid. That is not my idea of fun. I know you can't help with the Thursdays and the time with Harold's mother. I am not complaining 'cause it's out of your control. But as far as I'm concerned, the deal is: you catch up on Fridays."

"Which I have been doing, Jerry," she said defensively. "And just to give you some news here, I'm not catching up with dial tones. People now, they don't hang up. They are used to machines. That is not the problem here, that we have got to face. Where we've got the problem is with people who did talk, waited for the beep, and left their messages as ordered.

"Those nice people," she said, "and a few that are not nice—I write down what they've recorded, on these little fucking slips." She waved the messages at me again. "These things, Jerry. See them? Make them out and put them in your messy In box there. Before your ass hits that chair on Fridays, all those calls are logged.

"And what do you do then, you bastard? You ignore them all. I put the little pink slips in there, with all of the others, and you come in and disregard them. You don't even look at them."

"I glance through them," I said, my turn to be defensive. "Names I recognize and so forth. I look through those calls."

"You look through them," she said, "like you look through trees and flowers. 'There they are,' you say to yourself, and go on to something else. If it's one of your pals calling, him you will call back. But anything or anyone that you do not have fun with, you put those ones right back down, and you don't think about them."

"That's not strictly true," I said. "I don't always do that. What I do, it's like the mail—I treat it like the mail. Just because I get a letter, doesn't mean I have to answer. Some dumb asshole buys a stamp, I don't have to reply. Half the crap that comes in, any busy office, you can leave it where the Good Lord threw it and it takes care of itself."

"Your estimate's way high," she said, flipping through the slips. "These are not the Rotary. These are not admirers. These are people who are calling and they want to hear from you. You ignore them, they get mad. They call back on Fridays. This means I get shit from them, which I have to take. I throw out the shit and write another message slip, drop it in your box. Which means you have got another one to ignore. They call back on Mondays, some again on Tuesdays. Wednesdays, even, people call back: 'Is he dead or something? Have you had his pulse checked lately? Or is he drying out?' These guys have got lots of dimes, millions of them, I think. Some of them must live in phone booths, maybe have them in their homes. I am getting so, the Thursdays, I look forward to them. Good old Jenny is a bitch. I still hate her guts. But there is only one of Jenny, yelling in my ears. And if I don't enjoy what she says, I just leave her lie in shit.

"These ones," she said, "these are different. These are serious. These are people who can hurt you, they get mad enough. They do not like stalling, Jerry, and they are not bashful. They cannot get you to listen, they get nastier with me. Plus which, of course, some are jerks,· but they're persistent jerks. I cannot get rid of them. Only you can do that. And if you expect me to get any other work done, you are going to have to do that. Call them up and do it."

"All right," I said, "you've got me." I reached for the slips. "Gimme those and I'll work backwards."

"Not so fast," she said, snatching the slips back. "These're only part of it. Just· the easy part. I said we had problems, it was not just messages."

"Go ahead," I said. "This day's shot, it looks like."

The phone rang again as Gretchen opened her mouth. I reached for it and she frowned. "I should not do this?" I said. Gretchen, looking undecided, bit her lip and shook her head. "I don't think so, Jerry," she said. "Sometimes those are loaded. Better let me finish first, before you reform." I pulled my hand back. Gretchen looked relieved.

"My guess is, that's Calvin's mother," she said. " 'Mrs. Parker Beal,' as she says. 'Parker Beal of Randolph.' You'd think you were talking to some damned aristocrat. Mrs. Beal has not seen Calvin. She is very worried."

"Cripes," I said, "she shouldn't be. Calvin's in good hands. Got himself a lovely room, even without windows. Floors and walls are soft and padded and he's probably got a vest. Nice white canvas vest they give you, thick and warm, with sleeves. Does tend to constrict your movements, but he will not take a chill. Tell her that the charming lad was off to Bridgewater, last time I saw him, which I do hope's the last time."

Gretchen shook her head. "That won't do it, Jerry. I have told her you fired Calvin, and you paid his fee back into the court, and it doesn't satisfy her. She has got the idea that you want to talk to her. Says you gave it to her in fact. Told her she should call."

"I have never met the woman," I said, "damnit, Gretchen. She, I've never spoken to her. Never laid eyes on her."

"That is not her version, Jerry. That is not the way she tells it. She has seen you several times. She knows what you said. You said, and she heard it, Jerry, she should get involved. 'Courts and lawyers just can't do it,' that is what you said. 'By the time the kid's a client, in the justice system, all the harm's been done. Parents have to do some work.' You did say that, Jerry. She is just reporting in, wants to do her share."

"Television," I said. "She was watching television and she heard me say those things."

"Uh-huh," Gretchen said, nodding. "That is it exactly. You said that and she was listening. Therefore you said it to her. Now you've got to say some more, and you're going to have to do it. She calls every two hours, faithful as an oven timer, and you've got to ditch her, Jerry, before I lose my mind too."

"Okay," I said, "is that it? That the list of problems?"

"No," she said, "it isn't, really. I have several more." She began to leaf through the message slips. "Your bus driver," she said, "the one who likes the kids?"

"Colebrook Unified School District," I said. "Victor Danielson. Catch that total recall, Gretchen? Mind like a steel trap."

"Uh-huh," she said, "I'm impressed. Victor will be too. DA called from Essex. There are problems with the case. Victor's psychiatric report says that Victor should be put away, 'flash-frozen' were his words. 'Victor is a very disturbed young American, and he is dangerous.'"

"That is easy," I said. "Have him bring a motion. We'll go through a one-day trial. Victor goes away."

"It's not quite that easy," she said, "which is why the DA's worried. Said his name is Sam Cuneo, and you would recognize it."

" 'Sam the Slam,' " I said, "I do. Very nice young man. Played some decent basketball for BC some years ago."

"Sam says his problem is that he has got no case. Says the kids that fingered Victor as the guy that fingered them? They have all recanted and he cannot prove his case."

"That is interesting," I said. "What do we do now?"

"That was Sam's interpretation. That was what he said to me: 'Do me and your boss a favor—have him think of something. I think we have got a small bomb on our hands. Goddamned kids'—these are his words—'they are just too smart. What they did was spot this creep, before he acted up. So they put him in the glue for us, and now we are stuck with him. I dismiss and he is loose. He will probably do it. Then I look like turds of course, and Jerry is another. Ask him for me, all right? Say: "Can we shoot this menace?" ' "

"Put a longer hold on that one," I said. "I'll get back to Sam today, if he calls back before."

"Your musician druggie," she said. "One who jumped his bail? They have got him in Northampton, charged with robbery. DA in Middlesex wants him brought down to Woburn and arraigned for disappearing. 'Just a small formality, get it over with.' You're supposed to call Miss Goldser in the Woburn District Court."

"Right," I said, "of course I will. But first get the client's name. Always makes a bad impression, you don't know whom you're representing."

"Well," Gretchen said, "you could always call her up and say: 'Duh, da kid that ran away there when he wasn't supposed to? Had the grass and shit, you know? Him. That's my client.' "

"Right," I said, "and she could tape the conversation for the later use of Luther Dawes, to prove he was right."

"I'll check on that name," she said. "Now, I have here in my hand no less than eleven other messages that we have not discussed, all right? Are you sure you're ready for this? Because this is pretty heavy stuff that we are dealing with here now."

"Ready," I said. "Do your worst."

"Three of them are from the papers," she said, grinning at me. "Lady from the *Globe* says she is from the Living Section. I assume that means they have one also for the people who are dead, but I didn't ask her that. She said they would like to follow you around some day, do a piece about how a *real* trial lawyer spends his time. 'Playing with himself,' I said, but she didn't believe me."

"You did not say that," I said.

"No," she said, "I didn't. I was tempted, though, I can assure you. What I said was that I'd check with you and call her. Wanna do it, Jerry? Might be kind of fun. Might be good for business too, have that in the *Globe*."

"Tell her," I said, "I am busy, but I'm interested. Ask her if she can come over, so we work out some ground rules."

"Will do," she said. "*Herald*'s next. Guy was working on a story for a Sunday page. 'Checking quotes,' was what he said. Something from the TV? I thought of having him call Mrs. Beal, you know? She seems to have taken in every word you said. He says that it's urgent but it's not important, if that makes any sense to you, and you should call him back.

"*Commoner*," she said, "has got a piece on courts they're doing. I gather what this guy wants is some more of your bullshit about how guys who did the same thing don't get the same punishments. He said there was no hurry just as long as he heard back from you by three this afternoon."

"I will do that," I said, feeling pleased with myself.

"Next one," she said, "you will like. It's our pal Jack Rowley. Jack says he would like to 'explore certain avenues with you.' Doesn't that sound interesting? Really big-time, Jerry?"

"Absolutely," I said, "till he tells you what they are. Commonwealth and Massachusetts, those're avenues. He wants me to take a ride, maybe even down Dort Ave."

"Jack was very nice," she said. "Also full of shit. Said your stuff was a big hit. That he'd like to do some more. He said you're a natural, perfect television."

"Which means he thinks I'm a sucker," I said happily. "Me and Harry Mapes's dog, perfect for their needs. Able to do simple tricks, always want to please. We don't ask for anything except a bowl of water and a place where we can pee without someone hitting us and yelling at us for it."

"But you will call him, though," she said.

"Absolutely," I said. "I said he thinks I'm a sucker. I did not say he was wrong."

Gretchen nodded, her smile fading. She went back to the sheaf.

"That leaves seven, Jerry, from the weekend and today. Weekend means they came in after we left Friday. Anything past four o'clock or so, I guess it was."

"Okay," I said, "who they from?"

Gretchen nodded grimly. "I know, all right. Well, I've never met them, but I do know who they are. They are duplicates, okay? Every single one. Not the names, but the addresses. Office's the same." She looked at me with eyes full of misery. "All of them are five-two-threes, all the same exchange. Last four numbers vary but the first three stay the same, five-two-threes." She flourished them. "Every single one. And," she said, glancing at my In box, "there are lots more of them in there."

"I don't get it," I said. "What is five-two-three? I should know this number, maybe? Play it in the lottery?"

"People like us," she said, "have been lucky. That's why we don't know it. Five-two-three is IRS. Internal Revenue."

"Oh," I said, "that *is* good news. Internal Revenue. Just what I was hoping. 'Life has been too quiet,' I was telling Mack last night. 'What we need is some excitement, something interesting. Just like Mrs. Noah said to Mister Noah, you know: "We could use some rain, you know it? Things are getting dry." ' Who is it? That toad Wainer? Marvin? Merlin?"

"Malcolm," she said. "He's among them, Jerry. But he is only one of them, and I have counted four. Four so far I know of, that is. Could be that a fifth one checked in while we have been talking."

"Poor Lou," I said.

"Poor you," she said. "Never mind old Lou. They are pulling your returns this time. Jeremiah Kennedy—he is who concerns them. That is why they're calling, Jerry. They are after you."

32

MRS. PARKER BEAL of Randolph was a thoroughbred champion of her peculiar variety of people. "I am not exactly sure how her mind works," I told Mack that night. "Hell, I'm not sure her mind is working: I am giving her the benefit of a very large doubt by assuming that she even has a mind. But, on that assumption, either she thinks that each time she starts a conversation with a person, it is a totally new person, or else she thinks that the person she's addressing for the sixth or seventh time has the retention powers of a magic slate for kids, and no recollection of what Mrs. Beal said earlier. Whichever it is, I am beginning to see a possible explanation for why Calvin Beal went berserk suddenly. Only thing that puzzles me is why it took him so long."

Mrs. Beal had called four times on Thursday, while the machine was taking my calls. Each time she identified herself by name, place of residence, and maternal relationship to my client, "Mister Calvin Beal." Each time she complained that she had not heard anything from her son, "that is supposed to be in Quincy District Court today with Mister Kennedy, he told me and he told his father too." These protests were delivered during the very hours when Calvin was threatening me in Quincy District Court and being carted off to Bridgewater State Hospital, for some rest and some observation too.

Thursday night, Mrs. Beal called four more times. Gretchen was able to distinguish calls made during the day from the calls made after dark because the latter included not only Mrs. Beal's recitation of her name, residence, and maternal connection to Calvin Beal, but the newer information that Mrs. Beal had heard what I was saying and that was why she was calling. The second of the nighttime calls was very petulant, repeating all of what the first one had delivered, plus a declaration of her inability to understand why I did not return her calls, since I had requested them. The machine tape allowance for each call ran out partway through that recital. Mrs. Beal immediately called again and continued it on the third tape, shouting at the machine and the person whom she presumed to be sitting there beside it. The fourth nighttime call was shorter, although basically the same; Gretchen said that Mrs. Beal by then appeared to be either drunk or drowsy, "but still very much pissed off."

Friday, according to Gretchen, Mrs. Beal made three calls in the morning, one of which Gretchen took unwittingly; after that one, she had used the machine to screen all calls, waiting for the callers to identify themselves over the speaker unit before she picked the phone up. When Mrs. Beal had Gretchen actually on the line, she had once again gone through everything that Gretchen had already heard on tape. When Mrs. Beal was reduced to chatting with the box again, she did the whole spiel again on tapes. She made four more tapes in the afternoon, Gretchen said. Over the weekend she made nine more tapes. And she had called twice before my arrival on Monday morning.

"The woman is remarkable," I told Mack that night. "She is completely placid, I think. Querulous but placid. And she must have the same capacity for air that the Goodyear blimp has for helium, because she never seems to stop for breath." Mrs. Beal accepted my call with complacency. Notwithstanding the fact that I had called her, she told me who she was and where she lived and that she was Calvin's mother.

"Calvin," she said, "didn't come home Thursday night." I made the mistake of saying that Calvin, after all, had not been home for a good many nights, under strict orders of the Quincy District Court, Toner, J., presiding, pending resolution of the charges against him that he had attacked his wife. "Whaaat?" Mrs. Beal said. She strung the word out for what seemed like fifteen seconds. I repeated that Calvin hadn't been home for a good many nights because he was charged with beating his wife and the judge had ordered him not to go home. "To Hough's Neck," I said.

"Not there," Mrs. Beal said, with evident impatience at my stupidity. "I know he wasn't there. Here. To his house here, where he grew up. Calvin didn't come here Thursday." I explained to Mrs. Beal that Calvin had been given other accommodations Thursday, by the Commonwealth, reminding her that my secretary had previously furnished this information to her. Mrs. Beal said: "I don't understand that." Then she went through it all again.

"By now I'm getting smart," I told Mack. "I said 'Uh-huh' as the circumstances seemed to call for it, which was not very often. She went right on, telling me what she'd told Gretchen, telling me what she'd told me, always circling around back to Calvin's non-appearance at his boyhood home on Thursday night."

"The Mister come home late for dinner," Mrs. Beal told me. "He might've been a little drunk, but I know he understood me. He come home right when the news coming on. We sit there and watched it and I told him about it. We both seen you on that show there. You was talking. And I was telling him, the Mister, how I tried to reach you. And he said there you was, if I was interested, you know, in what you might have to say. That it might have something to do with why Calvin wasn't there. Was that judge you talked about, did he do something to Calvin?"

"No, Mrs. Beal," I said, "nothing whatsoever. Judge Dawes was not on Calvin's case. That was Judge Toner."

"Oh," she said, "I wasn't sure. But we watched that, or I did, at least, all of what you had to say, and then I called your office like you probably must know. And me and the Mister, we talked more about it, such as where Calvin had gone and so forth, and then the Mister said he would go up to bed, he thought, and he did that. And I called your office again. I was worried, you know. And then I went to bed.

"Then Friday," she said, "when I talked to your woman there, and that you should, that she ought to have you call me. Because I didn't see how anyone that says he is a lawyer that says he is helping people, you know, that he doesn't when they call him, that he don't call them back up."

"Mrs. Beal," I said, "I'm not helping you. I never said I was. You are not my client. Back on Thursday, Calvin was. Calvin was my client. Calvin's not my client now. Calvin threatened me. But that is neither here nor there, whether I call you. You are not my client. I just call my clients."

"I don't understand that," she said. "So then I keep calling Friday, and I guess your woman went out, in case you did not know she was doing this when she's supposed to be there and to talk to people for you. And Calvin, I still did not know where he was, except he wasn't home. And the Mister Friday didn't see him on the job or nothing, which I find out from him when he come home pretty late. And by then you were back on the television there, and I told him what you said. And he said he did not see Calvin, and by then it was quite late. See, the Mister when he gets through and it's Friday afternoon and he's through painting for the week, the Mister likes to drink a lot of beer then and he feels that it's all right. See, with the weekend and all, he don't have to climb the ladders. He says with the ladders, if he's had a lot of beer, he says it makes him feel, well, sort of funny the next day. Like he will fall or something when he's climbing up on them. Or maybe he will drop something, when he has to carry things when he's up on the scaffolding."

"I see," I said. "Mrs. Beal, I really hate to . . ."

"So the Mister," she said, "he came home and he was full of beer. And I asked him and I told him and he went to bed before me and I think he got it all, what I had to tell him you said. And I went up there with him and got his overhauls off there and he went to bed and stayed there except for once I heard him get up when he had to make his water. And I called your office some more but I guess you must have been, you were probably still out there where they make the television. Would that be where you were there Friday night, at the television station when I called you at your office?"

"No, I wasn't, Mrs. Beal," I said desperately. "I have never been inside that television station. Never in my whole life, Mrs. Beal. I haven't. I was not there Friday and I was not there Thursday either. Everything you saw on TV was filmed right in my own office."

"It *was?*" she said in tones of extreme agitation.

"Certainly was," I said. "Every picture that you saw on me was taken in my office. Except for the first ones that they showed on Monday night. Monday night or Tuesday—I forget which night it was."

"Well, Mister Kennedy," she said, "then I don't think that's very fair. If you was right there then when I called, you should have let me talk to you and answered when I called."

"I don't understand," I said. I really didn't either.

"Oh, Mister *Kennedy,*" she said with shock and horror, "you can't sit there and tell me that, that you don't understand. You just told me, you said so, you were in your office when you were on TV there. And that's when I was calling you, to ask about my Calvin. And you were just, just sitting there, and I was very worried. And you would not talk to me and I don't think that's fair. If you were not Calvin's lawyer, I would call the police on you."

"Mack," I said, "she drove me to it. I used the old part-sentence trick, sound like you're starting something and cut the connection in the middle? And I yelled out to Gretchen, the minute that I did it: 'Put the machine on again. I just cut her off.' And sure enough, with ten seconds, she was calling back. This time she was really angry. Said if I did not come on, she did not care if I was Calvin's lawyer, she was going to call the police on me."

"She probably did call them," Mack said.

"Oh, indeed she did," I said. "Rick Fowler called me from the plain-clothes unit there. 'Kennedy, you scumbag,' he says, 'are you turning yourself in? Or do we get a posse up and haul you in in irons?' Gave me a whole load of shit. But he did say she's harmless. 'Must be all the paint fumes,' he said, 'from old Parker's overhauls, all the washing, all the years. You ought to be flattered, though, company you're in. Last month it was Ronald Reagan that she wanted brought in here. He said something about pensions and she wanted him arrested.'

"Now," I said, "from that I go through the reporters. All of them seem sane enough. The *Globe* lady's coming by tomorrow to conduct an interview, see if there is something I do that is interesting enough to bump some designer off the feature pages one day. Then I'm having lunch with Rowley, hear what's on his fertile mind. And then Wednesday I am going to see Lou."

Mack looked dubious. "What can he do?" she said. "Him in jail and all. Doesn't he need all the records, all the stuff he used?"

"What he can do," I said, "is give me a quick education. Which I really think I need. I put the phone down from my talk with Mrs. Beal. Gretchen comes back in my office, looking like she's just been shot. 'Mister Everson to see you.'

" 'Who is Everson?' I say. Never heard of Everson, not in all of my born days. He is right behind her, though, sticking his head in. 'Richard Everson,' he says, 'mind if I come in?' Looks like an insurance salesman, David Mackin starting out, with the briefcase and the smile. 'Frankly, yes, I do mind,' I say. 'You have no appointment.'

"This does not faze Everson, not in the slightest. Comes right in and sits himself down, handing me his card. 'Richard Everson,' it says. 'Internal Revenue.'

" 'You're right, Mister Kennedy,' says Mister Everson. 'I don't have an appointment, but it's not for lack of trying.' Opens up his briefcase, which looks like it might be leather. Takes out an appointment book, one of those pocket calendars with a small gold pencil in it. Takes the pencil from the loop. Puts his glasses on. 'One, two; three, four; five, six; seven. Seven times I've called for one. You have not called back.'

" 'Look,' I said, 'as you can see, I am pretty busy. I'm just getting back to clients who called me last week. Have to put their interests first if I am going to stay in business.'

"That smile of his," I told Mack, "would survive a missile hit. 'Not to mention,' he says, 'four visits here by Agent Wainer, only one of them successful. You're a hard man to locate, Mister Kennedy, except for those who can be satisfied with seeing you on TV, and that won't do for our needs. You can understand my feelings, I hope, now that I am in here and I see you in the flesh. Few men in our office have accomplished this, and I do not want to leave.'

" 'Mister Everson,' I said, to try a little swerve, 'things have not changed in the slightest since I saw your Mister Wainer back a month or so ago. Lou Schwartz isn't talking and I won't advise him to. He has nothing to be gained and a great deal to be lost, and he wouldn't do it if I said that I now think he should.'

" 'Mister Kennedy,' he says, and gives Gretchen a sharp look. 'If you get your messages, you know that's not the issue.' So much for that little dodge—nice try and all that. 'This is about *your* returns. You have been selected for routine auditing. We have come up with a few questions about some of your deductions. There are also income items we're not sure we understand. In most cases, these small matters can be solved routinely. Just a matter of locating proper records.

" 'But,' he says, 'unless that's done, unless you cooperate, we have no choice but to disallow the items. You don't have to talk with us. That is certainly your right. You don't have to open records. That is also your right. But if you do not do those things, and reject this chance, we will disallow the items. We will have no choice. That will mean more taxes for you, plus interest and penalties that are not insubstantial.' "

"Ah, yes," Mack said. " 'Interest and substantial penalties.' Those guys like that little phrase. They just love to use it. The one that saw Francine and me, he licked his lips when he said it. 'Interest and substantial penalties.' Highlight of his day."

"You didn't tell me that you saw him," I said.

"You were sulking," she said. "Somehow what the tax man told me didn't seem the news that would be likeliest to pull you out of your bad mood. It's the deferred compensation package Ace and Roy set up. The insurance company that sells the annuities had the letter from their lawyers with the opinion in it that the plan was qualified under IRS rules and regulations. The people at the IRS do not agree with that opinion, so they're taxing us. All of us, and with a vengeance. 'We are going to get screwed,' was the way that Francine put it. And the only thing that we can do to stop this screwing, she said, is sue the insurance company and wait eight years to settle. Which of course is going to cost us still another bundle."

"Are you going to do it?" I said.

"We're not sure," she said. "Ace and Roy are thinking about it, and we're going to have a meeting. My guess is that we will not. It's just too expensive. Take our lumps and write it off. We have not got time for this, if we are going to make a living. That guy with the eight of us, he cost the company, we figure, four full days of our time plus another six of Francine's. We cannot afford that crap. It is too expensive. Which it will be too for you, of course, and which they're counting on."

"Not only too expensive," I said, "but very inconvenient. 'Mister Everson,' I said to him, with Gretchen standing there and wearing the same pleased expression she would wear for any snake, 'obviously I am not delighted to hear any of this news. But equally obviously, I know I had better sit down with you and see if we can resolve this. Problem is, as you can see, things are pretty hectic here. And, on top of that, you have my accountant in jail, and I'll need to talk to him. So, you will have to give me time, talk to him and then find someone else to represent me.'

" 'Mister Kennedy,' he says, looking kind of startled, 'you are an attorney. What we want to ask you about isn't all that technical. Besides, we see from your returns for last year that you're capable of doing them, in Mister Schwartz's absence.' "

"Oh my God," Mack said, "you didn't do that, Jerry."

"Mack," I said. "I did do that. What choice did I have? Cooper refused, point-blank. Said he would not do them. Told me he's using H and R Block this year for his own returns. 'It's embarrassing,' he said, 'but bugger the embarrassment. Take the papers down to the Sears store in the plaza, get the numbers filled in and mailed off to Uncle Sammy. I've got too much on my mind, screw around with this.' And that left me with Mendel, Lou's young nephew there. Mendel's not in Boston and I don't know him anyway. April fifteenth rolls around, I'm procrastinating. Business with Dawes comes up, then the crap with Calvin. I just did the damned returns, same as Lou did last year. Wrote the checks and sent them in."

"And after all these years," she said, "of giving good advice, lawyer Jerry does what he's been telling everybody they should never do themselves."

"Yeah," I said, "and it gets worse. I made some mistakes."

"Like what kind?" she said. "You forgot to put down income? Should I be looking out for cake recipes with files?"

"No, no," I said, "it's not like that. Perfectly innocent. I just assumed that overhead, the items were the same. Not that the numbers stayed the same—I am not that innocent. But that the categories were the same as last year, when Lou did the returns, and so all I had to do was get the numbers for this year and just plug them in.

"Which I therefore did," I said. "Rent, I get the check that Gretchen wrote for May and I know it didn't go up after that, so I multiply by twelve and that's what I deduct for rent. And postage is about the same, and the phones, and I estimate the same mileage and depreciation on the car that Lou did last year, and so on. And I am perfectly confident that everything is neatsy-keen and I send the returns in.

"Now," I said, "this is the furthest thing from my mind when I am jawing with Mister Everson there and Gretchen is looking sort of stricken, and the phone machine is gobbling up all kinds of calls and losing business for me because people still do not like chatting with machines. And Mister Everson tries discreet threats and flattery combined to try to talk me into sitting down with him all by myself, and I am not having any of that shit, thank you, and he finally sees that this isn't getting him anywhere, so we strike a goddamned deal. I will go and see Lou, and I will get new counsel or something like that to assist me, and he will get the hell out of my office so I can get some work done. And I will call him up by Friday and tell him who my new counselor is, and we will set up a definite appointment for Mister Everson to torment me about the last two years that Lou did my returns.

"So, the bastard leaves," I said. "And Gretchen is still standing there like somebody hit her on the forehead with a good-sized ball peen hammer, looking like she's going to cry. So we can hear the door open and close, and she starts to say something, and her lower lip is quivering, and I shush her and get up and look out into the reception area, and there is Mister Everson, all by himself, very quietly putting on his goddamned topcoat there. So I say, just a little bit sarcastically, maybe: 'Oh, Mister Everson. I heard the door and I thought someone must've come in. Or that you went out.' And he smirks at me, like he knows it was a cheap trick but there's no harm in trying, and he says: 'Door? I didn't hear any door, Mister Kennedy.' So I stand there and I watch him get all dressed and pick up his hat and start for the door, and I say: 'Don't forget your briefcase, Mister Everson. Don't want you having to come back for that.' And he picks it right up, like he would never stoop to such a thing, and goes on his merry way. And I let the door close behind him and then I go right out there and I lock the goddamned thing.

"Now," I said to Mack, "I go back in my office and I say to Gretchen: 'Spill it.' And she looks absolutely miserable. Got her right hand under her left boob and now she does have tears in her eyes, and she looks like there is no blood in her body north of her neck there. 'But first sit down,' I say, and I put her in the chair. 'I think you could use a drink,' I say, and all she can do is nod, so I go out into the file closet where the bottle of Jack Daniel's is and I pour two goddamned stiff shots, one for her and one for me. Because when Gretchen looks like she's been poleaxed, and she doesn't want to tell me why, I am pretty sure it is something I will need a drink to take.

"And it was," I said. "Gretchen knocks the booze back and the blood returns to her face. She looks at me. 'Jerry,' she says, and then she breaks down again. Shakes her head and cries some more, then looks up at me. 'You want to slug me, go ahead,' she says, 'because this guy Everson, this whole thing with him is my fault, that he's after you. And what makes it worse is that I did something else which now that he is after you, he can probably get you.'

"The long and short of it, Mack," I said, "was that I haven't paid my taxes, like I said I did."

33

GRETCHEN STOOD up with her empty plastic cup and snuffled. "Be right back," she said. "Lemme get a Kleenex." She came back with a wad of tissue and the jug of Jack's. I had not touched mine. She poured her glass nearly full and took a tug at it. "Jay-zuss," she said, shaking her head, "that'll get a man's attention." She coughed and cleared her throat three times.

"You okay?" I said.

Gretchen shook her head. "No," she said, in a very husky voice, "I am not okay, but I think I can function." She sat down heavily and flopped her arms down on the chair arms. "Jerry," she said, pursing her lips, running her tongue over them, dabbing with the tissue at her nose, and brushing her hair back at her left temple, "I have got you in the shit.

"This guy Everson," she said. "He does not exaggerate. He has called you seven times. Seven times at least. First time, I think it was, he got the machine, because I was out or something."

"Probably a Thursday," I said, trying to be helpful.

"No," she said, "it wasn't. That came after that. Anyway, he left his name and the outfit he works for. This was back right after you ran into his pal here, the guy that said his name was Wainer and he wanted more of Lou. I didn't think too much about it: Mister Everson. Figured he was just another Wainer and they're working Lou together. Put the message in your box, and you of course ignored it.

"Next time that he called," she said, "Everson got me. You had Calvin Beal in here, and I wasn't going to interrupt you for some bastard of a tax man. Asked him what he wanted and he wouldn't tell me that. I of course therefore assumed that he is after Lou. So," she said, "I lied to him. Told him you were out. 'He is out a lot,' he says. 'Yes,' I say, 'he is. He tries cases for a living and they don't hold court in here.' I admit I could have been a little more polite, but I don't like this fellow, Jerry, I don't like his attitude. So he leaves his number again and he says you'd better call it. You don't call it, he says, and he'll drop in unannounced. Says if you will not see him, maybe he can see you. I wrote all that up for you, and you of course ignored it.

"Apparently," she said, "he called back again that Thursday. Three calls he made that day, and the box received them all. Friday he got me again. Now he is sarcastic. 'Before you say he is out'—this is what he says—'tell me for my own information: Is he ever in?'

" 'Look, Mister Everson,' I say back to him, 'like I told you, he tries cases. He is all alone. Cases come up in the courts and he goes where they are. He does not just sit here, you know, waiting for your calls.'

" 'Okay,' says Mister Everson, 'tell me this then, all right? Where was Mister Kennedy when I was calling yesterday, you want to tell me that?'

" 'Sure,' I say, I'm on firm ground, 'Quincy District Court. Commonwealth vee Calvin Beal. You could look it up.'

" 'I will do that,' he says, and that is the end of that.

"Three or four hours later," she said, "Everson calls back. You'd think I was his mother and he'd just found out the stork doesn't bring the babies like I always told him it did. 'You told me Mister Kennedy was in Quincy District Court,' he says. 'Yes, I did,' I said. 'I just called there,' he said, 'and they have no such information.' He is very huffy with me—now he's really got me. Since he is a public servant, he cannot say 'fucking liar,' but he can make it very clear that he would like to say that.

" 'Mister Everson,' I say, getting very huffy back, 'this here is a busy office. Small but very busy. I have not got time to teach you all about the district courts. I have work to do this morning, and this afternoon as well. I cannot explain to you what goes on in the courts. I bet if you called up ten courts that are in session right now, you would find at least five people who would tell you that there is no judge in their buildings.'

"Well," she said, "he can't say 'fuck,' and he cannot say 'liar.' But he's allowed to get stern and nasty, and he does that pretty well. 'Maybe you're suggesting,' he says, 'that I had the wrong number?'

" 'I am not suggesting a damned thing to you,' I say. See, I am not a public servant. I can swear if I want. 'Neither am I going to look up your numbers for you. I do that for Kennedy, but I work for him.'

"That lit his wick for him," she said. "Now he's screaming at me. 'I talked to the clerk of the Quincy District Court,' he says. 'I talked to her myself.'

" 'The clerk down in Quincy is a man,' I say to him. 'You got an assistant.'

" 'Don't give me that,' he says. 'She told me she has not seen Kennedy since last July, in that District Courthouse.'

" 'Very possibly, she hasn't,' I say, sweet as pie. 'Probably out having coffee when he spent last Thursday there.'

" 'I will take her word, I think,' he yells back at me, 'on that point at least. And you should take my word on this one, if you like your boss. You tell Mister Kennedy, young lady, when he finally decides that he has come into his office, he had better call me up or I am coming over.' Oh, he was really quite fierce, Jerry. Very fierce indeed. 'If he does not return my call by the close of business today,' he said, 'I will see him there on Monday.'

" 'If he's in here,' I say, 'I don't know his schedule yet.'

" 'I will be there,' Everson says. 'I will be there irregardless. Irregardless of his schedule, I will be there at his office Monday afternoon, and I will wait there for him until he shows up to talk. And if he ducks me Monday, miss, then I will come on Tuesday. And if he stays out Tuesday, I'll be at his house on Wednesday.'

" 'Gee,' I said to him, 'you are quite determined. Must be the government doesn't have much work for you, you can spend a couple days just camping in some office.' "

"Wonderful," I said. "No wonder that the bastard made his debut Monday morning."

"Jerry," she said, "I got mad. He's a total prick. He thinks he can just call up people and start ordering them around, and if they don't do what he wants, the minute that he says it, he can throw his weight around and frighten them or something."

"He is right, and that's the trouble," I said. "He has got the weight to throw. That's what Lou says, and he should know, eating prison chow. They get on somebody like this, and their own time is nothing. It becomes a damned crusade. Someone's flouting them, flouting their authority, pissing on their boots. He'll go to my house, hang around down there? Yeah, he probably will," I said. "Talk to all my neighbors and make sure they know who he is, what outfit he represents. And all because some clerk in Quincy, some assistant clerk, who didn't see me show up in her court that morning because she wasn't up in her court that morning, this agent thinks I'm avoiding him. To him that's going to mean there's something wrong with my returns, something more wrong than what he thought there was when he started out."

"Yeah," she said, now genuinely regretful.

"Well," I said, "I suppose it can't be helped. Now tell me what else happened that got you so upset."

"Yeah," she said. She fished the soiled Kleenex out from between her thigh and the cushion of the chair and dabbed at her nose and eyes again. She twisted the tissue in her hands after she finished that. She pursed her lips. "Well," she said, "the problem really is, Jerry, there is something . . . you have got something wrong with your taxes."

"Like what?" I said. "I paid my taxes. I filled them out myself, like an idiot, but I didn't claim exemptions for the starving millions in Cambodia or anything. And I sent them checks that made me weep to write them, and those checks came back canceled with my bank statements."

"Not your income taxes," she said. "Your employer taxes. The taxes for unemployment insurance that you have to pay because I work for you?"

"You mean the penalty I pay for creating a job?" I said.

"Yeah," she said miserably, "those."

My flesh began to creep. "I," I said. "I, ah, I thought you always paid those."

She nodded twice. "I do," she said. "I did, at least. Every quarter, every three months, you know? I would pay those unemployment compensation taxes. 'Employer's Contribution to Unemployment Compensation' is what they are called."

"Yeah," I said.

"And," she said, "it's really quite a lot of money. Now. It didn't used to be that much, and I would just pay it out of the office income, you know? When it came in. It wasn't always on time, but it was right around when it was supposed to be paid. A few times I even paid it early. When we had a fairly big case come in and you got a retainer, then I would see that it wasn't very likely you would get another one right off, although you might if you got lucky, so I wouldn't take any chances. I would pay the thing.

"Then, though," she said, "in the past few years, it began to get kind of rough. The withholding from my pay and the social security and all of that went up, and then the employer's contributions went up, and it was about, it was almost another thousand dollars every three months that I had to send in. And the state as well, they also have a tax like that I have to send in."

"Don't I know it," I said.

"Well," she said, crossing her legs at the ankles and pursing her lips again, clenching the tissue in both hands in her lap and looking at the old oriental rug I obtained from Doctor Carey as a part of my fee for his trouble with the drug boys so many years ago, "then I stopped doing it."

"You stopped," I said.

"Yeah," she said. "Well, it wasn't like I said: 'This is too much now and I'm not going to pay it anymore.' Nothing like that. I don't mean that. It was just that when Heather started school there last year, up at Dartmouth?"

"Yeah," I said.

"Well," she said, "you began doing something that you didn't used to do before. Before that, when she started college, you would always if you got a fee from somebody and you didn't happen to be in the office at the time, you would bring it back with you, or when you came in the next morning, and you would give it to me. And if you needed money for something, like say if you were going out to buy a car or something and you needed more cash than you ordinarily take out of the office, all right? Then you would have me write you a check."

"Right," I said.

"But then a year ago this summer," she said, "you stopped doing that all of the time. You still did it most of the time, but there were a few times when you got a fee and you just came back here and told me how much and from who, and I would write it down. And you would put the money in your own checking account. So none of it ever came through here."

"It was a small matter," I said, "of covering some fairly major checks which I sent up to Hanover, New Hampshire."

"I know that," she said. "It's not like I was saying . . . Look, Jerry, okay? It's your money that you were collecting. You're the one that needed it. If you wanted to put it into your account directly, what the hell reason is there that you shouldn't?"

"None that I could think of at the time, at least," I said.

"Me either," she said. "So, I didn't say anything. It was not my place to say anything. And there was always still, you always put enough into the office account for my salary and the rent and the other stuff like that, which we had to have." She paused and looked up at me pleadingly. "The trouble was that there was not enough for those goddamned contributions that they make you make each quarter."

"You, ah," I said, feeling ridiculous but feeling as though I really had to make some sort of disapproving remark, "you really should have said something to me. At least called my attention to it or something."

She looked at me pityingly. "Jerry," she said, "you didn't have any more money. If you'd've had enough dough to keep on running the office account like you always did before, you would have kept on doing that. But you didn't. No," she said, putting her head back and blinking several times, "I should maybe not have taken my regular Christmas bonus when you said to, or something like that."

"No," I said, interrupting her, "that's part of your pay, really. You depend on getting that every year. You think I want to spend half a day hanging around perfume counters trying to get something that won't make you smell like a skunk?"

"I know," she said, "and you're right that I depend on it. Absolutely right. And it was Christmas when the second one, the second payment that I missed, when that came due, and I said: 'Shit on them. I'm buying Christmas presents. Jerry's doing Christmas shopping. Fuck the fucking government if they think we are going to give them our damned Christmas shopping money that we earned so they can turn around and give it to a bunch of lazy bastards that won't work for a living.' And I didn't.

"So," she said, "that made two I missed, and I was thinking after the first of the year I would catch up, but then you were doing it again, you had been, back there in December, for the second-semester tuition, and I had to stall off quite a lot of bills until February or so. And when the first quarter for this year was due, which was back in March there, well, with those new cases you got to get almost even."

"Almost," I said.

"We still owe one," she said. "I paid the first one for this year, because of penalties. Way they've got it set up, and I first learned this from Lou, pay the one that's current if you get some money, all right? Because the ones that you've missed, they've already got the penalties on them. So, first you pay the new one, so there's no new penalties. Then go back and pay the old ones, if you get some more dough in." She took a very deep breath. She exhaled it loudly. She looked down at the rug again. She looked back up at me. "See what I mean, you've got troubles?" she said forlornly. "You have got them and they're my fault. I am really ashamed."

"Because I said on my own return that I had paid those taxes," I said, "when I haven't paid them."

"That is a false statement," Mack said when I finished telling her.

"That is what it is, all right," I said. "Without question. I didn't know it was false, and I didn't mean to make one, but the IRS will not believe that and no jury would either."

"You," Mack said, looking worried, "we have got some problems here. I bet this will be expensive."

34

"WELL," LOU said to me out on the prison patio, "now do you believe me, maybe? That they are coming after you?" He had a heavy jacket on; I kept my topcoat on. We sat in the April sun, which did not warm us much. "Look," he said when I arrived and looked doubtful about sitting out of doors, "humor me on this one, all right? Out and in, these are things that don't mean a lot to you. Me, I have to have a good reason to go out, and then I am supposed to be getting exercise or something. Besides, I always did feel better about talking to a guy about things when I was outdoors, you know? They can still pick up what you say, but it's harder for them."

"After me," I said. "Yeah, I guess they are. But then I try to keep in mind, you know, that it could be coincidence. Lawyers, doctors, everybody, all of us go through this. Self-employed professionals. The bastards do not trust us. And we can count on that, all of us, that they do not trust us. So, paranoia, you know, Lou? Have to watch for that."

Lou had taken up pipe smoking; he had a rough-briar bulldog fully stoked and going. He had also grown a beard. I asked what had brought that on, and he laughed at me. "Oh," he said, "let's see. Partly to see what one would look like on me. I was always curious. But when I was out and working, finding out was not practical. In here, what difference does it make, I look like Yasir Arafat? Who is going to see me except a bunch of goddamned crooks? And then it was because of the food, which I do not recommend. That was part of it too, Jerry, I guess."

"You wanted to grow your own strainer?" I said.

"No," he said. "See, it is boredom. The food here is not really bad. It is just boring. So I ask around a little, other guys been here a while, and there is only two things, maybe three things, you can do about the food. First one is that you decide you're Orthodox, all right? And you got to have it kosher, which they will do for you. Trouble with that is, kosher's also boring. And once you get locked into that, you are stuck with it. Plus which, I think I might have some trouble, selling them that line. These guys, or the ones that put me in here, they have got a book on me. It does not show anywhere that I'm a devout Jew, let alone an Orthodox one. So that is the problem.

"This leaves me with two other things that I can do about it, get myself a different menu because meals become important. Vegetarian is out, and that is one of them. So that leaves just allergies. Maybe there is hope.

"Trouble with the allergies," Lou said, grinning at me, "is that I don't have them. I don't even sneeze at ragweed. What is this with food? For that I will need some symptoms, and that leads me to the beard. I go in and see the doctor, say my skin is acting up. He looks at me, nothing's wrong. That is what he tells me. 'Doc,' I said, 'you know your business. I don't argue with you. But I am telling you, it burns. Ever since I came in. Has to be the diet here, 'cause this is something new. When I shave, it's killing me. Feel like I'm on fire.'

"Now this guy is not stupid," he said. "He knows about us fakers. So he looks at me and says: 'Maybe it is shaving. Why don't you lay off the blades and see if it improves? Then if it still bothers you, come back in and see me.'

"So," Lou said, "I do that, and it makes me itch like hell. But I get through that and I go back and I say: 'It was not the shaving, Doc. I still got the burning feeling. I think it is the diet.'

"'So do I,' the doctor says. 'You don't like the food. Very few men like it, but there is no help for that. Get yourself a hobby and stop thinking about it. I bet that your skin improves. You will feel much better.'

"So," Lou said, "that didn't work, but I did try the pipe." He puffed into it so that a fat cloud of heavy blue smoke boiled up out of it. "Dirty, and it stinks, I guess. Takes about as much equipment as the average plumber uses. Makes you drool and it sounds awful, you get water in the bowl. But it does keep you busy and it doesn't hurt your lungs." He took the pipe out of his mouth and stared at it critically. He took a pipe cleaner from his pocket and rammed it down the stem. He pulled it out, all bent and brown, and held it up for me. "Look at that, will ya?" he said. "If that isn't one disgusting piece of shit to have around you where you happen to be sitting, I don't know what is. I must be related to the goddamned spaniels there."

"It is pretty gross," I said, employing one of Heather's discarded favorite terms without thinking about it.

"It's a fucking metaphor for life, is what it is," he said, holding it up to the sun. "Just like my artsy-craftsy second wife always used to be saying about runny fried eggs, flat tires, any goddamned thing she came across that wasn't to her liking." He shifted his voice into a falsetto. " 'It's a metaphor for life, Louis, a statement of the whole human condition.' Bullshit. What it is is a pipe cleaner that is all shitted up, and what the fuck do you do with a thing that's made of wire and that you have made so shitty you can't bear to put down? Eat it?"

"That'd put some roughage in your diet," I said.

"Yeah," he said absently, and put the cleaner on the table. He rested his forearm on the edge of the table and looked at me as though I was a student on academic probation, and he was the dean of my college. He shook his head at last and gave me a woeful smile. "I dunno, Jerry," he said.

"About what, Lou?" I said. This was not the kind of admission I had grown accustomed to from him. It bothered me to hear him say it.

"I have got a pretty good conscience," he said. "It's never given me a lot of trouble. I would think of something I would like to do, such as with my first wife, Cheryl, when she really got so she was giving me these huge amounts of shit because I didn't like her fucking country club broad friends or something, and I woke up one morning after hearing her mouth going all night before I went to bed, and I said to myself: 'I am going to get rid of this broad even if she did give me my kids. Fuck her and all her fucking noise.' And that is what I did. And my conscience just sat there in my head like it was an old man getting some sun in Boca in the winter and it didn't let a peep out of it.

"The same thing with my second wife," he said. "I knew when me and Sally just decided to get married, this was not a thing that you'd expect to work. I was forty-three years old. I read a book once, several of them in fact. They were all about accounting, tax regs, proposed changes in the filing dates, what you should do for your clients that're getting their heads bashed in with the new rules on debenture payouts. All that kind of thing. Here is this broad who is twenty-two, and she has got four things in the world. Two of them are her tits, the right one and the left one—very, very nice tits by any man's standards. The third thing is her brain, which apparently was just about the best that come along in about ten years in the BU graduate school. At first I thought perhaps those profs that said she was so smart were actually ripping off a few pieces of her ass, giving her mind all those good grades so her tits will come to classes. But then I ask around some and I find out I am too suspicious. Sally is actually really very smart. So her brain was the third thing. And the fourth thing was that Sally was ambitious. Really was determined she was gonna get that doctorate, and also equally determined she is going to live good while she's getting it and afterwards. She was very up-front about that. 'Graduate school sucks,' she said. 'The food is lousy, where you live is lousy, the people you go out with don't have any money so they can take you places, and in the winter when you get a good vacation, you don't have the cash to go off anywhere that ever heard of room service. I have had it with this. I am going to get my degree, and I am going to teach, but one way or the other I am going to get some money for myself while I am doing it.'

"It was a straight cash transaction," Lou said. "No players to be named later, no deferred payments in the contract. I offered first to set her up in an apartment, give her all the things I'd give her if she was my wife, treat her better than most men treated their wives, probably, and then if it did not work out, no hard feelings, toodle-oo. This she did not want. 'Lou,' she said, 'that is fair. But when I get the damned degree, I've got to land a job. And there is lots of competition for the jobs I want. I'll be up against a lot of other people, some of whom will be women, so I won't have that going for me. And they will try to knock me out of the running by spreading stories about me if I do that, what you say. They will say I worked my way through school by doing a reasonable amount of hooking. And that will demolish me. So either I will have to say that we get married, or you will have to be satisfied with dating me like we are now, knowing I am dating other guys to see if I can find one with some money who will also marry me. I'm sorry that it is this way, but that's the way it is.'

"I thought that was fair," Lou said. "I married her. Maybe it would work out and she would still like me after she was running the department somewhere at some school where guys who look like I do until twenty years ago were known as *sheenies*. Not anymore, though, at least not to our faces—too many of us on the faculties these days. Then again, she might teach at one of those schools, meet some dip-shit who inherited a lot of money so it didn't matter if he spent his entire fucking life reading books nobody ever heard of, by some guys like him who lived about four hundred years ago, and decide that she liked being with him more than she liked being with me. In which case we would get divorced, no alimony on account I told her if that was the deal I wanted an agreement down in writing before we got ourselves married. No big deal, all right?

"Well," Lou said, "I was a little off, I guess—what she met at some conference was not another guy, but another broad—but otherwise I had the whole scenario correct, and so I get divorced from Sally. Once again, I sleep like a baby. No grief from my conscience. And now I'm in the can, all right? My present wife, Joanna, she is not what you would call the sort of woman who ought to've been a nun, all right? I meet her in Vegas. It was if you want the truth a business arrangement, not the first of those for either one of us, but still quite a bit better than most of the other ones that either of us had. So I see her for a second date, a third one and a fourth one, and we get along together great, better every night. We like the same things even when we're not in the bedroom. And finally I say to her: 'Joanna, all right? In the first place, while you are obviously the best piece of ass God ever let loose on the world, and while I've made a number of wise investments in my time, this is running into money. In the second place, there's a limit on how long I can stay out here in the desert, seeing shows and betting a few dollars here and there when I get the urge. I stay here long enough and when I go back I will find my nephew Mendel taking calls and telling people not to worry even though I am dead, because he's a better guy to do their work than I am. So I have got to haul ass back to Boston.' So I propose to her, and she says she has tried this once before and he turned out to be an asshole as a steady guy for her, but she supposes that don't mean every man's an asshole and besides, she's getting older and she should think of the future. And once again, it's all right, although I have got to say I hope she don't get serious about some guy while I am in here, if she isn't really keeping her legs crossed like she claims she is.

"You see what I mean," Lou said. "That is just about all of the dealings I have had in my life where I got involved in something that included other people. My kids, all right, I didn't do so good with, but they were mostly Cheryl's idea anyway, and I supported them. Otherwise I have been fair with people, I believe. I did not ask them to do something that was not maybe exactly in their own best interests, unless I came out and told them I was asking them to do something that might put them in the shit. So far as I can see, nobody ever ended up in the shit because of something I did, but that is more luck than good intentions. I was honest about things, and that's all I really deserve any credit for.

"Except, Jeremiah," Lou said mournfully, "where you are concerned. Where you are concerned, I have got some serious problems with this nice quiet conscience of mine. You should not have got involved in this. I should not have gotten you involved in this. I told Frank that in the first place, when it is first becoming obvious that since they cannot lay their hands on Uncle Nunzio there and do mean things to him, because I will not allow it, they are coming after me. 'Frank,' I said to him, 'we are now in the situation where they're saying: "Aw right, wise guy, let's see just how good you are." Things are about to start getting very hairy, very interesting.' Frank knew what I meant, but he was sick. 'You got to have a lawyer,' Frank tells me as though I can't see that one for myself. 'This I am aware of,' I tell Frank. 'You are not telling me something that I did not know before I talked to you.'

" 'I am sick,' Frank says to me. This I also knew," Lou said. "It was getting so when somebody saw Frank walking down the street, having lunch in Locke's, or getting on a plane to go somewhere, it is an event. People call each other up and spread the joyous news. 'Seen Frank headin' down to Florida the other day. Said he's gonna get some sun, take a little rest. Didn't look good, Frank. Kind of green around the gills. Claimed he felt all right, felt fine. You think Frank is gonna be all right? Tell me, Louis, all right? Man to fuckin' man? You think Frank Macdonald's really gonna be all right?'

" 'I know Frank is sick,' is what I would say to these guys," Lou said. "I would say to them: 'The fuck do I know if he's gonna be all right? I see him and he tells me, he is taking care of himself for a change. Looking out for his health, now that he is getting old. What can I tell you?'

" 'You think Frank looks good?' they say. What am I supposed to say, you wanna tell me that? Frank looks good if you spend all your time in funeral parlors, all the people that you see are lying down and guys are coming in and saying how they look so natural. Of course Frank doesn't look good. I should lie, perhaps? What good does that do? 'No,' I say to them, 'I don't think Frank looks good. I think Frank looks shitty. But you tell me he is going down to Georgia. Maybe he will get a nice tan for himself, play a little golf and eat some fruit or something, so he should feel better for a change, and then if and when he comes back here, he will look like he is better. But I don't know, all right? I am not Frank's doctor.'

" 'Frank,' I say, 'I know you're sick.' This is when I need a lawyer and he tells me he is sick. 'I am the guy it seems like is the information desk for you in Boston where the guys check in that love you and would like to have some news about how you are feeling. And you're telling me you are not feeling so good, Frank? You want maybe I should stop all of this talking about tax collectors and them guys and start rolling up my sleeves so I can give you high colonics?' And Frank says no, that is not what he means. And this is when I am fighting there with him and Nunzio, that I am getting you for my case and that is the end of it. And I say: 'Frank, all right? We both know what is going on here, which is something Jerry doesn't. And if it happens, what I think, after they get me, they will come back again and see if maybe they can work him over some. And when that happens, Frank, you know, as it probably will, you are going to have to come through, without no apologies.'

" 'Well,' he says, 'if I am better, naturally, I will.'

" 'Frank,' I say, 'that does not do it, if you are feeling better. Maybe you will not be, and then what happens, huh? Jerry will go in and he will do this thing for me. And after Jerry does it, Frank, I will be in jail.

And then it will be your turn, Frank—he does not know Nunzio. And you will have to do it then, and just come through for him.' And Frank says: 'I know this.'

"So," Lou said to me in the logician's sun that provided light but no heat which would have warmed us, "now the time has come and you have got to cash that chit. What you need is Magazu, and I can't get him for you. Frank can get him for you, Jerry, and he has to do that. Call him up and tell Corinne, let you talk to him. Tell him that you talked to me and what I said to do. Do not let him bullshit you. Don't let her do it either. Frank is well enough for this. He can make a phone call."

"Lou," I said, "I can't do that."

"Jerry," he said, "bullshit. Take your fucking pride and shove it. This is serious. You are now the TV star? You are on the news? You tell me this asshole, Rowley, wants you once a week? You come down here like a jerk and tell me all this stuff? Channel Eight is gonna pay you what my lawn guys used to get, and that makes you important? Jerry, pay attention here. This is serious."

"Lou," I said, "listen to me. Serious, I know. But I have not got Frank's phone number, all right? I can't call him, Lou. I already tried that. If I want to call him, Mousie Feeley has to tell him. I assume that Mousie called him and he told him what I said. Frank did not return my call. That is what I mean. Mousie won't give me the number. I cannot call Frank."

Lou looked at me speculatively. "I don't know about you, Mister Kennedy," he said. "Sometimes I think you're making progress. Other times: you're hopeless."

"You have got Frank's number?" I said. "Tell me, and I'll call him."

Lou put his head back and laughed. "I do not believe this," he said, "how damned gullible you are. No, I do not have Frank's number. I don't have my files here, you know, or my call director. But if I did and I felt lazy, I would not need them. I would just dial up nine-twelve, and ask the operator."

"Ask the operator," I said slowly. "As in Information?"

"As in Information, Jerry," Lou said, grinning at me. "Nine-twelve and then you dial three fives. After that dial twelve twice. And don't come back down here and tell me there's no twelve on the phone. Ask for Frank Macdonald's number, in Sea Island, Georgia. While you're at it, get Corinne's, case his line is busy. Call the fucker up and tell him, what I said to you. Tell him: 'Call Bert Magazu. This is serious.'"

35

THE MIDDLESEX ASSISTANT DA was an older and less polished version of the federal prosecutor, Mike Dunn, who had put Lou in jail. His name was Stephen Ranney and he hated evildoers. He eyed Teddy narrowly and ushered me aside. He leaned back against the wall in the courtroom corridor and kept his vision on the floor while murmuring to me. "I don't like it, Jerry," he said, looking pinched and angry. "You come in here with this guy, and we know who he is. Tell me that he won't cooperate, and then you ask for favors? You want favors, Jerry, you know, you have got to trade. Why should I let you guys go, make your lives easier? He is going to Fifth me in there, okay, that's his right. But my right is to keep him waiting, till I'm good and ready. Sorry, since that means you wait—I'm not mad at you. But he's your client, Jerry, and I'm doing him no favors."

"Steve," I wheedled, "for Christ sake, what does this accomplish? Keep me standing here all day? What good does this do? Bring him back again tomorrow, for another witness fee? This how you guys trim the budget, wasting dough like this? This is asinine for God's sake. Let us out of here."

That was the wrong choice of words. I saw that at once. Ranney's gaze came up and pierced me. "What are you, a wise guy? What is it you tell me next? You'll get me on TV? Everybody's equal here, Mister Kennedy. Everybody that comes in here gets exactly the same treatment. We don't care who they are, who they know or who knows them. You decide you don't like us? Shoot your mouth off on TV? Fine, go ahead and do it, Jerry. I will take that risk." Then he gave me a defiant look that ran on high-test envy.

"Steve," I said, "for heaven's sake, be reasonable, will you? That stuff I'll be doing with Jack Rowley is just general commentary. Two or three times monthly, on general legal issues. It's not personalities, or anything like that. Merely advice for the laymen, general interpretations."

Ranney looked at me as though I had been pimping him. "That is not what I heard, Jerry," he said. "I saw Rowley just last night. That's not what he said. Said that you'd be real hard-hitting, no holds barred and that crap. 'Jerry Kennedy knows courts, and those who work in them. He'll be speaking out on issues, making sense of things.' "

"Okay, okay," I said, "you can have it your way then. Maybe you have got a point. Maybe this crap should be exposed, now that you mention it. You've as much as said to me, you're harassing us. Is this a new tactic here, a fresh abuse of power? Yeah, I think you're right, Steve. Thanks for calling this to my attention here." Then I walked away from him, working on his glare.

"Teddy," I said, "I have got bad news for us. DA doesn't like you and he's not too fond of me. Don't make any concrete plans for today or tomorrow. He is going to keep us here until we both have bedsores."

Teddy sucked his teeth and smirked. "Not too impressed with you?" he said. "What is he, some kind of yokel? Doesn't realize who he's dealing with?"

"Actually," I said, taking Teddy to a bench, "his principal dislike is you. He doesn't like your ass. Pisses him off, you know, all this Fifth Amendment crap. Dangerous criminals out there, preying on the people. Guys like you frustrate the cops. Steve does not approve."

"Huh," Teddy said, gazing into space. "Wonder if he ever had a Cadillac I got?"

"Cadillac?" I said. "I don't think so, my friend. Steve is more the Pinto type, four or five years old."

"Hey," Teddy said, looking interested. "Those are the ones that explode, hit them from behind. Maybe we can work this out, I can get some calls made."

"Calls," I said, "don't talk to me. I'm losing faith in that. The ones I get cause me great pain, and those I place don't work. Last night I was a basket case, waiting for a call. It finally comes through and the guy busts my balls for me."

"Who is this guy?" Teddy said. "Has he got a Cad, perhaps? I could swipe it just for practice—put it in a pond."

"Teddy," I said, "this is Frank Macdonald, hard as that is to believe."

"Frank Macdonald," Teddy said. "I thought he was dead. Thought the booze took Frank out there, several years ago. Still alive, but dead."

"No," I said, "it didn't. But it sure did not improve him. He did something last night that I would not have believed."

"Well, Counselor," Teddy said, "we've got lots of time, from the looks of things."

Both of Frank Macdonald's numbers called machines. Both machines had Corinne's voice, smooth and unemotional. Neither recording actually conceded that the caller had reached Frank Macdonald's home. Each said simply that "we cannot take your call just now, but we will return it. Leave your name and number, and the time you placed your call. We start placing our return calls at six-thirty, EDT. Please don't be discouraged if you do not hear from us. Callers with extended messages may call our Boston office." Then it gave the Boston number, for those in need of more stalling.

It was nearly midnight by the time Corinne called back. "Jerry, Jerry," Mack said, when it was still relatively early and I had already driven her close to distraction with my pacing in the living room, sitting down abruptly to fret in one place for a minute, getting up again almost at once to walk around, "can't you light someplace for God's sake? You will drive me nuts. I'd've known you'd be like this, I would've stopped on the way home down at the plaza pet store. Bought one of those gerbil treadmills for you, damn it all. You'll have a heart attack, just like Frank Macdonald. You haven't had this much exercise in months."

It was the frustration, the infuriating feeling that people who were virtual strangers to me, except for their occupations, were at that very instant making plans and scheming to demolish me and my family, without my being able to anticipate what they would do or take any steps to defend myself against them. Ever since Heather had first gone away from us, to college and to work, I had complained that she called too infrequently. "You should be happy," Mack would say. "If there was something wrong, she would. We haven't heard from her? That's good. Everything is fine." I would then protest that I would like the kid to call me up and tell me that, that everything was fine. I declared in no uncertain terms that I did not like being merely Him Whom You Call When the Shit Is in the Fan. I said the phone company would not mind in the slightest if for once they asked me to accept a collect call placed for the purpose of delivering good news. Or even one that delivered no news whatsoever, except for the happy tidings that there was no news at all. I would say that I could take it in my stride if Heather called to report that she hadn't fallen irretrievably in love with some man who is older than I am, some man whose wife, the mother of his four lovely children, does not understand him. I said it would be fine if she called to say that she was still not using drugs and did not need the Blue Cross number for the people in the admitting office. "But last night, Teddy," I said, "I was scared to death the kid would call to say she loves her daddy."

"I think you are batty," Mack said when I muttered that I hoped that Heather wouldn't call. "Here you have been sulking at her shadow for about a couple months, and now you're saying you don't *want* a call from her, for God's sake?"

"Not tonight," I said. "Not until Frank calls me back tonight, I'd rather not. Then I hope she calls, and I will gladly talk to her. But if she calls tonight, the chances are I'll make things worse."

"You have gone round the bend," Mack said. "I think when the IRS boys come to see Francine again, I will take them aside and ask them if they want to save the government some money. 'If you're doing this because you want to drive my husband nuts,' I'll say, 'you can take the rest of this year off, because you've succeeded and he is. Mad as the March hare, the man is. You've done what you wanted.' "

"Did the kid call?" Teddy said. "I assume she did."

"Absolutely," I said. "Right at nine o'clock."

"What did you do?" Teddy said. "Tell her to get off?"

"No," I said, "I didn't. I do have a little sense."

Heather's gambit, which I recognized, was to seize what she thought was a happy moment for me. Join in my elation over something quite apart from us, and thus slide right over what divided us. "Congratulations, Dad," she said. "I've seen you and you're good. You're really very good on TV. I was proud of you."

"Now," I said to Teddy, "this is coming from my daughter, whom I love. My daughter who has not been speaking to me for what seems like several years. But she is up in Hanover, and that is in New Hampshire. Or at least she's supposed to be there, and therefore I get suspicious. 'How did you see Channel Eight where you are?' I immediately ask. She gives me the patient sigh, the one that kids have for slow learners."

"*Daddy,*" Heather said, "welcome to the last quarter of the twentieth century. Mother taped it at the office, on the Beta there. She sent the tapes up to me, so I could see them here."

"This was news," I said to Teddy. "My wife's really smart. Commandeered the Sony hook-up that they have at the office. Set it to record my debut and the second night as well. I can't talk to Heather and the kid can't talk to me? Okay, Mack will change the subject from the boyfriend to the courts. I will talk to Heather plus a quarter million others about harmless shit like Luther Dawes that also gets me upset, but does not get Heather lathered like our chats about her jaunts with her damned boyfriend there. I admit, I was impressed. I was just about as jumpy as a racing dog or something, because every minute Heather's chatting, Frank cannot get through. But at the same time, I was flattered. This had taken thought. You do not just piss on something that has taken that much work. So I had a long talk with my lovely grown-up daughter, and when she mentioned Charlie I was nice and did not bark.

"This does not mean I was calmed down when she finally hung up," I said. "I was happier about things in the world in general, but I was still waiting for that call from good old Frank. You know when that bastard called me? Midnight, for Christ sake. And when the goddamned call came through, it was Corinne at first."

Corinne was apologetic, clinically so. She said she hoped that it was not too late for me. I assured her it was not. I was very tense when I spoke because I didn't want her massage. What I wanted was her husband, not her silky guff. I didn't dare to tell her that because she'd cut me off.

She said that Frank's medicine had completely usurped daylight and darkness as strong factors in the control of his waking-sleeping cycles. She said that he was sometimes disoriented when he woke up and had to be quiet for a while. Then at other times, she said, he woke up fully alert but became disoriented gradually as he remained awake. She said that that night he seemed fine when he woke up, but it was possible that he might lapse into vagueness in the course of our conversation. She said she hoped I'd understand, if that sort of thing should happen.

I agreed with everything she said which seemed to call for such endorsements. I murmured what I hoped would sound like understanding regret at those items that she mentioned which seemed like they called for that. I assured her that I would not keep him on the line for very long.

She said she was depending on me for that courtesy. She wanted me to understand that she had reservations about allowing him to talk, to almost anybody. She said she permitted this to very few of those who called and wished to speak to him. She said she was doing this because Frank had seemed extremely interested in the fact that I had called. "He said the others might not matter, but he had to talk to you." She said that was the basis of the decision she had made, to let him talk to me, "but briefly," because he so wanted to. I had the feeling I now knew exactly how it must have felt to be the father of a young lady of ordinary intelligence whose consuming wish to enter Mills College was about to be denied. If Corinne had not possessed the power to prevent me from talking to Frank, I would have told her to go shit into her hat and pull it down around her ears.

"Jerry," Frank said, when she at last permitted us to talk. His voice was familiar in its cadence, unchanged in its pitch, but strangely husky and quite faint. It was more a hoarse whisper than a normal speaking voice. The timbre had gone out of it. Frank Macdonald sounded far away, in time as well as space. "How ya doing, pal?"

"Frank," I said awkwardly, forcing as much cheerfulness as I could without wanting to convey the erroneous impression that I felt at all cheerful. "The fuck you doing, huh? You got the shit scared out of everybody up here 'cause we never see you now."

He attempted a sort of hacking laugh. It made him cough somewhere near the top of his throat. It was the cough of a man who is being very careful about easing a small tickle, fearing it will hurt severely if he puts some muscle in it. "Everybody, huh?" he said. "You wanna know what scared is, they should spend some time with me. Going through what I been through, that is scared, Jerry."

"I can imagine," I said. I could not imagine and I did not wish to do so. What I said seemed like a harmless enough lie in a situation which appeared to call for something like that.

"Yeah," he said, and pondered. "Fucking helicopters. When I had that last one, my attack in February, they used one of those damned things to get me out of here. Airplanes, Jerry, okay? Those're bad enough. But helicopters? Jesus. If I hadn't been so sick that they had me all strapped down, they would never've been able to get me onto that damned chopper." He paused and uttered the fragile cough again. "Never let 'em get you in a fucking helicopter. Tell 'em if they do that to you, they are cut out of your will."

"I'll keep that in mind, Frank," I said desperately. It seemed as though for the first time in all the years that we had owned the house that we lived in, I could hear appliance motors separately and clearly. I could hear the motor in the wall clock in the kitchen. I could hear the refrigerator fan. I could hear the bedside clocks in our bedroom and Heather's. I could hear the pump in the oil burner in the basement. Each of them was quite distinct, and all of them, together, seemed almost deafening. "Frank," I said, disconcerted, "I . . ."

"Yeah," he said, his voice now faintly guttural, "Corinne said you sounded urgent."

"I am, Frank," I said. "I think I've got some trouble and I really need some help."

"Why the hell did you do it?" he said. It was not a reproach. It was nothing like a rebuke. It was simply an expression of real curiosity, the variety of question that a parent would put to a child who had just finished removing all the stuffing from his favorite bedtime toy, and absolutely ruined it. The question almost stunned me.

"Do it?" I said. "Do what, Frank? This isn't something that you do, or that I did, as far as that goes, we are talking about here. This is something that happens to you. You react as best you can."

There was a long silence at his end of the line. I did not know what to make of it. Certainly he could not have become angry at me. I decided I would say more, to get some response from him. "You and I both know, Frank," I said, "that Lou had to have a lawyer. You were sick. You couldn't do it. Someone surely had to. Lou asked me and I did it. I don't see a choice there."

"Lou?" he rasped. "Is Lou all right? Has Lou Schwartz gotten sick? Whole damned world is getting sick. We're all getting old."

"Frank," I said, "Lou is in prison, but his health is fine. This is my own problem, that I called you about."

There was another pause. "Well," he said with much phlegm, "it'll probably blow over. Those things do that, you know. Look like they're gonna end the world, and then they disappear. Luther, you know, there's no power. He's got no real influence. Little while out in the limelight, then he'll go away."

"Luther?" I said. "Luther Dawes?"

"Yeah," Frank said thoughtfully. "The judgeship thing with Luther Dawes. That's chickenshit, Jerry. Luther wanted and he didn't, didn't get it. He will go away in time. People, people just get tired."

"Frank," I said, "the thing with Luther? That's not . . ."

"He's been calling here," Frank said. "Fucking Mousie stonewalled him, but Luther got the number. Must be one smart person in his family somewhere. Night he got it, he called here three times that night. Corinne didn't let him get through, didn't let him talk to me. Told him I was sick." He paused and he coughed three times. "Which was the truth, Jerry. I can assure you that. She was not lying to the guy when she said I was sick."

"No," I said. I had absolutely no idea of what to do next.

"Next day, I guess it was," Frank said meditatively, "Luther called again. Four more times, Corinne said. Still wouldn't let him talk to me. Day after that, the same thing, only not as many times. And then finally, about three days after Tierney picked the Belvedere broad there, Luther called again while I happened to be up." Frank chuckled through catarrh or phlegm or something, so that his amusement rattled through the phone to me. There was another pause then. I thought I could hear him swallow, with some difficulty. "I made Corinne let me take that call. Pretty obvious he wasn't going to let either one of us get any rest until I talked to him.

"He was all upset," Frank said. "Blamed it on the governor, for not appointing him. Wanted me to call the fucking governor, you beat that? Call him up and get him to reverse his own decision. 'Luther,' I said, 'Luther, for the love of Christ, man, all right? You should not be doing this. All those battles I had, I was always having, you know? I don't pick the judges, Luther. I just fought with them.'

"Luther says: 'Somebody did this. Someone did this to me.' I told him that of course it was somebody that did it to him. 'These things don't just happen, Luther. They're not accidents. Somebody must have remembered, thought of something that you did. Dropped a dime on you, Luther. Made a couple calls. The world works like this, Luther. You got people that don't like you? Can't be having these ambitions of yours, then. They will croak you if you have them, and they see a way to hurt you.' "

Frank forced that hideous chuckle again, and the same rattle followed. "Funny," he said, "good old Luther. Never had big balls. All the time he's talking to me, doesn't dare to ask me. Did I do it? Was I the one that called the governor? So naturally, I didn't tell him. He still doesn't know." There was another pause then. Frank coughed twice and said: "You still on there, Jerry?"

"Yeah," I said. "I guess so. I'm still holding on."

"Yeah," Frank said, "well, that's good. Anyway, I thought that was, that was the end of it. Couple weeks go by, I guess. Maybe it was three weeks, though could've been a month. Fucking drugs I'm taking, you know? Lose your track of things. You are in this situation, and your mind gets all fucked up. I got more drugs in me every day than all the kids have, put together, one of them rock concerts they have." Frank managed a soft laugh. "Junkies knew the stuff I got, they would be amazed. I've billed guys fifty grand in my time, representing them when somebody arrested them with less stuff than I've got here, right in my own house. And it's all legal too, my stuff. Every last bottle. 'Cept, of course, they want to sell it, want to take it too. And I don't want to do that. Feel like I missed most of the whole fucking summer and then the fall after it. Winter too. I missed the winter. Missed the whole damned year. Course it's warmer down here. You don't notice it as much. Seasons, you know? Seasons. We don't have them here." He paused again and sighed. "I feel like I'm gonna die, if I didn't die already. Maybe I would rather, you know? Maybe I would rather."

I did not say anything. The wall clock in the kitchen rumbled like a locomotive, and the clocks in the bedrooms sounded menacing.

"You think I'm gonna die, Jerry?" Frank said plaintively. "You aren't saying much to me. Is that what you think?"

"No," I said, startled, fumbling and too vehement as a result. "No, Frank, I don't think you're going to die." It was now my turn to force a laugh. "Not yet, anyway. Someday, maybe. We all will. But you've got Corinne with you now, taking care of you. You'll be all right. Take it easy. You'll be better soon."

Frank thought about that. "Maybe," he said softly. "That is possible. It's what I think too, of course. These new drugs they've got. It would be better, though, I didn't have the cancer. That's a rough one, Jerry, you know? Get the cancer too. With the heart, there is the pain, but it gets over, you know? Hurts like hell, you cannot stand it, there is so much pain. But then it goes away, or you do, and you just feel shitty.

The other thing they say I've got, that doesn't quit, you know? If you're not sleeping, Jerry, then you have it. Always have it." He paused again. "But I think I'll make it. That is what I think."

"Sure you will," I said.

"Doyle don't think so, though," he said.

"Doyle?" I said stupidly.

Frank answered absently, as though I had brought Doyle's name up where it had no place. "Yeah," he said, "Al Doyle there. Out in Springfield there. He told Drew Boyster I was dying. Drew was on the civil side, Hampden Civil Session. Doyle I guess did not know that I knew Drew Boyster from way back, and told him I was dying. In a lobby conference. I was finished, Doyle said, fucking little bastard. On my last legs. Checking out. Drew called me that night. Corinne said I was sleeping, but Drew was all upset. Had to call him when I woke up, like I'm doing you. You and Drew both know now. I am doing fine. Not as good I could wish, but better, Jerry. Better."

"Frank," I said, because I had to, "look, I hate to keep you. You're not feeling well, and so forth, and I realize that. But I am calling because I have got this problem, see? And Lou says you're the man, can help me. Said I should call you."

"Lou," Frank said thoughtfully. "This would be Lou Schwartz, you mean. How is old Lou, anyway?"

"Lou is fine," I said. "But, Frank, all right? The reason I am calling. Lou says that I need to get Bert Magazu to help me. It is with the IRS."

"IRS," Frank said. "Yeah, Bert is good at that. He's an amazing fellow, Bert is, on that goddamned tax stuff. Know what he does? He's a diver. Underwater diver. Years ago now, we were planning, I was going with him. Go with him when he went out on some damned expedition. Never did it, though. Usual excuse. Never seemed to have the time. Now, of course, I can't. Let that be a lesson to you, putting things off like that. Always a goddamned mistake. Always, Jerry. Always."

"Yeah," I said. "Look, Frank, all right? Will you call him for me? Call Bert Magazu and put the word in for me now? Because the way I get it, that is how he runs his practice. Strictly on referrals. No trade in from off the street. So, since you do know him, would you call him for me and tell him he should represent me with these motherfuckers?"

"No," Frank said regretfully. "I can't do that, Jerry." He cleared his throat, or tried to, and the stuff in it clattered. "See, Bert Magazu, he never sent me cases. And you know how I was about that, how we all have to be. It's reciprocal, you know? So I can't do that, Jerry."

"I don't get it," I said, and I didn't get it either. "You are saying you won't call him because he never sent you business?"

"Yeah," Frank said. "That's it. Rules in any business, Jerry, you should know as well as I do. That was always mine, someone like him was concerned."

"Frank," I said, "you sent me business. You sent me lots of cases. I did not reciprocate. I did not send you business."

"Jerry," Frank said, "that was different. We were not competing. You and me, you know? We weren't. We were not like that. Magazu and me, we were. One of us is best. Way I see it, it was a draw. But I never sent him business."

"I couldn't get it through my head," I said to Teddy the next day. "I could not believe it. Here is Frank Macdonald, whom I always knew and liked. I am asking him for help. One goddamned phone call, all right? I am in the need of help because I covered Frank. Frank was sick, and I took Lou, and that's how this all started. And here is this old egotist, and he will not help me. Might ding up his pride or something, to call Magazu."

"Frank," I said, "I can't believe this. I'm not hearing this. I need help here, really bad. Magazu can give it. All I need from you is just a simple telephone call. How the hell else do I do it? You're the only one I know, knows this Magazu."

"Jerry, I am sick," Frank said. "Have to understand that. What I'm doing's hanging on, until I get better. My law practice, you know, that is my whole life to me. I am down here, sick. I have to protect it. That is why, a guy like Doyle? Someone like that hurts me. Telling people I am dead? That is murderous. That was why I called Drew Boyster, just as soon as I woke up. Just like I'm doing you. Tell him not to worry. I am getting better. Not so very fast, but getting better, though."

"I'm glad to hear it, Frank," I said.

"So'm I," he said. He let another period of silence pass while we reflected on that. Then he cleared his throat, very gingerly, I thought. "Anyway," he said, "I thought that's what you called about. Luther. Luther and his fucking seat on the Appeals Court."

"No," I said.

"No," Frank said. "Well, that's good. Luther thinks you did it, you know. Put the boots to him."

"I figured that he would," I said.

"Yeah," Frank said. "Couple days, maybe a week, Luther called me up again. Same thing as before. I was always sleeping when he called. Finally he got me. 'It was Kennedy,' he says. He was even more upset'n he was the first time I talked to him. 'That goddamned Kennedy,' he says. 'I'll fix that rotten bastard if it's the last thing I do.' I told him to calm down. He would be in the same mess I'm in, if he got so excited. 'I mean it, Frank,' he said. 'I'm going to kill him. Someday he is going to have to appear in my court, and when he does I am going to ruin him.' "

"Great," I said to Frank.

Frank managed another chuckle. "You know Luther," he said. "All bullshit and about four feet deep. 'Come on, Luther,' I said, 'you're a bigger man than that. Besides, how're you so sure that it was Kennedy? Him and this new governor big asshole buddies now? That what you're telling me, Luther?' He says no, that isn't it. Says he's watching television and he sees this guy he sentenced, that you represented. Some guy with a dog?"

"Harry Mapes," I said.

"I didn't get the guy's name," Frank said, wheezing slightly. "All I got was Luther saying this guy with a dog was on the television there, and he said on the television you were the prime guy that sank old Luther's chance at the Appeals."

"Yeah," I said disconsolately.

"*Yeah?*" Frank said, his voice suddenly much louder. "You *did* do that to Luther?" He began coughing uncontrollably, deeply in his chest. I heard an extension clicking open on the line. "What the fuck did you do that for, Jerry?"

"Frank," I said desperately, "I did not do that. I didn't do . . ."

Corinne's voice interrupted me. "Frank," she said, "hang up." I heard one handset drop. "Mister Kennedy," she said with some severity, "I'm hanging this phone up." She was obviously highly pissed off at me.

"I didn't," I said, and the line went dead.

I stood there like a fool with the phone in my hand, looking at it as though I'd expected some sort of printed message to appear on the earpiece. Mack stared at me, her face displaying anguish. I put the phone down in its cradle. "No help, kid?" she said. I shook my head. "At all?" she said.

I shook my head again. "No help at all," I said. I thought about it for a minute. "I think," I said, "I am not sure, but I am pretty sure, and I think I have reached the point now where I'm going to have to be a real big boy and not think anybody else can help me anymore."

"You've been doing that for years," Mack said comfortingly. "You can handle that all right."

"No," I said, "I haven't. I thought that I was. I really believed it. I thought it was so. Now I am going to find out. Oh boy, am I gonna find out."

"So," I said to Teddy, "that is why I'm sick of calls. Make them and you find out things you didn't want to know."

"This guy Magazu," he said, "he's that hard to find?" I gave Teddy a rundown on the elusive Magazu. "I bet I know a guy," he said, "who can get you in to see him."

"Teddy, Teddy," I said, "this guy does not deal in cars."

"No," Teddy said, "I know that. There is very few guys do. But we know each other pretty good, and sometimes we can do things. Lemme call up Royal Belcher. Royal can do something."

36

"I DO NOT explain things twice," Bertram Magazu told me when I visited his office for the first time on the morning of Good Friday of the year in which I became forty-six years old. I told him that was fortunate, inasmuch as I was getting along in years myself and had no extra time to spend listening to people repeat things they had already told me. "If that's impolite," I said, "I guess I'm slightly sorry. But only very slightly, Mister Magazu, and not very sincerely."

"Good," he said, leaning toward me over his enormous rosewood desk. It was a free-form slab, the edges left unbeveled like the edges of my life—the desk was glossier. His windows high in 28 State Street faced north and they were tinted on the inside, so that light from God's sky did not seem to affect much the gray and maroon decorum of his

Art Deco furnishings. He was a compact man, perhaps five-ten, with a curly black Afro hairdo and a sort of Middle Eastern face. He wore a heavy gold Rolex GMT Master watch and a blue shirt made of silk which had been woven to resemble oxford cotton cloth. "That will save time. Tell me what is eating you and why you think it should be. Give me just as much detail as you think I might need."

He gestured over his shoulder at the long rosewood credenza behind him. I noticed two silver microphones, aimed so they converged upon the chair where I was sitting. "Those will get what you say," he said. Then he glanced up at the ceiling over my head where two more of them were aimed down at his chair. "Those will pick up what I say." He touched the edge of the desk with his right forefinger. "I am arming the system now," he said. "Except for those little gadgets, this room is quite dead. That switch I just hit cuts off power to the phones," which were not visible to my inspection, at least, "and even though there is no way for anyone to get in here, I have the place swept every night. That is every single night, Mister Kennedy, okay? This room is secure, in other words, and I can guarantee it. Nothing that you say in here will go anywhere but into my transcription system. Tapes from that system are sealed and locked until I have a need for their transcription into print."

"Understood," I said, and I began at the beginning. I told him how Lou Schwartz had accepted the fact that Frank Macdonald couldn't defend him, and approached me with the burden. I told him about Nunzio, as much as I really knew about that remote mafioso whose life seemed to have affected mine adversely. I described my meeting with the charming Agent Wainer, and my conversations with the prosecutor, Michael Dunn, of the U.S. Attorney's Office. I reported the ominous predictions Lou had made to me about the tax men. I told him how Lou's statements had echoed what Frank said to me, so many years ago. I gave him as much information as I had from Mack about the audit of her taxes. I was candid about my portion of the goods of this world, pausing for an instant to allow him to interrupt me and conclude the conference if it should seem to him that I was not worth his consideration, but he remained silent and I resumed my report. I informed him of my meeting with the genial Mr. Everson, and the obligation I had to call him that afternoon. I gave him all the background about Everson's colloquies with Gretchen. I told Bert Magazu that Gretchen, unbeknownst to me, had failed to file three quarterly employer's unemployment compensation contributions when they were actually due. I assured him I had filed those returns on Monday, the two that were then still owing. I opened my briefcase and removed from it my copies of my tax returns for the past five years, and I told him that the fat expanding folders tied with ribbons which remained inside the briefcase were my supporting documents—canceled checks, accountant's worksheets, and explanatory notes for the tax years Mr. Everson had designated. Without speaking, Magazu made it clear that he wanted those fat files as well, and I put them in all their shabby disrepair on the shining surface of his lovely rosewood desk. I stopped talking for a moment and reflected.

During all of that long monologue, Magazu had not stirred enough for me to notice. Irrelevantly I tried to guess just how old he was; I concluded he was somewhere between thirty-one and sixty-one, and therefore that I would most likely never know for sure. "I guess that's all," I said. "It's all that I can think of at the moment, at least."

He now made an imperceptible movement which, when he had completed it, left both of his forearms resting on the desk. "Have you had a recent private audit, Mister Kennedy?" he said. I shook my head and told him I have never had one. "We'll want to conduct one," he said. "To encompass all your assets. Those in which you have a beneficial interest as well as those which are in fact and public record in your name."

"That would just be the two houses," I said. "They are in my wife's name, and they're pretty much paid off."

He nodded. "How's your throat, Mister Kennedy?" he said.

"Well," I said, "I did consider cutting it, but I've heard good reports about your special talents, so I postponed that idea until I had talked to you."

He did not smile. "I meant," he said softly, "do you find it dry?"

I nodded, as I swallowed to see whether he was right. "Very," I said, "now that you mention it."

He nodded once. He made two motions with his right forefinger along the edge of that big desk. "I've just shut the system off," he said. "One of the ladies will be in in a minute with some water. Please do not say anything further until she has left the room and I have rearmed the system."

I started to say I would not say anything, caught his small smile at the incipient inadvertent disobedience, subjugated myself like a small child caught in a foolish lie, and nodded back at him. A woman with blond hair, wearing a gray silk business suit, entered the room soundlessly behind me, came to the desk with a polished wooden tray carrying two small bottles of Perrier water, a small glass dish of cut limes, and two glasses, and set it down. The bottles and the glasses were beaded with condensation. The woman without saying anything then turned and left the room. Magazu leaned forward, inquired with an eyebrow whether I would like lime, accepted my nod and squeezed one wedge into each glass. He poured the water bubbling over the lime wedges, took the glass nearest him, gestured that I should take the other, and leaned back again. We drank in silence, thoughtfully, like two monks taking our refreshment after matins, before a long day to be spent illuminating manuscripts. When he had finished his, he touched his right forefinger tip delicately to the center of his upper lip in what was clearly a concession to the preposterous possibility that there might be a single stray drop of the mineral water there, found none, and employed the finger to reactivate the sound system. I hurried to finish my drink. I was not sure whether drinking was permitted while the mikes were on.

"I prefer to start with the general," he said affably, "and proceed from it to the particular. If you have no objection?" I shook my head that I did not.

"What you have to understand," Magazu said, "and I mean: you really have to understand it, get it through your skull so you can almost feel it there when you are dealing with these guys, is that you make them very, very nervous. See, you are not *like* them. Their entire world is based on the idea of regularity, everything from bowel movements to Christmas coming in December, not in April this year and September, maybe, next year. People like us bother them."

"People like them bother me," I said.

"I know," he said, "but this is supposed to help you with that. These people get paid every two weeks. Do you know what that means? Every fourteen days a check arrives. It is always for the same amount, unless they are increasing it for some reason. Government checks are never for less than the checks that came before them. And when one of them is for more than the checks that came before it, the ones that come after it will be for that newer and larger amount. Never less."

"Those checks are always good, too," I said. "This is not always a feature of the checks that I receive."

"Right," Magazu said, nodding, "always good and always printed on stiff green paper that is almost cardboard, with purple marks on it that say how much they are for and a printed picture of somebody's name with wavy lines around it so you can't copy it or anything. And they have little holes punched in them. They say: 'Treasury of the United States' on them and they always come on time and they are always good. The company is always solvent.

"This is why," Magazu said, "they get so upset when somebody tries to get them to believe, say at the beginning of the year, that he doesn't know how much he will have made by the end of it."

"Or managed to collect out of what he has made," I said.

"That too," Magazu said. "People who work for the government, and the vast majority of people who are employed by the private sector, always know at the beginning of the year how much they will have made by the end of it. No, strike that: they always know *at least* how much they will have made by the end of it. They may turn out to have made more, but never less."

"It must be a great comfort to them," I said.

"It is not," he said. "It would be if they thought about what it would be like not to know that when you wake up New Year's morning with a mild hangover, not to have that assurance, but that is not something which appears on their screens as a possible version of the real world. Therefore they do not take any more satisfaction, or relief, or whatever you choose to call it, from it than they do from the fact that they can breathe the air and live that way. They have regular and secure incomes. That is the way things are. Therefore everybody has regular and secure incomes. Basically, when you start handing them papers that claim you do not, they do not believe you."

"Well, damnit," I said, "it is the truth, after all. Those are the goddamned facts."

"Bear with me," Magazu said. "The part of their brain which does addition and subtraction, which prepares questions and interprets answers, that part of their brain pretty much goes along with the idea that you don't have a regular income, and that the income which you do have fluctuates. But it sort of does that *arguendo*, you know? 'Okay, Jack, you say you live from hand to mouth, and we'll go along with that

for now if saying it makes you happy.' But their lizard brain, the one
which tells them to put warmer clothes on when it gets cold out, go inside when it starts raining, evacuate their bowels after they have their
morning coffee: that does not go along with this idiotic notion. All the
time they are sitting there, looking at your forms and listening to you
tell them that you made this much last year and it cost you that much
to do it, but you only made two-thirds as much this year and it cost you
about twenty percent more to do it, and that is really all the money that
you have, or had, back in their heads that beady little lizard brain is
saying: 'Bullshit.' It is nudging at them every single minute not to forget
while you are talking about this four-thousand-dollar fee and that
eleven-thousand-dollar fee and how this guy that hired you for eight
grand only paid you six, that all of these large chunks of cash are just
what you're admitting to, see? You don't ever say anything about what
you were always making every two weeks in addition to that, which
was your regular check that they think everybody gets because they
do."

"Despite the fact that I don't get one," I said.

"Right," Magazu said. "You get, say, ten grand as a fee. It happens to
be the only fee you have taken in this month, and the only one of any
size that you are likely to get for the next month. You see it as eight
weeks' salary for Gretchen. Two months' rent for the landlord. Two
payments on your house mortgage. The light bills, the phone bills, two
payments to the guy who delivers oil to your house, something for the
MasterCard, and maybe a hundred bucks a week down at the super-
market. This is the money you are going to live on until you get some
more money. You hope."

"Right," I said.

"These tax guys that are calling you," he said, "they look at that ten
grand in terms of what it would mean to them, if they got it. It would
be ten thousand dollars *extra*. Those checks every two weeks already
take care of the mortgage and the credit cards, the phone bill and the
lights. After those bills are paid, there isn't anything left, or much of
anything, but those bills are still all *paid*. That ten grand is two weeks
on the Riviera, if that is what they want to do with it, or maybe a new
boat with a motor and a trailer. It is also, unlike what they get in those
checks, not subject to withholding. They know they would not enjoy
paying the estimated taxes on it, and they know you don't like the idea

either, and because they think that ten grand which you got is all gravy, they believe you should pay half of it to them the minute you get it. And when you don't, because it wasn't all gravy, they think you are cheating."

He paused and stared at me the same way I look at new clients who have just finished solemnly assuring me that the arresting officers are lying and they would never dream of committing the foul deeds alleged against them. The clients always treat this as my accusation that they are lying to me, and it isn't that at all—what it is is my inadequate effort to assess whether the client has the fiber to stick to his story, and the talent to make twelve reasonably skeptical strangers believe it. Its truth or falsity doesn't matter to me in the slightest. It is not my job to decide whether the story I have been told is what actually happened, because whether it is that is no concern of mine. What I need to know is whether it is plausible enough to warrant its presentation to a jury, or so lame that the client had best plead guilty, even if what he is blathering is the truth as the Lord spoke it. Magazu was trying to decide how bright I am.

"It is almost impossible," Magazu said to me slowly, "to convince two or three of these people that you really are not cheating. You may overwhelm them with so many documents and statements that they will concede at last that they can't *prove* you cheated, but as you might expect, this does not make them feel happy. They take it to mean that you are an unusually good cheater, that you think you are too smart for them to catch, and that you are gloating at them. Sneering at them from behind their backs."

"But are they graceful about it?" I said. "Do they admit their defeats and go home quietly?"

"Very seldom," Magazu said. "Almost never, in fact. What they do, when they can't prove you cheated them out of a lot, is what amounts to silently accusing you of cheating them out of a little. The chances are you won't be able to prove that you did not. Therefore when the final report goes upstairs in the Service, it will show that the agent was at least as smart as you were, because you didn't get away clean. He collected something from you. Generally he tries to make that an amount which is large enough to justify some of the effort he put into chasing you, but small enough to make it uneconomic for you to fight him any further."

"It's an ego trip," I said.

"Yes," Magazu said, "but isn't everything? And it is something else too, at the same time: it's the agent's only reliable means of making his regular salary checks bigger than the cost-of-living adjustments would have made them if he just sat there and breathed."

"They get bounties for us?" I said.

"Essentially," Magazu said. "They deny that's what it is, but that is what it is. Merit promotions, grade jumps bigger than you'd get anyway from longevity, and lots faster ones, are not distributed within the IRS according to how many honest and trustworthy taxpayers the agent has provided with clean bills of health. If he puts you through a full field audit and fails to come up with anything, he's wasted a great deal of time. He looks like a fool. Fools don't find their names at the tops of promotion lists, not very often, anyway. And besides that, keep in mind this guy has been motivated in the first place by some office manager who looked at your return and decided you were up to something. He assigned you to the agent, who then motivated himself a great deal more by beginning with the assumption that you are a crook and he is the relentless lawman out to catch you. These agents don't entertain each other over coffee by telling stories about all the honest taxpayers they're investigating—they talk about the thieving bastards who think they can get away with bullshitting the IRS. You can guess who the heroes are in those stories."

"I get the impression," I said, "you are trying to tell me something that I think I probably don't want to hear."

"Correct," he said. "I realize that nobody with tax problems is completely rational about them, no matter what he does for a living. But you are an attorney, and I have to be aware that you're a little more sophisticated about things than the fellow who comes in here and tells me he drives a truck for a living and they're giving him trouble about his travel expenses. If I level with you, you're not going to like what I say, maybe, but at least you're not going to hate my guts for blowing smoke at you, and that is better.

"Therefore," he said, "no bullshit. I am expensive. I do a lot of underwater photography because I enjoy it. I do it in places like the Great Barrier Reef. It costs a lot more than I make from selling pictures to fly me down to Australia. It takes a lot of time as well. I allocate my time carefully between the work I have to do to get the money that I need, and the avocation that I spend the money on. This means I am pretty dear for my clients. I don't have many of them, and I don't expect to bill the ones I do take for more than about twelve hundred hours a year. That is thirty weeks of work, forty hours each. Most people actually work about forty-six weeks every year. I like to live as well as they do, which is selfish of me, maybe, so I charge roughly fifty percent more for each hour that I work than they do. I get away with this because I am very good and besides, I don't need to convince many clients at those rates in order to have enough to support me."

"I appreciate this candor," I said.

Magazu grinned at me. "This operation costs me about five thousand every week," he said. "That is close enough to a quarter million a year so the difference is not worth niggling about. Half of that overhead comes from the work I do myself. The associates bring in the other half from the work that they do. My fee is two hundred and twenty-five dollars per hour. My net after overhead from that is about one hundred and a quarter. Two dollars a minute, plus a little change."

"Cripes," I said, "if you ever decide to stop spending so much time with the fishes and the kangaroos, you could make yourself a lot of money."

"It's a living," he said, smiling. "Your consolation, if it is any to you, is that I am a deductible luxury. It costs you probably about sixty percent of what I'm billing to you. The taxpayers of the United States have to make up the slack in your tax bill, which their agents are responsible for causing in the first place by this harassment that brought you in here."

"I suppose," I said, "there's no professional courtesy I can invoke here."

"Sure there is," he said, the smile fading slightly. "You had that when I agreed to see you. I'm not kidding, Jerry. I don't accept just any client who comes in here looking worried. Without Buddy Belcher's introduction, and what I heard on the street already about how you got yourself into this box with the tax guys, you would never have gotten this bad news. I don't hustle clients, Mister Kennedy. I don't need to."

"We have got to stop here for a minute," I said. I suppose it was my ego, getting in its licks, but I'm not good at being humble and I cannot keep it up. I did not mind Bert Magazu putting on his airs and graces as some sort of secular pontiff reigning over the mysterious realms of

Taxes, where lesser mortals such as I were to be condescendingly instructed to remove footwear before we entered. What bothered me was his inept effort to speak what he thought was my language, patronizing me by coming down to my level with his phony backchat. "Just out of curiosity here, Bert, what street is this you were on when you picked up this information about me?" He was startled enough to be guilty of a fleeting gape of surprise. "And while I'm at it, I do not know Buddy Belcher."

Bert Magazu was not used to being challenged and he didn't like it either. He required time to regroup, but he was rattled enough so that he did not feel comfortable allowing it to pass in Trappist silence. "Buddy Belcher," he said, "Jerry, is an old school chum of mine. Buddy reached me last night, down in Hamilton. He was at La Quinta and he said I had to help you. He said you were in some trouble I could probably assist you with, and that you were the sort of guy that I would not mind seeing. I had the impression that the two of you had met. Buddy is an old friend, and a client too. Are you sure that you don't know him? He was very high on you."

I was very sure about that, but I didn't say it. What I knew was *about* Belcher; I had gotten that from Teddy. "Who the hell is Belcher?" I said. "Some damned crook pal of yours? Why should this guy help me out, that I don't even know?"

"Simple," Teddy said to me. "I did him a favor. And he owes me one."

37

"Mister Magazu," I said, in that recording office, "I would not know Buddy Belcher if he blew into my ear. If he'd served the Perrier, instead of that young lady, I would not have recognized him. This does not mean I don't feel obliged to him—all it means is that I don't want false impressions working here."

Magazu looked perplexed. "Well," he said, "I don't know. Maybe you know him as Roy? Royal Belcher?"

"Oh," I said, subsiding. "Saratoga, then. Of course. He'd be Chico's friend."

"Chico," Magazu said, looking more perplexed. "I don't think I know a Chico."

"Chico is the guy with Royal," I said helpfully. "Chico *was* the guy with Royal, up at Saratoga last year? Then I guess something happened to him, later on in San Diego."

Magazu looked downright baffled. He shook his high-priced head once. "I definitely don't know that Chico. I'd remember that."

I shrugged. "Well, doesn't matter, I guess. Chico was with Royal, up at Saratoga. Probably just some guy he met. Pal of Nunzio's. Happened to be with him."

Magazu leaned back in his chair and studied me a while. "I really must try to remember," he said very slowly, "not everybody went to the same schools that I attended at the same time that I did. And that those who went with me met other people later."

"Right," I said, in his long pause. I wasn't sure he wanted any comment from me, but supplying one seemed harmless.

"Buddy and I," Magazu said carefully, "we were at Choate together." He did not say when, I noticed, making that admission. "I guess I assume that if he was Buddy then, he has been Buddy ever since."

"Uh-huh," I said, "that leaves: which street?"

"Street?" he said, looking perplexed again.

"Street, street," I said, somewhat impatiently. I am not used to being a good little boy for very long stretches of time, forced to keep my hands folded in my lap and not allowed to talk to the kid next to me, or when the mike system is shut off. "You said you heard things about me on the street. Which street?"

"Oh," Magazu said, nodding twice and raising both eyebrows. He had recovered what he deemed to be his command of the situation now. His next step would be to restore my subordination to him. Bert Magazu did not like matters getting out of his control any more than I did. I was heartened to see that. His next few ploys were going to be designed to make me feel quite uncomfortable, and I did not relish that prospect, but at the same time, I hoped he'd be successful. This son of a bitch was hiring himself out to me as a fighter, my own mercenary to defend me against some real bastards with a shitload of firepower. I did not know a great deal about this fellow, except that he went to Choate with some rich sucker Teddy Franklin sort of met at Saratoga. It would make me feel more cheerful if he had the balls to take me down a peg, at least. "You mean: Whom did I call, after I talked to Buddy?"

"Something like that, yeah," I said.

Magazu smiled at me. "Mister Kennedy," he said, "I should say: None of your business. But I will be kind. Can you keep a confidence? Sure, of course you can. I called Ed Maguire at home. Asked him about you. Judge Maguire was high on you, and he was sympathetic. 'Jerry Kennedy,' he said, 'is one of hundreds of good people who got caught in traps like this. Partly through his own volition, partly by accident, he played Frank Macdonald's game and he got burned. If you can help him, Bert, you should. He is an honest man.' Ed Maguire said you were all right, and that was enough for me."

"Gee," I said, "it is for me as well, I'd have to say. Didn't know that Judge Maguire was that respectful, what I did for Lou."

"Lou?" Magazu said, puzzled. "Ed said nothing about Lou. What he talked about was different. He said: 'The crusader.'"

"The crusader?" I said. "Now I'm really baffled."

"Oh, come on, Jerry," he said. "I told you this was confidential. Levitable, Jerry, okay? Richard Coeur de Lion?"

"Joseph Vaster?" I said. "How does Ed Maguire fit in?"

Magazu looked at me with pity and amusement. "All I know is what Ed said, and he did not say much. He did not have to say much, of course, and I didn't press him on it. 'The crusader, Bert,' he said, 'came in to see Frank. This guy and Frank got together, long before I got wind of it. One of them did something, back when I was still in practice. Near as I can gather, they cooked up a little scheme. What they did was fix a witness, I think, but I never tried to prove it. Tampered with him, you know? I just got small snatches of it, but it smelled to very heaven.

"'I went in, confronted Frank, without knowing a whole lot. Told him he'd suborned the man. I wouldn't stand for it. Told him to get out of it, wash his hands of it. He protested innocence, said he had done nothing. I didn't buy Frank's story, not by a long shot. If the witness did it on the client's action only, Frank still knew about it and he had to report it. I said: "Frank, withdraw from this. Get our firm out of this. If you stay in, I'll report it. I will have no choice." Frank agreed he would get out, if I would keep my mouth shut.

" 'Jerry Kennedy accepted that case,' Judge Maguire told me. 'Took it in all innocence, and naturally, he won it. He did not know what went on. No one ever told him. But those who have suspected it, they have never believed that, and they never will. What he's going through these days, it's the consequence of that. Long delayed and long deferred, but that's what it came from. Underground, the cops believe that he bought off a witness. Paid a guy named Ranger Damon to forget he knew the client. Cops are right—he was paid off. But Jerry didn't know it. Give the guy a break if you can. He could really use the help.' "

I did not say anything. I just sat and gaped. "I take it," Magazu said, "you, ah, lacked this news?" I managed to nod. Magazu frowned very slightly—he does not do very much of anything that he deigns to do at all. "So I gather," he said. "Look, try not to be upset. No more upset, anyway, than you were when you came in."

"I had no idea of this," I said, feeling stupid. "That guy, really, I was certain. He was innocent. Ranger Damon, he could fake that? I just don't believe it. I cannot believe it's true."

"Jerry," Magazu said, "let's try our best to stick to business. Things that happened, long ago, we cannot change them. What we have to do, this year, is deal with the IRS. Why they're chasing you, all right? If it really is the reason, what the cops must think happened, that does not concern us here. That is not our problem here."

"Yeah," I said, "that is certainly the truth."

"So," he said, "let's have it clear here, make sure that we understand each other, so we can get you out of this. You are not here on the say-so of anyone named Chico. Buddy overstated matters, and I'll deal with him myself, but Buddy did get me to call Ed, and I will accept your case. But not because some crypto-mafioso is in back of Buddy. Are we clear on that?"

"Yes," I said, "we are quite clear. We're in full agreement."

"Good," he said, "let's move along. This is what I can do, and it's all that I can do. I cannot prevent the IRS from inspecting your returns. I cannot preclude them from demanding documents. I cannot block them from disallowing items. I cannot stop them from making findings of deficiencies, and issuing assessments which are based upon such findings. If you do not pay up when they complete their auditing, they will hound you to the point at which your grandchildren will remember. I cannot prevent that either. They have singled you out here. You have helped them in this process. And what you are doing now—first the Schwartz case, now the TV—that is making it still worse. You stick out from the landscape. That celebrity will cost you. It's a good thing you're not rich—then it would cost you more. They have so decided.

"Their base motives in this," he said, "do not matter in the slightest. You are going to end up paying them something. You will also have to pay me. They must justify what they do for administrative reasons. I must justify mine by keeping those damned ego charges down to minimum. These guys know two things about me. One is that I'm tough. The other is that I am quite expensive. Therefore while I fight them hard, it costs you a lot to have me do it—they are aware of this. After we have sparred a while, and they have grown a little bored with chasing a small fish like you, they will sit down by themselves and make a rough guess about how much they can hit you with, as a final assessment. The figure they arrive at will be their approximation of about two-thirds of my additional fee for contesting that assessment in the Tax Court or the Court of Claims. It will be almost exactly sixty-six and two-thirds percent too. Keep in mind that I file tax returns too, just like you. They know precisely what I charge my clients, and they do not have much trouble figuring what my fee will be for any given service. My advice to you, when that day comes, will in all likelihood be that you pay the assessment. It will be less than the cost in money and anxiety of fighting any further. If you're sane, you will pay it. If you aren't, you'll pay me and we'll fight some more. It will be up to you when that day comes. Understood?"

"How much in front?" I said.

"Five thousand dollars," he said.

"Twenty-two point something hours of your undivided attention," I said, calculating what remained of Teddy's dwindling envelope.

"I'll be a sport about this," Magazu said with another small smile. "Call it twenty-five whole hours, okay? I may need a break someday when I'm caught driving under. But be prepared for more. These cases are not quick."

"Cripes," I said, "I'm not surprised. Nothing is, these days, if the reports I get are true. Even death is slowing down, taking its sweet time."

"Well," Mack said that night when I finished briefing her, "is he big-time, Jerry?"

"I guess he must be," I said. "He sure is expensive."

38

FAIRLY EARLY in the morning of the Wednesday before Memorial Day, I put our single trash can at the end of our driveway for collection, under the surveillance of the young male Doberman the Coreys had acquired at Easter as a present for their kids. "Gee, Jim," I had said, when the dog had first gotten into our yard, bounding between urination stops he made to stake it out, "things've changed a lot, I guess, since Heather was their age. Back when she was little, we could still get tinted chicks."

Jim was somewhat winded from pursuing his new dog. "Oh," he puffed, in disapproval, "they don't do that. They won't let them. Not anymore, at least. That was cruel to animals. If the dye they used didn't poison the little chickens, then the mauling that they got from little kids just killed them off. We thought if we got Bluster—that was Robbie, Robbie named him—he could sort of, you know, he'd grow up with them. And even though he's very gentle, actually, Jerry, well, they do have a reputation. Dobermans, I mean. So that he'd protect them, you know? Just by being with them." He gazed at the dog admiringly. "Dobermans are very smart," he said, "and they're beautiful."

"And this one, by the looks of things," I said as Bluster peed, "has the bladder capacity of a transatlantic tanker."

Bluster was indeed quite smart. By May he had already learned that Kennedys ate meat most nights, and they left tasty scraps and bones. He had learned that by approaching our trash barrel like an NFL linebacker, knocking it over and popping the cover off. I knew his procedure because I'd seen him do it twice, waiting until I had backed my car out in the street, then leaping into our yard while I drove away from it, watching from my rearview mirror as he made his attack. That May morning, therefore, we looked at each other with the mutual respect of animals in our positions. He spent perhaps a minute wandering around his yard, sniffing here and poking there, elaborately aimless, futilely intending to delude me into thinking that he didn't plan to raid my garbage just as soon as I was out of there. I for my part made a pretense of intending to stand sentry over my offal either until he was called back into his house or the hippo truck arrived to remove it from his reach. I had no more success in my effort to fool him than he had had in his attempt to bamboozle me. After a short while he sat down and stared at me with his tongue out. "All right, Bluster," I said softly, "I guess you have won." Bluster stood up fast and gazed at me hungrily. Then he sat down once more to wait until I actually did leave. I backed my car down the driveway, hearing the forsythia branches scraping on the finish, got it out into the street and put into drive. The instant that the car moved forward, Bluster jumped across the line. He had the barrel dumped open before I had reached the stop sign at the end of Kevin Road.

Miss Goldser in the Woburn District Court that morning regarded me in the same way that I had regarded Bluster. I had cut a deal with the DA for my musician druggie, who had jumped his bail on charges that he had a half pound of grass. He had been tried in Northampton on the convenience-store armed robbery. He had gotten Concord prison, indeterminate ten years—this meant that he might get out in one if he was lucky, but it also meant that he could not afford a second felony, because that would crease his chances even if the sentence were to run concurrently with his first one. I had therefore bargained with the DA himself. Dennis Patrick, the DA, is a decent man; he has some jerks, like Steve Ranney, doing things for him, but he, like me, could see no point in blocking the kid's parole. He reduced the grass charge from possession with intent to distribute to a civil offense of possession for personal use. In court that morning, on my strong recommendation, the kid admitted to sufficient facts to enable the judge to enter a finding that he was guilty as charged. Pursuant to the General Laws, he was duly found to have committed no previous offense of possession and placed upon probation for a period of six months, and his case was ordered filed without an entry of the finding therein, said charge to be dismissed and the record of it expunged if he should complete his probationary period successfully. Inasmuch as he was going to spend that period in the Massachusetts Correctional Institution at Concord, where drug use is not unknown, that was by no means assured, but it was possible. The kid was ordered to pay court costs of one hundred dollars to the clerk, and to report forthwith to the probation office, where Miss Goldser brooded in extreme and dark suspicion.

The kid, his reddish blond hair in need of cutting and his freckled complexion making him look like a scared country boy and not an armed robber, his wrists back in handcuffs and his mind bewildered by the court proceeding which had been conducted at a pace that reminded older listeners of the old Lucky Strike commercials, featuring the tobacco auctioneer, sat at Miss Goldser's desk and tried to look undaunted. Miss Goldser, a woman about fifty with gray hair and gray eyes and lines of fatigue in her face, took what comfort she could from Kool cigarette smoke and expressed her disapproval. "Straight possession?" she said, and her eyebrows arched. "On half a pound of pot, for God's sake, he pleads out to straight possession? Hasn't Dennis read the statute, where it says: 'half an ounce'? You must be quite a lawyer, Mister Kennedy."

"Miss Goldser," I said, "Dennis and I, this is strictly wrapping up that we are trying to do here. My client has been sentenced on those other charges there. There is absolutely no point in just making this thing worse."

She shook her head. "I don't think so," she said firmly. "I just do not think so. If you ask me, Kennedy, what should have been done here . . ."

"I did not ask you, Miss Goldser," I said, "and the DA didn't either. The judge knew about this and he didn't seek your views. Only reason we are in here is formalities. Why don't we just get them finished, so we can get on to other things?"

"Look," she said, "celebrity, this is my office here. I decide how it is run. Not some guy like you." At that instant, the phone rang, and she took it wearily. "Goldser," she said, "whatcha want?" Then she reared back in her chair. "Yeah, what of it?" she said. "So what if he is?" She paused then and glared at me, while she listened to her caller. "Yeah," she said, "now look, Gail, I don't like this. This is where I do my business, and it isn't taking calls. This guy's in here and we're busy, and I see no need of this. Just barge in here like some colonel, in my old days in the Army, everything just has to stop. I don't like it, see?" She leaned forward then and whomped both elbows on the desk. "You tell Patrick," she said, "he can go ..." Then she paused again. My client sat there and studied her, perfectly serene. She made an impatient gesture at him, which startled him. His face showed hurt amazement. She looked at him angrily. She put her right palm on the mouthpiece. "Quit your looking at me, damnit," she snarled at the poor kid. "The hell do you think this is? Some damned circus here or something?" Then she removed her hand from the telephone. "All right, all right, have it your way. Anything you say. Just let people come in here and walk all over us. That's the way you want it, Gailsie, that's how it will be. Yeah, that is what I think." She handed the phone to me. "It's for *you*, Mister Kennedy," she said, "you big man, you. Hurry up, for God's sake, will ya? We've got work to do in here."

"Who is it?" I said on reflex as I took it.

"How the hell do I know?" she said. "You think I'm your secretary?"

Gail, Dennis Patrick's secretary, answered when I spoke. "Mister Kennedy?" she said. "It's Frank Macdonald's office. Someone named Ray Feeley, if I can just get him patched in."

Feeley came on after ten or fifteen seconds of complete silence. "Jerry?" he said, sounding relieved when I replied. "Jerry," he said, "sorry for this. For the interruption. But it's sort of urgent and Gretchen said you would be there. Frank died. Frank Macdonald? Passed away early this morning."

"Oh," I said with Goldser glaring and my client looking addled. "Oh, well, gee, Ray," I said. "I'm real sorry to hear that."

"Yeah," Feeley said, almost abruptly. "What I wanted ..."

"Was it cancer?" I said. "Or another heart attack?"

"Well," Ray said, "right now, at least ... We're not saying yet. Okay? Cause of death's not known."

"They're having an autopsy?" I said. I was treading water.

"Yeah," Feeley said, "well, I don't know. Maybe they're having one. But Corinne said: 'Don't say anything.' So that is what I'm doing."

"Yeah," I said, "well, gee, I'm sorry."

"Yeah," he said, "we all are. But, why I was calling, Jerry, all right? Asked the DA to find you. Corinne wants you to call her, all right? I think you have got her number."

"Call her?" I said. "What for, Ray? What good will that do?"

"Well," he said, "it's what she wants, and she is all upset. She called here and talked to me and told me about Frank. And then she started telling me, the things I had to do. And one of them was get in touch with you and do it fast. So, and I said you might not be, not be in your office. And she said I should find you, call your office and I should get ahold of you somehow and tell you that she wanted, that she wants to talk to you. But she did not say what for, when she said that. Just: 'Do it right off.' You know?"

"Ray," I said, "for heaven's sake, I'm in a meeting here. After this, I've got to go over to East Cambridge there, for an arraignment, all right? This is not my office. This is not my phone. I am tying up somebody else's phone here, and I cannot be using it to make my private calls."

"Jerry," he said, sighing, "will you just call her, please? She is all upset and everything, and she's . . . She wants you to call her."

"I will call her, Ray," I said. "You can tell her I will call her."

"And you've got her number, she said."

"Not on my person," I said, "no, but I know how to get it. Now I'm hanging up, Ray. And I'm sorry that Frank died." I gave the handset back to Goldser, who was looking very pissed. Adders have looked friendlier than Miss Goldser did that instant.

She banged the handset in the cradle and said: "Now, Mister Kennedy? Can we get our work done now, or do you have some other business before we can get to that? You and your pal, good old Dennis, who's amending laws these days."

"Look, Miss Goldser," I said, "I think you are right. That was not an urgent call, they put through to me. But they did not know that it was not urgent when they did it. And, after all, Miss Goldser, when you plugged me into it, I did not know either, that it really wasn't urgent. So don't blame me and don't blame Dennis. It was someone else's fault, and she's nowhere around here. As for me and Dennis, playing snuggle-bunny with the law, that is not true, lady, and you're full of shit on that. If I had an in with Dennis, I would not be leaving this joint so I can be with my best client for arraignment on a chickenshit indictment that should never have been brought."

"*Oh*," she said, grinning at me, "have you got yourself a car thief? One of those nice fellows that they're bringing in this morning?"

"I have got a client," I said, "who is no part of that action. But he's in it, thanks to Ranney, and I don't have time to waste here."

"Did you call Corinne?" Coop said, when I got back in time for lunch.

"No," I said, "I didn't. I got out of Woburn and I went to Superior. Ranney's showing off today, for the media. Makes himself a big speech on these vicious criminals he's got. Asks for fifty thousand bail each, with recognizance. Teddy Franklin, I thought, was about to add a charge of murder one to his conspiracy indictment. 'Look,' I say to him, 'siddown. We can beat this one. You deck Ranney and we lose.' Then I came back here. And frankly, Coop, in my own rankings, lunch with you looked like more fun than calling old Corinne."

Coop pondered over pot roast. He drank some dark beer. "I suppose it's possible, Francis killed himself?"

"I suppose it is," I said, "but I don't think it happened. Nothing they could trace, at least, not with all the junk he's on. If they did a blood test, you know? Sure, they would find traces. But he was all doped up quite legal, so that wouldn't mean a thing. Did he overdose? He could. But he was so drugged anyway, it could be an accident."

"Maybe Corinne killed him," Coop said. "Wants you to defend her. After what he did to you, you might be effective."

"Uh-uh," I said, "I won't do it. I might get excited and get that damned bitch acquitted. Then what would I have on my nice peaceful conscience? I do not seek pain."

"Hah," Coop said, attacking meat, "that's what I told my doctor." He chewed zestfully. "Bastard tells me: 'Almost finished. Three more months of visits and we'll have you good as new. You will have the dental structure of a young buck in his twenties.' 'Screw you, Doctor,' I said, when he got his fingers out. 'This is it, *fini* and finished. This is my last visit. You have been tormenting me since Yaz was in his second year. Yaz is old and so am I. I am even older, and now I am retiring. I have had it with this crap, paying you to hurt me. My damned teeth fall out, I will pick them up. But I will not subject myself to no more shit like this.' "

"Whereupon he told you," I said, "that you should stockpile Polident."

"Words to that effect," Coop said, spearing a large carrot. "Said I would regret my rash decision, and he wouldn't give me guarantees on what he's done already. 'No,' I said, 'of course you won't. I knew that before I started. But if I stop now, I won't give you a goddamned new Rolls-Royce or something, and I won't cry when I think of eating.' "

Cooper nodded satisfaction. "That is what I said. Then I went home and decided: I am on a roll. So I said to Karen: 'All right, here is what we're going to do. We are going to take Peter out of his damned expensive kindergarten for big juvenile delinquents. None of that crap works at all, hasn't for him, at least. He can go to work or something, and find out what money is. And if he takes up full-time pushing, he'll make my pal Jerry rich.' "

"How did Karen take that?" I said.

"Shocked and horrified," he said. "I think that describes it. Looks like I just hit her with a goddamned two-by-four. 'Weldon,' she says, 'we can't do it. Peter is our son.' 'Right,' I said, 'he is that, and I don't object to that. But he has also got bad habits, so that means he's lots more things. He is, for example, our place in the Caribbean. He is my little motorboat, and my secure old age. He is trips to Europe and he's dinner out at restaurants. He is also, I might add, his own college education, which he's pissed away without a by-your-leave. But those are all the things that Peter's going to be. All the things of mine, that I've got left, at least, I am getting selfish about.' "

"I admire your courage," I said.

"Courage?" he said. "Bullshit. *Selfish* was the word I used, and it was what I meant. 'Kennedy has got a beach house'—this is what I said to Karen. 'In the summer he and his wife can go swimming in the sun. I'd prefer the winter, and a southern ocean for it, but we have not got enough left to get what I'd prefer. So I am going to buy a beach place. Something nice and new, and fairly close to here. And then at least, when summer comes, I will have that pleasure and we both can have some fun."

"Any place in mind?" I said. "Besides: nice and new?"

"Uh-huh," Cooper said. "I've thought about it some. Cape is out, I have decided. I will not fight that damned traffic. Then last Sunday I am browsing in the real estate ads, see? And I see where this outfit that your wife's with's got some nice stuff. Looks like just what I would need. So, I think, I'll get all the information. And then if it still looks good, I'll make Jerry do the deal. Mack works for Southarbor still, am I right?"

"Oh yes, Cooper," I said. "Mack works for Southarbor."

"And they are the ones," he said. " 'Commodore Islands Village, on historic Buzzards Bay.' "

"Coop," I said, "I am not sure you should just plunge into this. That stuff, you know, can be tricky, on the waterfronts."

That did not discourage him. "Yeah," he said, "I know, I know. But I'll look over the brochures and then decide. Take a ride down there someday, check the places out. But if it looks good, I am buying. Get in on the ground floor, when the prices are the cheapest. Before all that good shit goes up and the riffraff comes in, bidding."

"Jerry," Mack said, when I told her, getting home that night. "What did you say, Jerry, when he said that stuff to you?"

"Relax, Mack," I said, "I said nothing. He may change his mind. And if he doesn't change it, well, he is a big boy now. He said what he wants is his own place on the water. And then he said: 'A big storm comes? Then it's my own place *in* the water. Certainly no riskier'n having teen-aged kids.'"

"I suppose I should say: thank you," she said.

"Either that," I said, "or I should. When I got back to the office, had a call from the expensive Magazu."

"Oh," she said, "has Magazu, has he worked something out?"

"Nah," I said, "it's way too early. He has found some things out, though, and that was why he called me. You know what that bastard Everson told him? That they know I'm cheating on my taxes because I say I pay Gretchen to work for me full-time, and Gretchen's never there. 'Goddamnit, Bert,' I said, 'she reports what I pay her, on her income tax. And I pay those damned withholdings, and all that other crap.' And he says they just laugh that off, say Gretchen pays taxes in a lower bracket than I do, and we're splitting what I save."

"That's insane," Mack said. "Who would think of that?"

"Your government, my dear," I said. "They have suspicious minds."

"They should be committed," she said.

"Ah," I said, "but sometimes, lover, those madmen are right. People tell them stories, you know? And those stories are not true."

"You didn't do that," she said.

"I didn't mean to," I said. "I did tell Mister Magazu some things that were not true, though, and that was his second discovery. 'Jerry,' he says, 'with these tax guys, you know how it is. Got to have all your facts straight, even if theirs are wrong. This real estate of yours and your wife's, with your beneficial interest? You said both those houses, that you own them free and clear.'

" 'Well,' I say to Magazu, 'pretty close to that. If there's any payments left, she'll make them all this year.'

" 'Jerry,' he said, 'you're mistaken. Both of those parcels are heavily mortgaged. My man checked them both out, at the Registry of Deeds. You, well, not you, but your wife owes quite a lot of money. Challenge Equity Investments has a sixty-thousand-dollar mortgage. Salt River Savings is in for another twenty thousand. Both of those loans went on since the first of this year, Jerry. Am I breaking up your marriage, or have you been lying to me?' "

Mack did not say anything. She looked at me and tried to, but the words would not come out.

"Well," I said, "which is it? I said: 'Bert, I did not lie. Right now I am hoping there's a third alternative.' "

"Jerry," she said, "listen to me. Just hear what I have to say. First, of course, his man is right. We have four investment units in the Commodore Islands plans. So far I have binders that will cover two of them. If the whole thing goes as planned, and it looks as though it will, I'll retire those mortgages by Labor Day, the latest. And if we don't sell another one by then, we will have a profit then of thirty thousand dollars. If we sell the other two, as we will be able to, I'll come out of this with a net gain of another hundred thousand dollars. These things, they are cheap today, in the market that we have. Fifty-five grand, Jerry? People think that that's a bargain. If we hold the two that aren't sold, and just keep them for a year, they'll be worth a hundred each."

"If we have no storms," I said.

"If we have no storms," she said. "That's the chance I took.

"Now," she said, "I am not sorry. I am not apologizing. I did not like doing this, without telling you. But I know this stuff, Jerry. It's my job to know it. And when you, when you kissed it off, and wouldn't even listen, I got mad and said: 'Well, all right, I'll get rich alone.'

"I am willing," she said, "I guess, to leave that question up to you. I won't want it, rich alone, but I did take that risk. If that ruins things for us, I am really sorry. But you do not know everything, and sometimes you are wrong."

39

IT WAS very warm and sunny, on Memorial Day. Mack and I went to the beach, down at Green Harbor. We spread the blanket out and she flopped down and went to sleep. I sat there in my trunks and a dark green Dartmouth tee-shirt Heather gave to me for Christmas and listened to the ball game without getting much involved. The beach was sparsely populated even though the air was warm; the ocean was still chilly, too cold even for the kids. Out two or three miles from us there were seven sails shaped like balloons, striped with red and blue and yellow, and I wondered idly if Mack's quietly devised plans would require me to transfer to one of them from my old blanket.

After a while Mike Curran came by, doing his self-appointed rounds. Mike was in place when we arrived as owners of the summer place so many years ago. In his early sixties then, forced into retirement by an ailing heart, a stern doctor, and a numerous and concerned family, Mike had more or less adopted us into his own clan, and vouched for us to other members who'd been earlier admitted. Mike must therefore be near eighty, but he doesn't look it. He still has a rug of white fur on his broad and muscled chest, and he still looks capable of running his old printing business as he did when he was young. Mike is called the Mayor of the Beach by all his friends; he still patrols it daily, as the doctor told him to, doing his two miles a day without ever getting more than three hundred yards from his big white house that looms above the seawall, gleaning gossip, dispensing advice, commenting upon affairs, and supervising matters. His doctor is long dead, he told me, with some satisfaction. "Didn't walk enough," he said. "Always worked too hard."

"Senator," he called me, as he has from the beginning, hunkering down next to me and rumbling his greetings, "I've been watching you on television, with your commentaries there. It's a fine job that you're doing, you know, with the courts and everything. Standin' up for decent people and acquainting us with things."

"Thank you, Michael," I said, reaching for the cooler. Our tacit arrangement is that Mike delivers the news and I furnish the refreshments. I pulled out a can of Diet Coke and set it down on the blanket. "And what the hell might that be?" Mike said. "Is that tonic there or something?"

I removed a Michelob from the cooler second. I cracked that for Mike and popped the Coke for myself. "I cannot believe my eyes," Curran said to me. "And here this is a holiday, the first one of the season, and I with my own eyes am seeing this sacrilege?"

I gestured toward Mack, sleeping there. "Boss's orders," I said. "Nothing decent before luncheon, and damned little after that."

Mike at once revised his thinking. He nodded approval. "Ah, well then," he said, "if that's the way of it. Probably the best idea. This stuff can get to you." He drank deeply, nonetheless, of the Michelob. Mike would say that it was best for me if he caught me in the act of eating dog turds off the lawn if I told him Mack said that I really ought to do it. Mike treats good-looking and nice women in the classic Irish way; he still finds them quite attractive and he's afraid they'll find out. Mike thinks that they know something, and does not know what it is. He fears they may tell him, and it will embarrass him. "A man like yourself could do worse, than hear what she has to say."

Yes indeed, Mike, I thought. You have no idea. "That's true, Mike," I said. "She takes care of my best interests."

"And of course," he said, "I'd assume, with the television thing, you must have to watch your weight and think of things like that."

"Are you telling me I'm fat, Mike?" I said, laughing at him. "After all these years of pleasant conversation and good feelings between us, are you now at the sad point where you are telling me I'm fat?"

Mike touched my arm with his hand and shook his head. "Jeremiah," he said, "do not entertain such thoughts. Merely saying only, since you are a star and all, have to make adjustments in the way you have been living."

"Oh," I said, "well, in that case, yes, I would agree. Reach the point in life that I have, you are certainly quite right. Why, people now know who I am, even in Fall River. Gotten so I'm recognized, in Newton and East Cambridge."

"It must be a burden for you," Mike said. He looked very serious, and I remembered not to take things too far, lest he miss an irony and become uncomfortable.

"Oh," I said, "not really, Mike, I was joking, really. I do the TV thing there because I had some fun at it. But you would be surprised, Mike, at how few people see it. And those who do see it, I think, do not pay much attention. The only ones it seems to bother are the ones that didn't like me, but couldn't give you a good reason until I started doing that. And now they can."

"I know," Mike said sorrowfully. "It is always that way, isn't it though, Jerry? When I came here, you know, I was only a lad then fresh as paint, and right out of Cork City, so I thought I knew the score. And I got my first job, you know, and everybody liked me, it seemed like it was in those days. And they wished me well, you know. And I got myself married, and we had ourselves a family, and I had to work me arse off to keep them in vegetables. But everybody I met seemed to like me pretty well, and what money we could save, well, we just put it by. And then I start the business, and it was tough for quite a while. Livin' hand to mouth, you know, and not a pot to piss in. But I stuck to it and I worked, and by the time that I was fifty I had myself and family pretty well fixed there. And that was when we bought this house, where I am living now. And thirty years or so ago, Jerry, it was an imposing place, and I was proud of it and maybe proud of myself too. That I came from Cork City to a land I did not know, without much in my pockets and not a whole lot in my head, but I had worked, and I worked hard, and I had done this much.

"And then," he said, "I noticed, there were strange things going on. Things like people saying things about me, don't you know? Talking about me, they were, saying things behind my back. And I was shocked, I was. I even went to one or two of them, before I learned my lesson, and I would say: 'Well, Tom,' or 'John,' whatever their name was, 'and what is this fine stuff you have been putting out on me? That I do not deal squarely, or you can't rely on me?' And one of them, I heard about, he said I was a drunk. And this a man that I knew well, from the Holy Name. And I went up to him and I said: 'Joe, ya rotten barstid. Here you are a friend of mine, and saying this about me. And you've been drunk yourself, I think. I've seen it with my eyes. And who are you, you barstid, that I always treated well, to go around and bad-mouth me and say these rotten things?'

"Now, you know, Jeremiah," Mike said, "that he couldn't answer me. He tried there to deny it, and he couldn't do it, of course, for I had the goods on him. And I said: 'Joe, I'm not denyin', there are times when

I've been full. Once or three times, I admit, I've had a jar too many and I got too jovial. But that is not the same thing, Joseph, as the things that you've been sayin'. And it's hurting business, you know, and my hard-earned reputation.'

"And he gives me this look," Mike said. "You'd think he always hated me. And he said: 'Hurtin' business, is it? While you're dancin' with the swells? And down at your fine summer place, with all your fancy friends? Don't tell me, Curran, hurt your business. Don't you try to give me that. You are doing very well for yourself, Mike, and anyone can see it.' And that was when I realized, he really did hate me. Hated me because I had more fortune than he did. And that was when I dropped the barstid, if that was the way he felt. Better off without him, I say, than a man who's jealous like that. Forgive me anything except the fact that I'd done well. So don't take it seriously, Jerry, if that's happening to you."

"Oh," I said, to reassure him, "they're not getting to me. That's not what I meant, Mike, that I was getting down."

"No," he said, "well, I hope not. I've been a little worried. That Saturday, for instance, when you came down by yourself? And we sat in your kitchen there, and had ourselves a glass? I thought when I saw you then, there was something on your mind. And you remember, when we talked, I asked you about that."

I remembered that grim Saturday quite well. "You mean the day the heater busted, and I couldn't get it fixed."

"Yes," Mike said, "that was the one. Back when it was still the winter there and there was nobody around. You were down here by yourself, and I wasn't used to that. Seeing you there at your house, and Mack nowhere around you."

"Ah, well," I said, "that was nothing. Just a routine sort of thing. Making sure that things were all right. Which of course meant that they wouldn't be, and it would cost me money."

"Did you do what I said?" he said.

"You mean: the circuit breakers?" I said. "No, I didn't, actually. Guy I had come down here said they're perfectly all right. Just some little gadget that he fixed for fifty cents. And charged me eighty dollars for the service call, of course."

"No, no," Mike said, "not that, with the circuit breakers. When I said that you looked troubled, and you should see Father Boyle."

That too, I remembered, because Mike had been persistent. When he finally resigned himself that gray, wet, and cold March Saturday that I was not about to confide in him, he had embarked upon a long description of the benefits of the sacrament of penance. "Look at me now, Jerry," he said. "I'm a man of many years. But I still go there faithfully, at least once a month. And I go in there and kneel down, and I confess my sins. And I'll admit, of course, they're not, not too exciting these days. With the girls, you know, and that stuff, and out hellin' with the lads. But I don't mind admitting to you, I still have my faults—I do. Get short-tempered with my family, and God knows, they don't deserve it. Sometimes fail of charity, and other things as well. And I go in there and kneel down and I just say: 'Bless me, Father,' the way you're supposed to do. And tell him what is on my mind, and that I'm truly sorry. And you know, Jerry, it does wonders, it does wonders for me. Father Boyle is young, he is, probably your age. But he's a kind man and a good one, and he is considerate. You know what he does for me, the old tad that I am? When he gives me absolution, he says, *'Ego te absolvo,'* just like when I was growing up there in my mother's house in Cork. And the penance that he gives me, it's not really very heavy. But it eases my mind, Jerry, and I think it would ease yours."

All the while Mike talked that day, I kept my troubles silent, I searched anxiously for ways to deflect him harmlessly, without hurting him by saying that I wouldn't take his advice. It was on the edge of my tongue to inform him of what was nagging at me: daughter unchaste, wife rebellious, my close friend in jail, and I without the vaguest notion of what to do for them or me. And then to proceed to tell him what I knew he must suspect: that Mack and I quit listening to what was said in church, the day that our priest told her and repeated it to me: that we could not use birth control to protect her from another pregnancy that would probably kill her. I remember Father Bliss's words today: "Artificial means of birth control are sin. You cannot use them. If you do, you violate Church teaching and God's law. Every time, each time you do it, you commit a mortal sin. And I cannot absolve you of it, unless you promise, and you mean it, you will not do it again." No exceptions, Father Bliss said, and no "damned extenuations." Mack and I, it was God's will, must spend our days faithfully wedded, but fearful every time we made love that the consequence would kill her. I looked at her when he said that, and she shared my first reaction. "Well, then," she said, and we both stood up, "as my father often said: We have heard what you've said and it doesn't make us happy." Father Bliss stood up as well: "Joanie," he said, "Jerry, I know this is hard for you. But God will bless your union and support you in this pain."

"Suck eggs, Father," I said, and we left the rectory. Holding hands, I might add, and most sublimely happy.

"No, Mike," I said to him, on the beach that holiday, "I did not see Father Boyle. I just worked on things in my own mind, and got them straightened out."

"Ah," Mike said, "well, that is good. Long as you've been helped."

"Oh yes, I've been helped," I said. "I've been helped abundantly."

"And your fine daughter there," he said. "Will we be seeing her?"

"Oh, briefly," I said, "briefly. For a couple days, at least. She'll be down next weekend, before her Cape job starts. She is growing up, Mike, you know. She's become a visitor. Just passes through these days."

"Isn't that the way, though?" he said. "And it goes so fast. Hard to get it straight in your mind, that they're really on their own."

"Regardless whether," I said, "you approve of that or not."

"Ahh," he said, "we're never ready. Not for anything. Not for kids that grow up when we're not looking. Not for friends who let us down. Not for friends who die. You get to be my age, you know, and they're gone before you notice."

"Not just at your age," I said. "My friend Frank Macdonald—there is one example. My old friend Frank Macdonald, I mean. Been years since I've seen him. I guess I won't see him now."

"Ahh," Mike said again, "he was that? He was a friend of yours? The famous lawyer, you mean, passed away this week."

"More or less," I said. "More or less, he was. This is a tough business, the one I am in. We are always seeing people, that are in deep trouble. People at their worst, you know? That is when we see them. Happy people, working people, people with good lives: they don't get in trouble and we very seldom see them. So we get used to the hard stuff, and we sometimes mimic it. Not intentional, I guess, but that's the way it is."

"Tell me, Jerry," Mike said, shifting on his haunches, "this Macdonald fellow there—do they know what killed him? I mean, from the television, sounded like it could be suicide."

"I don't think so," I said. "I talked to his wife. She was having him cremated. No postmortem on him. He was on a lot of drugs, I know. But when you're in that shape, you know? Who's to say what killed him?"

Corinne, as a matter of fact, was prepared to say what killed him. She was bitter when I reached her, on the telephone Wednesday night. "Jerry," she said, forgetting *Mister Kennedy* as her preferred mode of address, "you should have reversed the charges. I would not have minded."

"I don't see . . ." I said, "I don't mind paying for the call."

"No," she said, "but then you could have called me earlier. Instead of waiting like this, until the rates go down. Mousie said he talked to you in some courthouse this morning. Told you about Frank and you said you would call me."

"He did reach me and I said that," I said, getting mad. "I also told him I was tied up, in somebody else's office. And that from that office I had to go to another court. I said I would call you when I got back to my office. But when I got back there, I had other things to do. So I'm calling you tonight. It's the first chance I have had."

"Jerry," she said, taking a deep breath, "I suppose it doesn't matter. Frank is dead now, and I'm learning. Things change very fast. People when he was alive were pleading, wouldn't let me off the phone. 'Please, just let me talk to Frank. He can help me, Corinne.' But now Frank is dead, and all of that is over. Notwithstanding the fact that it's such people who killed him. Badgered him and bothered him, and wouldn't let him rest. Poor man would've been dead years ago, if I hadn't stepped in to protect him as I did."

"Corinne," I said, seeing no future in this talk, "what is it you wanted from me, that you called me for?"

"I'll come to the point," she said. "This is long-distance, after all, and you are very busy. Frank did not want a funeral. I'm honoring that wish, as of course I would. His ashes will be scattered in the sea tomorrow morning, and that will be the end of him as mortal man.

"Nevertheless, Jerry," she said, "something must be done. Some attention must be paid, when Frank Macdonald dies. He was one of few; very few, I might add. So, to honor him for being what he was in life, we are scheduling a brief memorial service for him, at the Marsh Chapel at BU a week from Sunday."

"I will be there," I said, "of course. What time should I come?"

There was another deep breath taken, down in the warm darkness of Georgia. "Naturally, you'll be there," she said. "But that isn't why I'm calling. As I said, Jerry, and I am sure you will agree, Frank was a rare man in this life. Some attention must be paid. I know you have contacts now at Channel Eight in Boston. Therefore, I want you to arrange for TV coverage. Dave Reed will be coming in, to make a brief address. Cole Younger's coming up from Abilene, Duncan Reo from Wyoming. Jennings Mills down in Orlando, he is quite sure he will be there. If you can cut through all the red tape and take this concern from me, I will be most appreciative, and you know Frank would be pleased."

"Coverage?" I said. "You want this covered on TV?"

"Yes," she said. "Is that surprising? After all Frank did? I know just as well as you do, they would not leave him alone. Surely, with a milestone like this, they will cover it."

"What did you tell her?" Mack said, when I had hung up the phone.

"That if the news department thought it should be covered," I said, "they would cover it. That I will not meddle with this. I did not say I'm astonished and appalled, but I think she guessed that anyway."

"What did she say?" Mack said.

"She said she assumed that meant I wanted to be MC of the ceremonies," I said. "I told her that I didn't and I wouldn't and 'Goodbye.' She was saying something while I was hanging up, but I'm not sure what it was. I did catch the word *bastard* but very little else."

"Maybe she did kill him," Mack said.

"Mack, my own beloved," I said, "if I were living with her and I was too sick to move, I would save the broad the trouble. I would kill myself."

"Ahh," Mike said, that afternoon, "that is a sad thing. Man like this Macdonald fellow, dying slow like that. Still, I suppose it's God's mercy, painful though it is."

"Mercy?" I said. "How is that? How is cancer mercy, or a heart as weak as his?"

"Why, Jerry, for the time," Mike said. "The time to reconcile. Make your peace with God, you know, and Holy Mother Church. That's what all our time is for, that we have here on earth. Sickness, when it strikes us, is just God reminding us. Trouble, worry, all of that—God is warning us to make our peace with Him."

Mack rolled over and sat up. She looked at Mike with interest. "Is that what it's all about, Mike? Is that what you think?"

Mike looked surprised she would ask. "Well, sure," he said. "Of course."

Mack shifted her gaze back to me and raised both of her eyebrows. "You know, Jerry," she said, "that would explain a lot of things that I don't understand."

"Yes," I said, "wouldn't it? God's just having a few laughs."